**The deck steps behind her creaked.
Rita froze, holding her breath,
straining to hear what she couldn't see.**

Rita turned her head as a tall figure loomed over her. Rough hands grabbed her wrists, pinning them behind her back, and crushing her body into the door. Her car keys jangled loudly as they hit the porch. She opened her mouth to scream but couldn't make a sound.

"Don't move a muscle and you won't get hurt!" a deep voice growled inches above her ear. Hot moist breath brushed against her neck as she tried to think.

She struggled to break his grasp, to escape the intense smell of musk and salty sweat. The muscles of his abdomen tensed into her back, his chest hair scratched like bristles on her shoulders. Sand scraped her wrists as he clamped them together with one huge hand. She was in good condition but no match for his strength. His free hand pawed her breasts, searched the cleavage of her spandex sports bra, slid down her stomach and over her tight knit shorts, stopping only when he felt her smooth thighs. "No," she moaned, tears flooding onto her cheeks. "Don't!"

She panted, her chest cramped. Scream? Who would hear her above the surf?

"Please," she begged, "Please, don't hurt me."

Dangerous Sands

by

Karen Bostrom

To Dorothy,
Thank you for
your support + energy!
Enjoy! Karen Bostrom

Dangerous Sands

Cover art by *Kim Mendoza*

The Wild Rose Press
PO Box 708
Adams Basin, NY 14410-0706
Visit us at www.thewildrosepress.com

Publishing History
First Last Rose of Summer Edition, 2011
Print ISBN 1-60154-864-8

Published in the United States of America

Dedication

With love to my family of storytellers,
to my wonderful critique partners,
Nancy Quatrano, Gail Freeman, Daria Ludas,
Andrea Mansue, Robyn Sayre, and Pat Marinelli,
as well as many other women writers and friends
for all their time, talent, support,
and encouragement,
and to a very special man named Carlos.

Chapter One

"Damn!" she muttered. Plenty of sticky paint and dirt but no key. Not under the mat, not under the pot of geraniums she'd knocked over in the dark. Wiping her hands on her sweaty shorts, she rose. "Where is that blasted key?"

A shroud of fog blanketed the secluded stretch of sand - no moon, no stars, no porch light. The only sound was the rumble of waves pounding the beach just beyond the dunes as Rita searched for the spare key to unlock the back door of the dark three-story house. Being alone on the porch with a dead flashlight and no neighbors nearby would never have made her nervous before. To her, this was home, a safe haven. But something felt wrong about being back this time. She didn't need a power outage and oppressive humidity to make this homecoming any worse.

Stretching her arm as high as she could, Rita fumbled again for the spare key on the narrow ledge above the doorframe. It'd been kept there for as long as she had lived with her aunt at the Jersey Shore. Now there was nothing, not even a cobweb.

Rita opened the screen door to reach for the knocker, but the brass anchor was gone. Instead of wood, her hand skimmed over smooth glass panels and rough metal ridges. A stained glass window? Since when?

The deck steps behind her creaked. Rita froze, holding her breath, straining to hear what she couldn't see.

Rita turned her head as a tall figure loomed over

1

her. Rough hands grabbed her wrists, pinning them behind her back, and crushing her body into the door. Her car keys jangled loudly as they hit the porch. She opened her mouth to scream but couldn't make a sound.

"Don't move a muscle and you won't get hurt!" a deep voice growled inches above her ear. Hot moist breath brushed against her neck as she tried to think.

She struggled to break his grasp, to escape the intense smell of musk and salty sweat. The muscles of his abdomen tensed into her back, his chest hair scratched like bristles on her shoulders. Sand scraped her wrists as he clamped them together with one huge hand. She was in good condition but no match for his strength. His free hand pawed her breasts, searched the cleavage of her spandex sports bra, slid down her stomach and over her tight knit shorts, stopping only when he felt her smooth thighs. "No," she moaned, tears flooding onto her cheeks. "Don't!"

She panted, her chest cramped. Scream? Who would hear her above the surf?

"Please," she begged, "Please, don't hurt me."

"Easy now," the man whispered as if he were calming a wild pony. His bare chest rubbed against her. What had the karate master at the gym told her to do when attacked from behind? Don't fight. Let go. She forced herself to breathe out, to surrender. Her body went completely limp.

As soon as her captor eased his grip to catch her dead weight, Rita rammed her foot into his shin with all the energy she had.

"You little bitch!" he cursed. She smashed her elbow into his gut and broke free, taking off around the side of the house.

Now what? Run for her truck and roar off down the winding driveway? She couldn't. *No keys*. She'd dropped them when he'd slammed her into the door. She'd left her bag, and her cell phone, in the truck. Route 35 wasn't far - maybe flag down a passing motorist for help? *Who'd stop for a crazy woman running down the road at this time of night?*

She darted to the vacant lot next door. Her only chance was to do the unexpected. He was bigger and stronger, but she was fast. She knew the area better than any stranger. She'd catch her breath by the run-down building next door. Follow the low shrubs north to the closest pay phone on the beach. Punch in 911 and blurt out a quick message. That's all she'd have to remember.

Underbrush scraped her legs and slowed her down. She inched around some fir trees, leaned against a prickly pine to rest a moment, to listen. Glancing behind her, she scanned for movement. There was only blackness; no sound of anything moving, just the thumping of her heart and the rhythm of the waves ahead and to her right. A far-off flash of heat lightning outlined a solitary garage against the dunes ahead. It was all that remained of the old Victorian house next door which had burned down last year.

She dropped to the sand until the blackness returned, then took off toward the garage. She wanted to kick off her sandals, but couldn't risk cutting her feet on a broken beer bottle or a rusty nail.

At last, she made it to the safety of the building and leaned against its rough cedar shakes, inhaling deeply. She had to stay calm. *Just a few blocks to the only public entrance to the beach.* There used to be a pay phone by the benches. "Please," Rita prayed. "Let it still be there."

There were a few year-round residents further down the beach; would anyone let in a frantic stranger pounding on a door for help in the middle of the night? What if she made too much noise and the attacker found her before the police ever came?

Rita gasped for air and winced as she held her aching sides. Her shins burned from running in the sand, but she moved on, ducking low near shrubs and deck fencing by each deserted home.

Now that she was closer to the eerie glow of the fog hovering over the streetlights ahead, it was easier to see shapes, to dash more quickly to the next possible hiding place. Reaching the last house that bordered the street, she paused in its shadows to look around and listen. Nothing. Had she lost him?

She jumped over the snow fencing protecting the dunes and headed toward the gazebo on the short boardwalk. Next week, a summer badge checker would sit there, ready to keep the riff raff off the beach, but now there was no one, nothing to hear but the crashing waves beyond.

"Thank God!" Twenty feet ahead under the old-fashioned gaslight stood the phone. Rita forced herself to walk calmly on the asphalt street leading to the gazebo, hoping not to be noticed if the stalker had tracked her. She picked up the receiver, ready to stab the buttons with 9-1-1 and froze.

"Where's the dial tone? Come on! Come on!" She pumped the metal clicker frantically. "Nothing! Damn it! Now what?" She'd have to head for the highway after all. Could she make it?

Her hands trembled from hunger and her head throbbed in time with her pounding heart. No one even knew she was in town. When the casino cancelled her shift at the spa and told her to pick up her final check, she'd finished packing up the rest of her belongings, turned in her condo keys a week early, and headed for the Garden State Parkway and home. She hadn't counted on the accident that tied up traffic for three hours, the power outage in the neighborhood, or her flashlight dying. "If only... Yeah, if only. If only my life weren't so damn full of 'if only' this or that, imagine how great it would be. I wouldn't be standing here scared to death, hungry, tired, hot and..."

She replaced the receiver and paused to catch her breath. A sports utility vehicle turned the corner from Route 35 and drove slowly in her direction. Could she trust a complete stranger to give her a ride to police headquarters? Rita had never even hitchhiked in daylight before, but who else could help her? Running toward the approaching headlights, she suddenly stopped. Not only did the black Jeep look like hers, it was hers. He was hunting her down in her own truck.

The driver jammed on the brakes, cut the ignition, and leaped out of the vehicle. Within seconds, he was inches away and towering over her again, long black and silver hair visible in the headlights. His eyes gleamed at her from under thick black eyebrows. His chest was taut and flexed, as bare as his feet. "You won't get away from me this time."

Rita opened her mouth to scream, but he clamped his hand over her lips, his other arm engulfed her body. "And don't even think of pulling that shin trick again. Just shut up and listen if you don't want to get hurt."

Rita stopped struggling, but the stranger's hands remained firmly cupped over her mouth and gripped around her waist from behind. "I'm not falling for that nonresistance crap so forget about running. Who are you and why the hell you were breaking into the house?" He paused a moment. "I'm gonna take my hand off your mouth now. Stay quiet. No biting or screaming, or I'll tie you up and take you to the cops myself. Understand?"

Rita nodded. He slowly removed his hand from

her lips and gripped her shoulders like a vise. "Now talk."

"You jump me in the dark, maul me, steal my truck, and you're threatening to take *me* to the police? Are you nuts? Who the hell are *you*?"

"Listen, lady, I'm the one asking the questions. You were the one trying to break in."

"You attacked me. What do you want? If it's money, I only have twenty bucks. I don't know how much money's in the house. Can't be much. Dozens of vacant ritzy houses to rob, and you pick the poorest one. Didn't you see there's no security system, no Mercedes, no triple car garage? How about the peeling paint?"

"What's your scam, lady? I know you don't own that house. What did you really want? When the power went out in the neighborhood, did you figure you'd go door to door helping yourself to a few goodies?"

"For God's sake, no," Rita whispered. "Please, just let me go! Take my Jeep and go on your way. By the time I walk to the police station, you'll be long gone. Take the twenty in the glove compartment, wipe off your fingerprints, and leave the truck somewhere. Just don't hurt me, or my aunt."

"Your aunt?" He loosened his hold on her slightly. "Calm down. I'm gonna turn you around slowly. But don't try anything stupid," he warned.

Rita wondered if it was too late to get away as he eased her around to face him. "Aunt Liz. Where is she? You didn't hurt her, did you? We don't have much money. Please don't hurt us." Rita's eyes widened, brimming with tears, and she shut her mouth. *Why did she blab so much? If he wanted ransom, now she had nothing to bargain.*

The tall man looked puzzled. "Your Aunt Liz? Liz Chandler?" Suddenly, a look of recognition flashed across his face and he loosened his grip.

"She's fine!" he boomed.

Lifting Rita's chin upward toward the streetlight, he examined her like an artist studying a nude in a figure drawing class: wild brown curls escaped from her disheveled ponytail and her trim body strained under a paint-smeared black sports bra and skintight shorts. Her defiant eyes looked directly into his.

The hint of a grin tugged at one corner of his mouth. "Well, now. Maybe you're not a criminal after all. You must be Rita Madison," he said softly and released her arms. "The house is full of pictures of you. Yes, you look like Liz. Same eyes, same chin. And the same stubbornness. I thought you were showing up on the doorstep next week."

She eyed him warily. "Yeah, and I didn't intend to get here this late at night, either. But forget that for now. Just tell me where Aunt Liz is. And who the hell are *you*?"

"Mitch Grant. I work for your aunt, and she's spending the night at the fancy spa across town where the electric's still on. When the power went off, she took advantage of some rich friend's offer to stay there since I was away. She left me a note in case I got back."

"Yeah, right. I've never heard of you and she's leaving you notes? And why were you hanging around our house during the blackout?"

"My own long story. Out of town, trouble with my truck. You name it, it happened. When I couldn't reach Liz by phone, I hitched a ride home." He motioned to the Jeep. "Anyway, I checked the registration in the glove compartment before I came after you. 'Margarita Myers,' it said. That's *you*?"

She nodded. "Another change I need to make. I go by my maiden name now, Rita Madison."

Mitch noticed her rubbing her arms. Good muscle tone, but she'd have bruises where he'd been clutching her, bruises to match the swelling of his throbbing shin. "Sorry if I was a little rough, Rita, but we've had some robberies in town. I thought you were breaking in. Maybe one of Liz's strays coming back to help themselves to something while the power was out. You know how she always invites those flaky types over for a swim or a cup of tea on the porch?"

"Gee, thanks," Rita said sarcastically. "First I'm a robber. Now I'm a flake. How do you know my aunt, anyway? You certainly weren't working at two a.m., were you? Or borrowing a cup of sugar in the dark? Getting notes from a seventy-five-year-old lady?"

He stiffened slightly. "I told you. Liz hired me to do some work on the place. Carpentry and whatever else needs doing. I've been staying above the garage." Extending his right hand, he added, "How about a truce? I was only looking out for your aunt and her property."

Rita hesitated. She studied his outstretched hand and shook her head. This was too much. "Oh, so you're the 'silver-haired gentleman' Aunt Liz invited to live in the garage apartment? She said you needed a little time at the beach, and she needed a handyman. Knowing Aunt Liz, it's rent-free, too. I know the house needs a lot of work, but don't you think she's a little old for you to mooch off? You're hardly the down-on-his luck senior citizen I pictured!"

Looking at Mitch's smooth, almost unlined face, Rita guessed he was closer to forty-five than retirement. Tan and rugged but not weathered like most of the construction workers she'd seen. No trace of a beer belly, just the six-pack abs men envied and women dreamed of touching. His broad shoulders and v-shaped torso hinted at hours of physical labor or daily bodybuilding.

She'd been staring, and Mitch withdrew his hand. "Well, lady. Have it your way. I don't care what you pictured, but who are you to talk? Hell, I heard you're pushing forty and running back home for a 'rest.' And I bet you're not in the habit of paying the going rent here either." His eyes narrowed and his jaw tightened. "I leave the mooching to relatives with problems. I don't need this job."

"Listen, Mr. Grant, right now I don't care what you've heard about me or why someone your age is drifting around doing odd jobs. I've had a rotten day. Now I know Aunt Liz is okay, I'd just like to take a hot bath or get some ice packs and go to bed. Alone. I don't care if the house is dark or empty or full of paint fumes. I need sleep. I assume you have a key that works? And you'll let me in?"

"Fine, get in the truck. I'll take you back."

"No, it's my truck. I drive, unless you'd like to walk."

"You've forgotten. I don't have to walk." He smiled and dangled her keys above her head, close to a foot below his own six-feet-two-inch frame. "I may be just the hired help, but I'm the one with these, plus a new house key that unlocks the door. If you want to get to bed sooner, get in the truck."

Rita sighed and walked around to the passenger side. "Okay, play chauffeur or macho or whatever your thing is. Drive. I'm too tired to argue. I've been awake since five o'clock yesterday morning and I just want to crash."

Mitch started the Jeep and drove back in silence, wondering how Liz Chandler's niece would react in the light of day when she saw everything he'd done to the house during the past few months. Liz was one hell of a special lady, but even after a year of getting to know her, Mitch still wasn't sure if she was a foolish old woman or the gutsiest broad he'd ever met. Maybe both. But if anyone could deal with this whirlwind in the passenger's seat, Liz could.

He glanced to his right as he braked to turn into the driveway, and shook his head at the sight of Rita's head slumped against the window, already asleep. She clutched a huge black tote bag like a child gripping a teddy bear with one hand, the other curled into a tiny fist. As the truck rocked gently on the gravel and came to a halt, she opened her eyes and pretended she hadn't dozed off.

"Wait here till I get a working flashlight," Mitch commanded. He shut the door and disappeared into the nearby garage, returning within seconds. "I don't need Liz bugging me because I didn't take care of you," he muttered. "Just take the bag you need for tonight. I'll help you unpack the rest in the morning."

"I won't need your help. Just open the front door now, okay? I can find my own way from there. I lived here, remember?" She hopped out, slipping the tote bag over one shoulder and an old khaki duffel bag over the other. "My keys, please?"

"Here, let me carry those," Mitch leaned in close and grabbed the straps, but Rita wouldn't let go.

"Thanks, but no thanks. I'm a trainer. I lug heavier equipment than this all the time."

"Yeah, so do I. But it doesn't give me as much trouble as one tiny woman and a couple of bags. Here, be in charge of the light." He shoved the flashlight into her hand, scooped her up, bags and all, and carried her to the front porch where he placed her on her feet. Unlocking the door, he pushed it open ceremoniously and handed her the car keys. "Sweet dreams," he said. "I'm going to bed. It's been a tough day," he added and vanished into the darkness.

"What nerve," Rita mumbled as she flung her bags inside. "Where did Aunt Liz ever find him?"

She shut the door and rested against it. She took a moment to scan the living room with the flashlight, smiling at the familiar mixture of contemporary and antique furniture blended with flowers, pottery and knick-knacks that somehow looked just right.

She sighed. Climbing the staircase seemed like scaling Mt. Everest. She made her way cautiously upstairs to the old tower room that had always been hers. It had made her feel like a princess, like Rapunzel in a tower awaiting rescue, or a queen surveying her castle grounds.

She went to the window and looked toward the ocean, remembering childhood dreams of sailing the seas and owning a place like this on the endless sand, free to swim or build sandcastles that never washed away. What a fantasy! She shuddered as she studied the darkness. Why did she feel like she was being watched? She closed the blinds and locked the door before flinging herself on the familiar canopy bed with relief. At least some things were still the same, she thought, and fell asleep clutching an old quilt.

Chapter Two

Rita slowly opened her eyes to soft morning light filtering through the lacy curtains. No matter how tired she was, she always woke up at six, her favorite time of day, full of possibilities and new beginnings. But today she wished she could sleep forever, curled up in the soft quilt Aunt Liz had helped her make during her first summer at the shore when she was ten. Sun and moon, stars and starfish, rainbows and teddy bears. Anything Rita had drawn, Liz had transformed into cloth.

"Making dreams, a block at a time," Aunt Liz had said. "Whatever you want, you can have. You only have to know what it is and go for it, girl! You can make anything happen." Rita had believed her then. Now she wasn't so sure.

Still, after so many years of struggling for her dreams, it was good to come home and maybe believe in possibilities again. Right now, her only plan was to visit with Aunt Liz and relax in the sun.

Rita moved to the window seat, peered out, and inhaled deeply. There was nothing like the smell of ocean air and a walk along the beach. But first, she'd unload the Jeep before that man woke up.

Going down the stairs in her bare feet, Rita smelled coffee and toast, heard the familiar rattle of an old percolator. Though a firm tea drinker, Aunt Liz's morning ritual began with one cup of steaming black coffee every morning. She refused to replace the ancient coffeemaker she'd received as a wedding gift with a modern drip one. Rita hurried toward the kitchen, eager to talk to her aunt over a Fiestaware cup of strong coffee resting on an unmatched saucer.

"Hey, Stranger, how about a walk on the beach?" Rita called out. She smiled as she entered the kitchen in her oversized New Jersey Devils T-shirt shirt ready for a hug. Instead of a familiar white-haired aunt, there *he* sat, grinning at her over a mug of coffee, reading the morning newspaper as if he lived here.

"Thanks for the offer, but I'll pass on the walk. Recent shin injury. Plus the hired help is too busy. I'm supposed to have this job done before the princess of the house arrives next week." Motioning to the percolator, he added, "Electric's back on. Want some coffee?"

Rita looked around. The Fiestaware and percolator were all that remained of the kitchen she remembered. Gone were the quaint but scarred pine cabinets with heavy black latches, as well as the dated green Formica countertop with dented chrome edging. In their place were custom Shaker style hickory cabinets, sleek granite countertops, and a custom tile backsplash with accents of shells and seagulls. It was breathtaking, like something out of an ad for *House and Gardens*.

"I can't believe it! A new kitchen after all these years! And what are you doing in here? I thought you lived in the garage apartment."

"I do. But I need to finish the inside trim and painting before I start on the siding. Liz thought you'd be surprised. Too bad you got here early and spoiled it."

"Maybe I'm not here early enough. Whose idea was it to redo the entire kitchen?"

"Why? Don't you like it?"

"Of course I do. It's incredible. But it probably cost a fortune. What are you doing? Milking a handyman job into a career renovation project?"

Mitch's smile vanished and lines creased his

forehead. "Sorry, lady. I work for your aunt, not for you. And don't you go telling her how much this should cost, okay? I got great deals for her, and I don't want you making her feel bad about fixing this place up instead of always looking out for everybody else."

He stood up abruptly. "I'll be back in a few minutes to work in here so why don't you grab something to eat and get out of my way? Go collect shells along the beach."

He motioned toward the magnet-covered refrigerator. "Liz's phone number at the spa is on the business card. Her car's in for repairs, and she wants to be picked up as soon as possible. You might as well get her. I'm busy and my truck's not back yet. You know, for some reason your aunt thinks you're something special, but as far as I'm concerned, you've been one royal pain in the ...shin." He washed and dried his cup and replaced it behind one of the stained glass doors of dolphins. "Oh, and the rest of your bags are in the living room. Welcome home, Princess Rita." He raised his eyebrows slightly and bowed his head.

"Who the hell do you think you are? You don't even know the first thing about me!"

The screen door slammed behind him as he strode off toward the garage. "I told you. I'm Mitch Grant, and I don't think I need to know anything else about you for now. Have a nice walk."

Rita watched his silver and black ponytail disappear. What a rude man. And why hadn't Aunt Liz told her about all the work he'd being doing around here?

The whine of a power saw broke the early morning stillness. Rita poured herself a cup of coffee, wandered out to the back porch, and curled up on the wicker rocker. She had important decisions to make, more important than how to avoid arguing with some handyman. She sipped her coffee and rocked, twirling a few stray curls absent-mindedly as she watched a lone fisherman move his tackle box and pole further down the beach, following the gulls feeding in the surf. What to make of Mitch Grant? She needed to ask Aunt Liz that question.

She'd planned to take a long walk on the beach but was too eager to see her aunt to do more than run to the water's edge for a few minutes. She bolted down to the surf, scaring the sandpipers and freezing her toes. The air was warm; the water was not.

She ran back to shower quickly and unpack a tangerine sundress that swirled just below her knees. Thank God for wrinkle-free fabrics! She cinched her waist with a macramé belt, grabbed a straw hat, and slipped on sandals. She applied coral lipstick in one smooth circle, smudged on a bit of mascara, and smiled at the mirror as if it were a camera, checking her reflection before she left to meet Aunt Liz. Creamy skin, green eyes, only minor crow's feet when she smiled big. One dimple when she smirked. Two when she laughed. A few wispy brown tendrils framed her face from under the wide-brimmed hat. *Looking good. Certainly not her age and not worried about turning forty, Mitch Grant,* she thought as she scrunched up her face and stuck out her tongue. She pushed away images of ticking biological clocks and women having their first children in their forties, even fifties. *Talk about jumping the gun. Hell, she wasn't even dating!*

She cringed at the thought. If only she could skip the dating process and be involved with a perfect soul mate right now! She wasn't into the bar scene or personals on the internet. She couldn't picture herself blending in with the ladies at the local yacht club, chatting about the best private schools for privileged offspring or comparing successful husbands making corporate deals over golf swings or martinis. Could she swap stories with them about ex-husbands and their bankruptcies? Even though Rita had never wanted that kind of life, it was out of her league now.

It was time to put Kevin and all that behind her, and she'd do it, step by step. She'd have to start back to work again soon, but not right away. Today she planned to take it easy. Yet with the hammering and sawing, how could she relax and enjoy doing nothing?

Mitch's words still taunted her. *"Someone pushing forty... mooching off relatives...plenty of problems."* How had she ended up like this? After years of substitute teaching, filling in for others' maternity leaves, working part-time casino jobs as a personal trainer and massage therapist, she'd saved enough money for a down payment on a fitness center. Then she had lost it all. Actually, her now-ex-husband had, but the IRS, the credit card companies, and the local bank didn't seem interested in which spouse was to blame. Outsiders ended up with whatever Kevin hadn't spent or gambled away during thirteen years of marriage. He'd filed for bankruptcy and left for Vegas with a rich older woman soon after the divorce.

Last week, she'd finally paid off her share of the debts Kevin had acquired before their divorce. It was definitely time for a fresh start. But first, wasn't she entitled to two months of peace and quiet, doing nothing but lying on the beach and drinking iced tea? She didn't have to explain herself to some overdeveloped carpenter with a tongue sharper than a saw.

She added a colorful beaded necklace, grabbed her straw purse, and fished out her key ring. Remembering she had no house key, Rita walked toward the garage and stopped at the entrance.

Breathing in the smell of fresh wood shavings, she sighed. Mitch sliced baseboard with precise, short strokes, and tiny sawdust particles clung to his arms. As a fitness trainer, she admired his muscle tone, the shape of his calves above his white socks. If it weren't for the silver-streaked hair, he could pass for forty, maybe less. She was dying to ask him how old he was but didn't want to give the impression she was interested in him as a man, or worse, suspicious. Which she was.

When he shut off the motor, she waited in the sudden silence. He grabbed a stack of trim, turned around, and almost dropped the whole pile when he noticed her. He paused, studying her body from her wide-brimmed hat to her trim ankles, and nodded. "Not bad, Princess. Ready to enter the social scene already, huh? Well, step aside. Some of us have work to do."

"Be glad to. I hate to stop a man from working, but I need a house key. I'm going to surprise Aunt Liz at the spa. Do you have her car keys, too? I couldn't find them in the usual spot. In fact, I couldn't find the usual spot or the board with the hooks. You've been quite busy making changes here since my last visit."

Mitch put down the wood and pulled a familiar set of keys from a pocket of his denim cut-offs. "Sure have. No key hooks or keys under a pot around here. Only a damn fool or a trusting soul like your aunt keeps a set hanging by an unlocked door. Even with the recent break-ins, I had a hell of a time convincing her to lock doors when she leaves and keep her keys out of sight. Why invite scumbags in like that?"

"Well, Mr. Grant, we finally agree on something."

"Mitch."

"Right. Mitch, the silver-haired gentleman. But

how did you get her to give in? The spare key has been there as long as I can remember. Are you that charming and persuasive when you want to be? In case you haven't noticed, my aunt is very...determined."

"You mean 'stubborn' like you?"

"No, stubborn is a man insisting on driving a woman's truck. Determined is what *we* are when we're being persistent and dedicated to something we believe in. So, how'd you manage to change a habit of fifty years in a few short months?"

"It wasn't easy, but I reminded her that she keeps telling me to trust the Universe. Says it gives you exactly what you need to learn. It may not be what you thought you wanted, but it's the perfect lesson. So I suggested the Universe sent me here to bug the hell out of her till she took care of herself, and somehow it made sense to her."

Rita smiled. "Sounds like Aunt Liz. And what about you? Do you trust the Universe?"

"Me? If I've been getting what the Universe thinks I need, I'd like to know where to return the gifts. I'd just like to be left alone to do what I want, and what I want to do is get back to work. Simple."

"No problem. Give me a house key that works and I'll get out of your hair. Or do you want to play macho chauffeur again and drive us both?"

Mitch tossed her the keys. "Too busy, Princess. Drive yourself. Oh, and her car is ready. Garage closes at three today. Now can I get back to work?" He gathered his boards and squinted in the bright sunlight as she hurried toward her Jeep and climbed in. She waved and drove off too fast, gravel spitting from under her tires. He nodded and headed toward the house with the lumber. As he hammered the remaining trim in the kitchen, he tried to forget how the flimsy fabric had clung to the curves of her trim body, how her wild dark hair blew in the wind after she'd tossed her large straw hat onto the passenger seat and roared off.

****

The smell of chlorine emanating from the deserted Olympic-size indoor pool at the Bayside Club and Spa overwhelmed Rita. She scanned the area to spot Aunt Liz with no luck. Not lounging by the oasis of live palm trees or sitting in the hot tub. The young man wiping off the white-strapped lounge chairs had let Liz swim a few laps before he added the pool chemicals, even though no one was officially allowed to swim until ten o'clock. "Don't tell anyone," he begged Rita. "But I couldn't say no. She reminded me my grandmother," he added as he finished folding a basket of striped towels for guests. "Check the sauna or the locker area around the corner from the juice bar." He pointed toward the workout section. "She left about twenty minutes ago."

Rita headed in that direction, appreciating the design and décor around her. No expenses had been spared in landscaping and furnishings. Rita had heard that after recent renovations, the spa was a popular meeting place for local movers and shakers to hang out and network. Like the nearby country club and yacht club, it offered expensive yearly memberships and society column references in the local paper. Rita touched the equipment in the weight room lovingly. Brand-new and state of the art. The turquoise, white, and black décor was almost what she had envisioned for her own health club, the one she'd been ready to start near Atlantic City before her ex-husband had helped himself to her savings and skipped town. *Never another joint account for her—not unless the other party supplied the funds.* If life gave you what you needed to learn, that's one lesson she'd learned from Kevin. Expensive lessons such as don't trust people with your dreams. Build your own.

Rita passed the Stairmasters and rowing machines. She couldn't picture Aunt Liz on a treadmill on a sunny day, but with her, you never knew. When Liz wasn't there either, Rita moved on to the sauna area. The nearby showers were immaculate, the lockers gleamed, and the eucalyptus room smelled as comforting as childhood memories of a whiff of Vicks from a blue glass jar. Her last stop was to peek into the steam room. Rita gasped as the hot vapor poured out. She started to shut the door quickly so her hair wouldn't curl anymore. "Help!" a familiar voice called from the mist. "Help me."

"Aunt Liz?" Rita charged into the cloud of steam and guided her aunt into the cool hallway. "Are you all right?"

The older woman steadied herself against Rita and paused. "Whew! I'm a little out of breath and overcooked, but I'll be fine in a moment."

"What happened?"

"I swam in the pool and wanted to check out the steam room. I had trouble finding the temperature control without my glasses. Damn bifocals. Can't see anything without them anymore. I guess I turned the dial the wrong way. And then it got so hot in here I panicked when I couldn't get the door open. The handle wouldn't budge. I could have sworn somebody was holding it shut, but I couldn't see anyone through the glass. It was so hot; I thought I'd faint, but you came just in time. Isn't that what I always tell you? Don't worry and things will work out."

Rita went back in and tried the knob from the inside. It moved easily. "Funny, it seems fine now. I'll turn the temperature down for the next person, though. And we'll mention it to the attendant. What if someone with a bad heart got stuck in that heat?"

"Well, dear. You know I'm strong as an ox, so

don't fret over my health. Now, let's look at you!" Liz gave her a once-over. "A bit thin, aren't you? Never mind, you can come along to the ice cream parlor and have a big lunch with the nice young man who owns this place. This is perfect. I think you two should work together. He's tall, dark, and handsome, as they say, and successful, too. He's got big plans."

"Aunt Liz. Remember what I said last week? No matchmaking this summer! I mean it. If it weren't for men, I'd be successful, too, instead of starting over at almost forty."

"Nonsense, girl. Forty's young nowadays! You're beautiful and talented, and every morning's a new start when the sun comes up, no matter how old you are. Besides, I'm not matchmaking, I'm introducing. When Tony heard you were a fitness trainer, a massage therapist, and a physical education teacher, he said he had the perfect job for you."

"Aunt Liz! I'm not working right away, and I don't want to get involved with anyone. The last thing I need is a man tying me down, especially one with big plans. Been there, done that, as they say."

"You were too good for Kevin, dear. Someday you'll find the right man like my Carlton was. And it will be magic! But I wouldn't dream of picking him out for you. You're so stubborn."

"Independent."

"As I was saying, so stubborn you'd send him packing if you hadn't picked him out yourself. Now stop fussing over me like I was some old lady about to keel over and let's get going. And since when have you ever taken it easy? It's not the Chandler style, or yours. We're doers, not watchers. You know that! You need to keep busy, not lie on a beach getting a tan."

As Liz stood and tightened the tie on her robe, footsteps approached. "Liz? Is that you?" a deep smooth voice called out. A tall lean man with a perfect tan and wavy dark hair appeared. "I should scold you. First you charm the attendant into letting you swim early. Then you end up here in the workout area without supervision. I thought you were checking out and we were having lunch together." He glanced at Rita and smiled before looking back at Liz.

"Oh, Tony, dear. I was just talking about you. I know I'm late, but I did a little exploring and got trapped in your steam room."

"What? Are you all right?"

"I'm fine now. Maybe a bit weak from hunger. I only did twenty laps in the pool. Used to do my age in laps, but I'd need a lifeguard or one of those rescue dolphins around to do that now."

"But what happened in the steam room?" Tony asked.

"I couldn't open the door to get out, but Rita came along and had no trouble. It's over now. Oh, where are my manners? Tony, I want you to meet my lovely niece, Rita Madison. She's the one I was telling you about, perfect for your new spa. I invited her along for lunch."

Liz took them both by the arm and ushered them toward the elevator. "Why don't you two get acquainted while I go to my room and get ready to go home? And no arguments about eating at the ice cream parlor either! You young people worry too much about fat grams instead of enjoying your food! I'll meet you in the lobby in fifteen minutes."

Liz smiled sweetly as the elevator doors closed, leaving Rita alone with Tony gazing down at her. His aqua eyes mirrored the color of the nearby pool as well as his impeccable knit shirt. Armani sunglasses were casually propped on top of his thick black hair. His teeth gleamed as white as his creased slacks. Rita wondered if his bronze skin was the product of the nearby beach or the spa's tanning bed.

He looked amused and waited for her to speak.

"Sorry about my aunt. She tends to arrange things on the spur of the moment and expects others to go along with whatever she comes up with."

"I know exactly what she's like. It's part of her charm. And I can see that charm and beauty run in the family, too."

Rita blushed, and then turned even redder from the embarrassment of not having outgrown the habit. "She didn't expect me until next week, but it's a good thing I came early. I think you'd better check the steam room door. What if someone else gets stuck in there?"

"You're right; I'll have it taken care of immediately. I insist you join us for lunch, though. If you're half as good a massage therapist as your aunt claims you are, I'll make you an offer you can't refuse. Excuse me for a minute." He pulled a cell phone from his waistband and ordered maintenance to check the steam room right away before turning back to Rita. "Sometimes I'm concerned about Liz being alone in that big house. I know she's spunky and full of energy for a person half her age, but she seems to think she's still nineteen and invincible. Often acts impulsively. That can lead to trouble when you're in your seventies, as you saw this morning."

"Yes, she tends to forge ahead without considering consequences," said Rita, "But everything seems to work out for her, as least this far. Still, it's a different world nowadays, and my uncle isn't around anymore to rein her in …or try to keep her safe."

"Well, it's good you're here to keep an eye on her this summer. With all those stairs and the upkeep, eventually she won't be able to maintain, much less afford to stay in, that old three-story house by herself. And it's never too early to think ahead."

"Yeah, I guess so. But sometimes plans get ruined and you have to start all over."

"True, but every problem offers an opportunity to succeed."

Rita smiled. "Spare me the motivational speech, okay? It's a lot easier for someone born with a silver spoon in his mouth to make his dreams come true - especially if you've got a rich daddy with connections and the local good ol' boy network to send you clients or bail you out. I imagine it helps you deal with any unfortunate 'opportunities' that appear." Rita stopped and blushed again. "Sorry. That was out of line."

Tony laughed. "Let's call it 'refreshingly blunt.' You know, most women I meet seem to be sizing me up as future husband material. They consider family money, solid social and business connections, and several thriving companies as assets. It's so rare to meet someone with such a beautiful mouth who is so eager and capable of putting her foot into it. Bravo." He clapped and bowed. "Let me guess. You're recently divorced and mad at all men, including me."

Rita took off her hat and looked down. "Tony, I apologize. I've been through a lot lately and I was upset when I saw Aunt Liz gasping in the steam room. And then I saw you after all these years, looking as perfect as you did as the local star basketball player for that snooty prep school that had no use for us mere public school graduates. I figure you've had a pretty easy life."

"No one has an easy life," Tony said with a smile. "Never assume that. When you've always had an abundance of material things, you realize how priceless the simple things are—family, love, friends, and health—people of substance, not glitter..." His voice trailed off.

"Well, Tony, I confess you're right about me being divorced, but I swear I'm not mad at all men or you. At the moment, I'm just not interested in any kind of man or husband, rich or poor, ex or future. So please forgive my little outburst, and I'll overlook your wealth and good looks." She held out her hand and added, "And I'd love to join you for lunch. Besides, Aunt Liz would skin me alive for being so rude to you, especially after your generous offer to let her stay here last night."

"Apology accepted. Now why don't you go gather Liz from Room 325 before she explores something else and we have to track her down? I'll meet you at the entrance in ten minutes." Tony reached for her hand and brought it to his lips, kissing her fingers lightly. She didn't know what to say. Guys only did that in the movies, yet it looked so natural for Tony. A shiver went down her back. Or was it a tingle? No, she would never look for magic again. She'd trusted Kevin and lost almost everything. The last thing she saw as the elevator doors shut was Tony grinning at her with his perfect dental work and bleached teeth.

Chapter Three

When Rita entered Jackson's Ice Cream Parlor with Aunt Liz and Tony, she was amazed at its transformation. Instead of chipped Formica tables and vinyl seats sutured with duct tape, thick oak tables gleamed under coats of varnish. Red hurricane lamps glowed and old photos of the shore area hung on expensive paneling. Gilt-framed portraits of Victorian ladies and framed copies of crinkled yellow newspaper pages complemented the antiques hanging from the ceiling. And if the line of people waiting for a seat was any indication, Rita could see visitors were willing to pay extra for the new décor. Her stomach grumbled as she looked over the list of ice cream flavors, reminding her she'd only had coffee for breakfast.

Tony called one of the waiters over and whispered in his ear. He motioned for Rita and Liz to follow the red-and-white striped shirt to a back booth. A couple waiting ahead of them with a whining toddler grumbled. Tony said, "We have a reservation, but the waiter said for you to sit right there." Tony pointed to a table up front where the hostess stood with menus.

"How'd you manage that?" Rita asked.

"I always have a reservation. I know the owner." Tony smiled and waited for Rita and Liz to slide into the booth.

Rita scanned the menu, looking for something reasonable. The prices had changed dramatically, too.

Tony leaned over and put his hand on Rita's.

"My treat, remember?" Had he read her mind? "I recommend the deli sandwiches, but save room for dessert. Old man Jackson's recipe for ice cream is still the best."

Rita listened as Aunt Liz and Tony discussed the spa and Tony's plans for expanding the wellness and elder care programs in the community during lunch. Aunt Liz was relentless in her praise of Rita, and Tony often smiled in Rita's direction as she polished off a huge corned beef sandwich.

"I'm sure she's very talented," he agreed.

Rita's cheeks burned and she shook her head. She felt as embarrassed as the huge matron at the next table enduring a birthday song being sung in four-part harmony by waiters in fake handlebar mustaches holding a massive banana split with three sparklers. "Aunt Liz, will you stop bragging about me? Tony's spa is awesome, but I don't want you twisting his arm to give me a job. I'm not looking for one. I'm fine. I'm on vacation, remember?"

At last, the waiter cleared their table and passed out dessert menus. The cheapest hot fudge sundae cost three times more than one at Dairy Queen. Still, Rita couldn't resist indulging for old time's sake.

"Mmmmm," she murmured as she closed her eyes and savored the chocolate ice cream. "Even better than I remember."

Tony stirred his coffee. "How wonderful to see a beautiful woman enjoying dessert instead of counting calories. Your aunt is right. You simply must come to work for me at the spa. When word gets out you can put away an entire hot fudge sundae and one of Jackson's famous sixteen-ounce sandwiches in one sitting and still stay so slim and trim, all the ladies will want to know your secret. And the men, too, of course."

"Tony, I appreciate the offer, but I need some

time off. No boss. No time clock."

"I understand, but promise you'll reconsider. You could teach aerobics classes. Give massages. Make your own schedule with no overhead. And our members are notoriously large tippers. What do you say?"

"I'm flattered, but..."

"Will you at least think it over?"

"Okay, I'll think about it." Rita smiled.

The waiter placed the check on the table and began clearing things away efficiently. Rita drew her wallet out of her purse.

Tony swiftly grabbed the check. "Put that away. You're my guests." Rita was relieved he insisted on paying the tab. After supporting Kevin for years, it was a welcomed change.

Tony spoke briefly with the cashier, then steered Liz and Rita outside. "Well, ladies, would you like to go anyplace else today?"

"Thank you, Tony, but I want to walk," Liz said firmly. "I missed my stroll on the beach this morning, and that treadmill at the spa isn't the same. Machines take all the joy out of walking - no fresh air or scenery, just flashing lights and a lot of buttons to push."

Rita added, "And I want to see what the local business section of town looks like nowadays. But thank you for lunch and for the job offer."

"My pleasure, Rita. You'll find a lot of the stores have gone downhill. I appreciate local history and old buildings, but some of those little stores were ugly when they were new. Unsafe, too. Real firetraps. Restoring them is next to impossible, and the town needs more ratables, more upscale shops. Anyway, don't get me started again on business, or I'll start badgering you to come work for me again." Tony winked as he opened the door of his white Lexus.

"Have a great day, ladies! And if you ever need to stay over again, Liz, call me, okay? Carlton and my father were always close, and I promised Dad I'd take care of his friends after he retired to Myrtle Beach!" He rolled down the top of his convertible and waved as he eased into the flow of traffic.

Liz turned to face Rita. "So?" she asked.

"So, let's walk a little. I'm stuffed."

"That's not what I meant, young lady. And you know it," scolded Liz. "I mean, what do you think of Tony Jennings?"

"Smooth, attractive, and too good to be true. You know, like puppies and babies, so cute you can't resist at first. Then the puppies grow into huge dogs that eat massive amounts of expensive dog food and need to go to the vet. Adorable babies grow into teenagers who play rap music and hate you, unless you're using your charge card at the mall to buy CDs, video games, or overpriced trendy clothing for them."

"My, my, aren't you cynical now? I didn't ask you to marry him, adopt a puppy together, or have his babies. I just asked what you thought of him. You've been divorced from Kevin over two years. I know he wasn't good enough for you, but don't you think it's time to stop hating all men just because one man hurt you?"

"I don't hate all men, Aunt Liz." Rita said slowly. "I just don't trust most of them. Unfortunately, they're not all like Uncle Carlton was. You don't know what it's like to be betrayed. I'll need a job soon, but I want to be my own boss, not work for anyone else, male or female. I'll think about Tony's offer as a back-up, but not right now."

"Fair enough. Now, let's go window-shopping and walk off some of that whipped cream. We'll come back for your truck later and get my car from the garage on our way home."

Rita took Liz's arm, and the two ladies in their straw hats strolled toward the seasonal gift shops and restaurants on the next block.

Liz headed for a small outdoor café decorated with overflowing baskets of ferns and impatiens. Dozens of moon and star mobiles chimed in the light breeze. A hand-painted sign announced "Jewel's Tea Cup Café" next to "Serena's Body & Soul Gift Shop." Liz sat down at one of the white resin tables. "You would have loved this café. Too bad it closed. I met such interesting people here. Not like most of the women in the Garden Club who never pot their own plants or pull their own weeds for fear of breaking a nail. You know, you can tell a lot about people from their hands, and I don't mean those fortune-telling lines, though Serena swears she can read the future.

"Serena?"

"Remember your friend Sally Starr from high school? The tall girl with the frizzy red hair and the Ouija board? She's changed back to her given name Serena since then. Sounds better for a fortuneteller, I guess. She owns the shop now. Inherited this old building and a lot of debts after her grandfather died from a hit-and-run last year. She came back from California to try to make a go of it. She's always been a bit...unusual but very nice."

Rita sat down on a plastic chair to rest. "Aunt Liz. You think *everyone's* nice. It's a wonder you've survived this long still believing that!"

Liz took off her sunglasses and stared hard at her niece. "You sound just like Mitch. He gives me such a hard time about people I meet. Reminds me of my Carlton. Always telling me not to trust strangers and be careful and all. Anyway, I used to have tea here every day before Jewel left town. She'd rented the café from Serena and just when she was starting to make a little money, she packed up and disappeared. No warning or forwarding address.

Just a note saying she was moving on. Very odd."

Rita shook her head. "Is there any local gossip you don't know?"

A bell clanged as the gift shop door opened. A tall redhead in a purple caftan stood with her arms wide open. "Well look who's back in town! I can't believe it's you, girl! Give me a hug!" Rita grinned and stood, dwarfed by the woman with the dangling crescent moon earrings.

"Sally! You look gorgeous!"

"Thank you, I've been transformed. I'm Serena Starr now. No more 'Too Tall Sally' or 'Mustang Sally' for me. That was a previous life or non-life if you remember high school." She winked. "Come on in. My tearoom's not open today, but I make exceptions for special ladies. I've got all kinds of varieties, a state-of-the-art espresso machine, and so much cool stuff you'll go nuts."

The shop was full of good smells, incense, chocolate, teas, and coffee. Angels, moons, and stars hung from the ceiling. Curious New Age products crowded the shelves: astrology pins, candles, tarot cards, Indian scarves, wind chimes, and books on everything from aliens to Zen. "Sit here and I'll do your cards after I get your tea. I'm very good at it."

"My cards? Honest, Sally…"

"Serena. I'm not joking. I don't answer to Sally anymore. Do you still use your married name?

"No, but…"

"No buts. Adios and 'Rest in Peace' to 'Mrs. Kevin Myers' and 'Sally.' There's a time to stay and a time to move on, and honey, we are moving on, right?" Serena paused to pour hot water into three small teapots and set an assortment of herbal teas on the glass table.

Rita nodded as she selected a teabag. "So what's your story?"

"Well, I've been with a few jerks myself, but

some nice guys, too. Came close to remarrying again, but I'm happy with life. I've learned a lot. I have two wonderful sons back in California, practically launched into adulthood. One's planning a naval career to get away from his dad the philosophy professor. The younger one's in film school near his dad the screenwriter. He's less of a jerk than my first ex, and we've tried to cooperate with raising the kids. My concept of Mr. Right is evolving...like me. And I've evolved into Serena, not Sally, okay?"

Rita grinned. "Okay, 'Serena' it is. I might slip from time to time, but I'll try. You're still the nicest kook I ever knew. Graduated from late night Ouija boards to tarot cards when you went to California, huh? I bet the tourists love it, especially from a tall, red-headed gypsy."

"Damn straight. And by the way, I have a confession to make. You were so gullible I used to push the Ouija slider to whatever you wanted to hear. I even spelled answers backwards. But these cards are legit and I have a gift. I take it very seriously. Ask your Aunt Liz. Am I good at this or what?"

"Yes, dear. You are," Liz agreed as she dunked her chamomile tea bag up and down. "You serve the best cup of tea in the whole town, and the best brownies, too. And that is a hint, even though we're stuffed."

"That's not what I meant. Remember the day you won big at Atlantic City? Who told you to go that morning when you didn't want to? And what about the fire I warned you about?"

"What fire, Aunt Liz?"

"Just a small electrical one. Started by the bug zapper outside. It was my usual day for going to Atlantic City on the bus, and if Mitch hadn't come home for lunch early and discovered the fire, the whole house might have burned down! He replaced the old outlet and redid the entire deck. So like I tell you, things work out for the best, even a fire."

Serena passed the brownies over to the older woman. "Yeah, well, I hope so, but Liz, I still want you to be real careful. Last time I did your reading, something was not quite right. Some kind of loss, something missing. Like a balloon about to pop. Remember that image of being too close to the sun?"

"Yes, Serena, but remember, they're just cards. Life is about making wise choices and following your heart, not picking good cards."

"Don't listen to her, Rita. Come on. I'll do your cards. You'll see." Serena grabbed Rita's hand and dragged her over to a small table behind a fringe of dangling beads. "Nice touch, huh? You always said I reminded you of that psychic Lady Fatima on the boardwalk, minus the scraggly black hair and ugly mole. And I don't even need a crystal ball with these." Taking out a round deck of cards, she shuffled them expertly. "No medieval scary stuff, just cool drawings based on Native American mythology, animal spirits, and goddesses. Now open yourself to what's coming. Clear your mind and let go. Let come what comes."

Rita settled into the chair and sighed. "The last time I let go and did something without planning, I ended up married. And I'm real clear I don't want to do that again anytime soon, so no 'tall, dark, and handsome' cards, okay?"

"Shhh! Relax. Stop trying to be the boss. You're not in charge, anyway. Haven't you noticed things happen you can't control? Aren't I right, Liz? Now close your eyes, Rita. Take a nice deep breath and pick a card with your left hand - it's more intuitive. Then describe what you see."

Rita selected a round card and opened her eyes. Flipping it over on the table she said, "I see a hunter in the forest aiming his bow and arrow at a target surrounded by animals and wooden shields. He looks like a cross between Robin Hood and a medicine man. What does that mean?"

"It's all about archetypes, you know, the hero's journey. This guy is a powerful, grounded male on a quest, a seeker of something important." Serena turned a page in a thick paperback manual and paused as she skimmed. "Oooh, you'll like this part: The Hunter is earthy and revels in sexuality. Someone good with his hands. He could stand for the active part of your own personality, or a new man coming into your life. The target represents focusing on goals. Was the card tilted, upside-down, or upright, the way you have it now?"

"I didn't notice. Does it matter?"

"Of course. I should have looked. Reversed can mean bad news or a blockage of your energy flow. Anyway, the first card stands for where you are right now and what's most important to you. An upright Hunter could mean it's time to look for your right work and accomplish goals. Maybe romance with a great guy. A slanted or upside-down card could indicate obstacles to your dreams. Sorry I still have to keep consulting this explanation book, though I don't let my paying customers see me checking it out. Come on, pick another card. I'll be more observant about which way it's facing. The second one in this three card spread represents challenges in your near future."

Serena watched Rita turn over another card from the array on the table and shook her head. "The Tower card can be a rough draw, Rita. It often predicts major life upheavals and destruction of existing relationships and structures..."

"Too late," Rita interrupted. "I've already done that. I'm starting fresh."

"Ever the optimist. Well, the card was almost upright, and I do see change and romance in your future. Just beware of possible danger. Now tell me about the card."

Rita studied the image. "Well, Lady Serena, I see a very weird card of a woman perched on a tower being struck by lightning and about to be demolished by a tidal wave. That may signify something to you, but I don't need cards or a book to tell you what my immediate challenge is. After a short vacation, I need to start a new job and avoid getting fixed up, romanced, or trapped by a man. My quest? To take it easy for a change and enjoy myself. I'm just going to walk along the beach and spend time with Aunt Liz. I can't afford to not work forever but right now, I intend to do nothing. Tony Jennings offered me a job. I told him no, but I'll keep it in mind."

"Tony. *The* Tony Jennings, mover and shaker? I bet he pays really well. One of his real estate agents wanted to list this property, but I told the guy I wasn't ready to throw in the towel. Not yet. Depends on my kids. I may want to move back to the West Coast, but if my younger son switches to the stage, he might be interested in living closer to the Big Apple."

Rita sighed. "At the rate I'm going, if I ever have kids they'll be playing with your grandchildren!"

Serena laughed. "Bite your tongue, girlfriend! I'm not ready for that. But why not consider Tony's offer?"

"I admit it's tempting, but I want my own business. No more working my tail off for someone else's Mustang payment or gambling losses. I saved every dime I earned and Kevin blew it all, so I can forget about owning a fitness club for a long time. In a few weeks, I'll start looking for a couple of rooms to set up my massage therapy business. I've done massages at homes by personal appointment, but I don't like being on someone else's turf and lugging equipment anymore. I don't want to deal with potential weirdoes, either, but I might have to take the chance if I can't afford the summer rent for an office."

Serena closed her book and grinned. "How about renting some space from me? With the café closed, I could use a tenant in the vacant office on the other side of my shop. And your clients would be exactly the kind of customers I'm looking for: interested in holistic health, spirituality, and spending money on their bodies. It'd be great for both of us."

"What about my questionable cards? Aren't you afraid of the possible danger coming into my life and destroying your structure?" Rita teased.

"I think 'danger' was a bit strong. Maybe 'unsettling' or 'uneasy' are better word choices. Besides, change is often uncomfortable, not bad. Maybe you're only in danger of losing beach time if you fix up this place." She grabbed a set of keys. "Come check it out for yourself. You, too, Liz."

Serena jumped up from the table and headed for a door in the main part of the gift shop. She inserted an ancient passkey into the keyhole. "This used to be a doctor's office. It would be perfect for you, Rita. If you help me out with the store sometimes, I'll rent it to you real cheap. It'll be fun, like old times."

Rita edged around piles of old furniture and file cabinets coated with dust. There was a side entrance to the parking lot and three rooms. The large one could be her waiting room and office, and the other two were the perfect size for massage rooms. She imagined soft music and candles. "I love the space, Serena, but it needs a ton of work. And this grimy carpeting has to go."

"You're right, Rita," her aunt said from the doorway. "But after Mitch gets done with it, you'll have the perfect place for your business."

"Aunt Liz, I'm not asking Mitch to help. I can do

things myself."

"Nonsense, dear, you can paint, but you're no carpenter. Mitch wouldn't charge much, if at all, and Lord knows he's running out of things to do at my house. Maybe you could do something for him in exchange for his labor. He doesn't take money."

Rita grumbled, "I can't imagine what I'd want to do for him. And that reminds me. I didn't want to say anything around Tony, but Mitch is hardly the 'silver-haired gentleman' you mentioned on the phone. I got in late last night and he practically mauled me on the doorstep. He said he was only protecting your house in the dark, but it didn't take that long to discover I wasn't armed and dangerous."

Serena raised her eyebrows and grinned. "Oooh. And you said there wasn't any danger in your life." She turned to Liz and patted her arm. "Liz, have you been keeping secrets from me? Who is this Mitch you have living at your house? Is he single and available? Or do you have your eye on him?"

"Serena! Get your mind out of the gutter, young lady! He has streaks of gray in his hair, but he's much too young for me! I imagine he's single, but I don't know. He's just a nice young man who keeps to himself and takes care of the place for me. Sometimes I think he's a little sad, but I'm not one to pry. When he wants to tell me something, he will."

Rita chuckled. "Aunt Liz, for someone who's not 'one to pry' you sure know everybody's business. Perfect strangers in the checkout line in Shop Rite tell you their most intimate secrets. So why hasn't Mitch told you his life story? He's lived above your garage longer than a year and you don't even know if he's single or married? Either you're slipping, or maybe he's hiding something..."

"Nonsense! I know good character when I see it, and I like having him around. He may not say much about his past, but I trust him a lot more than those slick talkers like the one you married, Rita. Big talk but no action—or not the right kind. I'll never forgive that so-and-so Kevin for hurting you."

Rita hugged her aunt. "Thanks for being on my side, Aunt Liz, but my ex-husband is ancient history. And I saw what Mitch did to your kitchen. It's beautiful. If you think he's a good guy, I promise I'll ask him for advice about fixing this place." She didn't add that Mitch didn't like her and he wouldn't want to help her anyway, so why argue about it with Aunt Liz? Even as a child, she'd learned that was pointless.

Liz squeezed her niece's hand. "That's my Rita. You won't be sorry." Rita smiled and already wished she hadn't agreed to consult Mitch. He was probably still sore about his shin and her sarcastic comments. Even if he agreed to help her because he liked Aunt Liz, he'd probably charge her more. She couldn't offer him free room and board.

"Well, Rita, if he's good-looking," Serena purred as they reentered the gift shop, "I'm sure you could think of *some* way to compensate him. You said you didn't want 'tall, dark, and handsome.' How about tall, silver, and handy? If you don't want him, send him over to me for a reading or some palm work. I do wonderful work with my hands, too. And speaking of hands, you have one last card to pick, the indicator of what comes next in your future. Come over here and choose the last one."

"We don't have time. We've got to stop by the garage to get Aunt Liz's car. It closes early today."

"It'll only take a second to humor your future landlord. Pick a card. Now."

"Okay. I give up. You're both relentless." Rita went over to the small table, grabbed a card, and stuffed it into her friend's pocket. "Here. Now let's get going, Aunt Liz, before she breaks out her Ouija board or puts me to work. Serena, I'll get back to you about the rental."

"Hey, aren't you curious about the card? Want to know what's coming next in your life?" Serena called out as Rita rushed Liz out the door and back into the sun.

Rita shook her head and waved.

Serena pulled the round card out of her pocket and studied the disturbing image. A viper displayed its fangs as it coiled through a skull atop a heap of wrinkled brown leaves. *Death.* "Be careful, Rita," she whispered. Good thing she hadn't looked at it while Liz was around. You never knew how people would take the Death card. You could tell them a million times that it was symbolic, and not always sinister, and they'd still take it literally...worrying about who was going to die or if their best black dress was ready to wear.

Serena slid the card back into the deck and shuffled without focusing. Depending on the slant, even the archer on that first card could be troubling. Was Rita the hunter or the target?

The Tower card cautioned Rita to prepare for drastic change, but would she listen? She hadn't seemed to take the cards seriously. Yes, her reading could be positive: death to the past, shedding an old way of life and giving birth to a new business, a new partnership. Or not. Either way, Serena vowed to keep an eye on her friend. She wouldn't mention the Death card, not unless Rita asked about the last selection. And maybe not even then...unless Rita needed a warning.

Chapter Four

As soon as the car doors slammed, Mitch got up from the front porch glider and limped down the steps. "Welcome home, Liz!" he hollered. "Here, let me take that." He bent down to grab the handle of the small suitcase from Rita's hand.

Rita gritted her teeth. "I can manage, thank you."

"You know, Liz. You could have warned me this niece of yours was such a handful. She attacked me in the dark last night when the electric was off and almost broke my leg!"

Liz laughed. "I heard something about that, but Rita made it sound like she was the injured party. You ought to be ashamed of yourself, Mitch. Almost a foot taller than she is and you got the worst of it in a tussle? I thought *you* were here to protect *me*."

Rita put the suitcase on a rocker. "Aunt Liz, the only protection you need is from yourself. You trust people to be as good as you are. And, believe me, they're not."

"Such cynicism, young lady! You're complaining like that dreadful child at the ice cream parlor who had to have a ten-dollar banana split. Now you two might have started off on the wrong foot last night, but we're family, and family helps each other."

"Family?" Rita glared at Mitch who winked.

"Think of me as the brother you never had. Unless maybe you'd like to think of me in a different way, especially after our close encounter last night."

"Yeah. Dream on. You're more like a long-lost relative who should have stayed that way. Or the black sheep that bothers the rest of the flock."

"Mitch, don't pay attention to her. She's a sweetheart. Deep down." Liz put her two hands on Rita's face and squeezed her cheeks as if she were a toddler.

"Rita needs your help. She's going to start her own massage business in town. We'd like you to look over the building and do a few things to get the place ready." She rummaged through her purse and pulled out her keys. "Here. Be a dear and drive her over there to check it out. I need to take a little nap and then we'll decide how we're going to celebrate Rita's homecoming. Okay?"

Liz dropped the keys into Mitch's hands, picked up her suitcase, and opened the screen door. "And Rita's right. This bag is too light for her to need your assistance. I didn't raise her to be helpless, you know." Liz smiled and disappeared into the house.

Mitch leaned against the railing. "So you need the black sheep's help, huh?"

Rita hesitated at the door. "Not if you don't want to. And I'm sorry about putting you on the spot. Aunt Liz has always been a bit pushy...and sometimes a terribly obvious matchmaker. I think she was trying to fix me up at lunch, too. That's just how she is. So don't feel obligated."

"You're right. I don't have to do anything I don't want to. But how about that truce I offered last night? You know she'll bug the hell out of both of us till I check out the building."

Rita twirled her straw hat and considered the options. "Well, you're right about that. Let's go take a quick look. No promises, no strings. Deal?"

Mitch nodded and shook her hand, holding it a few seconds longer than she expected. His brown eyes studied hers for a moment before he spoke. "Rita, I like my life simple and uncomplicated. I'm not looking for anything from you, understand?" He gave her a lop-sided grin. "Of course, I don't know what *your* intentions are. Maybe I should be the one who doesn't trust *you*!"

"Oh, please! Let's just go and get this over with. It's the old doctor's office by the New Age gift shop north of Jackson's Ice Cream. And remember, we're only humoring Aunt Liz." Rita put her hat back on. "I'm ready when you are. And if it's too much trouble for you or too much money for me, we're both off the hook."

"Deal, Princess," Mitch extended his hand again and shook hers firmly. His felt strong but surprisingly soft, with few calluses. She stared at their hands; his large tan one engulfed hers. His nails were trim and neat, without the dry rough hangnails that edged hers. She remembered the tiny plaster of Paris handprint she'd made in kindergarten that had shattered long ago during one of her moves: pale, vulnerable, easily broken.

She realized she was still holding on and massaging his knuckles with her thumb. She looked up and released his hand. "Sorry, I couldn't help noticing how big your hands are. Smooth…and nice." The image of the archer on the card and Serena saying "good with his hands" popped into her mind. Rita turned red, imagining how her words must have sounded. "Damn. Can't believe I still blush. Not to mention my bad habit of blurting things out and thinking later. Sorry."

Mitch studied Rita's pink cheekbones. "No problem. And thank you. I mean about the nice hands. Come on, let's go," he added quietly. "We'll pick up some food on the way home so Liz won't have to cook. Sometimes she's more tired than she admits."

Rita followed Mitch to the driveway. *Home.* It sounded so natural the way he said it, as if he'd lived here for years.

"Liz doesn't have a set of tools in her car so we'll go in my truck. I picked it up while you were gone." He opened the driver's side door and motioned for her to slide in. "The passenger's lock is jammed from the outside, but you can escape from inside if you need to. Or want to." He looked directly into her eyes and put out his hand to help her into the truck. "After you."

They drove along in silence. A million questions ran through Rita's mind before she settled on one. "So how did you end up living above Aunt Liz's garage?"

Mitch took a moment to check his rear view mirror and adjust the outside one. "What did she tell you?"

"Not much. The week I was here last summer, you were away fishing. She made you sound like a polite old man who was staying temporarily to fix a few things. I felt better knowing someone was here to watch over her."

"And now you don't?" Mitch asked.

"I didn't say that. But you're not exactly what I expected."

"Expectations." He paused and turned briefly to look at her. "The quicksand of life. They'll get you into trouble."

Rita studied Mitch's profile. "That's an odd statement. Everyone has expectations. Or have you given them up along with a regular job?"

"There you go again. And I thought we had an agreement to put down the pistols." Mitch's jaw hardened slightly. "If you're so uncomfortable with me being around and keeping an eye on Liz, why don't you check me out?"

"I asked around. Her friends from the Garden Club raved about how helpful you've been. Fixed their minor plumbing problems and did odd jobs. I figured I didn't have to worry about you."

"You don't. Stop worrying. Relax." Mitch chuckled. "You're in the relaxation business. Isn't that what you came home for?"

Rita nodded. "Yes, but…"

"Let go of the 'buts' and the past. Last night, I thought you were a cat burglar. Before that, I thought you were a burned-out high school teacher who did massages on the side. That's what I expected."

"I wasn't burned out. Just tired of knocking myself out on a substitute's pay, juggling other jobs on the side, and waiting for a permanent teaching position. With all the bills, I needed more than a pat on the back or an empty promise of a job opening someday."

Mitch smirked. "Three jobs? Did the Jersey Princess charge too much on her credit cards?"

"No. Not that it's any of your business. I'm the one who should be grilling you. Despite your silver streaks, you must be in your forties. If you're such a great carpenter, why aren't you earning more money and living in your own home? And why are your hands so smooth?"

Mitch slowed down to let a pedestrian dash across the two-lane highway. Rita saw the edge of his mouth curve slightly and watched a dimple deepen in his cheek. He glanced over at her with a twinkle in his eye. "I knew you liked the feel of my hands on you last night. The way you started panting and squirming…before you kicked me, that is."

He reached across the seat and lightly traced the outline of her thigh over the gauzy fabric. "You have such smooth skin, too. Maybe you could use a special massage yourself, you know, to loosen you up."

Rita picked up his hand and placed it back on the steering wheel. "My interest in touching men's bodies is *purely* professional..." Flustered, she began again, "I meant I'm in it for the money." She felt her cheeks heating up again as Mitch laughed.

"And stop teasing me, Mitch! I've had extensive training in the field and years of experience. I was the most-requested massage therapist of both men and women at the best hotels in Atlantic City."

"You do both men and women?" Mitch raised his eyebrows and looked shocked. "In hotels?"

"In the spa, you fool! It's therapeutic! Not X-rated!"

Mitch smiled. "I don't have a certificate, but I know what feels good. Tell me, what happens if a guy starts getting turned on? You're an attractive woman...when you're not whining, kicking, or arguing."

"Massage is sensual, not sexual, when it's done professionally. It's a joining of mind, body, and spirit." Rita sighed and looked out the window. "I don't expect you to understand."

"I understand," Mitch said quietly. "But I do enjoy teasing you. You turn a bright shade of pink. Kind of refreshing in a woman, especially one of your age and level of experience." He pulled into the parking lot of Serena's Body & Soul Gift Shop and studied the sign. "So what happened to your friend's mind?"

"What are you talking about?"

"Sorry, bad joke. You know, it's usually body, *mind*, and soul, but her sign only has two out of three. Is she one of those mindless, touchy-feely flakes your aunt is so fond of bringing home?"

"No. By the way, she was my best friend in high school. Please don't embarrass me or give her a hard time, okay? She may not think you're as charming as Aunt Liz does."

"Listen, if I decide to take the job, it's only because I think so highly of Liz. Maybe you'd find me charming, too, if you stopped being mad at the male half of the population."

"I'm not asking for your charm or your charity, and I intend to pay for your labor."

"I won't take it. Not when it's for someone I know. I don't work for money."

"Right. Are you independently wealthy or something?"

"Let's say I prefer barter or just doing things because I feel like it. Seems to work out pretty well." Mitch shut off the ignition and turned to face Rita.

"Mitch, this whole project might be hopeless. Let's go in and check it out first. We can always haggle later, right?"

Mitch silently propped open the truck door and paused. "Okay, Princess. Or should I say 'Boss?' Let's see what you've gotten yourself into." He extended his hand and helped her out of the truck.

As he followed Rita to the entrance, Mitch studied the front of the old Victorian. Good quality and full of potential. Original wood. Porch slightly sagging but basically sound. Massive custom trim around the huge bay window in the front, filled with statues of wizards and unicorns, books, crystals and geodes. He turned the glass-handled knob and noticed the lock, a true antique. This place would be so easy to break into.

Door chimes announced their presence as Mitch pulled on the massive oak door with its original stained glass and carvings. Indian music wailed from another room.

He ducked to avoid bumping his head on a star and moon mobile and stopped in the center of the room. Without a word, he scanned the ceilings, walls, and floors. He walked a full circle and took a deep breath. Exotic smells hung in the air, musky, earthy, incense blended with coffee and chocolate. Zodiac signs and calligraphy of Buddhist sayings covered the faded wallpaper while small fountains gurgled on display cases and antique cabinets.

He'd always felt houses had spirits. A sense of history, an imprint, a story of all the terrible, amazing, and boring things that happened to the people within. Not that he believed in ghosts, but somehow people left their mark on a place. More than physical traces like tiny pencil marks and dates on an old closet wall showing how tall long-gone Johnny or Susie had been.

In years of restoration work, he'd found a few secrets left behind. An old cigar box of trinkets hidden under a closet floorboard, a love note tucked behind an old piece of paneling and forgotten. A journal, a map. He'd thought about turning them over to the owners but had kept them all instead. He respected their secrets.

Mitch touched the intricate molding and shook his head. This fine old house must be shuddering with all the New Age paraphernalia in it.

"This will be the entrance to my place," Rita said as she motioned him to the left.

"Look at the wood on this door," Mitch exhaled softly and lovingly stroked its surface. "Solid oak, almost two inches thick! Hand-carved panels, probably from Italy, and some idiot painted it blue! And whoever stuck thumbtacks in it to hold up a stupid astrology poster ought to be shot. Who the hell would do something so stupid?"

"And who the hell are you, Cowboy? The building inspector? Or the style police?" A tall redhead in a long purple dress breezed in from the kitchen with a plateful of brownies and stopped in front of Mitch.

Rita cleared her throat. "Hi, Serena. This is Mitch. You know, the *charming* carpenter Aunt Liz mentioned? Thanks to her badgering, he came to check out the renovation project. He's the 'silver-haired gentleman' she spoke so highly of."

"Gentleman? This guy?" Serena frowned as Mitch stared back at her without a word.

"Well, Aunt Liz thinks so. Right now he's disguised as a smartass handyman who might help us get going faster. Gentleman or not, here's Mitch Grant. And Mitch, meet the so-called 'idiot' you just insulted, my friend and local 'New Age Goddess' Serena Starr." Rita paused and watched her long-time friend put down the plate and sit on a stool. "Hey, guys, say something. I'm not the mother hen Aunt Liz is, but if she were here, she'd have you promise to play nice together and share some brownies."

Mitch narrowed his eyes and stepped forward with his arm extended to shake Serena's hand. "Sorry, I get pissed when people screw up a beautiful old building. Do art museums give Mona Lisa a new hairdo when they touch her up? Trim the thighs of those fat Renaissance ladies? No. I'll refinish the door for you after Rita's job is done."

"Who said I hired you?" Rita asked. "You haven't even seen the place, and we never agreed on a price."

"Not a problem. You pay for materials. No charge for labor, but if you're uncomfortable with that, I'm sure you'll think of something you can do in return. I always leave my customers satisfied." Mitch gave Rita a look that could melt ice in a blizzard.

"Oh, really?" Serena softened and slipped her arm through his. "Well, in *that* case, let's take the grand tour and see what magic you can do."

"Coming, Rita?" Mitch glanced over his shoulder and then turned his attention back to Serena. "Serena Starr, is that your real name?"

"Yes, I'm a victim of hippie parents who still live on a commune. My grandfather used to call me Sally, but now I'm back to my cosmic roots. But tell me about Mitch Grant, handyman to the local seniors. Where have you been hiding? Whenever I stop in to see Liz, you're never around. I would have remembered you."

Serena smiled as she glanced at Mitch's tight T-shirt and tanned biceps. "Liz didn't mention you were more my age than hers. That silver hair is deceiving."

"You have a thing for silver, huh?" Mitch looked down at the turquoise and silver rings she wore on every finger, the heavy crescent moon earrings swaying from her ears.

He bumped into a dragon mobile that started clanging. "Tall woman like you should know mobiles are dangerous things if you're not short like Rita. Smart women also know when to ask for help, like when not to paint a solid oak door blue because it's an incredible piece of craftsmanship."

"Tell that to the idiot who painted it pink before me, Cowboy. Listen, if you can help Rita fix up the rooms next door, that's great. Someday, I might restore this old place. Maybe I won't. Maybe I'll paint more doors blue or purple or neon yellow." She fumbled with the ancient skeleton key. "But for now, let's look over the space I promised Rita, and if you're extra nice, I'll give you one of my best-in-the-world brownies."

"Brownies like your flower-child mom used to make? With a little extra something slipped inside?"

"Yeah, a touch of cosmic love. No illegal substances. You better watch your manners if you want a brownie...or the privilege of working here. We 'goddesses' have to watch out for pushy guys like you. Right, Rita?"

Rita forced a thin smile and nodded. She followed them into the old doctor's office. Grime and dust covered everything.

Mitch examined each room before speaking. "It'll

take about two or three weeks. What are you ladies willing to give me in return for my hard work?"

Serena looked at Rita staring at the floor. "Well, I don't know about my massage friend here, but I'll feed you lunch or dinner anytime I'm here. Fifty percent discount on tarot readings, and all the aphrodisiac incense you can use." She grinned. "You look pretty good, but with your personality, you might need some help. Hell, you can have free tarot readings if you're as good as Liz says you are."

Mitch shook his head. "Forget the cards, throw in free brownies, and it's a deal."

Turning to Rita, Mitch went on, "Now, Miss Rita. What special talents or skills are you willing to share?"

Rita looked up at him. "You don't need a personal fitness trainer from the looks of you..."

"Nothing like stating the obvious, Rita," Serena interrupted. "But I've got a better idea. How about a free massage after a hard day's work? What do you think, Mitch?"

"I think I like you, Serena Starr. Never had that offered in trade, but I don't know if she can control herself around me. I bet she didn't tell you how she attacked me last night. And we didn't even know each other's names!"

Rita turned red. "Serena, you're supposed to be my friend, not his. I want to keep this businesslike. Mitch, I'll pay you as soon as clients pay me."

"Oh, no. You don't get the easy way out. I won't take money. No strings. I just like teasing you."

"I don't expect to get anything for free."

"Fine. No such thing as 'free' anyway."

"Well, I don't want to owe you anything either. I've never been dependent on a man and I never will be."

"Rita, if you feel obligated, that's your choice. I'm sure you could come up with something to do for me," Mitch said with a wink. "I'm not doing this for you anyway. I'm doing it for myself. I'll love seeing the way this place looks when it's done right, plus it'll make Liz happy." He looked out through the sooty windows. "I know. Buy my gas to and from this place and be my go-fer on the job. Then we'll get done quicker, too."

Rita paused. "Well, all right. I wanted to do a lot of the work myself, anyway."

"We start tomorrow. Up at six, here by seven. Any problems with that?"

"No, that's fine with me, Mitch."

"I need to take a few measurements, make a list, and then we're out of here." Grabbing a couple of brownies, he added, "You don't mind if I test some of these while I work, do you, Miss Starr?"

"Help yourself, Cowboy," Serena said and watched approvingly as he disappeared into the shop next door. "And call me 'Serena,' okay?" she hollered.

As soon as Mitch was out of earshot, Serena walked over and put her arm around her friend's shoulder. "Rita, don't you think my massage-a-day idea could be quite therapeutic for both of you?"

"Thanks, Serena, but since we're living under the same roof, a massage might be a little too close and personal."

"I saw him look at you. I think he might feel very comfortable getting a massage from you. Maybe you're the one who'd be uncomfortable. Is it hard to resist touching an attractive, muscled man like that, especially one that wants to help you fix things around the place? Imagine what a massage might lead to with a passionate, sweaty hunk like that."

"Serena, you're supposed to be transformed and spiritual. If I didn't make this clear before, here goes: I need to focus on getting myself back on my feet, not swept off them.

"Besides, I'm a little worried about Aunt Liz. I

was so busy working extra jobs at the casino—giving massages and dealing blackjack - to clean up Kevin's financial mess, I guess I neglected her. Maybe she wouldn't be so dependent on Mitch if I'd visited more instead of only calling every week. And I've heard a lot of lines before, especially at the casino, but never Mitch's line: 'I don't charge.' Who does he think he is, Gandhi?"

"Honey, I'd love to see Mitch in a little loincloth like Gandhi's, but I definitely wouldn't be thinking spiritual thoughts, or even passive resistance. You know, I have a book on some Hindu practices that totally connect the body and spirit. I could loan it to you."

"Thanks, but no thanks!" Rita laughed. "You haven't changed much, Serena. Still as irreverent as ever. And don't think for a minute I believe everything you say. Or that our Cowboy in there is just a noble do-gooder who rescues elderly damsels with his carpentry magic and no thought of personal gain. He's keeping an eye on Aunt Liz, and I'm going to keep my eye on him."

"And maybe more than your eyes?" Serena snickered. "Now that could be fun! Help you get over that money-grubbing ex of yours."

Rita shook her head and hugged Serena. "Thanks for offering me the space. I'll help out here in the store whenever I can, and if it doesn't work out, at least you'll have the place next door fixed up to rent."

"Well, if we don't make a go of it, I may leave town. The taxes are killing me and my kids are a continent away. Almost independent young adults, but I miss them at times. Now that Gramps passed on, I don't have any family left here. Besides, it's hard to go to the beach when you own a store. Remember the days when we wished we were grown-ups? We didn't know how good we had it."

Mitch stood in the doorway, clipboard in hand. "Ready to go, Massage Lady?" He strode across the room to where Serena had resumed untangling old jewelry spread out on the display case. "Serena, I'm going to make this a showplace. You'll have customers coming in to drool over the molding." He watched her free an antique cameo locket from a twisted chain and place it in a black velvet box.

"As long as they drool and buy enough of this stuff for me to pay my mortgage, they're welcome." Serena extended her hand and shook Mitch's firmly. "Thanks for the help. Rita has the keys. I don't do early mornings. Brunch at ten. My treat, remember?"

Mitch nodded and headed for the door. Rita followed and stopped to look around. Less than twenty-four hours ago she thought Mitch was going to rape and kill her on the beach and now they were practically partners. What was she getting herself into? Taking a deep breath, she shut the chiming door behind her and raced to the battered old red truck, its engine already running.

Mitch got out and let her climb in. "How does Serena get her merchandise, you know, like that old jewelry?"

"Some on commission I guess. People get tired of things or need money. A few find things at the water's edge with metal detectors. I bet she buys pieces mostly at garage or estate sales. I remember we used to spend Saturdays picking through old memories. Some treasures, some junk." She looked at him curiously. "Why?"

"Nothing," he murmured. "Just seems sad to think that bits of people's lives, their special occasions and memories, get reduced to trinkets worn around someone else's neck."

Rita hesitated. "That sounds pretty bleak. Why not imagine how happy the locket's new owner will be instead of how depressing it is that someone lost it or had to let it go? Like Aunt Liz says, it's all about attitude. I'd rather visualize how great my office will look than wonder what happened to the poor old doctor who used to practice here. Maybe he's dead...or maybe he's playing golf in Florida. Better to picture him practicing his swing in crazy plaid pants than pushing up daisies! Besides, I like daisies."

Mitch nodded. "You're more like your aunt than I thought. Now let's get you home and order some pizza. Your choice of toppings. We've got a lot of work ahead of us tomorrow."

Chapter Five

Rita's first day of renovation was devoted to demolition and removing debris. She tossed out the faded calico curtains, scraped the doctor's flaking black and gold name off the side door, and stripped old wallpaper from the plaster walls in the bathroom. By the time Mitch got back from the home center with an armload of molding, lumber, stain, and other supplies, her back ached, but her heart soared.

"Break time!" he called out. "Coffee's in the truck. Could you get it? Mine's black. Yours has lots of milk and sugar."

Rita stopped to stretch. "How did you know that's how I take my coffee?"

"I watched you in the kitchen yesterday morning. After our memorable first night alone together at the beach house."

Rita rolled her eyes. "Aunt Liz should have warned me you were a horrible tease. You better not repeat that to anybody. I'll deny it."

"Did we, or did we not spend your first night back in town alone in the dark with no electricity?" Mitch paused and smiled. "But enough small talk. Get the coffee and I'll tell you what to do next."

Rita dusted off her hands on the back of her tight jeans and headed for the door. He'd thought she looked good in exercise shorts and that flimsy sundress, but what she did for a pair of jeans was beyond words. He watched her rounded backside as she moved away from him, quick and purposeful.

When she returned and handed him the coffee,

he looked down at her T-shirt, covered with old paint stains. Her tiny nails were bitten slightly crooked. He grabbed the steaming cup, and reached out to pick some pieces of old plaster out of her curly brown ponytail.

"Wearing your work. I see from your shirt that you've painted before. Are you any good?"

"I don't know what a professional would say, but I get the job done."

"That's what's important, unless you do it badly."

"Never had any complaints before, but then I always did my own work. Never had an expert or a partner to help or critique. I don't mind suggestions, but I don't like taking orders or being pushed around."

He nodded and looked at everything she'd accomplished. "I hope you're as good at construction and painting as you are on the tearing down and garbage phase. None of my other helpers ever got this much done and looked so good. And the black bra under the 'Penguin Lust' cartoon shirt? That's hardly a uniform for a house painter, but it works for me."

Rita blushed. "You were honking the horn. I grabbed my oldest T-shirt and didn't think about the color until later. You weren't supposed to notice."

"Right. Well, if you don't want to be noticed, don't wear tight jeans and threadbare shirts. We construction workers are only human, you know."

"I've heard that rumor. Thanks for the coffee. Can we get back to work?"

"Liz never said you were a slave driver."

"I want to get a lot done and knock off early. Maybe go to the beach. It's been so long since I just sat on the sand, felt the sun, and listened to the waves. Is that okay with you?"

"Fine. First thing you said that made some

sense. I was beginning to think you were all work and no play."

"Well, I intended to play and rest all summer, but I don't expect Aunt Liz to support me. I need to focus on making money."

Mitch shook his head and sighed. "You *make* a life. You *earn* money. Easy to confuse the two, real easy. But back to business. Want to see how this crown molding's going to look? Not only classy but will hide the imperfections in the corners. Climb that ladder and hold the end of this up." He watched her climb to the middle step and turn around, waiting for him to hand her the other end.

"Well?" she said, with one hand reaching down, the other steadying herself on the top of the aluminum ladder. "What are you waiting for?"

"Sorry. The view distracted me. Maybe you should wear sweatpants if you want me to get this job done."

Rita laughed and shook her head. She grabbed the molding, placed it on the corner, and looked toward Mitch holding the other end up. "I guess you know your stuff, Cowboy. It's perfect. Now if you'll excuse me, I have an examining room to tear apart."

They worked in different sections, Rita ripping things down and dragging debris to the dumpster Mitch had rented. He knocked out two walls. By lunchtime, he'd taken out everything he could: old cabinets, battered examining tables, even the stained industrial gray carpeting. Underneath were beautiful hardwood floors, with light to dark variations that would gleam with resurfacing.

To Rita's horror, though, Mitch had broken the toilet and sink, leaving only the claw foot bathtub intact. "Are you crazy, Mitch? Why did you wreck those?"

"We'll refinish the tub. It's an original to this addition, but the other things were cheap and cracked. Not worth restoring."

"But functional. You should have asked me first. I could have made do with them for now. I don't want to spend a fortune here. Do you know how many massages I have to give to pay for a new toilet?"

"I guess it depends on what you charge. Do you have any idea how little it will cost?"

"No, but anything's more than what I wanted to spend. I may not be paying you cash for your labor, but I told Serena I'd pay for half the materials. She doesn't have much money on hand, either."

"Don't worry. I'll get some things wholesale, others for free. You can't imagine what some of these rich people on the beachfront throw away when they want to change colors or remodel in the latest style. Trust me. It won't cost you a dime for a lot of these things."

Rita knitted her brows close together and eyed him suspiciously as if he were a magician who had just pulled a quarter from behind her ear and she couldn't figure out where the coin had been hidden. "I don't want to be surprised with a big bill at the end of all this. I want to be informed about expenses at every step of this project. I've been kept in the dark before and I don't ever intend to be that stupid again."

Mitch put one finger gently on her lips. "Shhhh. Look at Liz. Do you see her complaining about my prices?" Rita shook her head, distracted by the tingle spreading across her face as he traced the outline of her mouth.

"Less talk. More action," he whispered and turned back to taping the new sheetrock.

Serena had popped in, left a plate of brownies with two mugs of milk, and hurried away. A slight drizzle had inspired some of the early season tourists to wander in from the beach, and business was brisk from the occasional chime Rita could hear over the buzz of Mitch's saw or the pounding of his hammer. He often tapped her on the shoulder or called her over to help with something heavy or awkward.

Around one, Serena brought them pitas stuffed with vegetables and sprouts. Mitch eyed the pocket warily and waited for Serena to leave. After one small bite, he removed the sprouts and ate the rest. "Healthy food," he said and washed it down with a glass of green tea. "I wonder if she has any peanut butter and jelly for tomorrow." Rita smiled. They sat outside on the porch with its peeling paint and watched the visitors flock back to the beach with the first ray of sun.

Rita was exhausted, but wouldn't admit it. She liked working on a project, making things look better. She'd once imagined that's what her life with Kevin was going to be: fixing up a home and sharing her dream of building a gym and spa complex complete with daycare for their clients' children as well as their own. Kevin would manage the business details and she would be the people person. Well, she had learned a lot about business and people the last few years. Not all of it good.

But today was different. She was nobody's victim. She felt powerful ripping this place apart and rebuilding it. With each crack of broken wood and every time she tossed a load of old blinds or other garbage into the dumpster, she imagined letting go of Kevin. This would be *her* place, a haven for those seeking relaxation and wellness. Her excitement was growing, and she closed her eyes and smiled.

"I'd offer a penny, but from the look of bliss on your face, you probably wouldn't sell your thoughts for so little," Mitch said.

Rita opened her eyes and realized she hadn't been listening to him at all.

"Sorry, I was thinking how great this place will look. What did you say?"

Mitch pushed his sunglasses on top of his head and put out a hand to help pull her up. "I said you have a nice smile when you let go. Now, if you want to hit the beach later, lunch - if you want to call it that - is over. The boss has spoken."

"I thought *I* was the boss and you're the hired hand," Rita protested.

He grunted. "I'm not 'hired.' That would mean you're paying me. Getting to be boss is another perk of not charging for labor!" Mitch pulled her hand with more force than she expected, and Rita suddenly found her face pressed against his chest. "Sorry," she muttered as she struggled to untangle herself and still hold onto the plate in her hand. She wrapped one arm around his neck and fell backward, pulling him over, too, and crashed onto the glider. His mug shattered on the porch as he landed on top of her.

Inches from her face, he paused and studied her green eyes. "Ms. Madison, do you always attack men on porches...or just me?"

His lips were so close to hers. Her heart raced and she held her breath. It had been so long since she had been this close to a man face-to-face, felt warm breath tickling her neck, the lingering scent of aftershave mixed with sweat and her own cologne.

"I'm so sorry. I'm not usually so clumsy. I swear! I used to be a gymnastics champ."

"A little rusty I guess. How long has it been?"

Rita blushed again, feeling exposed as if he'd read her mind. "Well, I've been divorced for almost three years, and it had been awhile before that, even before Kevin moved out. And I haven't dated anyone long enough to..."

Mitch looked puzzled and then laughed. "I meant, how long ago were you a gymnastics champ?

What did you think I was asking about? This maybe?" Mitch pressed his mouth to hers, softly at first, then firmly, nudging her moist lips slightly apart before backing up ever so slowly. He gazed into her questioning eyes as if he'd suddenly awakened from a dream.

"I don't know what to say," he mumbled. He got up abruptly and turned to see Serena standing nearby with a pitcher of lemonade and some chocolate chip cookies.

"I can see you two enjoyed lunch," Serena said after a short pause. "Want some dessert? Or have you already had some?"

Mitch walked past her and grabbed a couple of cookies. "Time to get back to work. Thanks for the green sandwich, but how about something less good for us tomorrow? Higher on the fat food chain? Like burgers? Grilled cheese?" His work boots clomped on the porch and he disappeared inside.

Serena smirked as she sat down on a creaky wicker chair. "I knew there was chemistry between you two. Tell me everything."

"Serena, there's nothing to tell. I tripped and we fell over and somehow...It's been awhile. Must have been some kind of automatic reaction. But it won't happen again, so don't make a big deal out of a little kiss, okay?"

"I sense something simmering below the surface here, and remember: I'm psychic."

"*Psycho* is more like it. Now, thanks for the lemonade and cookies, but I don't have time to sit around and chat." Rita bent to pick up the pieces of the broken mug.

Mitch stuck his head out the doorway. "Serena, door chimes and customers." Without waiting for an answer, he went back inside.

Serena leaned over to whisper in Rita's ear. "Watch yourself, girl. Remember the archer? Stay focused. The Cowboy seems like a real hunk, but don't screw up this arrangement before he gets the job done. I don't want you getting hurt again, either."

"Serena, I'm a big girl. I can control myself, and right now, we both need to get back to business."

For the rest of the afternoon, Mitch and Rita worked in separate rooms, and unlike earlier that morning, he didn't ask for help. When she had a question about the next job to do, he'd answer her in a businesslike tone, demonstrate how to do the work correctly, and watch her begin the task before leaving the room.

A few hours later, he reappeared. "Quitting time, Massage Lady. Tell Serena we'll be back tomorrow. I'll get my tools and lock up here."

They drove home in an uncomfortable silence, not the easy kind of quiet they'd shared at lunch. Before that kiss. Finally, Rita couldn't stand it. "Mitch, are you mad at me? I didn't mean to pull you down on me."

"Mad? Not at you. I'm mad at myself for kissing you. Not that it wasn't nice. Too nice, in fact. I don't want to complicate my life, or yours, by getting over-involved."

He drove the truck up the driveway and parked next to Liz's old clunker. "In some ways you remind me of my kid sister, and I'd like to keep it that way. I always loved to tease her. She'd turn red and tongue-tied like you do." He shut off the radio. "Rita, I don't want to risk having to leave here. Can we just be friends?"

"Sure," she smirked. "Do you really think you're such a gift to women I can't resist an accidental kiss? Get real."

Mitch's caramel eyes twinkled. "What a relief. You're back to insults. I was afraid our relationship had soured into something sweet. Or was leading to something meaningful." Mitch raised a suggestive eyebrow. "Look, Rita, how about we go back to our original deal? That is, if you can keep your hands off me."

"I'll fight my urges," Rita joked before turning serious. "Mitch, I don't know exactly what we have, but Aunt Liz likes you and that's good enough for me, as long as you don't have any hidden agendas."

"What you see is what you get," he grinned. "Or don't get." He slowly inched his arm around the back of the seat as if he were a teenager in a drive-in movie of long ago. He started to play with a few escaped curls resting on her neck. "It might feel so good to give in, though, wouldn't it? Even better than imagining it? Or fighting over not doing it?"

Rita playfully swatted his wandering hand away from her. "Mitch, you are incorrigible. Are you sure Aunt Liz didn't pick you up at one of those tacky singles bars in Seaside?"

He shook his head slightly and turned off the engine. "Drinking and sex don't fill up the emptiness. The funny thing is there really is no escape, yet we're always looking for one. That, or security. And it's never somewhere else."

Rita studied his features. "Mitch, you are intriguing. I'm not quite sure what those philosophical thoughts are about, but it sounds so poetic. And yet I know from experience it could all be bull."

"You're absolutely right. Enough talk. Get the hell out of my truck and go sun yourself. You're the palest Jersey Girl I've ever seen!"

"Thanks. And you may not like to hear it, but thank you for your help. For me, and for Aunt Liz. I don't know what I'd do without her, and I want to get back to work so I can help her out if she needs it. She seems a bit anxious about something. Maybe money. And that's not like her."

"Rita, I know you two don't like to accept help. You're used to giving it and doing things yourselves. So you're welcome, both of you."

He hopped out of the truck and held the door open for her, resisting the urge to tap her behind as she slid past him. What was he thinking of?

He'd thought he'd never be attracted to anyone else after he'd lost Ginger, and now his heart beat faster just thinking about Rita removing her belt, shimmying out of her dusty jeans, throwing black lace panties in the hamper, and pulling on a swimsuit. What would it be? A bikini or a sensible black tank? One with strange cutouts or tempting zippers? Living on the beach, he'd seen them all; until now, he thought he'd never want to lie on a beach blanket again with a special woman sharing the sun, sweat glistening on her shoulders.

He'd better shower in very cold water. He had to stop visualizing a tiny bikini, or hoping Rita might need his assistance with suntan lotion if he went by at the right moment. God, what was happening to him? He'd only barely survived the pain of losing Ginger. He needed to stay a loner, but it was suddenly getting harder.

Chapter Six

Rita stripped off her dusty T-shirt and struggled to peel off her sweat-soaked jeans. She studied the three swimsuits on the bed. When was the last time she'd agonized over a bathing suit, much less worn one? Working three jobs hadn't left much time for playing in the sun.

She closed her eyes and grabbed one, leaving the decision to Fate. Not the bikini, but at least it wasn't the sensible navy one. She pulled on the one-piece black suit with the plunging neckline and fishnet Vs on the sides and checked it out in the mirror. It would do. A bit Fredericks of Hollywood flashy, but it still fit. It looked great, in fact. *Eat your heart out, Kevin, wherever you are!*

She doused herself with spray-on sunscreen. Such a practical invention for single people with no significant others to spread lotion on their backs. Another reason she didn't need her ex-husband. She shoved a towel and a book into a canvas bag, slipped into sandals, and headed for the beach.

She smiled remembering the first time she'd been to the beach without Kevin after their marriage dissolved. She'd thought she'd covered her entire back with sunscreen, but missed a tiny section between her shoulders that remained a weird-shaped tan spot for the rest of the season. Branded. Every time she'd seen it, she'd cursed him for betraying her, for not being there for her. She'd known it was irrational even then, but now she could laugh at it. Maybe she was healing after all.

She threw her things on the sand and ran into

the surf. Plunging into the water, her skin turned to instant goose bumps. Definitely not the bathwater temperature of South Beach! Three years ago, she'd flown down to Miami for a bit of motherly sympathy after the final break-up with Kevin. The water was warm, but Rita's mother was as cold as ever. She seemed more concerned with protecting her hairdo, her condo, and her retired third husband from sand, sun, wind, and any disruption of their daily routine. Dealing with a divorcing daughter was uncomfortable.

Do widows have trouble understanding the pain of divorce, or was it only her mother who had a problem? Wishing two husbands hadn't died from natural causes and left you was a lot different from wishing that a scheming, cheating one had never existed on the planet to begin with. Kevin was lucky Rita hadn't killed him when the bastard told her he'd secretly had a vasectomy when she'd gone off the pill after ten years of marriage. Kids. Another thing she'd wanted someday with Kevin and wouldn't have.

"Be thankful you didn't have children," her mother kept repeating, even now. Not exactly the comfort Rita wanted to hear at age thirty-nine. She pictured her own dad in faded photos and tried to imagine what he might have said to his little girl. She hoped it wouldn't have been, "Be glad you didn't have kids." Unlike her widowed mom, Rita had no child and no life insurance to collect, just debts to repay.

Funny. Rita's mother looked like a younger version of Aunt Liz and even lived on the same ocean a thousand miles away, yet she'd always been too busy or too distant no matter where she was. When she'd remarried and moved to Florida almost thirty years ago, Rita had begged to stay with Aunt Liz and Uncle Carlton to finish school at the Jersey Shore.

This was home, not just the spare bedroom of a senior citizen condo where she always had to be quiet when she visited. And somehow northern summers seemed sweeter when you had to survive a freezing winter to get to them.

Right now, though, Rita's sore muscles longed for warmth. This Jersey surf was invigorating but too chilly! If only she could give herself a massage!

She shivered and ran for a towel, shaking her head and squeezing the water out of her curly hair. She patted herself dry and anchored the sheet she'd grabbed from the clothesline with her paperback and sandals. Smiling, she nestled into the heat of the sand shifting below her and stretched out. At last, she let go. She breathed in the peace of the salt air and exhaled all the troubles and schedules and worries about making a living.

She sank slowly into a deep rest, into the warmth of the afternoon sun and the safety of being home, dreaming of sandcastles, and collecting blue and green sea glass smoothed by years of gritty sand.

****

In his apartment, Mitch ordered materials for the next day and snapped his cell phone shut. If the rain held off, he'd finish sanding and spackling in two days. Another two to install the trim before painting. Rita had painted one wall already and he'd help her with the rest. Damn shame about the water damage, though. Between the repairs and picking out wallpaper, the bathroom would take longer than he'd originally estimated. It'd take two weeks, tops.

He'd planned to stay later on the job today, but he needed a break, too. Needed to cool off. A little surfing usually cleared his head.

He still couldn't believe he'd kissed her. What had he been thinking? Nothing! That was the problem. He hadn't been thinking at all. He'd let his guard down. What started out as good-natured teasing had somehow changed, but it wasn't too late to get out of this quicksand.

He emptied his pockets and tossed his sweaty T-shirt into the hamper. He grabbed a towel and a root beer and headed for the ocean with his board.

He scanned the beach. Nobody in the unprotected surf. Where the hell was she? What if she were swimming alone? He should have been quicker. Three college students had already drowned on the barrier islands this season. At least Liz had the sense to tell him when she was going for a swim so he could keep an eye on her. But Rita?

Maybe she'd changed her mind. Did she go back inside or to the pool? He paused to take a deep breath, to stop the panic from growing until he spotted her at last. There she was, closer to the dunes than he'd expected, clutching a beach towel on an old sheet. He approached without a sound and put his things near hers. He admired the curves of her trim body, felt the urge to touch the tangled mass of soft, damp curls resting on her neck. Her pale skin was turning a little pink already. Should he wake her to smooth suntan lotion on her? Would she be grateful for the offer? Or cranky?

Fifteen minutes of surfing and then he'd risk it. Mitch blended into the rhythm of the waves, the constant ebb and flow, back and forth. Out here, he didn't have to figure anything out. Just be aware, pay attention, and be present. He relaxed into the sheer simplicity of the process: paddle out, wait for the right wave, and ride it back to shore.

Images of Rita and the taste of her lips vanished until he saw her move from a distance. She sat up and extended her arms to the sun, leaned far back and stretched down on her stomach again like a cat readjusting its body for another nap.

He'd been surfing longer than fifteen minutes.

The sun was lower, its rays less intense, but if Rita didn't go inside soon, she was going to be in pain later. He paddled back to shore.

He thrust his surfboard into the sand near her and leaned over for his towel. It flapped in the breeze, blasting Rita's back with tiny grains. "Hey!" she yelled, sitting up and squinting his way. "It's a big beach. Get your own spot."

"Sorry." Mitch grinned as he wrapped the towel around his shoulders. "You're turning red. Again."

"Don't flatter yourself. It's only the heat. Now, if you'll stop bothering me, I'd like to get back to sleep."

"I'm talking red from sunburn, not embarrassment. You won't feel so good in the morning if you fry yourself the first time out. Want me to put some suntan lotion on you?"

"I already did."

"Doesn't look like it, but suit yourself. Just don't complain about it tomorrow."

"Oh, so that's it. You're not really being a nice guy, just saving yourself grief?"

"Hardly. What do you call *this* conversation?"

Rita laughed. "You're right. Sorry I jumped all over you."

"Hey, you're the one who said touch is good for you. Therapeutic. Are you telling me Ms. Health Conscious bakes her skin to a golden brown? Or cooks it lobster red?"

"Neither. I was careful. I put on lotion before I came out."

"Almost two hours ago. Before swimming and dozing off." Mitch sat down on her sheet and opened his warm root beer. "What's the matter? Afraid you can't resist a man smearing sunscreen on your body?"

"Yeah, you have such a great towel-side manner. It's a real struggle to fight the attraction. But I don't need you. I've got my own spray, see?" She reached into her bag and pulled out a tube. "Well, not this stuff. I have a pump." She rummaged around with no success. "I guess I left it in my room. This one must be two years old."

Mitch knelt on the sheet and squeezed some of the cocoa butter lotion onto his hands. "It's better than nothing. Now lay down on your stomach. Unless you're afraid..."

Rita mumbled something and plopped down.

"And relax." Mitch teased. "Isn't that what you tell your clients?" He gently traced a path up and down her spine in tiny swirls, applying slight pressure and then easing up. He squirted more of the warm liquid onto her back and smoothed it over an untouched spot. He felt the tension ease under his fingertips. He skimmed his fingers over her back, rolling with the rhythm of the waves crashing on the sand, the flapping of a distant flag.

He watched his tan fingers inch their way under those inviting curls to stroke her neck. He traced the edge of her earlobe and left a trail of small ovals across one of her temples.

He slid his hands down to her shoulders and smoothed the lotion swiftly up and down her arms. Then both of his palms were on her thighs, hard and soft, alternating long slow strokes with probing circles, exploring, slightly separating her legs and nudging the bottom of her swimsuit. Her body tensed and he smiled. He leaned close to her ear and whispered, "Relax. Other side. Keep your eyes closed and roll over." Rita moaned but did as she was told.

Mitch spread the cream lightly across the bridge of her nose, her high cheekbones, smoothed her tightened brow, and traced her jaw. He studied her full lips as he carefully applied the lotion around her eyes, paused a moment, and bent over. He thought of kissing her but didn't. "How's that?" he said softly.

She smiled. "Mmmmmm. Maybe I should hire you as my assistant when I open for business."

"No way. But I'll tell you what you shouldn't do. Don't swim alone this summer. Go with a friend. Buddy system only. If I'm not around, head down to where the lifeguard is. And have your cell phone. No more solitary swimming. You know the riptides are treacherous. No one can predict them...or fight them."

Rita opened her eyes and stared defiantly into his, just inches away. "Mitch, it's not your job to worry about me. And I've been swimming alone my whole life."

Mitch stared back at her green eyes without flinching. "Doesn't make it smart. If you don't care about yourself, at least think about your aunt. She couldn't take it if you drowned."

Rita paused and closed her eyes. "No, I guess not. But what about you? You'd be the favorite child around here. Course I bet you'd miss me bugging you. Or rather you bugging me."

Mitch sat up and gazed at the passing clouds. "Be serious. We're talking about your Aunt Liz. Hasn't she lost enough?"

"Oh, all right. I'll never go in above my knees if I'm alone, okay, 'Dad?' Just stop nagging." She sat up and poured lotion on her hands. "And I can finish this." She started applying the cream on her arms and legs. "You sure know how to turn a Kodak moment into a safety lecture."

"Better a lecture than a funeral," he said abruptly and got up. "I'm going inside. Pizza in an hour. Mushrooms or plain?"

"Doesn't matter. I'll be in soon." She'd never admit to Mitch her muscles were screaming for a warm, relaxing bath, or that she could feel the slight sunburn on her back already.

She watched him head for the garage. His erect

posture and long silver-streaked hair reminded her of a shaman she'd once seen during a brief bus tour through the Southwest. Aloof and mysterious, part of the landscape. A male with magic in his hands. An enigma. Possibly dangerous.

****

By the time Rita came downstairs for supper after a long bath, Liz was bringing in a tray of used plates from the deck. "We ate already, dear. Mitch said to say goodnight. Oh, and to be ready to leave at 6 a.m. sharp. Your pizza's in the oven and the salad in the green bowl is fresh from the garden. Let's sit out on the back porch, okay?"

Rita felt strangely disappointed. Was Mitch avoiding her now? She filled her plate and joined Liz outside. No voices, no sounds except the breaking waves and the creak of their wicker rockers.

"Almost like old times, huh Aunt Liz? Sometimes I wish I could go back and do it over. Better. It was all so simple back then and somehow it got all messed up."

"Dear, old times only seem like the best times. Funny how we forget the bad things that happened, the arguments, the broken promises, the things we couldn't afford back then. Yes, everything was cheaper, but we earned less money, too." Liz stopped rocking and picked up a stack of mail from the small glass table. "Still do..."

Rita looked puzzled. "Still do what? Earn less or forget?"

Liz shook her head as if she couldn't recall what she was going to say. "Never mind. You can't go back, Rita. No matter how much you think you'd like to. We're here right now, this minute, smelling the sea air and feeling the wind blowing on our faces. Nothing like it. Makes you forget your troubles most of the time."

Rita looked at her aunt's profile in the

candlelight. "What troubles? Is something wrong?"

Liz sighed. "No dear. Just a little mix-up with the water and the electric companies. Happens from time to time. I stuff all the bills and papers into a tote bag and take it to my accountant to fix. Not to worry."

"Do you want me to look it over? I'm pretty good at straightening out financial messes by now."

"Oh, no. It's fine. He'll take care of it."

Rita yawned and stood to stretch. "Well, if I'm getting up before six and doing hard labor, I'd better get to bed." She bent over to kiss her aunt's silver hair. "It's good to be home. You've always been here for me, and I'm going to make you proud of me."

"Rita, honey, I've always been proud of you, no matter what you do. You're the daughter I never had. The one I've been lucky to share with your mom. Just be happy."

Liz got up and collected her things. "I'm ready to call it a day, too." Liz put her other arm around Rita and steered her into the house, locking the door behind them. "See? Aren't you proud of me? Mitch even has me locking deadbolts and cranking these jalousie windows shut tight. Latches secure on all the other windows."

Liz went to her roll top desk in the corner and crammed the envelopes into a drawer. Pushing it shut, she added, "Tomorrow's another day. Goodnight, dear." She hugged Rita and headed for her room without stopping in the kitchen to make her usual cup of tea.

Something wasn't right. Rita wanted to sneak back into the living room and check out the papers in that drawer, but what if Aunt Liz came back out? Rita dragged herself up the stairs. She'd have to wait until morning to satisfy her curiosity. For now, setting her alarm early and getting some much-needed sleep was her only agenda.

Chapter Seven

Rita groaned at the sound of the alarm and slammed the off button. She leaped out of bed, took a quick shower, and dressed quickly. Five early mornings and long days on the job and she still hadn't been able to check out those papers in Aunt Liz's desk. She tiptoed down the stairs and headed toward the living room, but stopped at the sound of clanging pots in the kitchen. "That you, dear?" Aunt Liz called out. "Ready for coffee and oatmeal?"

Rita glanced at the clock. Almost six. "You're up early again, Aunt Liz. Didn't you sleep well?"

"Rita, it's nothing." Liz paused to spoon some blueberries into two bowls of cereal. "Well, actually, I'm feeling a bit weepy. It was four years ago today Carlton passed on, and I miss the old coot. Still mad at him for leaving me behind. Not just when I mess up the business things he used to handle. And you don't have to tell me I should have learned more about what to do! Writing checks and so on. It's the little things I miss most - having coffee together every morning on the porch, his corny jokes, his old stories, our walks along the beach, still holding hands after all those years."

Rita hugged Liz's shoulders. "I know it's hard on you. I miss him, too. And I'm sorry I was so busy with my own problems these past few years that I didn't help you out more. I should have been here more often."

"Oh, no, young lady. No 'should haves!' We all do the best we can. Enough sad talk. Think of good memories." She motioned for Rita to sit down. "I intend to keep on enjoying life, starting with these perfect blueberries."

They ate in silence for a few moments before Liz added, "I hate to admit it, but I'm lonely sometimes without him. I still crave my solitude, my quiet times, but it's been hard being alone. I'm grateful that Mitch came along. This place doesn't seem as empty. He was real quiet at first, but now he can be a big tease, just like Carlton."

Rita looked up at the ceiling before responding. "Yes, Mitch is a great teaser. But I'd hardly compare him to Uncle Carlton."

"Well, he's kind of protective and nags me like Carlton did about being safe. I must admit, this town is changing a bit...more robberies, fires, crank calls, old friends having heart attacks. The crazy drivers are worse than ever. They never caught the guy that ran Serena's grandfather's bike off the road. Poor man died soon after the fall. I'm not afraid, but I do feel better having Mitch around. And of course, having you home, too. Do I sound like a foolish old lady?"

"Never, Aunt Liz. You are the wisest person I know - wise enough not to care about looking foolish. And you'll never be old to me."

"Thank you, dear. Now let's both stop being maudlin! I'm going to take my morning walk and you have work to do."

Rita cleaned up the breakfast dishes and waited until she saw the top of her aunt's straw hat disappear over the sand dunes. At last! She rushed back to the desk, pulled out the drawer crammed with papers, and started flipping through the correspondence. A red "shut-off" notice from the water company. A past-due collection letter from the Community Medical Center. An emergency room visit back in February? For Aunt Liz?

The sudden pounding on the screen door made

her jump. A familiar deep voice boomed, "Looking for something?" She turned to see Mitch staring.

"Yes, I am. What's it to you?" she snapped as she shoved everything back into the desk and almost smashed her finger closing the drawer. "I need paper to write a note to Aunt Liz."

"Didn't she just leave?" Mitch walked in and headed for the kitchen where he poured himself a cup of coffee. "I want some coffee, if you don't mind. Save us stopping at the 7-11. I'll get you a notepad from the refrigerator."

Rita sighed. "Thanks," she called out, and muttered to herself, "for the lousy timing."

He tossed the pad in front of her and stood by the desk. "Well, write the note and let's go. We'll be done sooner if we start early every day."

Rita scrawled a vague message to Liz and left it under a paperweight. Damn! Real estate people had it all wrong. Location wasn't the most critical thing, it was timing. Now she'd have to wait until tonight to find out more. How could Aunt Liz have financial problems? She and Carlton had never been rich, but they'd never had trouble paying their bills. After fifty years, the house mortgage must have been retired. Carlton wasn't the kind of man who would leave his wife without a decent income should he die.

As much as she hated snooping, Rita vowed to get to the bottom of that drawer and whatever was bothering Aunt Liz. Overextended or just disorganized? Did she need protection from herself, or from someone else? Maybe that kitchen project had been too expensive. If Mitch had anything to do with these problems, he'd pay.

"Coming?" Mitch held the door open for her but kept his distance as she passed by. "A bit jumpy today, aren't you?"

"Just tired. And in a rush," she mumbled. "I work for a slave driver."

Mitch laughed. "You're the one pushing *me* to get done. Who's the boss here?"

"The way you bark orders and cut lunch short, you'd think I was promising you a bonus for early completion. I want to get my business going, but I don't want to kill myself doing it."

Mitch shrugged. "They say you don't always get what you think you want, but keep trying. You'll get what you need."

"Great! Philosophy 101 from the Rolling Stones at six in the morning. Now I know what you meant when you said, 'Nothing is free.' You work for me and refuse to take money, but *I* pay the price of putting up with your bossy personality, unsolicited advice, and unasked-for platitudes."

Mitch smiled and motioned for her to get in the truck. "It's part of my charm," he added. He winked and held out his hand to help her up. "You love it. Admit it."

Rita slid over to the passenger window and studied his profile as he drove. "Now there you go again, changing gears. First you're 'macho' male ordering me around and telling me what I'm doing wrong whether it's painting with short brush strokes or hating men. Which I don't by the way, I just see them for what they are. Next you're the silent brooding male looking soulfully out at sea. Then you're Liz's adopted bad boy child competing for her attention. And just when I'm ready to tell you where to go, you smile and tease. What are you, schizophrenic? Full of multiple personalities?"

"No, just Mitch. One person, plain and simple."

"Well, 'Just Mitch,' how are you at simple answers? How much money did Aunt Liz pay you for all the work you've done on her house?"

Mitch's jaw tightened slightly. "I told you. It's none of your business. But since you seem determined to pry, Detective, it wasn't a fraction of what it's worth. I saved her thousands using leftover materials from other customers' jobs. I've installed new cabinets for rich people one day only to have them tell me to rip them out the next. Why? They changed their minds about the color. Some owners would rather toss something away than be bothered with paperwork in returning it or selling it to someone else. Call it 'wasteful' or 'recycling.' I get stuff free or cheap and use it in other jobs. Perfectly legal.

"Liz doesn't complain so why should you? Do you actually think I'd hurt your aunt?"

Rita hesitated and looked at the enormous beachfront mansions they passed. "No, not really. And I know how wasteful these people can be. Believe me, it wasn't easy being middle class here, going to school with kids driving new Porsches and charging on their own credit cards at Macy's. But I've made big mistakes trusting people before, and I don't want anything bad to happen to Aunt Liz."

"Then trust me. I don't have any ulterior motives about Liz...or you. Let's get this job done and be pleasant. Me helping you isn't a lifetime commitment. And I don't expect some favor from you, either." He braked for the stoplight and turned to her. He put his hand under her chin and tilted her face towards his. "Unless there's some favor you have in mind. I'm only human, you know. And I bet you think we men all have only one thing on our minds..." Mitch wiggled his dark eyebrows and grinned. "Right?"

Rita shook her head. "There you go again, shifting gears. I'll assume you're joking. In fact, I'll be grateful from now on when you're surly and silent. Maybe it'd be better for both of us if we kept a little more distance between us."

"Fine with me," Mitch switched on the radio and tapped his fingers on the steering wheel to a country western tune until they pulled into the lot near the back of the building. He turned off the ignition, slid out, and headed for his tools in the back of the truck without offering to give her a hand.

Rita hopped down by herself and slammed the door. "Hey, what happened to chivalry?"

"Make up your mind. You asked for distance, remember?" Mitch smirked and handed her the drill and sander. "Here, able-bodied female, carry these inside, okay? But three steps behind. Distance, you know." He grabbed two heavy toolboxes and walked to the side entrance. Rita bit her lip and followed. When he slid the key into the lock, the door pushed inward with the slight pressure before he even twisted the key.

Mitch frowned. "Did you leave the door unlocked last night?"

"Of course not!" Rita's heart started racing and fear gripped her stomach. That same queasy feeling when she'd come home to an unlocked apartment and found Kevin had taken most of the furniture along with his clothes. "You were rushing me, but I'm positive I twisted the knob to make sure it was locked."

"Well, it's not locked now." Mitch pushed the door all the way open and cautiously stepped inside. "Oh shit!" He stopped suddenly.

Rita bumped into him, but squeezed around him to see. "Oh, no!" Her mouth dropped open as she scanned the room. Red paint sprayed across her freshly painted blue walls screamed: "Surfs up!" and "Your screwed!" Yin and Yang symbols. A stick figure couple in a lewd posture. Her gut tightened and twisted. She felt attacked and violated. All that hard work! "Damn, damn, damn!" she yelled. "And they don't even know how to use apostrophes or contractions! Or draw!" she added. *Apostrophes? Too many years of checking students' papers.*

"Punk kids wreck a week's worth of work and you're bitching about their grammar?" Mitch shook his head.

"Punctuation, not grammar."

"What difference does it make? That room was almost done. Damn rich kids probably did this as a lark, never thinking about what it might cost someone who has to work for a living or clean up their mess. Why didn't you lock the door?"

"I did lock it. You were honking the horn, but I double-checked it. I swear."

Mitch went inside and checked the windows. "No broken glass and the latches are locked. Your door's intact, so I guess they could have used a credit card to get in or picked the lock. These old locks are garbage." Mitch strode across the room and tried opening the adjoining door. "Let's see if they hit Serena's place." The knob wouldn't turn.

"The locksmith was here yesterday. Remember Serena told me she'd feel better if she changed the front doorknob? That she didn't want to take chances with her merchandise?"

"No, no one told me. I would have changed the locks myself. And for less money. Why didn't she ask me? Kind of odd that all of a sudden Ms. Flighty is Ms. Security Conscious. Why didn't she change yours, too?"

"I don't know. What are you implying? That Serena knew we'd get vandalized?"

"No, just thinking out loud."

"Well, you're not making any sense. She's my friend. And she has rent to gain once I get started. Why would she want to jeopardize that?"

"Beats me, but let's take a look. Do you have the key?"

Rita pulled out a huge ring of keys and inserted the bright gold one with green plastic on it. "She said to remember green to get in, green for gifts, and green for money."

Mitch followed Rita into the gift shop. "No graffiti and nothing missing. Not that I can see. All this weird shit kids buy: CDs, incense, posters, paraphernalia for God knows what! Once they got into your place, why didn't they go a little farther and actually take something they might want instead of defacing your empty rooms?"

"Mitch, who knows? They're kids. Maybe they ran out of paint or time. Or a police car drove by and they got scared. Maybe they weren't out to steal anything, just trash a place."

Mitch leaned against the counter and took a deep breath. "Well, no use standing around doing nothing. Now we're behind schedule. Call Serena. Maybe she heard something. Then call the cops so we can get back to work."

"Don't order me around, okay? I was already dialing her number." Rita sat down at Serena's fortune-telling table with the portable phone and motioned Mitch away. She ignored Serena's choice words on being awakened so early and filled her in on the vandalism. Though groggy, Serena said she'd be right over but that she hadn't heard a thing until some ex-friend woke her.

Rita phoned the police dispatcher, who promised to send someone right away. She started shuffling the deck of round tarot cards. Mitch stopped pacing and stared at her. "You don't need cards to predict your 'immediate future' as Serena would say: more time wasted, more work, and an alarm system."

Rita continued to shuffle and glared at Mitch. "Hey, you pace, I shuffle. What's the difference? We're both upset and killing time."

Angel chimes on the kitchen door announced Serena's arrival. The tall redhead looked pale and haggard in a faded leopard caftan and no makeup. She gave up trying to twist her wild red hair into a lopsided bun at the nape of her neck and shut her eyes. Holding her palm up toward them she growled, "Don't even *talk* to me before coffee. Mornings are hell, even without vandalism."

She walked around the gift shop examining cases and shelves. "Looks fine in here." She disappeared into Rita's side for a minute and reappeared, holding her head and leaning against the entranceway. "Major disaster in there! Nasty S.O.B.s..." She paused before ambling toward the kitchen. "I'm making espresso. Got any aspirin in that shell of a bathroom?"

"Not yet." Mitch answered. "Medicine cabinet went in yesterday. It's empty."

Rita followed them both to the kitchen. Serena took a whiff from the bag of coffee beans. "Nothing like Kona," she murmured and started her new espresso machine. "So tell me, how'd they get in?"

"Probably through the side door to Rita's office. No forced entry, nothing broken," said Mitch.

"I'm almost positive I locked the side door," Rita offered tentatively, "but maybe it wasn't shut tight. Haven't you ever thought you'd left the iron plugged in or the coffee pot on and driven all the way home to check? Ninety-nine percent of the time, it's off...but there's always that one percent chance you messed up."

"Rita, don't start second-guessing yourself!" said Serena. "The locksmith said that old hardware wasn't very secure. I only wish I'd sent him over to change your locks, too, but I figured Mitch was in charge." Serena went over to Rita and hugged her. "I'll get the guy back here after the cops leave."

"Don't bother," Mitch interrupted. "I'm installing new lock sets and deadbolts for her myself. And you're both getting separate alarm systems."

"Forget it, Mitch. It's not in the budget," Rita said.

"Amen," Serena added. "Money's tight for me, too. We'll make do with better locks for now." She paused to pour three espressos and headed for the card-reading table with hers. "Help yourselves, guys. Yours has milk and sugar, Rita. I gotta sit down."

Mitch followed the two women. "Your safety and peace of mind are worth the cost of a security system. Ask the cop when he comes. Plus you need protection, and not only against vandals or robbers, Rita. It's not safe for you to be here alone, giving massages to strangers when the other shops are closed. What if some transient psycho picks up your card from the health club or Serena's shop, thinking you're going to massage more than his aching back?"

"Mitch, one problem at a time, okay? I'm only going to schedule people I know and trust after hours. New clients will have to make daytime appointments."

"I'm not taking no for an answer about the security system. I can get it for practically nothing. Do I have to tip off Aunt Liz and get her on your back, too?"

"Don't you dare tell her about this! I'm here to take care of her, not have her anxious about my safety or imaginary psychos. I'll agree to an *affordable* alarm system, but the sky's not the limit. I want to know the exact cost *before* you get it."

Serena downed her third cup of black coffee by the time Officer Murray arrived. He glanced around and surveyed the damage. "Sorry I'm running late. The natives were restless in this part of town last night." He jotted down their information for the police report on his clipboard. "If it makes you feel better, you weren't the only target. We logged similar incidents of vandalism last night: missing trashcans, graffiti on the deli, park benches sprayed with red surfer symbols and the words 'Wet Paint.' The usual things. You know, like changing the '35' on the speed limit sign to read '85?' "

"Do you have any leads, Officer?" Rita asked.

"No, ma'am. With typical kid stuff, it's hard to find the perpetrators. No evidence, not even an empty can of spray paint left behind. Without a video camera or an eyewitness, we don't usually catch these summer punks. At least an alarm system scares them off before they do much damage."

Mitch cleared his throat and interrupted. "We were just discussing that when you arrived. I'll order it today."

The patrolman nodded and put his clipboard under his arm. "Good idea. Until that's installed, we'll have our patrol units swing by here more often at night, but an alarm system's your best bet to prevent this from happening again." Officer Murray shook everyone's hand and nodded to the cards Rita had been shuffling absentmindedly. "Hope a better day's in the cards for you, Miss Madison." He chuckled. "At least you didn't lose any money or merchandise, Miss Starr. But you may not be so lucky next time."

Serena waited for the door to shut. "Too bad we're not next to a doughnut shop. Then we'd be safe without an alarm, right?"

Mitch laughed. "Give the guy a break. If you want better police protection, you should have offered him a brownie. You'll have your alarm system by tomorrow, but for now, it's back to work, Rita, or you won't have a business to protect."

Rita hurried to shove the cards back in the worn cardboard box. "Here, let me do that," Serena offered and reached over to get them. A single card fell to the floor as Rita left. Turning it over, Serena prayed it would be upright. It wasn't. And it was the Tower again, the symbol of major upheaval and destruction. What a perfect match to the vandalism.

She closed her eyes and recalled the Tower's ominous warning: *Dramatic challenges threaten you. Like it or not, you must be careful. Protect yourself against illness, attacks, and accidents. Do not let your guard down!*

Rita didn't even want to hear about alarm systems. Would she be open to hearing about a cosmic warning? Serena slid the card into the box with the others. Probably not, but some things couldn't be ignored. Not when your best friend's safety was at risk.

Chapter Eight

The week after the break-in had been hectic, but with long workdays and no new vandalism, Rita's office was almost ready for the grand opening on schedule. She unpacked her books and treasured belongings from storage as Mitch hung pictures on the pale blue walls. The scent of lavender, rosemary and a Native American smudge stick lingered in the air. Serena had insisted on conducting a space cleansing ritual to ward off accidents, misfortunes, and the dreaded upheavals and destruction she'd been warning Rita about. All this from an upside-down Tower card.

Mitch adjusted the corners of a large Monet print of water lilies to make it level. "How's that, Boss Lady?"

"Perfect!" said Rita. She stepped back and admired the waiting room and reception area. Mitch had installed new wall-to-wall carpeting from salvaged remnants and lined one wall with custom oak bookcases that matched her desk and computer station. A Zen fountain with a golden Buddha gurgled on a table behind a navy blue couch covered with exotic pillows of blues and purples. "Mitch, it's all perfect, so professional! How can I ever thank you?"

Mitch picked up his hammer and slid it slowly into his tool belt. "Oh, I don't know. What did you have in mind?" Tiny crinkles appeared around his eyes, and his mouth stretched into a smile. "How about a massage for a tired old carpenter?"

Rita mirrored his grin and threw a pillow at

him. "So the old Mitch is back at last! I thought you'd forgotten how to joke around after the break-in and our argument about the security system. Which reminds me, you still haven't told me about the cost, even after you installed it."

"I'll get to it. I've been preoccupied with deadlines…"

"You mean grouchy," Rita interrupted. "Giving orders and grunting short answers, working late and escaping to your garage apartment early all week long. Aunt Liz thinks I did something terrible to you." Although Rita had asked him for distance, she wasn't going to tell him she'd missed seeing his crooked grin and hearing his funny comments.

"I'm never grouchy. Only trying to get things done on time. Not easy with only two of us, but we made it!"

"Yes, we did, and only a few boxes left to empty." Rita went back to unpacking books on spirituality, fitness, and holistic health. "I love being surrounded by my favorite books and things again." The final box was full of small whimsical animal ceramics, some framed quotations, and more angels. She placed them on the last remaining shelf with a loud, "Ta da! Finished at last!"

"So many books," Mitch muttered. "And angels. With all the suns, moons, and stars you and Serena have hanging around, you could start your own universe."

Serena knocked once at the entranceway and rushed in. "Not to eavesdrop, but speaking of stars, here's a little something for your wall to make it official." She handed Rita a framed dollar bill she'd stamped with stars. "Your first dollar earned for your very first massage here! From your best friend and first customer." She hugged Rita and shoved a wad of money into the pocket of Rita's jeans.

"Oh, no, Serena. I'm not taking your money. You

get a massage on the house."

"Sorry, but this one's not for me. I bought a gift certificate for a friend. He'll be in soon. And if you want to make a second sale, you better get out to the gift shop right now and wait on the rich lady by the cash register. She's waiting to ask you about a massage and a reflexology book. So get a move on. Mitch and I will hang this."

Serena waited until Rita left and turned to Mitch. "And this, sir, is for all your hard work." She handed him a silver envelope. "You are the official first customer of Shore Therapeutic Massage."

"Serena, you know I don't take payment."

"It's not a *payment* certificate. It's a *gift*. You're not going to insult your favorite brownie maker by trying to give back a present, are you? Or bring on the ire of Liz Chandler by refusing to let her favorite niece practice on you?"

"You mean her only niece," muttered Mitch. "Thanks, but give it to someone else. I don't think it's a good idea anyway."

"Why not? She's the best massage therapist you'll ever have. And considering your limited income, she's probably the only one you'll ever have. What are you afraid of?"

"I'm not afraid of a massage, for God's sake!"

"Well, Grumpy, you sure sound like you need one! Loosen up and enjoy yourself for a change! You've been a real pain in the butt lately. Humor me. Ease my guilt for having such great work done around here for practically nothing. Hey, maybe it'll improve your personality."

Mitch couldn't help smiling. "From one pain in the butt to another, thanks, but I prefer to do my relaxing by myself. I don't need any woman in my life soothing my body, telling my future, or trying to figure me out. Or nagging."

"Sorry you feel that way, but I suggest you make

an exception this time or I swear I'll get Liz after you. And you're not insulting my best friend, so get in there and strip down to your birthday suit." Serena shoved a pair of blue silk boxers covered with stars into his hand and chuckled. "Here's another gift. Stars for you, too. Put these on if you're shy...or don't, if you're more European." She led him by the arm to an Oriental screen in the darkened room. "You can change behind this."

Mitch stood with his hands on his hips and looked around the massage room. Candles flickered and soft music played faintly. A hint of something musky drifted through the air, the scent of Rita's neck. He held up the silk boxers and shook his head. "Stars? I can't do this, Serena."

"Come on, Mitch. Please don't let me down. I told Rita her first customer would be in soon. A friend of mine." Mitch raised both eyebrows and snorted. "Okay, maybe I stretched the truth a little about the friend part. But I wanted to thank you for everything you've done, and frankly, I don't do nice gestures very often. Don't back out like some ungrateful macho bastard and spoil my surprise for Rita!"

"But she'll think I asked for it, and I don't need that. I like my life simple."

"Then simply go along with it. Think of yourself as a trial run for her. Be a charming guinea pig and I won't tell Liz what a pain you really are. Deal?"

Mitch sighed. "Well, I guess the old muscles could use a little relief. But tell her to go easy on me. It's been a rough week. And that this wasn't my idea."

Serena pushed him toward the screen and motioned toward the massage table. "Sure thing, Cowboy. Now take your clothes off." She laughed. "What a great line of work! And when you're naked, or close to it, lie down on your back and cover yourself with the sheet...Oh...and enjoy. Or at least pretend to! I have to get back to the store. She should be here in about five to ten minutes. You can hang that framed dollar later."

Mitch disrobed and left his work clothes folded on a chair. He thought about staying in his briefs, but slipped into the silky boxers instead. Ridiculous. He sat on the edge of the padded table and slid quickly under the sheet. He felt like a kid in the dentist's chair about to get his first filling.

And yet it was so peaceful. No glaring lights or sterile antiseptic smell. No traffic noises, just the hum of a small fan that made the sheer fabric draped over the skylight flutter slightly. He felt his pulse slow in spite of the nagging impulse to leap off the table and get the hell out of the room, away from Rita. But how could he back out now?

No, he'd stay. It would be fun to see the look of surprise on her face. And maybe the massage would feel good. Hopefully not too good. He slowed his breathing in time with a flute melody playing quietly over the ebb and flow of recorded waves. After a while he stopped listening for Rita's footsteps and drifted off to sleep.

****

In the shop, Rita wrapped a seashell mobile and a book on foot reflexology for a gray-haired woman in a gaudy red-white-and-blue sundress. "Thank you so much for your help, dear. I'll try working those reflexes you mentioned. If my husband decides to stay another week, I'll call you about that massage."

After she left, Rita hooted. "Hey, Serena, she might be my first walk-in customer! And she bought one of your gifts, too! This is working out great for both of us!" Rita smiled and hugged her friend.

"I have a surprise. Your first customer is already waiting for you as we speak."

"I didn't see anyone come in. Who is it?" Rita

looked directly into Serena's eyes. "Oh no, tell me it isn't Mitch. Did you sell that gift certificate to him?"

Serena shrugged her shoulders. "What makes you think that?"

"How could you do this to me?"

"Do what?"

"Cut the innocent crap, Serena. It's me, your friend from high school who knew all along when you cheated on the Ouija board. Who covered for you when you told your grandfather you were at my house when you were actually headed for a rock concert in New York City or the Stone Pony in Asbury Park. Stop matchmaking - or at least admit when you're doing it!"

"Oooh, I think you're protesting a little too much. What's the matter? Can't stay professional when you're attracted to him?

"Of course I can. I mean, Mitch is attractive in a rough sort of way. That doesn't mean I'm attracted to him. Think about the situation. I see him at home all the time, I don't know much about his background, and I certainly don't want him thinking I want to get involved with him."

"So what's the big deal? This is my way of thanking you both for helping me. A gift. Period. You get the chance to practice on someone whose business you'll never lose. He probably can't afford it and he won't come back for more. A simple trial run before you start on the rich clients down from the city like the lady who just left the store."

"I don't know. It doesn't feel right." Rita sat down on a stool behind the counter and propped up her head with her hands.

"Honey, just do it! If he gives you a hard time, smack him with one of those heavy-duty chops. What are you afraid of? That you can't act like a professional when you're touching him? Or maybe you can't get an uptight, secretive guy like Mitch to let go?"

"Serena, you're baiting me. But I'll show you anyway, I can give any guy a massage and stay detached, and unlike some people, not fall in lust or love!"

"So get in there and prove it. Now! You've kept him waiting too long as it is. And guess what! You're both nuts! He hated the idea, too."

Rita frowned. "He did?"

"Yes, so don't flatter yourself, kid. He's not going to jump your bones." Serena took Rita's arm and led her to the office entrance. "Now go take care of your customer, you ungrateful friend! Me? I've got to save some brownies from burning and unpack a shipment." She headed for the kitchen shaking her head.

Rita closed the door to her office and paused. So he wasn't behind this. It was Serena's scheme. Good. She'd show both of them how professional she was. She flipped the "Massage in Progress" sign on the door and entered the darkened room. She eased the door shut without a sound and inhaled the slight hint of sandalwood, her favorite scent.

The room was perfect. Candle flames glowed through blue glass and the air-conditioning vent hummed softly. The gauzy white curtains draped over the skylight were like billowing clouds in a gentle breeze. Aware of her breath, she exhaled slowly, releasing the tension in her stomach. No need to be nervous after all her years of experience. It was only Mitch. And this wasn't his idea. Or hers.

She approached the table noiselessly in slippered feet. She squirted some massage oil on her hands, rubbing them quickly together. Hands had to be smooth and warm. She visualized the momentary pleasure of putting cold fingers on Mitch's back and watching him leap up in shock; she smiled briefly, but she'd never actually do that. Not in here. Not even if he deserved it for all his teasing and gruffness.

His breathing was so quiet. Was he asleep? Maybe she should leave. She leaned over and whispered, "Mitch?"

"Yeah?" She jumped at the sound of his voice. "Took you long enough, Massage Lady. I was about to use the ten minute professor rule and slip out."

"Jeesh. You startled me. I thought you were asleep." Rita stepped back, her heart racing. "And how do you know the ten minute rule? You went to college?"

Mitch opened his eyes and studied her. "Would that shock you, me being a handyman, a carpenter? Did you have me pegged as a high school dropout?"

"No, but I'd rather not discuss your educational background now. The massage is better if you stop talking and close your eyes. Pay attention to your breathing. Are you comfortable?"

"As much as can be expected spread out like a mummy in silk boxer shorts. Another present from your friend."

"Client's choice. Take them off, unless you feel less threatened with them on. Total body massage doesn't mean *all* the parts, you know. I know where to stop."

"Oh really? You know, I never had a professional massage before, at least not one you pay for." He smirked. "It was always before or after, if you get my drift. Underwear wasn't part of the plan. It was more in the way."

Rita felt her face turn red. She moved to the CD player and restarted it. "Let's start over from the beginning. I don't want to shortchange you on time. How about ocean waves and piano this time?" She turned back to face Mitch who was now propped up on his elbows, his hair flowing loose on his shoulders. "Listen, we both know this was Serena's brainstorm. You're good practice for me, and she wanted to do something nice for you. Who knows? Maybe a massage will do wonders for your disposition, or at least shut you up for an hour. Are you ready?"

"Almost." Mitch smiled and wriggled under the sheet. He tossed the blue boxers across the room, put his head back on the table, and closed his eyes. "Okay, now I'm comfortable. But control yourself - no tickling or funny business. I'm not easy, you know."

"Believe me, I know how difficult you can be. So hush…and enjoy the music."

Rita sat on a stool behind his head and began stroking the tiny lines etched across his forehead. He looked like a little boy despite the streaks of gray in his long flowing hair. She rubbed his temples and rotated her fingers on his scalp, inhaling the musky scent of shampoo she remembered from their first encounter on the beach. That seemed like ages ago. Gone was the rough tension gripping her, the raw fear of being hurt.

Now she looked down at him stretched out before her and felt his powerful muscles surrendering to her touch. Now she was the one in control, in charge. She would make him melt, not in pretense, the way she'd tricked him and escaped that night. Now she was perfectly detached and he was just another body. Yes, just another client.

She gently lifted his head and inched her hand down the cleft between his shoulders, loosening, loosening the taut fibers of his back until his skin was pliant and probably tingling. Or was it her fingers tingling? She always visualized chi, the life energy, passing through her hands during massage, but somehow it felt stronger today. She could feel the chi pulsating, warm and glowing between her fingers and his neck. It was probably the perfect atmosphere that enhanced the feeling. The room was wonderful.

She eased his head back on the table and rose. Moving to his side, she uncovered his chest and continued moving her hands across his torso, around his shoulders. Softly, gradually, rhythmically, like the tide flowing in and out on a calm day.

He moaned slightly as her hands caressed his long muscled arms. She massaged each hand, pulling his fingers gently from their base as he eased deeper into the sheet below him.

Her hand skimmed up to his shoulder and across to the other arm. She tucked the soft sheet in around him as if encasing him in a silky cocoon. She noticed a slight smile on his lips and his lashes fluttered briefly. She wished she knew what he was thinking. She reminded herself that a professional massage therapist would never intrude by asking, and shouldn't be wondering in the first place. And she prayed he'd keep his eyes and his mouth closed. *Just be a body, not Mitch.*

After his left arm was tucked in gently, she sat down behind him again and slowly slid her hands up and down his chest to his trim waist. No hint of love handles on this body, unlike many of the men she used to do at the casino. Many had been overfed, under-exercised corporate types with pale flabby skin. A few were gym junkies proud of their tanned muscles and lean stomachs. But Mitch was all natural, his lean muscles and taut abs built through outdoor work and play. She caught herself remembering how he'd looked sawing crown molding with his shirt off or the way his biceps flexed as he pulled a fish from the surf. *He's just a client on the table, a collection of muscles and joints and nerves.* Rita glanced at the clinical anatomy charts he'd hung on one wall. She had to focus.

Keeping one hand on him at all times, she covered his chest and arranged the lower part of the sheet to expose one leg at a time. Her hands traveled from his thigh to foot. Massaging each reflex of his toes, she wondered if she might be affecting another part of him, at least a little. She blushed and reminded herself to get a grip. Thank God, he'd never know what she was thinking!

Covering him again, she extended the headrest of the massage table, applied more lotion to her hands, and whispered near his ear, "Please turn over slowly. It's time to do your back now."

She watched the slow rise and fall of his chest. "Mitch?" she whispered again. "Are you asleep?"

"Almost."

She felt his warm breath on her cheek. "Roll over and move up a few inches," she directed. "Rest your head on the extension."

Mitch sighed and slowly turned over, sinking his nose through the hole in the headrest. "You are so good," he murmured as Rita repeated the routine, head, neck, shoulders, arms, legs, back and buttocks. She felt him tense as she skimmed her hands over the side of his firm cheeks. "Hey, watch it!" he mumbled. His muscles gradually surrendered to the back and forth of her soothing palms. Had he drifted off to sleep?

She covered him gently and wondered how it would feel to touch her lips ever so softly at the nape of this neck. He wouldn't even know if she did it right next to her fingers. But she didn't; it wasn't the professional thing to do. Shock and guilt for even thinking about it flooded into her.

Whoa girl! Take it easy! She reminded herself Mitch was only a client and she was a detached massage therapist. That's all! And she hadn't done anything wrong. She lectured herself. *You don't really know him. And you don't want to either. He seems to be a nice guy, but a loner.* Certainly not someone to risk her entire future, her livelihood, and

Aunt Liz's security on. Attractive? Yes, but not irresistible. What was she thinking? He'd never let her hear the end of it if he were awake and felt a kiss. Obviously she needed distance.

Rita slipped out of the room and caught her breath. She sat at her computer desk to pull herself together before going out to the shop. Rita had never been able to hide anything from Serena, and she didn't want her friend seeing how touching Mitch had affected her.

She had to admit it to herself: she was attracted to Mitch. That was a good thing to know. She'd have to avoid him from now on. Go out of her way to let him know she wasn't interested in him.

What did she or Aunt Liz really know about him anyway? A carpenter who kept to himself, rarely drank beer like most of the construction guys she'd met, and shunned making extra money. A mysterious sort of Robin Hood who did favors for elderly people or damsels in distress like Serena and herself. Powerfully built yet with no calluses to speak of. And he'd been to college. Evaded answering her questions. Maybe she should look into his background in a more official way. Aunt Liz never would. If only Rita had done that with Kevin, maybe she wouldn't have gotten involved with him in the first place.

Suddenly the door from the shop burst open and Serena popped her head in with a big grin and whispered, "Hey, girlfriend. How'd it go?"

Before Rita could answer, Serena put her finger in front of her lips. "Hold that thought. Tell me all later. You have another visitor. This one bearing a gift in expensive wrapping! Told me he wanted to be your first customer, but I told him that position was already filled."

"Mitch is asleep. I don't have another appointment, so I'm letting him rest. He's actually quiet for a change. So who's out there?"

"Come see for yourself."

Rita followed her friend into the gift shop. Tony Jennings bent over a display case, studying an assortment of stickpins and miniature snuffboxes. At the sound of footsteps, he said, "You have some charming things here, Ms. Starr. Genuine value, not mere trinkets for tourists." He moved on to examine the pins and pocket watches without looking up at her.

"Call me Serena. And you're right. Some of the seniors in the older section of town bring in jewelry or knickknacks on consignment. I have the items appraised so they get a fair price, and I make a small commission on the sale, so everybody's happy. Is there anything you'd like to see out of the case?"

"Not today, but maybe in the future. Is Rita free yet? You know I also came to see her about a job opportunity." He turned and smiled when he saw her. "And maybe something you'd be interested in, too."

"Hi, Tony. I'm free to give a massage, but I'm not hiring anybody at this time. If you leave your number, though, I'll let you know when there's an opening."

Tony laughed. "What a kidder. I brought you a business-warming present, but I wanted you to know I could still use a good fitness trainer at the spa. You'd have fewer worries at an established business like mine rather than opening up a small outfit on your own. Safer, too, than this quaint but somewhat run-down business section. I assured your aunt my job offer was still open, especially since we're expanding our wellness program. What do you say?"

"Same thing I've said before. I appreciate your offer, but I like being my own boss. I've done the casino-hotel-spa massage and fitness routine. I need a change."

"If you want change and excitement, perhaps I could interest you and your fortune-telling friend here in joining the staff on my wellness cruises. It's like taking a working vacation. Think it over and get back to me. Today, though, I stopped in for a massage and to bring you this." Tony handed her a small package wrapped in embossed silver paper and a shiny purple ribbon.

Rita set the present on the counter and carefully unwrapped it. Inside the box was a snow globe with an angel inside. "Your aunt once mentioned you liked angels. I happened to see this at an auction the other day and I thought of you."

Rita shook it and watched the white flakes swirl. "Thank you, Tony, but this is far too expensive for an office-warming present. I can't accept it."

"Of course you can. Think of it as a present from a friend of the family and a grateful customer." He held up a silver envelope. "I thought it would be nice to be your first client."

A deep voice interrupted, "Too late for that." Mitch stood in the doorway buckling his belt. "I had her first. And she's not available at the moment. We have a little unfinished business."

Tony eyed Mitch from head to toe as Mitch leaned against the doorframe with his hands folded over his chest. Rita's face burned. "And you are?" Tony raised an eyebrow and returned Mitch's icy gaze.

"A friend of Liz's and Rita's."

Rita broke the awkward silence, "Sorry, I didn't realize you two hadn't met. Mitch, this is Tony Jennings. Tony, this is Mitch. He's been helping us fix up the place. Did a wonderful job, but now he's leaving for the day, aren't you, Mitch?"

"Well, Hon, we hadn't quite finished what we started. We need to discuss a couple things before I go home."

"I don't think so. In fact, I'm sure it can wait. I have to take care of my second client of the day, and the grand opening's not even until next week." Rita took Tony's arm and ushered him toward Mitch who was still blocking the way. "And look at the lovely paperweight he gave me." She lifted the snow globe to Mitch's eye level before turning to Tony and adding, "Thank you so much, Tony. I have the perfect place for this."

Mitch stepped aside and watched the door close behind Rita. He glared at Serena.

"Say, Mitch, you don't look very relaxed for someone's who just had a massage. Something bothering you?"

Mitch pointed to the closed door with his thumb. "What do you know about that guy?"

"Tony? Rich, rich, and rich. Very big wheel in this town and into everything—society, entertainment, businesses. His real estate firm offered to list this place for me but I said not now. Poor guy—he's even movie-star handsome, too. But then, I'm sure you noticed that."

"Married?"

"Nope, forty and never been married. From what I see in the paper, he's too busy going out with young models and society blondes to settle down. The best catch on the Shore, if you'll forgive the pun. But who knows? Maybe's he's decided to troll for a more mature, late thirties brunette. He seems quite taken by Rita. What do you think?"

"I don't like him. Slick phony. Why did you sell him a massage from Rita?"

"Hello! Earth to Mitch. She's in business for that purpose, and he paid cash for the full works, the same as yours. Any problem with that?"

"Of course not. I just don't like his type." Mitch looked down at his jeans and T-shirt and started pacing.

"What type? You mean rich? As opposed to your type?"

Mitch stared at Serena and took a deep breath.

"Sorry about that crack, Mitch." Serena's face softened. "I'm not rich, either. And I don't think it's his money you dislike. Maybe you're a bit jealous for a different reason."

"Me, jealous? I don't want his dough and I'm not involved with Rita. But I don't want her getting hurt by some sleazy Don Juan either, no matter how much money he has."

"Mitch, it's a therapeutic massage. It's not like Rita and her clients are having sex. You should know. You just had a massage. It didn't turn you on...or did it? Oooh, tell me the juicy details."

Mitch shook his head. "Serena, you are a troublemaker, you know that?"

"Yep. Always have been and proud of it. Makes life more interesting. But you avoided answering the question, didn't you? Like you always do."

"Serena," Mitch began. "I'm beat. I'm done here for the day and almost finished with the whole job. Thanks for the massage and I'll miss your brownies, but I won't miss your third degrees. If Rita wants to know where I am, tell her I went fishing. Fish don't talk back, and sometimes it's even better if you don't catch one." He paused to put on what Serena called his Indiana Jones hat. "And watch out for her, okay? If you really are her friend."

Serena nodded and pointed a finger at him. "And you watch out for me, Cowboy, if you ever hurt a friend of mine."

Mitch sighed and left.

Had he imagined the butterfly kiss on his neck? So light, so quick? It had to be part of his daydream, not something she would do to anyone, not to him, not to anyone else. At least that's what she'd claim. And he wasn't jealous, either, just protective. He

101

couldn't let himself care again, not that way, maybe not ever.

So why did he hate the thought of Tony lying naked on sheets in a darkened room with Rita? After all, she'd been married to a greedy loser. What disturbed him about her attracting a rich, handsome husband? Whatever peace Mitch had felt a few minutes before on the massage table had vanished as he backed his truck out and headed for the beach, a fishing pole, and a cold beer. Not root beer this time.

Chapter Nine

Rita hadn't intended to keep the snow globe, but she was furious. How dare Mitch act like a possessive caveman in front of Tony! Implying he was more than a client, as if they were romantically involved. *And "Hon?"* She placed the snow globe on her desk and forced herself to smile at Tony. "I have two massage rooms," she said brightly. "Come this way. I wasn't expecting another client today, but I only have to light the candles."

Tony followed her inside and examined it wall to wall as she lit three candles and started a CD. "Very soothing atmosphere."

Rita motioned to a three-panel screen covered with one of Aunt Liz's seascape quilts. "I'll give you a few minutes to disrobe and hang your things there. You know the routine, right? Slide under the sheet on your back." She left Tony unbuttoning his black silk shirt.

Rita glanced at the clock and exhaled deeply. She had to let go of her irritation with Mitch to focus on her client. She didn't want to work at Tony's spa, but she had to admit, she did want to impress him. And it was a good thing Mitch had created two separate massage rooms for her to handle clients that overlapped. Enough about Mitch. She had to get back to business. She quickly changed the linens where he'd been and returned to her office.

Two more minutes. She didn't want to barge in on Tony before he was tucked in beneath the sheet. She picked up the antique glass sphere and watched the tiny white flakes drift slowly to the base of the angel's feet. If only problems settled that quickly.

No sense giving Tony the impression his gesture had more importance than it did, though. It couldn't stay on her desk. She hurried across the room and placed it on the shelf full of angels. Just another angel in the flock. Nothing special.

Tony should be undressed and ready by now. Rita knocked gently. "Are you ready?"

"Yes, come in," he said. She slipped into the second therapy room and let her eyes adjust to the semi-darkness. She glanced at Tony's jet-black hair, his bronzed arms and broad shoulders looking as good against the pale blue sheet as he did in Armani. He obviously knew the routine, saying nothing as Rita went through the hour-long ritual of massaging essential oils into his lean muscles with her strong, capable hands. His body was smooth, perfectly aligned, and virtually free of any knots or signs of stress. It was easy to work on a body like his, one that had been pampered and maintained like a treasured Ferrari. She focused on the music, the haunting piano melody intertwined with the sound of a gurgling stream.

Rita became aware of the silence when the music stopped. She completed her final sweeping movements over his back and covered him with the soft sheet. The hour was over. Perfect timing, even on automatic pilot. As if reading her mind, Tony murmured, "I don't want you to stop. It seems as if you just began."

"I know, but take your time getting up. I'll be in the outer office or helping Serena," she whispered and left before he said another word.

She wasn't needed in the gift shop, so Rita sat at her desk and started to work on designing a new flyer on the computer. Tony came out after about ten minutes and handed her his silver envelope. "Amazing hands and computer skills, too. You're a woman of many talents, Rita. I respect your desire to be independent, but if you ever change your mind about working for someone, you must call me first. You were wonderful!"

"Thank you, Tony. You were easy to work on. I bet you get regular massages and weekly chiropractic visits, right?"

"Very perceptive. Yes, I take good care of myself. Now compared to my spas, your décor is a bit more, shall we say, 'New Age' than I'm used to..."

"I prefer calling it 'soothing' and 'peaceful'..." Rita corrected. "Or 'spiritual' might be a better way to describe the atmosphere and the process. It's all about healing."

Tony pulled a chair next to Rita's computer station and clasped both of her hands in his. He looked directly into her eyes with excitement. "The magic is in your hands, Rita, not the furnishings. But whatever you want to label it, I think your style would appeal to the corporate wives who come to my spas.

"Most male clients care more about networking and making business connections with a little relaxation thrown in. Sleek chrome is fine for their area. I want you to transform the ladies' areas with this feminine blend of cozy garden, touch of heavens, quaint quilt sentimentalism. Add some 'New Age' elements: aromatherapy, incense, inspiring sayings, whatever. A kind of marketing experiment. How about it?"

Rita tilted her head and spoke slowly, "You want me to help my biggest competitor? Marketing spirituality? What kind of businesswoman do you think I am?"

Tony dropped her hands at last and reached for his wallet. He handed her two business cards. "A smart one who wants to increase her income as a consultant and make the right connections. I'm serious. Card one, join the Chamber of Commerce. Card two, call me. I pay very well. And remember, we're not competitors, we're fellow business owners. There are enough backs in need of rubbing in this town for both of us to be successful."

Tony paused a moment. "And you truly would be the perfect massage therapist for my wellness cruises. Your friend could do card readings. Lots of opportunities to meet the right kind of people. Though on second thought, maybe I don't want you whisked away by a handsome stranger on a moonlit night. I might want to keep you for myself."

He reached over and lifted her hand to his lips before getting up to leave. "I'll definitely be in touch. No pun intended." He slid on his sunglasses and paused at the doorway, smooth, relaxed, and in control. "Think it over. You know where to reach me."

Rita was still sitting there a few minutes later when Serena appeared. "So, Rita, tell me. What's it like to have two handsome men vying for your attention? And to think you get paid to touch them both! I definitely went into the wrong line of work."

"Yeah, the fringe benefits are great. I get to touch them and get paid for it, and I don't have to wonder if I'll have to support and take care of them for the rest of their lives."

"From the looks of both of them, I think they can take care of themselves just fine...and probably satisfy a lot of your basic needs as well. And Tony? With his money, I bet he can fulfill your every desire, too. Play your cards right and maybe you won't even have to work anymore!"

"Serena, I should turn you in to the women's lib movement. I used to get mad when someone suggested I needed a man to take care of me, as if they were suggesting I couldn't do it myself. But after my experience with Kevin, I sometimes wonder what was so wrong with the old way. Uncle Carlton worked and paid the bills while Aunt Liz took care of the house and garden. She never felt any less worthy because he made all the money.

"And look at my mom. She slaved as a waitress after my dad died while Aunt Liz looked after me. When my first step dad proposed, she was happy to stop working and retire with him to a condo in Florida. Not that I find her life exciting, but who am I to judge? They're happy and they support each other. They don't keep score, they share. Is an equal partner too much to ask for? Someone who wouldn't dream of spending my hard-earned money on gambling or risky business ventures?"

Serena plopped down on the couch. "Well, friend, from what I've seen and experienced, soul mates are few and far between. Maybe you and I have been traveling in the wrong circles, at least until now. May I be blunt?"

Rita giggled. "Since when do you ask permission?"

"Don't evade the issue. Stop being a victim and become the hunter yourself. Remember that Hunter card? Maybe ol' Tony is hunting you. Let yourself get caught and fall in love. Or *you* could go after *him* instead of hiding out with your sad story."

"Serena, I'm not pursuing anyone. And where did falling in love ever get me? In a hole. The story's sad, but true."

"Here's a novel idea. Why not let yourself fall in love with a wealthy man? Tony seems to have his eye on you."

"Yeah, well from what you've told me about Tony, his eyes have been on younger, blonder women with more money and power than I have. And they don't have to deal with the issue of having kids or not in the next few years."

Serena shook her head. "You don't have to rush.

Nowadays, plenty of women have babies in their forties. And as someone who had two when I was young, it might be easier to have them later in life. Older partners usually have more resources and patience."

"Are you done lecturing, Ms. Tarot reader?"

"Almost. I think the Hunter has Cupid's arrows aimed at you. Let down that shield you're holding up and enjoy being pampered instead. You can be sure Tony's not after your money!"

Rita laughed. "I can't argue with that! But speaking of money, how about celebrating my first sales with me? Let's close early and go for ribs at the new place in Point Pleasant, the one that's supposed to be like the Southern House that burned down. My treat."

"Sounds great, but I can't leave right away. I scheduled a tarot reading in a half hour. Go home and take it easy. I'll pick you up at 7."

"It's a date. And the only kind I want in the near future, understood?"

Serena shook her head. "Not really, but what are friends for? Now get going, and say hi to Liz for me. Ask her if she wants to join us."

****

When Rita got back to the house, a note on the refrigerator explained everything. *"Going to AC with Dorothy. Be back around nine. Food's on 'the Donald.' Don't cook for me.—Aunt Liz."* She smiled. Liz and her pals often took advantage of the tour buses traveling down to Atlantic City. For an investment of $15, they got a round trip ride to the casino of their choice, a roll of quarters, and half price on the buffet, courtesy of Donald Trump or a different casino. Liz had once seen "The Donald" entering an Aretha Franklin concert with his blonde second wife carrying a tiny little girl in a red velvet dress. Of course, that was one wife ago. Men.

Rita caught herself before she charged down her well-trodden mental path about marriage and the limited males on the planet. *It took two to get divorced, and we grow through the challenges in life.* Serena was right. Time to stop dredging up her "sad story." Even she was tired of it.

Rita poured herself a glass of iced tea and checked the clock. No rush. Time for a swim and a quick shower before Serena came by for supper. By now, the seniors on the casino trip would be in line for the buffet. They'd catch up on gossip or complain about the one-armed bandits devouring their quarters. Then they'd sit on the boardwalk benches by the ocean and enjoy watching the characters walk by. In Mantoloking Sands, they'd never see hookers in five-inch platform shoes and spangled tube tops striding by, or a disabled vet playing "Amazing Grace" on a keyboard with his tongue. It provided a break in their routines and shocking topics for conversations.

Rita had only gone with her aunt and uncle on one of these bus trips years before. Uncle Carlton had been pretty good at blackjack and had taught Rita how to play by the rules. She'd been extremely lucky with his money as long as she thought of simply betting two red chips instead of ten bucks or one green chip instead of twenty-five hard-earned dollars. When she lost, she'd think of how many hours she'd have to work to get it back. No, she was not cut out to be a great gambler.

Rita changed into her black bikini and shoved her keys, a book, and a towel into a beach bag. She pictured her feisty aunt installed at her favorite Double Diamonds slot machine. Insert coin, pull. Insert coin, pull. The diamonds would line up, buzzers would ring, and an avalanche of quarters would clang into the tray. Aunt Liz was amazingly lucky. At least in Atlantic City, she'd be having a grand time this evening and wouldn't be back for hours.

Finally, the perfect opportunity for Rita to explore the roll top desk downstairs. Because of the vandalism and the renovation project, Rita hadn't had a chance to check on the shut-off notice and the other papers her aunt had shoved into the desk.

Better find out if Mitch were around first. "Gone fishing" was the note tacked inside the garage. His tackle box and surf pole were gone. That should give her at least an hour to investigate undisturbed.

Rita opened the side drawer of the oak desk. Damn! The mound of papers was gone. The desk calendar said "Accountant OK" next to a little smiley face. Obviously, Liz Chandler, the former schoolteacher, had been happy to turn over those bills.

Rita rifled through the rest of the drawers. Lilac-scented stationery, garden club notices, seed catalogues, coupons for local stores, a few business cards wrapped tightly with a rubber band. Credit cards and a library card stuffed under the blotter along with her checkbook. *Never take a full purse to New York, Philly, or Atlantic City. Keep your load lighter and have less to lose.* Aunt Liz practiced what she preached.

Gazing at the big blotter size calendar, Rita smiled. Liz's tiny manuscript printing logged the events of her life in various calendar squares: "Card from Aunt Myrt, Longarzo funeral 7:30; Hair cut; lunch with Rita—got German Chocolate cake recipe; Electric out; stayed at spa; Accountant Appt. OK; Order lily bulbs; sympathy card for Marilyn; Doctor appt. Bank."

Liz kept these calendars year after year, stuffed in a closet. She refused to throw them out. Uncle Carlton had been the one who started it. Flipping back through past months was like rereading history. All the forgotten details that add up to a life lived moment by moment, errand by errand. "Rita called—Coming for summer!" "Lunch with Mitch" "Cabinets delivered." "Doctor Cardio." Her heart? "Deck fire." What did those last entries mean? How strange.

The last two months had "Cruise?" entered in purple. Under the blotter was a slick brochure about the wellness cruise to nowhere Tony had been talking about. "Cruise into wellness…For your mind, body, and spirit. Rejuvenate, refresh, and restore yourself as you rediscover the fountain of youth bubbling within you." Photos showed elegant seniors dancing in front of a big band, females in sequined full-lengths gowns and males in sharp tuxedos.

Other shots featured trim silver-haired ladies doing graceful stretches on teal yoga mats or sipping tropical drinks with umbrellas perched on coconut shells. Scores of Sean Connery look-alikes smiled at the ladies, extending their arms with the promise of one last dance and an intimate stroll around a moonlit deck.

The brochure showed some younger adults in the background, but no children anywhere in sight. And the food! Buffet tables overflowed with huge platters of tropical fruits, piles of pasta, and shellfish. Chefs in towering white hats sliced roast beef to order as they stood by glistening ice sculptures of dolphins and sea goddesses.

The ad promised it all: Tai Chi, yoga, massage, swimming, dancing, and excitement. And for those who leaned more toward worldly pleasures and the other kind of spirits, there were pictures of elaborate bars, blackjack tables, and slot machines, legal once you sailed far enough offshore.

Aunt Liz would be the life of the party on one of these cruises. She had frequented health food stores before her time, chanted with the Maharishi before it became fashionable, took pictures of India and Buddhist temples before Richard Gere discovered the Dalai Lama, and danced around the house before aerobics classes in gyms and Jane Fonda workout videos existed.

Maybe Rita should consider Tony's offer. This kind of cruise might be a fun thing for them to do someday after her business picked up. She couldn't let Aunt Liz foot the bill, though. Or Tony.

"Planning a cruise with Mr. Moneybags?" Mitch's husky voice interrupted her thoughts.

"How long have you been standing there?" Rita stammered.

"Why? What are you up to?"

"What am I up to? I live here, *Hon*. I'm a relative. The question is what are *you* doing in here? Now the kitchen's finished, I didn't expect to see you in the house unannounced. Besides, I thought you'd gone fishing. *Hon!*"

"Ouch. I guess you're still mad about me calling you that in front of Tony, huh?"

"Yes, I am, and not only about the 'Hon' thing. You just barged in on me. What if I'd been running around the house naked?"

"I guess I would have been in for a treat," Mitch chuckled. He walked into the kitchen and got a root beer. "You're right. I'm sorry....that you weren't naked." Rita glared.

"Just kidding. I admit, I wasn't thinking. This past year I got used to coming and going whether Liz was in or not. My refrigerator's small so I keep some of my stuff in hers. But let's get back to the cruise. Don't tell me you're taken in by that slick guy and his mumbo jumbo sales pitch."

"This is Aunt Liz's brochure, not mine, and it might be nice for her to get away." Rita slid the brochure back under the blotter where she'd found it. "She seems a bit worried at times, but when I ask her about it, she says she doesn't need a mother hen at this stage of her life. But a few of her friends and husbands of others have passed on lately, and I think it reminds her of losing Uncle Carlton."

Mitch took a long swallow. "It's tough losing someone. Takes time and you never really get over it. It hurts less the next day... till something happens and pinches a memory, good or bad. But sometimes even stubborn independent women need a mother hen, and they don't realize it. So if you're watching out for your aunt, that's great. But while you're at it, I hope you're not blinded into getting involved with the wrong guy."

"Right now, all guys are the wrong guys for me. I'm not getting involved with anyone, and here's another news flash for you. I'm not asking for any advice either, so as much as I truly appreciate all your help at the shop, could you please knock off the unsolicited words of wisdom? Save it for your own life, okay?"

Mitch studied Rita's flushed face and her angry green eyes. "Sorry to bother you, but I care about what happens to Liz, and since you're important to her, you're important to me, too. I'll try to stay out of your way, but...I'm here if you need me." He tipped his NJ Devils cap, picked up his root beer, and turned away, taking care not to slam the porch door.

After he left, Rita sat down at the desk again. She knew why she'd reacted so strongly. She felt guilty about getting caught snooping in Aunt Liz's desk, and she still didn't have the facts. How could she help if she didn't know what was wrong or where to turn to find solutions? She'd trusted the wrong person before and paid the price. She didn't want the same to happen to Aunt Liz.

Mitch seemed so sincere and his concern for Liz genuine. But so did Tony. That didn't explain the antagonism between them. Could Serena be right?

Was Mitch jealous of Tony's attentions toward her, or did he envy Tony's success as a businessman and his wealth?

That didn't make sense either. If Mitch envied Tony's money, why help old ladies and new business owners without charging for labor? What was he living on anyway? Could Mitch be taking advantage of her aunt some other way? Rita searched the drawers for a checkbook without any luck. Aunt Liz must have taken it to the accountant to fix.

She'd have to confront Aunt Liz for information, but it would have to wait until tomorrow. Right now, all Rita wanted to do was stretch out on the beach and relax before her night out with Serena. *I deserve a break, too.*

When she arrived at the water's edge, she spread her sheet on the hot sand, sprayed herself with sunscreen, took a swig from her water bottle, and sprawled out. Squinting south toward the distant Ferris wheel of the boardwalk at Seaside Shores, she watched Mitch cast his rig into the surf and steadily reel it in, trying to fool a stray bluefish into thinking the flash of silver was a slippery mullet skimming toward shore. The fish weren't biting, or weren't there at all. Still, Mitch flipped the hook back out and repeated the process again and again as precisely as he cut lumber.

Rita closed her eyes, shielded her face from the sun, and dozed off, wondering what Mitch was thinking as he cast his line out again, picturing his strong tan arms moving rhythmically back and forth, feeling them under her hands again as she thought back to the massage.

Suddenly cold drops of water pelted her hot arms. Rita jumped and tried to remember where she was. She looked up to see Mitch dangling two large bluefish on a line and his fishing gear in the other hand. "Hey! What's the big idea?" she yelled.

"Well, Princess, you've been sleeping in the sun a long time. It's almost suppertime. Thought I'd wake you before you fry." Mitch held up the fish for Rita to admire. "How about sharing these with me, unless you have other plans?"

"Oh, my God, I do! And I'll be late if I don't get going." She scrambled to stuff her unread novel and towel into her tote bag. "Thanks for waking me up, though next time, I'd appreciate something more subtle than fish juice dripping on my arm. You really know how to charm a girl, huh?"

"Definitely, but it's not the bluefish that's irresistible. Compared to flounder, they're oily and fishy. It's my secret recipe for the best sauce in the world."

"I bet you have lots of secrets, but I can't stay tonight. It's not the bluefish or fear of your cooking. I really do have to go."

"Hot date?"

Rita hesitated. Her brows inched closer in a tiny frown before she relaxed and grinned. "Not that it's any of your business, but you could definitely say this date is going to be very hot!"

His eyes narrowed to glittery slits. "So who is this date, anyway?"

"Well, if you insist on knowing the details, it's going to be incredibly hot. You can't imagine what I'm going to indulge in tonight for the first time in years and how much I'm looking forward to savoring every sticky moment." She paused to remove her sunglasses and look him directly in the eyes. "You know how it is to go without something you really crave for a long time and then there it is, waiting for you to reach out and grab it? Spicy, tender, juicy. So messy and wonderful you can't resist the urge to nibble slowly until you're ready to burst." Rita's eyes gleamed. "And I don't want to be late, so excuse me for passing up that bluefish staring at me, but I've got to take a shower."

"And who's the main course, Tony? Mr. 'Flash-a-smile, kiss-a-hand, and drop-off-an-expensive-gift' Tony?"

"Mitch, I don't want to hurt your feelings, but who I go out with is my business, remember? How about cooking the bluefish tomorrow?"

"Sorry, but we won't be available tomorrow. This baby has a date with a frying pan tonight. Your loss."

Mitch walked a few feet away and turned back to face Rita. "Be careful. And if you need me, for anything, call. You have my cell phone number."

Rita stopped smiling, too. "Mitch, don't worry about me. I'll be fine. I'm not really going on a..."

Mitch interrupted and nodded. "No, you're right. You don't owe me explanations. Just take care of yourself."

Rita watched him walk toward the house. Maybe she and Serena should stay and eat supper with him instead of going out. He'd been so helpful. She started to follow him but paused. When Serena arrived instead of Tony, Rita wouldn't have to explain a thing. And he'd have to eat crow with his bluefish.

Chapter Ten

Mitch walked over to the picnic table near the garage. He got some newspaper from the recycling bin and grabbed a knife from his tackle box. With precise cuts, he started to skin and fillet the fish efficiently and swiftly. Why should he care if Rita went out with Tony? Rich, attractive in a slick kind of way, and attentive. Probably considered "quite a catch" as his mom used to say, especially for someone in Rita's position, getting over an ex who turned out to be a moocher and a bum. Mitch plunged the blade into the scrap of plywood he'd been using as a cutting board.

Even though she claimed she was tired of working all those jobs, he'd bet she was too stubborn or proud to ever let a man support her. She didn't seem to like him trying to help her.

Hell, he could relate to that. His family and former in-laws had told him he was guilty of too much pride more times than he'd wanted to remember. Well, he didn't need to prove himself to anyone, anymore. Didn't need to work for money or answer to anyone else. Life was simple. Catch a fish, eat it for supper, bury the guts in Liz's rose garden. Money and women complicated life. Live, be grateful, create beauty, care for things. And people...but from a distance. It hurt too much to get close.

Mitch dug a shallow grave near the American Beauty bushes, threw the fish remains in, and packed the dirt down firmly. He grabbed the hose, rinsed the fillets, and squirted the mound. Peat moss splattered all over. "Damn, look at me. Covered with dirt and sand, sweaty and stinking like bluefish. *I* don't even want to eat with me." He sprayed himself next.

He was rolling up the hose when Serena pulled up in her vintage VW microbus hand painted with angels, stars, and moons. She honked the horn to the rhythm of "Shave and a haircut." Spotting Mitch, she turned off the ignition and hopped out. "Hey, Mitch, what's up? Taken up gardening, too?"

"No, just fertilizing flowers with fish guts. Liz's instructions. If you're looking for Rita, she's upstairs getting ready for some hot date."

"A hot date? Is that what she said?"

"Not in so many words, but I got the message."

"Did she say who the lucky guy is?"

"No, but my guess is Tony. He looks her over like he's checking out the dessert cart at some fancy restaurant. And the phony hand-kissing he does, the way he moves in too close. Do women really like that?"

"Actually, yes, they do. They just rarely get it. But Rita's not going out with Tony."

"Well, who else does she know around here? Some old flame?"

"Do I detect a bit of jealousy?"

"Of course not. Just looking out for her - for Liz's sake, you know. So who's the guy?"

"Mitch, there's no guy. We're going to the rib joint in Point Pleasant to celebrate her first sales today. You know the place with the greatest ribs on the entire Jersey Shore? And the sweetest white corn drizzled with tons of butter? It's down home style with mason jars of soda and all the hot buttery rolls you want to use to sop up the special barbeque sauce."

"Oh. So that's the 'hot spicy' date." Mitch grinned. "She really had me going."

The door opened and Rita appeared in tight jeans and a red tank top.

"Yo, Princess Rita. I hear the only date you have is with a pile of spare ribs. You reject my bluefish supreme for a slab of baby back ribs? You don't know what you're missing."

Serena looked Mitch up and down. "Well, Mitch, why don't you come along? We'll wait a few minutes for you—but only if you get rid of the fish smell quick."

Mitch hesitated and glanced at Rita who was glaring at Serena. If they had been sitting around a table, Mitch was sure Serena's shin would be throbbing by now. "No, thanks," he said. "Another time. The fish is a lot better fresh, so if you girls don't want to join me and Big Blue at my barbeque, then go on without me." He beamed at Rita. "Have fun on your hot date."

"Admit it, Mitch, I got you! Enjoy eating your crow along with the fish." Rita smirked and climbed into the VW. "Don't wait up, 'Dad!' " she yelled as they drove off.

Mitch laughed and headed toward the grill. "Just you and me, Fish," he said. At least Rita would only be engaged in small talk with her best female friend, not enjoying the wine and French cuisine he'd imagined her sharing with the suave and slimy Tony.

After a solitary supper on the picnic table, Mitch washed the few dishes. He drenched his hands in the leftover lemon, trying to dull the overwhelming odor of fish.

He eased down on a rocker on the back porch and twisted the cap off his bottle of Coors. He'd never understood why some construction workers guzzled beer after beer on sweltering summer days. Not when you had to do a job right, operate a power saw safely, and make precision cuts. Beer, like most things, was best savored like dessert. Too much of anything wasn't good for the body or soul. But one beer, one glass of fine wine, one kiss was sometimes more pleasure than a man could stand.

He took out an old pocketknife, one he'd had as a kid, and started whittling a piece of driftwood he'd found. The best carvers didn't need much light. They could feel the shape in the wood. He hadn't graduated from college like his late wife, but she'd told him when it came to whittling, he was like Michelangelo freeing David from marble. It's only a matter of releasing the figure from the material that held him. She'd been right about that.

In the dusk, he could just make out the delicate wings spread wide and hands embracing the sky. A tiny angel with a wild curly ponytail. That was new. And tricky. Angels had always had long flowing straight hair before. He closed the blade and shoved it in his pocket, curved his fist protectively around the small being, and wondered what to do with it.

The murmur of Liz's old Crown Victoria came slowly up the gravel driveway. "Hey, Liz! You're home early. How you doing?" he called out. He went down the steps and opened the car door for her.

"Just fine, Mitch. How about you?"

"Pretty good. Caught a couple of bluefish. Had one for supper and saved you one. Fed the rest to your roses. Did you win big?"

"No, Dorothy wasn't up to the bus trip so we didn't go to AC. I guess I came out ahead, though. As my Carlton would say, 'If you don't go, you don't lose. If you don't gamble, you win. But never lose sleep even if you lose all your money.' Anyway, we played some pinochle at her house and went out for ribs. Didn't have to listen to all those old folks complain on the bus ride home. You'd think somebody forced them to stuff nickels or quarters into those machines the way they bitch and moan, excuse my language."

Mitch put out a hand and helped her out of the car. "You're excused, as long as you don't start bitching and moaning and acting like an old lady."

"No way. But what's this I hear about you being antisocial? Rita and Serena stopped by our table right before we finished dessert. Serena claims you wouldn't go with them. Is something the matter?"

"Nah. In fact, they wouldn't stay for bluefish so I enjoyed it myself. So did the roses. Hey, give me your keys. I'll pull the car into the garage. Now that the big projects are over, there's actually room for this baby in the garage. Got to protect her from the salt and rust again."

"Thanks, Mitch." She patted the old blue car. "This one is my last car. I'd better take good care of her. Now sleep well. I'm hitting the hay early. It's tiring being around old people, you know." She winked.

"Hey, how would I know? I don't know any old fogies yet."

"Charmer! Why don't you try using some of that on a pretty young thing? At your age, you should be keeping company with something more attractive than a bluefish. I can't believe you turned down a dinner invitation from my own beautiful niece and her colorful friend."

"Next time, she invites me, I'll tag along. Promise." He slid into the driver's seat. "Now go get your beauty sleep. You got to be ready to hook Mr. Right someday."

"Right. That'll happen...like when you settle down."

Mitch smiled, eased the car into the garage, and threw Liz the keys. "Good catch. See, you're as young as ever. I'm the one who's going to bed first!"

"Good night, Mitch, and sleep well. Remember, happiness comes when you least expect it."

"If you say so. Night, yourself." He trudged

upstairs and turned off the lights below. He threw his cutoffs over the computer stuck in the corner. Hadn't turned it on in weeks, and didn't want to anymore. Sitting in a rocker looking out over the ocean was more his speed now, easing himself back and forth in time to the waves. He wished he'd moved here years ago.

A little while later, he heard the sputter of Serena's van, a creaky door slam, and faint laughter. Would they have been laughing if he'd gone along? He wished he wasn't remembering how good it felt to twist her thick curls around his fingers as he crushed his lips to hers during that brief impulsive kiss, breathing in her scent, feeling the grit of sawdust between them.

He rubbed his hands together and studied them. Pretty soon he'd have his old calluses again, rough from sanding and hauling lumber. Sometimes his muscles ached from physical labor or from reeling in a fighting fish in the surf, no longer from pumping iron during sessions at a corporate gym, squeezed in after long sessions on a keyboard or the telephone.

Money had been so important not very long ago. Now it seemed like centuries had passed since he'd left that part of his life behind, tucked away like the framed photo hidden in his closet, a five-by-seven of a handsome long-haired groom shoving cake into the perfect lips of a beautiful younger blonde. That photo was his favorite, the only picture that hadn't looked rehearsed, perfect, and worthy of being in one of those damned bridal magazines.

He'd lost so much. He'd tried to find himself again by withdrawing. Then by helping strangers, but at a distance. He had vowed never to get involved again. And he'd been doing okay.

Part of him wanted to remain detached, a silent fisherman alone on the beach. Part of him wanted to eat messy ribs with a tiny spitfire that irritated as much as aroused him.

Yes, he was attracted to her. Hell, it'd been two years since he'd been with a woman. But some people need to be off-limits. He'd learned that lesson with a striking young blonde who turned into a stranger after they married. Or maybe he was the one who'd turned into a stranger. When he'd finally realized it, it was too late. He'd never know if she'd ever really loved him. Not after fights about her alcoholism, her spending and partying. Not after her accidental drowning.

And now he cared too much for a scrappy old lady who'd taken him in one misty morning. What if he had been a con man? A thief? A murderer? How did she know who he really was? Did she always have great instincts when it came to trusting? Lucky for her, he was the kind of man he appeared to be...for the most part.

Would she still like him, still trust him, if she knew the whole truth? And what if things went badly with Rita? He had to keep his distance. He didn't want to start over again. It was too hard to lose your place in a family. Ironic. Being here felt more like being home, more part of a family than anything he'd ever known. He didn't have to prove anything to Liz or rebuild relationships wounded by old jealousies and judgments.

He'd keep up his big brother act, as Rita called it, but it was getting more difficult. He was afraid of giving in to those lips, the taut body that might be soaking in a nice hot bath right now, or curled up defenseless under a quilt upstairs in her room. Would she, too, ever yearn for someone to cling to, another warm body to hold till dawn?

Chapter Eleven

Rita and Serena were too busy working long hours to celebrate or to see much of Mitch and Liz during the next few weeks. Summer rentals and store revenues soared with the temperature and "No Vacancy" signs dangled at the motels and bed and breakfast places along the shore.

By Friday afternoon, Rita was tired of running back and forth between the gift shop and her own office. She did her best to handle the shop's customers and phone calls while Serena was doing tarot readings, but by the end of the week, her own appointment book was booked solid.

Some massage clients were local referrals from Aunt Liz's garden club; others were business executives and their wives down for the season at their summer homes.

"Stimulating the economy is a tough life, Serena," Rita joked. "These ladies have to drive over here for a massage and lunch after a long morning poolside with their children and nannies. Sometimes they even squeeze in nail appointments, not to mention consulting you to see what their futures hold…"

"Hey, don't knock the wealthy!" Serena cracked. "If they keep coming in here for your magic fingers and then buy what they need from me to 'recreate the mood' we'll both be rich. I've already had to reorder those meditation CDs you play and the aromatherapy oils and candles you burn during their soothing escapes from reality."

Rita smiled and plopped down on the peacock

chair with the "Sold" sticker on it. "Don't you wish we had their reality to escape from? Then we'd be the ones lounging on our decks sipping strawberry daiquiris instead of working here six days a week."

"Not you. You're a workaholic. But me? I know when to quit. In fact, it's five o'clock at last. All work and no play..." Serena locked the door, flipped the dangling sign to read, "Closed. Please Come Back Tomorrow," and pulled down the shade.

"Stay put," Serena ordered and hurried to the kitchen. She returned with two goblets and a tiny bottle of Asti Spumante. "A toast!" she cried, and popped the plastic cork. "To us! Our best week ever! Live your dreams! Trust the Universe! Goddesses unite!"

Rita accepted the glass and clinked it into Serena's. "Cheers! But promise me you'll stop talking in bumper sticker phrases. I think the merchandise is getting to you. Maybe too much incense?"

"No, I'm happy to be making a profit!" She sank into a canvas sling chair and sighed. "Everybody told me I was nuts to start up this shop. Everybody but you and Liz - and even Mitch, I must say. But we did it. What a great combo, you and I!"

"The best," Rita agreed, "But seriously overworked!"

"Not anymore. You can't always be available in the shop so I hired a girl who stopped by looking for part-time hours during the day. Kelly Weston. She's enrolled at the community college in the fall and has good references from her waitressing jobs. Says she's worked as a cashier, too. She starts tomorrow and we'll see how it goes. I need to take some time off for fun, and so do you."

"I wish I could," Rita moaned, "but right now, I need more money and work, not less."

"Well, speaking about fun and what you need,

where have your 'boyfriends' been hanging out? Did you scare them away?"

Rita swallowed the last of her wine. "Serena, will you drop it? And if I've scared away everyone except customers, good!"

"Hey, if you don't want Tony, send him my way. I wouldn't mind lounging on his deck! Or on something more private."

"Tony's not mine to send. He's charming to everyone. Besides, he only wants me for my hands! Professionally speaking, of course. Now, let's get out of here and go to my house for a swim. No cooking, no crowds. We'll get take-out for supper."

Serena gasped. "Not tonight! Oh, my God. I can't believe I forgot to tell you. Liz called during your last appointment. She said it wasn't an emergency, but to call right back. Something very important about tonight."

Rita jumped up to get the phone and started pressing buttons. "About what?"

"She didn't say. Sorry. I got so busy it slipped my mind."

Rita frowned. Liz rarely called the shop. Ten rings and still no answer. This was the final straw. She was buying an answering machine for the house whether Aunt Liz wanted one or not. Rita'd tried before, only to have her aunt return it, saying she didn't need modern technology to be rude to her friends. "If it's important, they'll call back. I've been getting by just fine for seventy-four years without one of those gadgets."

Four more rings. Was Aunt Liz outside? At last, a deep voice answered, "Chandler residence. May I help you?"

Rita hesitated. "Mitch? Is that you? Is everything all right?"

"Yeah, why wouldn't it be?"

"Serena told me to call Aunt Liz and I didn't

126

expect you to answer the phone. Where is she?"

"Just got out of the pool and headed for the shower. Asked me to answer the phone and tell you to come home right away. And to call you again if you weren't on the other end of the line."

"What's up?"

"She'll explain when you get here. Nothing's wrong, but you have to come home right now, okay? I've got to run, too. See you later."

Rita was surprised at how much Mitch's voice sounded like a radio announcer's on the phone: smooth, deep, seductive. How could a man almost hang up on her and still sound seductive?

"Aunt Liz is up to something, Serena. I've got to get home. Sounds like she has big plans for me tonight. I bet it's related to her birthday and I've been so busy here I can't say no. How about a rain check on our celebration?"

"Sure thing. Now get a move on, girl. Enjoy whatever it is with a smile, okay? Let's see. What could it be? Square dancing? Tai Chi? A lecture on birding in the Pine Barrens? You never know with Liz, except you'll probably have a good time whether you want to or not. Me? I'll find someone my own age to play with tonight...if I have the energy."

Rita closed and locked the door between their businesses. She'd been looking forward to an early night and smiled at the irony of her social life. Not only was she destined to spend the evening with ladies close to twice her age, she might even have trouble keeping up with them.

****

By the time Rita arrived home, Aunt Liz was already pacing by the door in a lavender pants suit, fussing over which dangling amethyst earrings looked best with her outfit. "Hurry up, Rita. Sorry to spring this at you on such short notice, but you'll never believe who we're going to see tonight. Front row seats, too, and dinner at one of the best French restaurants in the world. Or at least in New Jersey."

"Who?"

Liz changed her earrings and kept talking. "Get dolled up in your best outfit, and I don't mean your best workout clothes. How about that slinky black satin and lace thing you wore to your friend Sherry's engagement party last year? Oh, and wear your hair wild and loose, and put on more make-up. We might even get to meet him after the show."

"Aunt Liz. Meet *who* after what show?"

"Tony Bennett. You know he's always been one of my favorites." She began singing one of his best-known songs.

Rita placed her hands on her aunt's shoulders. "Slow down. You're talking a mile a minute. We're going *tonight*?"

"Of course, tonight. Why else would I be all gussied up and rushing you to get ready?"

"But where?"

"One of the casinos on the boardwalk. I forget which one."

"We're going tonight and you don't even know where the show is. Where are the tickets?" Rita shook her head in disbelief. "Opening night with Tony Bennett. That's impossible to get at short notice."

Liz winked. "Not impossible if you have connections with the right people."

"And since when do you have connections?"

"We'll talk after you're ready. If I miss this concert, I'll never forgive you. It could be my last chance."

"Believe me, you'll have more chances to forgive me."

"No, Rita, I meant my last chance to see Tony Bennett up close. He and I aren't exactly teenagers, you know. Who knows how many years we have left?

Promise me you'll get ready as fast as you can! Now scoot! Even if you're too stubborn to see you need a night out, I know I need one and this means a lot to me. It's for my birthday. *Please?*"

"Oh, all right. Give me twenty minutes."

"Fifteen. Your hair's naturally curly. Just spray it and let it hang in wild curls. Sexier that way."

"Aunt Liz!"

"I was young, once, remember? At least I haven't forgotten how to live." She twirled around once and pointed to the stairway. "Get going, young lady!"

"But..."

"No 'buts.' My friend is driving us. I'm getting my purse, and I refuse to answer any more questions until you're a vision in black."

"Aunt Liz, you know I hate casinos. Not that I'm worried about bumping into Kevin anymore. But after his gambling and my stint at dealing blackjack, I..."

Liz called out from the living room, "Young lady, no more ancient history, which this concert will be if you keep yapping. Stop dawdling! Now you've got fourteen minutes." She turned on a scratchy LP from the '60s and started singing along with Tony Bennett in her alto voice.

Rita gave up and took the stairs two at a time. The hot steamy shower felt so good Rita wanted to fill the tub with bubbles, lean back with a good mystery, and relax. But Aunt Liz didn't often ask for favors, so three minutes later, Rita stepped out of the shower, unleashed her hair, and coaxed it into tangled ringlets. She smiled as she heard another of Liz's favorite hits booming downstairs.

She wiggled into sleek black slacks and a red satin top with a plunging neckline. She replaced her tiny gold studs with enormous braided golden hoops. Might as well go all out and complete the free-spirited gypsy look. She painted her mouth with bold red lipstick and applied extra eyeliner and mascara to accent her green eyes.

She arched an eyebrow and flashed a smoldering look at her reflection as if she were a teenager primping in the mirror, then erupted in laughter. Where was this sultry mysterious temptress going? Out with a pair of seventy-something groupies to see a silver-haired crooner. They'd share old stories about big bands and slow dancing with lost loves. Maybe Serena was right. Rita's social life left a lot to be desired. Though she wasn't ashamed to admit she loved Tony Bennett, too, she knew there weren't many almost-forty-year olds who shared her eclectic taste in music. Some exciting night out!

"Ready, Rita?" Liz hollered up the stairs. "Our ride will be here any minute."

"Almost. I have to stick the bare essentials in my beaded bag. Someone wise taught me not to take too much cash or credit cards to AC." She caught herself about to throw in a comment about Kevin's gambling and stopped. She'd vowed to give up her sad story and had promised Serena to be on "SOS" alert as they named it, no more "Same Old Story" or "Sad Old Shit" for her.

Rita grabbed her black Spanish shawl with the red rose embroidery and threw it over one shoulder. She slipped on a pair of three-inch heels she hadn't worn in years and approached the stairs. "These heels are slowing me down, Aunt Liz. Are you sure I can't wear my black Nikes?" she teased as she stepped carefully down the stairs holding the railing.

A deep voice was singing along with the record from the living room. Mitch's low radio voice crooned in perfect time to the old song. Rita stopped and stared when she got near the bottom of the stairs. There was Mitch, dressed in a perfectly tailored tuxedo, dancing with Liz on the hardwood floor as if they were Arthur Murray Dance Studio graduates. He twirled Liz expertly and finished with a dip.

"I don't believe it!" Rita exclaimed. "Is this the friend who's driving us? What's going on here?"

Liz straightened her outfit and laughed. "I think it's called fun, dear. Remember fun? Going out, good music, dancing, a handsome gentleman? Want the next dance? I'm sitting this one out. A bit out of breath. And I need my wrap, too." Liz hustled out of the room.

Mitch looked amazing. Rugged, sharp, and poised. She'd never pictured him all dressed up, and blushed as she recalled the last time she'd imagined him: taking off his sandy blue cut-offs and stepping naked into a hot shower, grinning that crooked little smile of his...and raising his eyebrows in invitation.

She'd been staring. "Where did you ever learn to dance like that?" she stammered. "Have you been hiding out at the dance studio this week while I've been slaving away over tense shoulders and flabby stomachs?"

"No, my mom forced me to take lessons as a kid. Doesn't come in handy much, except at weddings and big family get-togethers. Women seem to like it when I don't step on their toes. Especially with these big feet. But look at you!" Mitch gave her a once-over like a construction worker on a city building site. He let out a long wolf whistle. "You are one hot Cinderella, ready for the ball!" He held out his hand at the bottom of the stairway.

Rita turned even redder, smiled, and put her hand in his uncertainly. "And you sound like the Big Bad Wolf, but you look more like Prince Charming all dolled up in that tux. It's incredible, fits perfectly. But you in a tux? How long have you been planning this?"

"I didn't plan it at all. Liz asked me at lunchtime to tag along to AC with a friend of hers. Insisted I had to wear a tux and be an escort or she'd never forgive me. Plus, I confess, I've always wanted to hear ol' Tony in person. I offered to drive, but she's acting a little funny about the whole thing."

Mitch pulled her into the living room with one hand. He gently lifted up the arm of the old stereo and placed the needle on another selection. "So Cinderella, how's your slow dancing? As good as your hands?" He twirled her around and slid his arm around her back. He led her easily across the floor and sang along with the music from the sixties. "Embarrassing, isn't it," Mitch whispered near her ear, "to know the lyrics to these old tunes? This was one of my mom's favorite records. Still is. I swore I hated it at the time, but I used to sing into my screwdriver mike when she wasn't around."

Rita laughed. "Mine was a hairbrush. I didn't know guys did the mike thing, too. True confession time. Are you a shower stall Sinatra, too?"

"Want to stop by and find out sometime?"

Rita rolled her eyes. "You know what, Mitch? I bet you're all talk."

Mitch held her tight and did a few swift circles. "And I bet you're not. Want to try me out?" he whispered. "You know where my shower is. We could do one hell of a duet in all that steam. What do you think?"

Rita grinned. "I think you like to make a grown woman turn red. Why don't you pick on someone your own size?"

Mitch pulled away slightly. He looked down into her eyes and feigned shock. "Now you're talking size. And you claim you're not interested in men?"

"Mitch, will you stop teasing me?"

He drew her closer and resumed dancing. "Sorry, it's like riding a bike. You never forget how, and once you get started, it's hard to put on the brakes."

"Like trying to stop eating the chocolates in a sampler box?"

"Yeah, and with four sisters, you better believe I had lots of opportunities to tease, especially with all the sorry boyfriends they'd drag home."

"I'm surprised. You come from a big family? You seem like such a loner. So, mystery man, what other secrets and tricks do you have up your sleeve?"

Mitch's face relaxed and his eyelids closed briefly. "Hmmmm. I wouldn't be much of a mystery man if I told you everything or showed you all my tricks, now would I?" He stopped dancing, touched her lips softly with his index finger, and traced a path down her neck, sending shivers down her back.

The doorbell rang and Mitch abruptly dropped his hand. "Saved by the bell," he said softly before yelling, "I'll get it, Liz. I think your friend's here. And I'm not letting Dorothy drive. I want to live to see the show."

Mitch opened the door and stood there speechless for a moment before saying, "You're sure not Dorothy!" Standing there in an identical tuxedo was a slightly shorter but very elegant Tony Jennings. He looked equally surprised for a split second. He raised an eyebrow, examined Mitch's tuxedo, and then glanced toward the living room where Rita watched.

"How perceptive of you," Tony observed.

"My, you two look almost like twins!" Liz exclaimed as she breezed in with her beaded bag and turquoise shawl. "Do you know each other?" There was a brief pause.

"Yes," they answered in unison. "We've met."

"Oh, good. Tony generously offered to arrange a night out for us when I happened to see him at the Borough Hall. Imagine tickets to see Tony Bennett on opening night! And Mitch is the friend I mentioned might like to come along." Liz held her cheek out as Tony kissed it and took her hand.

"Well, I suppose I can share you two lovely ladies with Mitch here. Such good taste in clothes for a handyman. I didn't know they rented Armani around here on such short notice."

"I wouldn't know, but if you buy one from a reputable tailor, it's not a problem," Mitch said with huge smile.

Liz interrupted, "Mitch, I guess I didn't mention Tony was the friend who got me the tickets for my birthday. I never dreamed you'd think I'd let Dorothy drive! She can barely see well enough to stuff coins into those one-armed bandits. And Tony, dear, be nice to Mitch. He isn't too keen on casinos, but he promised he won't be grumpy. We're both big fans of Tony, aren't we?" She looked up at Mitch.

"Yes, Tony Bennett fans," mumbled Mitch as he checked the locks, windows, and the lights.

Tony and Liz headed toward the long white limousine. Mitch caught up to Rita and offered his hand to her as she stepped down off the porch, a little wobbly in her heels.

"Thanks," she whispered. "It's been awhile since I wore such impractical shoes. Takes a little practice, but it comes back. Wow, a limo!"

"Some pumpkin coach, huh Rita?" Mitch smiled and kissed her hand. "Is that as good as Tony's phony European gesture? See, even a lowly footman can be charming and debonair."

Rita punched his shoulder. "Turning into a rat already? I thought you promised to be a good boy tonight!"

"Only around Liz. You're fair game for teasing, remember? Anyway, what do you think old Tony's after with all this?"

Rita yanked on Mitch's arm and whispered in a barely audible voice while Tony got Liz settled and spoke to the driver. "What do you mean? With all his money, what could he possibly want from Liz or me beside friendship? Do you always have to be so cynical?"

"Who, me? Cynical? I thought you had that market cornered. I'm on my best behavior. Or at least I'll try. An hour and a half limo ride with Mr. Suave?" he said somewhat grimly. "What's not fun about that?" He flashed a smile and winked before turning solemn. "You keep an eye on Liz, and I'll keep an eye on you. Tony, too, for that matter."

"Mitch, I don't like casinos either, but promise me you won't spoil this show for her. Don't give Tony a hard time."

"Cross my heart and hope to die. I solemnly swear I'll be a good boy." He did the familiar motions of kids making secret pacts and held up his right hand. Rita smiled and gave him a high five on it.

"Let's get this show on the road then," she murmured and stepped into the extended white Lincoln town car under Tony's watchful eye as well. She settled into the plush seat with one of her "boyfriends" on each side like tuxedo bookends.

Chapter Twelve

As soon as they pulled out onto Route 35 and headed south, Tony moved to the other side of the limo and sat next to Liz. Friday evening traffic was already heavy as people from the city made their way through the resort towns of Ocean County. The skies were sunny and the forecast predicted perfect beach weather after several weekends of rain.

Tony promised a surprise once they got on the Garden State Parkway, but first they had to get through the string of traffic lights on the barrier island, over the Seaside Bridge, and through the stretch of Route 37 in Toms River full of car lots, fast food chains, and strip malls. Tony pointed out family and business holdings as they passed waterfront mansions, tiny summer bungalows, restaurants, and small businesses that depended on tourists in search of suntan lotion, ice cream, and mini-golf.

"Sounds like your family plays Monopoly for real," Mitch joked as Tony pointed at several pending real estate deals through the tinted glass. "From Baltic to Boardwalk, huh?"

"It's good business to diversify. Takes more skill than luck," Tony replied. "And hard work."

"Not to mention connections," Mitch offered.

Liz shook her head at another huge three-story home under construction on a tiny bayfront lot. "Tony, I know it's good business for you, but I can't help wishing we had more open space and less noise. Everything's so crowded now. Course we used to say that fifty years ago when the summer people came over a two-lane highway from Philly. Now there are six lanes and we still have traffic jams."

"People have to live and vacation somewhere. I provide services and products people want, and I always upgrade my acquisitions. It's good for me and for the community. But enough talk about business and the old days. We're on the Parkway at last. Time for a little toast for smooth sailing to Atlantic City."

Tony pulled out a chilled bottle of Dom Perignon, popped the cork expertly, and filled four crystal glasses almost to the brim without spilling a drop. He held his own glass high and toasted, "Happy seventy-fifth birthday, Liz, and many more healthy, enjoyable years ahead! And here's to a wonderful evening of celebration!" They all leaned forward to clink glasses and started to sip.

"Please help yourself to a snack." Tony opened the refrigerator and another cabinet and started to pass around plates of chocolate-covered strawberries, hot and cold hors d'oeuvres, crudités, crackers, and cheese. "Supper is after the show, so you may want to indulge now."

"Thank you, Tony," Liz said. "You think of everything, don't you?"

Tony eyed Mitch and said, "Almost everything, but you surprised me, Liz. I didn't realize you had your own personal carpenter or that you were bringing him along. I saw the wonderful work you did at Rita's place, Mitch. Are you available for custom projects?"

Mitch stabbed a piece of pineapple with a toothpick before he spoke. "It depends."

Tony waited a moment. "Depends on what?"

"What the project is and the people involved," Mitch replied. "I only take jobs I like."

"Like the Chandler home and Ms. Starr's building?"

"That's right." Mitch stared at Tony and chewed on a colored toothpick.

"Well, I'm not as attractive as these beautiful ladies, but come see me if you're interested in working on some upcoming remodeling projects. Money is no object for many of my real estate clients. Of course, the trend now is to buy a house for a few million, bulldoze it, and build an entirely new home on the lot for a few more million. In some cases, though, I can convince them to preserve the charm and history of the original dwelling."

"Well, I'm kind of choosy about my clients, Tony. Making money isn't my objective."

Tony laughed. "Well, in my experience, money is a big motivator, often the biggest. Even if you're referring to pride in your work or craftsmanship as goals, good quality brings you more money. And what's wrong with that? Most people have trouble when they don't make enough. I guess you believe the old adage, 'Money is the root of all evil?' "

Mitch continued to stare at Tony as if he were sizing up a fellow poker player and his pile of chips. "You misquote. It's the *love* of money that's the root of all evil. Attachment to money, the greed to accumulate a pile of dough for its own sake, that's what brings out the worst in people."

"I'm afraid you've got it backwards, Mitch. *Lack* of money leads to misery: unhappiness, robberies, drug use, domestic violence. There's nothing noble about being poor. Being rich affords you more time and resources to do noble things, not merely survive."

"Such as..."

"Well, I don't want to toot my own horn, as they say, but in my own case, people who earn the most, give the most. Check out the charity functions on the society page. You can't give what you don't have."

Mitch remained silent and helped himself to some crackers. "Depends on your motives. There's giving to give, and giving to get. They're not the same."

"Mitch, if you'd rather be a poor lone wolf than the leader of a successful pack, I wish you luck. You'll probably need it. But to each his own." Tony raised his glass and finished his drink. "More champagne, Mitch? You're still nursing yours. Never had Dom before?"

Mitch covered his glass with his hand and waved off the second tilted bottle. He looked upward as if he were trying to remember something. "Dom? Oh, I had an Uncle Dominick in Brooklyn who used to make dynamite red wine every year in his cellar." He paused and watched a small smirk spread on Tony's face. "But before you tell me how much this stuff costs, I already know. And it doesn't make me want to drink more. I don't drink much because I don't feel like it."

"How unusual for a construction worker," Tony said smoothly.

The veins on Mitch's temples started to bulge slightly as he eyed Tony. "Oh, really? I'm a carpenter, so you think I guzzle too much beer, never show up on time, break promises, and always pad my bill? I bet you think all senior citizens are old fogies, and fitness trainers are probably brainless bimbos or jocks.

"How's this for a stereotype, Tony? All real estate tycoons are unethical, money-grubbing S.O.B.s. Or is that only on TV?"

"Mitch! You promised you'd behave," Liz scolded as if she were speaking to a troublesome two-year old.

Tony laughed and said, "Touché, Mitch. I deserved that!" He turned to Rita and smiled. "I love this man! So entertaining! What a great time we're going to have tonight!"

Glancing at his Rolex, he added, "We're making excellent time. After the show, we'll meet Mr.

Bennett, and then have a late dinner at the French restaurant. Perhaps we can squeeze in a bit of gambling if you like before the ride home."

"It's up to the birthday girl," Rita said. "Aunt Liz, if you want to play a little blackjack instead of slots, I'm in, but not for long. I promise only to give advice when asked. We ex-dealers are notorious for telling people when they should hit or stay, often with disastrous results. Somehow we have the worst luck unless we're playing for the house."

Tony's eyes narrowed. "A dealer, too. Rita, you surprise me again. What haven't you done? And Liz. I pictured you as a slot player."

"I play slots when I come down with Dorothy, and I'm pretty lucky. But I used to have fun playing twenty-one with Carlton, and talking to some of the characters at a blackjack table is better than watching a soap opera."

"And how about you, Mitch? Do you gamble?" Tony asked.

Mitch chuckled. "Every time I pull out of the driveway in front of the tourists onto Route 35. Or sample one of Liz's new recipes."

Liz grinned. "Young man, you'd better apologize if you ever want to eat my chocolate chip pancakes again!"

Tony stared at Mitch. "Ah, yes. You're quite the joker, I see, but you didn't answer my question? Are you a gambler?"

"If you mean taking stupid risks and throwing away my money expecting to win? No. But I'll take chances when I believe in something, even if the odds aren't great. So I guess I am. We all like gambling when we win, when everything turns out okay. But even winning can be tricky. Hell, we get so busy trying to win, sometimes we don't realize what we're losing. And I don't mean money."

"Right. Back to that again. Your claim that

money isn't important to you. Intriguing idea, but I don't believe you. Tell me, what's your favorite game?"

"Poker or pinochle with friends around a kitchen table, not with a bunch of strangers at a casino. And you, Tony? What's your favorite game? My guess is baccarat."

"Perceptive again. I think I've underestimated you. Craps gives better odds, but it's so barbaric with all that yelling and hunching around the table. It's almost as distasteful as those pro wrestling matches. Baccarat has the best atmosphere and clientele, but I'll play blackjack tonight. I prefer the twenty-five dollar and up tables, though. Even better are those with no mid-shoe entry. Keeps the down-on-their-luck losers from jumping in with their last twenty-dollar bills before catching their buses. They ruin the flow of the table."

Rita shook her head. "If I had a dollar for every time I heard a player blame the 'flow of the table' or a fellow gambler when they lose all their chips, I'd be as rich as you, Tony! I was only a part-time dealer to help pay off some bills, but I had to quit. I couldn't stand the obnoxious characters with their cigars. Or the desperate faces of the people who couldn't afford to lose their mortgage payment or the week's food allotment, but did."

"Ah, Rita, being sentimental is no good on the casino floor, but absolutely wonderful in a person. You take after your lovely aunt." Tony turned to Liz and started telling her more about his wellness cruises and the assisted living retirement wing he was adding on to his spa.

As the limo sped along the Atlantic City Expressway, Rita and Mitch stared silently at the lights of the hotel skyline getting closer. When the driver pulled up to the curb of the casino hotel, Tony hurried to step out. "Here at last. Thank God for chauffeurs! We won't be late."

He held out his hand to help both Liz and Rita out of the car, spoke briefly to the driver and handed him a hundred dollar bill. He gently took Liz's arm and turned to Rita.

"Go ahead, Tony, I have Rita!" Mitch called out and steered her toward the revolving door. "Two can go faster than one!" He grinned as he pulled her close and entered a wedge of the door's circle with her. Tony looked back and frowned slightly as Rita emerged clinging to Mitch and giggling.

She shoved Mitch slightly and freed her hand. "You idiot!" she muttered. "I almost tripped over your big feet."

Mitch raised his eyebrows innocently. "Aren't you going to thank me for rescuing you from an embarrassing fall?" Mitch asked as he looked at the crowd waiting to check in at the front desk under the sparkling chandeliers.

"If you weren't around, I wouldn't need rescuing. I mean, I don't need rescuing, period!"

"I'll be back in a minute," Tony was saying to Liz as he waved to an employee at the VIP guest services counter. After a brief exchange, he took an envelope from a casino representative and guided them to the elevators like a seasoned regular. Up they went to the sixth floor, to the front of the line, and were escorted to a table right next to the stage. They had just enough time to order a cocktail when the lights dimmed and the music began. Rita looked at Aunt Liz's beaming face.

Rita felt relaxed for the first time in months, truly relaxed. And how odd to feel that way in a place that symbolized bad memories for her...Kevin's gambling, working three jobs to pay off his debts, and putting up with rude players and chain smokers. How wonderful to see an incredible man in his seventies singing his greatest hits and loving every minute of it.

Mitch was smiling, too, and tapping his shiny black shoes. She'd never seen him in anything but sandals, sneakers, or work boots and here he was looking as sophisticated as Tony. Well, maybe no one could look quite that poised, especially with Mitch's shoulder-length hair, thick, full, looking wild and windblown even indoors...and oh, those silver streaks, strangely exciting like lightning flashes crackling against a charcoal sky.

After the applause died down from his opening song, the singer moved closer to their front row table and spoke, "I'd like to dedicate my next song to a beautiful lady from the Jersey Shore who's going to be seventy-five years young tomorrow. This song is for you, Liz Chandler, as well as some roses from another Tony!" And with that, a waiter brought out a dozen roses and the orchestra struck the opening refrain to one of Liz's favorite songs.

Radiant. Aunt Liz looks radiant, thought Rita. Little tears glistened at the rims of her aunt's eyes all through the lyric right through the final phrase. Rita looked at Tony and smiled. "Thank you," she mouthed.

Mitch and Tony made eye contact and stared at each other a moment. Mitch looked at Liz. She was glowing. Was Tony sincerely interested in her well-being or only trying to make a big impression? No doubt about it, Tony scored big tonight. If this were a Monopoly game, Mitch felt like he'd landed on Tony's hotel on Boardwalk and wasn't going to make it to "Go." He remembered being ten years old and getting stuck with Baltic Avenue and bad rolls of the dice. He'd played by the rules, tried so hard to beat the big kids, but lost anyway. He thought he'd let go of his need to compete, to prove he was a success. Hadn't he learned anything from all the shit he'd been through?

A great concert, a great gift for Liz. He'd enjoyed it himself, despite sitting across from Tony. Now he had to make it through dinner and the casino floor. He didn't know how much more of Tony's generosity and know-it-all attitude he could stomach. He'd prefer a greasy burger at Checkers to enduring a gourmet meal with Tony. He remembered why he'd come along and glanced over at the two women. And what was Rita doing? Smiling at that snake and looking gorgeous, probably feeling impressed and grateful to Tony. Hell, he felt impressed, too. The guy had thought of everything.

****

Dinner was elegant, with servers outnumbering guests two to one. Mitch had one more sip of wine in a birthday toast to Liz and noticed Rita and Liz had only had one glass each. Tony, on the other hand, had downed several, but alcohol had no noticeable effect on his behavior. He tested the wine, sent soup back that wasn't hot enough, and had even arranged for a birthday candle to be lit in a slice of chocolate mousse cake Liz had selected from the dessert cart. "Make a wish, Liz," he'd encouraged.

"I've already got everything I need," Liz insisted, but looked lovingly at her niece. "But a wish for someone else can't hurt," she added before she blew out the candles. "Thank you all. It's been lovely."

"You're more than welcome, and the night's not over yet." Tony motioned the waiter over for more coffee. Liz switched to decaf and Tony ordered a cognac.

Rita waved her hand over the cup and said, "It was wonderful, but I can't eat or drink anything else or I'll explode! What I really need is a walk on the boardwalk. Want to join me, Aunt Liz?"

"Not tonight, dear. It's too late for an early bird like me. Besides, I intend to enjoy every forkful of my birthday cake. I'll walk tomorrow. Mitch, why don't you take Rita outside for a stroll? Tony and I will chat a little and maybe I'll play a little blackjack before we go."

"Good idea," Mitch agreed. He rose from his chair immediately and held out a hand to help Rita up as well. "I could use some fresh air. We'll meet you down in the blackjack section in a little while."

"Don't be too long," Tony stared at Mitch. "We'll play a bit without you if we get there first. Excuse me a minute, Liz. I'll make a quick phone call to see about a table. Terrible reception in here." Tony flipped open his cell phone and walked toward the balcony.

Mitch had to walk fast to catch up with Rita. "Slow down, Rita. I haven't worn these damn shoes in a couple years. I never thought they were uncomfortable before, but I'd give anything to take 'em off a few minutes."

"You're complaining? Who scrunched her Fred Flintstone feet into pointed heels three inches off the ground? Damn, I want to walk, but not in these. I'd kill for my running shoes."

"Take 'em off till we get to the elevator. Nobody's around." Mitch was right. Rita slipped out of her shoes and sighed as she walked on the plush carpet. When the floor bell sounded, she shoved her feet back into her heels and stepped into the elevator behind Mitch, leaning on him slightly to fix her shoe strap.

They made it to the revolving doors and out to the boardwalk, one by one this time. "Fresh air at last!" Rita exclaimed, "And an empty bench." She motioned forty feet away on the boardwalk. "Let's grab it." But by the time they got closer, three older women with custard cones and large shopping bags had beaten them to it and installed themselves.

"Screw the bench!" Mitch picked up Rita and headed for the stairs leading to the beach. "Our feet need sand!" He placed her on the bottom step, removed his shoes, and stuffed his socks in them. "Bring 'em with you. Let's check out the water. We've got time."

"Ahhh! Freedom!" Rita murmured as her toes dug into the sand. "A few moments of freedom!" She followed in Mitch's footsteps toward the lapping waves.

Mitch took off his jacket. "Here, we can sit on this," he said starting to toss it on the ground.

Rita grabbed his arm. "No, don't be silly. Not your tuxedo. We can use my shawl. It's bigger and doesn't need dry cleaning." It billowed out as she guided it down and sat down, patting the spot next to her.

"Thanks. But put my jacket around your shoulders. The breeze..." He dropped to the ground next to her and sighed. They both stared at the round orange moon poised above the horizon. The moonlight shimmered on the waves as they dug their feet in and out of the damp sand.

"This is much nicer than being inside." Rita turned to Mitch. "Thanks for letting Liz twist your arm to go for a walk."

"You're welcome. I was happy to escape. So what do you think so far of Mr. Tony's night out for Liz?"

"Well, the food was great but I hate when multiple waiters hover like high-class vultures waiting to zoom in and scrape away crumbs. Makes me feel like a messy eater. And you know what else bugs me in this day and age? Menus with no prices for ladies. And a dessert cart overloaded with evil, decadent chocolate creations I'm dying to eat but don't have room for."

"Not that I like Tony," Mitch said, "but Liz is having a great time."

"Oh, I know. It's wonderful for her. Forgive me for complaining, but casinos bring back bad memories, plus I felt kind of closed in and watched. Like I have to be on my best behavior, or be on my guard." She shivered and pulled his coat closer around her.

"Are you cold? Do you want to go in?" Mitch asked.

"Oh, no. I love it out here. Look at that huge orange moon, bright and ready to burst like a big sweet tangerine. This is the kind of moon to wish on." She closed her eyes and smiled.

"I thought it was the first star, you know, for wishes."

Rita shook her head. "Well, that, too. But I always liked to wish on a full moon. Turn around." Rita motioned back at the casinos and shops. "All those lights can't come close to the magic of a full moon. Doesn't it make you feel like one big smile?"

"Looking at you does," Mitch said quietly. "You remind me of a little girl who just learned how to blow enormous bubbles."

"Bubbles. My favorite. Did you ever let the wind blow bubbles on the beach? Did Aunt Liz tell you about my bubble habit?"

"Yeah," he grinned. "When I cleaned out the garage, I saw lots of bottles of bubbles on the tool shelf. I asked Liz if she had grandkids who visited. That was before I knew she'd never had kids of her own. She said she had a very special niece who used to live with her. Blew bubbles all through high school, college, and probably still did."

"That was me. I swore if I had kids, I'd blow bubbles with them, too. Be a mom like Aunt Liz was to me."

"You still want kids?" Mitch asked softly.

Rita paused. "I don't know if it's in the cards for me anymore." She took a deep breath and shrugged. "Think I should ask Serena for a reading?"

"Depends on what you want to hear. I'm hoping

life isn't all mapped out - that I can change the things I don't like."

"Well, I'd change the breeze if I could." Rita shivered. "It's a little chilly out here, but it's so peaceful. I don't want to go back inside yet."

"Get up a second," Mitch ordered. He got up and rearranged the shawl so she could sit in front of him between his legs. "Sit here, I'll shield you from the breeze. Just five more minutes." When she hesitated, he coaxed her. "Come on, I'm not going to assault you. No funny business...unless you start it, understand?"

She stood, uncertain, gazing into his eyes. "You think I'm being childish, don't you?" she asked.

"Maybe childlike. A hurt child who got burned and is having a little trouble trusting people, and herself, again." He patted the shawl. "Hey, take a chance. Sit down. You know self-defense. I had the bruise to prove it, remember? I swear I'll be a good boy."

She carefully sat between his legs and he wrapped his arms around her shoulders. She felt safe and warm, protected from the dampness and the wind. He started massaging her neck, ran his fingers through her wild curls. Leaning forward with his lips next to her ear, he whispered, "But you sure don't look like a child." Immediately he felt her tighten up. "Uh, oh. Muscles on teasing alert. Let go and relax, Rita. I won't hurt you. You're the massage therapist. I'm sure you can feel the tension right here, can't you?"

"Ummm. That feels so good."

A few minutes later, Mitch stopped circling his fingers and rested his hands on her shoulders. "I hate to go in, but we'd better rescue Liz from Tony's alleged charms. Besides, maybe we can skip the gambling if we catch them before they get settled at a table."

"Good idea," Rita agreed, and they began their walk back toward the flashing lights and the smell of cheese steaks, onions, and peppers from a nearby stand.

They paused to put on their shoes again. Rita leaned over the boardwalk fence to get her balance. Suddenly a figure slammed into her, snatched her bag, and took off. "Hey! That's my purse!" she yelled at the young man sprinting across the boardwalk. She threw a high heel at him and missed.

"Stay here!" Mitch ordered and took off in pursuit. He zigzagged through the crowd and chased the wiry kid down a side street. A half block down, Mitch tackled the runner and pinned him into a construction fence.

"I'll take that purse now!" Mitch grabbed the bag and slung it over his shoulder. "Put your hands up against the fence. Spread 'em." He patted the assailant's shirt and pants for concealed weapons. "Now turn around nice and slow."

"You got no right. You're no cop!" the young man with the backward baseball cap protested, but turned to face Mitch.

"Want me to get one? Must be fifty witnesses here to testify against you and you're demanding your rights?"

"No, man. I don't want no cop. Damn, I'm on probation. And my momma'll kill me."

"You're old enough for a driver's license?" Mitch asked.

"Yeah. In my wallet."

"Get it out, nice and easy." Mitch studied the picture and the information solemnly. "You José?"

"Yeah."

"Well José. You want to go to jail at 17?"

"No man. Let me go! I promise I won't do it again. I didn't mean to..."

"No bull shit. Of course you meant to steal the

lady's purse. You didn't mean to get caught doing it."

"Hey, some guy in a suit gave me fifty bucks to grab her purse and run. Said I could keep whatever cash was in it. Leave the license inside and drop it in a can around the corner. It was supposed to be some kind of joke or something."

Mitch paused. "Not very funny, now is it? And I don't suppose you know the guy's name?" When José shook his head, Mitch added, "Well, José, I've got a life-changing choice for you."

The small dark-haired young man looked at Mitch strangely. "Hey mister, what are you gonna do to me? You connected? Maybe I could help you out, work for you? I don't got a job no more, but I learn quick. I quit school and my momma keeps bugging me. I needed the money, but I guessed wrong about you. Most guys like you wouldn't run after me. You know, big rich guy all dressed up, 'fraid of a gun or knife. I shoulda known you weren't the average guy."

"Cut the flattery. Tell me, what church you go to?" Mitch asked.

"Church? My momma goes to church, not me."

"Then what's her church? Name it quick or we'll find ourselves a cop who's less understanding than me."

"St. Mary's, a couple blocks over. Why?"

"Well, José. You're going to stop in at St. Mary's tomorrow afternoon and see the good father there. I'm keeping your license for a while. You show up and ask Father...what's his name?"

"Father Mark, I think," José fumbled nervously as Mitch flipped over Jose's arms and checked them.

"You ask Father Mark or whoever is in charge for help. Tell him you want to get an honest job; that you want to give up drugs if you're on them and whatever else makes you steal from hard-working people. I'm calling St. Mary's tomorrow and he'll be expecting to see you. So José, it's decision time.

Right now. Are you going to stop breaking the law or do you want to go to jail?"

"What if I don't show?"

"Then the cops are going to get a phone call tomorrow night, complete with this license. I'll press charges and they'll pick up your sorry ass. Then you're history in this area, see? Or maybe I'll stop in personally. Talk to your momma. See if you're lying to me. I don't like my ladies abused on this boardwalk, understand?"

José nodded.

"Any part of the story you want to change, kid?" Mitch grabbed his shirt collar and pulled it up to his chin.

"No, sir. And don't tell my momma, okay?"

"Depends on you, José," Mitch released his grip on the young man's shirt and put both hands firmly on his shoulders. "Your call. You don't have to be a scumbag. Try earning your fancy sneakers. You wanna split before I change my mind?"

The teen in the baggy shorts backed away slowly. When he reached the intersection, he looked both ways and disappeared around the corner.

Rita had been standing at the boardwalk, ready to scream for help. No cell phone to call 911. That had been in her purse, too. What a relief to see Mitch walking back holding her small beaded bag! Thanks to him, she'd also have her cash and her driver's license. No one except teenagers taking their driving tests ever looked forward to visiting the DMV.

Mitch bowed and handed the bag back to her with a bow. "Your purse, mi'lady."

"Thank you so much!" Rita paused to check its contents before slinging the bag over her shoulder. "But what were you talking to him about for so long? He stole my purse and you let him go?"

"He only thinks I let him go." Mitch waved the young man's license. "But with this small card and a little luck, maybe there'll be one less scumbag in the world. It's like throwing stranded starfish back into the ocean. Sometimes you can save a few. We'll see."

Rita clasped his two hands in hers. "I don't really understand what you're talking about, but thank you, Mitch. My hero! You saved me from waiting in the DMV line tomorrow."

He studied her small hands gripping his and gazed into her eyes. "You're very welcome, my little gypsy. Now let's go get Liz before it's too late to go home early."

As they passed by, a figure in a rumpled suit and tie by the casino's entrance spoke softly into his cell phone. "Sorry, sir. The kid got away without the object." He grimaced as he listened. "No, sir, they both look fine...Sorry it didn't work out." He winced at the response and clicked his phone shut.

He turned and watched the couple head back into the casino and toward the escalator. "Sometimes you win, sometimes you lose," the figure muttered to himself. He lit a cigarette and walked down a side street to his usual spot at the corner bar. With any luck, maybe he'd get another call, another discreet 'job' offer, and this one would turn out better.

Chapter Thirteen

Mitch and Rita stepped onto the escalator and glided up to the second floor of the casino. She clutched her purse and glanced at the reflection of the smiling twosome moving upward in the beveled mirrors. She and Mitch. How strange. *We look like a couple,* she thought. *And no one seeing us would probably believe I just got mugged on the boardwalk.*

They stepped off and scanned the area for Liz and Tony. The mellow voice of a cabaret singer near the bar was muted by rows of clanging slot machines to their right.

"This way." Mitch put his hand on her back and guided her toward the blackjack tables ahead.

"Look for the red and yellow signs," Rita said, pointing to the plastic cards announcing the minimum bet at each table. "Aunt Liz prefers five dollar tables, but never more than ten. And it has to be non-smoking."

Mitch snorted. "Tony won't be at a five-dollar table. Let's find the yellow."

Sure enough, there they were, the sole players at a horseshoe-shaped table watching the dealer wash the cards, pushing six fresh decks together in a kind of massage. "Damn! The pit boss must have opened a new table for Tony," Rita whispered. "Now we can't leave."

Liz looked up and waved as they approached. "Have a nice walk, you two?"

"You look a bit...windblown," Tony observed. "And sandy." He reached over and dusted some particles from Rita's shawl.

153

"We took a walk on the beach. It's a full moon, and my feet were killing me," Rita added. "But going barefoot helped."

"You have to watch out for those full moons, you know." Tony said. "All kinds of crazy people come out they say." Rita and Mitch exchanged a glance and remained silent. "You're just in time to join us for a new shoe. They opened another ten-dollar, non-smoking table for us. The others were full."

"Well, I was kind of hoping to head home early," Rita said. Seeing Liz's smiling face, she added, "But I don't mind watching a few hands."

"Oh Rita, dear. How selfish of me. It's late and I know how you feel about gambling. Let's go!"

"Nonsense," Tony said. "Rita, I'll give you some chips to play with for one shoe. If you ladies want to leave when the dealer shuffles again, we'll go."

"I'm a big girl, Tony. Thanks for the offer, but you've done more than enough tonight. I have my own money to gamble with."

"I'll play with you," Mitch said quietly, tossing a fifty-dollar bill down. "I feel lucky. Sit down, Rita, and slip off those sandy shoes. I'll stand behind you and be a silent partner."

"Well, I'll throw in fifty, too." Rita said. "We can share this spot. Do you know the rules? You know, when to hit, when to stay?"

"I used to, but it's been awhile. You make the decisions, okay?"

"Deal!"

The red-haired dealer looked up, surprised. "I'm not ready yet, honey. New shoe takes more time."

"Oh, sorry. I wasn't giving orders to you. Just making a deal with my partner here." Rita grinned at Mitch, relieved she'd only be risking five dollars a hand. They'd last ten hands even with bad luck.

Tony's smile looked somewhat forced. He slipped out his wallet and put ten crisp one-hundred dollar bills on the green felt. "Green and black chips, please," he said to the dealer. Liz got ten red chips for her fifty, and Mitch and Rita ended up with two stacks of red chips. Tony played two spaces, and the three empty chairs quickly filled up with strangers.

Rita was relieved that even the strangers followed generally accepted blackjack rules of when to hit and get a card and when to stay. If anyone won or lost, it would be because of bad cards or bad luck, not stupidity or ignorance. She and Mitch played the same amount each time, winning two, losing one. Whenever they got a blackjack or the dealer broke, Mitch would put a white dollar chip on the dealer's spot to play or keep as her tip.

Liz's pile kept going up and down, but she would always win when she was down to her last ten dollars. Once, Mitch slid over two chips so she could double down on a ten and she drew an ace. "Blackjack!" Liz was thrilled.

Only Tony was losing more than he was winning. When his green twenty-five dollar chips were gone, he cashed in three of the hundred dollar black ones for green. "I'm bound to win sooner or later," he'd say, and increased his bets.

When he was down to his last two black chips, he placed one each on his two spaces. "Black action!" the dealer called to the pit boss, who came over to watch.

Rita felt the knot in her stomach tighten. Here she was ahead, and Tony was behind, after everything he'd spent on this night already. Why didn't some people quit or go easy when they kept losing? She was dying to say something to make him stop, but his face looked calm and smooth, no frowns or complaints. He would never bet the minimum.

The dealer had a six. Excellent for the players. Tony had two tens showing on his spots. Pulling more money out of his billfold, he asked for two black chips. "Double down on both spots," he said, tapping on the table.

"One card each?" the dealer asked.

Tony nodded. A two made twelve. A nine made nineteen. The dealer paused to say, "Twelve and nineteen. Dealer has six. Hope I break!" Chances were Tony could lose one and win the other. Better yet, the dealer would break by pulling cards and going over twenty-one. Everyone would win!

The table was full of low cards. "Break!" several of the players urged the dealer. The old man on the end stayed with a fourteen, hoping the dealer would draw any tens.

"Hope so," the redhead dealer said. She flipped over a queen. Sixteen. That was a good sign.

"Another ten, another ten!" chanted the lady in the sequined sweatshirt and champagne-colored hair.

The next card was a four. That made twenty. Everyone lost except Mitch and Rita who also had twenty. "Push," the dealer said and left their bet on the table. They'd expected to win but they hadn't lost. "Sorry," the dealer said as she scooped up Liz's two chips. "So sorry, sir," the dealer said to Tony. "You did the right thing," she added as she stacked up Tony's four black chips and removed them to the dealer's rows of chips.

Tony shrugged and said, "C'est la vie." He motioned for the pit boss to come closer and asked for a marker. The man nodded and scurried away to check his computer. Tony scribbled his signature on a small piece of paper the dealer put over the slot and pushed in with a piece of Plexiglas. "All black, please." The dealer uncovered the row of black chips and made two neat piles of five each. Another thousand dollars!

"Good luck, sir," the dealer said as play resumed again. At last, the dealer broke with a twenty-four and everyone won.

Rita tried to cover a yawn. "One last shoe, Rita? Liz?" Tony asked. They both nodded.

After three more hands, Mitch and Rita had two hundred and thirty dollars. Mitch leaned over and whispered in Rita's ear, "We'll quit when we reach $250 or $200, okay?"

"Fine with me," she said and sighed. Gambling was fun when you won, but she was tired and ready to cash in. They lost two more hands. Mitch leaned forward and picked up two red chips. He whispered in Rita's ear, "Time to cash in, okay, honey?" Rita pushed the rest of their chips toward the dealer. *Had Mitch really called her 'honey?'*

"Color in," the dealer announced, stacked and restacked the chips, and with the pit boss's approval, pushed two black chips toward them.

Mitch slid the two red chips toward the dealer and said, "For you."

The dealer tapped the chips on the tip box and announced "For the dealer," before slipping them down the slot. "Thank you very much!" she smiled at both Rita and Mitch.

Rita moved to get up, but Mitch put a hand on her shoulder. "Sit till someone new comes. Might as well be comfortable."

Tony stretched to place one of his green chips on their spot, saying, "I'll play yours, too. You can keep your seat and no strangers will pop in." He lost. Liz decided to quit after losing another hand, but Tony took over her spot, too. He chatted with the rich woman to his left about the best islands to visit and some mutual friends they discovered they had in Palm Beach. His pile of green chips was gone. "My goodness, I'm being a bad host. Let's put it all down on one and see if my luck changes." Tony put two hundred-dollar black chips on his original two spaces and lost them both.

Gone, just like that. Two thousand dollars down that little slot, and not even a tip left for the dealer. True, he had given the buxom waitress a five-dollar tip for his cognac, but Rita had never been a cocktail waitress. She'd been a dealer.

The ride home was quiet. Tony sipped a brandy and acted as if he hadn't even lost a dime. Liz and Mitch leaned against the tinted windows and dozed off.

Tony smiled. "Looks like we kept them up too late, Rita. How about a cognac?"

"No thanks, Tony. Then you'd be talking to yourself. I don't drink much and it hits me like the proverbial ton of bricks when I forget."

"A cheap date?"

"I haven't heard that phrase since high school, but no. And I know this evening wasn't cheap either. You spent a fortune on making Aunt Liz's birthday a special one. Thank you. She had such a great time."

"So did I. It wasn't only because of Liz." Tony raised his snifter in a toast, "Here's to you, the beautiful Rita. Believe me, the pleasure was all mine."

"No, we all had a good time. But I'm so tired. I don't mean to be rude, but after all that smoke, the wine, and the excitement, I have to close my eyes."

"Go right ahead. I'll switch the music to classical for you," Tony said and flicked on a different CD. She tried to stay awake but drifted off to the soothing sound of Chopin on the limo's stereo.

****

At last, the car was winding over the dark gravel driveway of the Chandler home. Mitch gently wiggled his shoulder to rouse Rita, who was leaning on him. "Wake up, Sleepyhead. My arm's falling asleep." Rita mumbled something incoherent and snuggled into his arm.

Liz tapped Rita's knee and said, "Wake up, dear,

we're home."

Tony spoke quietly to the driver and came back to the car door to guide Liz to the front porch. Mitch eased Rita out of the car and they followed Tony and Liz to the front door.

"Thank you for a lovely evening, Tony. It was wonderful. And I will think over what you said. I don't really like the idea, but I don't want to be a burden to Rita, ever."

"Liz, you may be in a tight spot now, but I'm sure I can help you out. My dad always told me to take care of his old friends like you and Carlton. I insist on checking this out for you. What are friends for?" He patted her hand before raising it to his lips. "Now promise me you'll have a happy birthday, and don't you worry about a thing."

"Don't worry about what, Tony?" Mitch asked as he came up the steps with Rita.

"Nothing. Everything's fine," Tony smiled. "Right, Liz?"

"Of course it is. I'm so blessed - surrounded by wonderful people and living in a beautiful home right on the shore. Plus I had a fantastic evening." She looked around at the three of them. "But right now, I'll say goodnight. I need my beauty sleep! Thank you all for a wonderful celebration."

Rita echoed her thanks and followed Aunt Liz into the house. After he closed the door, Mitch turned to face Tony. "So what were you and Liz talking about? What's not to worry about?"

Tony stared at Mitch for a minute. "It's none of your business, Mitch, but since you seem to have assumed the role of resident watchdog here, I'll put your mind at ease. There's absolutely nothing to worry about."

"I'll rephrase. What did you reassure her about?"

"Listen, I've known Liz Chandler a lot longer than you have. I think she's feeling a bit sentimental...and concerned about her advancing age. My mother went through the same sort of...wistful moments before she passed on. It's hard to lose someone. Maybe you don't know what it's like with older people. Are your parents still alive?"

Mitch folded his arms across his chest, and shook his head. "This isn't about me. And I don't buy it. Try again."

"Buy what? Try what again?"

"What's Liz worried about?"

"Mitch, you're making too much out of simple statement. Maybe she's worried about Rita. Maybe she wants to get away. A lot of her friends have passed on and she's getting up in years. Ask her. I simply offered to help if she ever needs my assistance." He held out his hand, and added, "It's late. Thanks for coming along. It seemed to mean a lot to Liz."

Mitch shook Tony's hand firmly. "Thank you as well. It was quite a show."

Mitch stood and watched the taillights of the limo disappear around the last clump of scrub pines. "I don't know what you're selling, Tony, but I sure ain't buying any of it." He hoped Liz and Rita weren't either.

****

Upstairs, Rita crinkled her nose at the lingering odor of cigarettes on her clothes and tossed them into the hamper. Comfortable in one of her soft large T-shirts, she crawled into bed and turned out the light. All she could smell was the stench of smoke from her hair. She didn't have the energy to shower, but if she opened the windows wider, maybe the breeze would air it out.

She heard voices below, Tony's and Mitch's. She strained to decipher what they were saying, but couldn't understand a word. Tony's voice was a smooth stream, flowing like a melody. Mitch's would break in with short staccato bursts.

Mitch had almost been rude to Tony at times this evening, baiting him. In fact, they both seemed to dislike each other, as if drawing a line in the sand and daring the other to step over. What in the world were they talking about? She couldn't make out the words.

They had been so handsome in their tuxedos. Tony, sophisticated and charming. Mitch, powerful and rough, but gentle with the dealers, Liz, and herself. He even seemed concerned about the young man who'd robbed her.

After the taillights vanished, Rita watched Mitch in the moonlight heading for the garage apartment. The light flicked on upstairs. She imagined him flinging his jacket on a chair, removing the tie he'd loosened in the limo, and tossing his shirt to the floor. Maybe he'd hang the slacks over a chair, slide his boxers over his legs, and shoot for the hamper.

He'd run his fingers one last time through his thick hair, punch his pillow, and slide under the sheet. Rita looked up at the moon, remembering the feel of his large hands massaging her shoulders. The shiver...had it been from the breeze or from being so close to him? How right it had felt to dance together.

No, she had to stop this fantasy. She remembered the kid's frightened face as Mitch loomed over him. She could relate to that fear. She recalled his little barbs about money around Tony. The mystery of how he'd come up with a perfectly tailored tuxedo in one short afternoon. Something wasn't quite right.

As the light went off in the window of the detached garage apartment, Rita remembered how wonderful it was to have his strong arms around her, to feel protected from the chill and the kid who'd stolen her bag, to have his hand gently resting on her back. How much fun she'd had playing for red chips with him, not worrying about losing money. How right it had looked for one brief moment when she'd seen their reflection in the mirror. They looked like a couple, comfortable even after the incident on the boardwalk. Without even discussing it, they knew neither one of them would mention the purse snatching to Aunt Liz.

She fell asleep under a soft sheet, wondering what it would be like to be curled up next someone again. Instead, she clutched a big teddy bear she'd won on a childhood trip to the boardwalk, but dreamed of a strong, gentle man with silver and black flowing hair.

Chapter Fourteen

Rita woke the next morning with a piercing headache. She squinted at the alarm and groaned. Nine o'clock. That explained the blinding sunlight, but the pain? She never got headaches. Then she remembered the trip to Atlantic City.

Unbelievable! A hangover after less than three drinks in eight hours, and her hair reeked of cigarettes. Another reason to hate casinos. Yet except for the incident on the boardwalk, she'd had a wonderful time.

Rita slowly sat up and reached for a bottle of water. Not there. Good thing she'd refused that last cognac from Tony or she'd feel even worse now.

She eased off the bed and headed for the medicine cabinet. Nothing helpful in there. And her reflection? "The Beautiful Rita" Tony had toasted last night now looked more like the Bride of Frankenstein without the white streak. She brushed her teeth and removed some smeared mascara before stepping into the shower.

She relaxed in the warm spray and thought about last night. Tony had been so charming and flattering, so considerate of Aunt Liz. And extravagant! A limo stocked with desserts, overpriced champagne, and fruit and cheese she hadn't washed, sliced, or arranged in her own Tupperware. Tony Bennett dedicating a song to Aunt Liz. Pit bosses hovering around Tony's blackjack table eager to do favors for him. He made life look so damn easy.

And then there was Mitch. She hated to admit

it, but she was attracted to him. Their brief dance, his crazy grin during the revolving door incident, his closeness on the sandy beach, feeling safe and cared for but with an edge of fun, of danger even.

She'd thought she was safe with a different man before, an "open book" who'd turned into a real mystery...a horror story. She'd met Kevin when they were seniors in college. An All-American guy. Who could be more stable and trustworthy than the insurance broker he'd become, a financial planner in a three-piece suit? He couldn't have been more different on the surface from Mitch or Tony, and yet he'd had secrets, big ones. Gambling and womanizing.

"You can't judge a book by its cover," Aunt Liz would repeat. Well, thank God the Kevin chapter in her life was over. It was time to stop distrusting everyone, especially herself. Another favorite saying of her aunt's popped in her head. "Trust your instincts." Yes, she'd made some mistakes trusting others, ignored red flags she didn't want to see, but she was learning. With men, her instincts were telling her go slowly...but be open to possibilities.

With Aunt Liz, Rita's gut was telling her something was definitely wrong. She wanted explanations for those disappearing bills and the cryptic conversation between her aunt and Tony after the limo ride, something about being a burden. What was that all about? Time to do a little more digging and not take "No" for an answer.

Rita dressed quickly and went downstairs for some aspirin and her morning cup of coffee. Aunt Liz's note said she was out for a birthday breakfast but she'd left a bag of fresh doughnuts. Rita's favorite - chocolate cake with chocolate frosting. God only knew how many fat grams were lurking inside one, but Rita bit in and savored it, promising herself to consider taking advantage of Tony's offer for her to use his fitness club. Why shouldn't she? Maybe it was time for her to let go of her resentment of people who inherited money, too.

For now, as much as she disliked snooping again, Liz's desk was her next stop. She sat down and started going through the mess on and in Uncle Carlton's once-orderly desk.

He had always handled the finances. It was a family joke. "I make the money," her uncle would say. "My accountant manages it, and my lovely Liz spends it and gives it away." The few times Rita had offered to go over the financial matters after her uncle's death, Aunt Liz had simply waved her off. "I may be old, dear, but I'm not incompetent. I still have the same accountant and he'll tell me what to do. I trust him."

Uncle Carlton would be horrified at the pile of mail stuffed under the blotter. The new bundle of envelopes crammed in the drawer was ominous. A collection notice from the water company and an unopened gas bill with "Urgent" stamped on the outside. Rita hesitated before ripping it open with her finger. "Damn!" she swore at the paper cut. "Past due. Pay upon receipt." The electric bill threatened a "shut-off" within ten days, and the phone company demanded immediate payment. Rita recognized her mom's number and smiled. Sisters who could still talk for hours. At least someone was close to her mom.

Another bill, this one from a bookkeeping service, for one hundred dollars. "Writing checks, phone calls, correspondence. Monthly fee." How many expenses could Liz possibly have to warrant paying that much money for bill-paying? Why weren't the bills getting paid?

Rita shook her head. This had to be troubling Aunt Liz. What else was in the drawers? Some credit card bills totaling a couple hundred dollars. Nothing disastrous there. Receipts for some hefty donations to Literacy Volunteers and the Audubon Society. Last, the checking account statement. A deposit of $10,000? From what? A direct deposit from Social Security of $398. Like that would support a widow. A check drawn for more than $9,000. What could that be? For the kitchen? The ending balance was less than one hundred dollars. Where was the checkbook so she could identify specific checks and deposits?

Suddenly, there was a rap on the screen door at the back porch. Startled, Rita turned to see Mitch waiting outside. "Morning, Lady. See, I remembered to knock first?" he said lightly. Rita shoved papers back into the bill drawer. "Well, can I come in, or not?"

"Sure, come on in," She turned away from the sunlight streaming in and focused on another drawer.

"Thanks, and how are you feeling this morning, Cinderella? Sleep well?" he asked as he came in with a travel mug.

"Yes, except for a slight headache, which seems to be getting worse despite aspirin, coffee, and chocolate. I don't feel much like singing or dancing at the moment so would you please keep the volume down?"

"Oh, a slight hangover," Mitch replied in a stage whisper. "Maybe Tony was right about the 'Beautiful Rita' being a cheap date."

"Hmmmm. If I remember correctly, that little conversation was between Tony and me while you and Aunt Liz were allegedly snoozing on the way home."

"I guess I must have heard it while I was dozing off. Having my eyes shut spared me from chatting with Tony." He motioned toward the kitchen. "Mind if I have some coffee? Somehow Liz makes it better than I do."

"Be my guest. Have a doughnut. Maybe you can answer a few questions for me."

Mitch poured a cup of coffee and bit into a chocolate one. "Ask away."

"Well, for starters, how much did the cabinets and these stained glass panels cost? And what about the deck? Isn't that made of some super expensive hardwood the rich people around here are always bragging about? What's it called?"

"Ipe. Spelled I-P-E. Sounds like "ee-pay." Indestructible stuff from South America. But I thought we were beyond this. I already told you. Everything was really cheap. The best quality, but very low cost. Or free from somebody who didn't want or need it anymore."

"Yeah, well, I've been told a few stories in my day. Even believed most of them until I got royally screwed by my ex. Let's be straight. You and Tony were talking about something bothering Aunt Liz. I don't think it's her health. Did he say anything about her finances?"

"I couldn't get anything out of Tony," Mitch said. "He said it was nothing."

"Well, this bank statement confuses me. She's a retired widow with simple tastes. Outside of home improvements, I don't see her buying expensive things, no new car or clothes. She's always been frugal. Generous yet sensible. Now she makes huge donations, goes to an accountant to take care of bill-paying, and has all these shut-off notices." Rita motioned to the stack of overdue notices and picked up the statement. "This says she spent over nine thousand dollars last month on something. What? The Jacuzzi? The cabinets? Your work?" Rita got up and paced the floor.

Mitch frowned. "Hell, no. I told you I didn't charge her for any labor. I get a sixty-percent discount as a contractor. A lot of the stuff was free from guys who did me favors. I didn't want to tell her or you, but I paid for some of it. You know, kind of like room and board when she refused to take any money. Her total expense wasn't even two grand."

"Yeah, right. All this custom stuff and I'm supposed to believe that?"

"Yeah, you are," Mitch set his cup on the counter with such force Rita thought it would crack. "Who do you think made that stained glass? Painted and installed everything? Me. It's the labor cost that kills you."

"You did that?" Rita said, pointing to the seascape in glass, with dolphins leaping above the waves and the sun rising at the horizon.

"Yes."

"It's beautiful. I had no idea…"

"Well, I suggest you find out what's happening with Liz's money because I didn't take it. May I see that?" he asked, looking at the bank statement in her hand.

Rita considered his request and passed it over. He scanned the numbers quickly. "Guess it could be quarterly taxes."

"Quarterly taxes? How could that be? That would mean the tax on this place is over thirty-six grand a year. A lot of people don't even make that much money. She doesn't on her widow's pension."

"Yeah, but most people in this neighborhood make six or seven figures a year. Most of these huge houses are vacation homes. Their bigger ones are back in North Jersey or Manhattan."

"I had no idea her taxes might be that high."

"Depends on the value of the house and land. Even taxes on a vacant lot here can be eight to ten thousand dollars."

"You're kidding. How do you know all this stuff?"

He paused. "Construction experience with architects, builders, and their clients with fat wallets. When they say, 'Get me the best and money is no object,' they mean it. The only thing they hate to pay is taxes."

Rita poured herself a glass of milk and selected another glazed doughnut. "When I was little, I thought Uncle Carlton and Aunt Liz were rich. Compared to me shuffling around the country from trailers to apartments to cheap condos with my mom, they were. He had a good job as a chemist and then a decent pension. Aunt Liz quit teaching once she got married and never had to work like my mom. Never had any kids, either, to raise or put through college. And the house must have been paid off long ago. They lived in it over fifty years. I thought she'd be fine."

Mitch studied the statement a little longer before passing it back. "Well, it looks like she's got plenty of income to balance that bill, as long as those direct deposits are monthly. Your uncle must have invested pretty well for Liz to have that kind of income, especially since she probably doesn't have much of a pension herself and his is gone. Maybe a few thousand from Social Security. It's no wonder some older people have to sell their homes. Even if the mortgage is paid off, sometimes they can't afford to eat and pay the taxes. Where's her checkbook?"

"I don't know. It's not in the middle drawer where my uncle used to keep it, or in any of the other ones. Maybe she carries it in her purse now."

"You've got to take a look at it and confront her. I don't want anybody taking advantage of a good-hearted person like Liz."

"Neither do I, Mitch. But today's her birthday and I'm not going to spoil it. We'll discuss it tomorrow. I don't have any massage appointments today, but I have to leave. I promised Serena I'd cover the cash register if she needs me while she's training the part-time girl."

Mitch rinsed his plate and slid it into the dishwasher. "Yeah, well, I have to make an important phone call myself. Don't put off talking to Liz. And let me know if she needs help." He glanced at the clock, refilled his coffee mug, and headed for the door. "See you."

Rita felt confused. He'd been so attentive last night, and now he didn't even linger for small talk. Of course, how did she expect him to react after her suggestion he'd overcharged Aunt Liz on home improvements?

Maybe it was time to mend fences and apologize. She'd invite him to a birthday barbeque for Aunt Liz before she left for work.

Rita ducked into the garage and walked up the narrow stairs to his apartment. His door was open and she overheard Mitch talking on the phone. "Yeah, I want this kid taken care of, off the streets. He shouldn't be snatching purses on the boardwalk. Claimed his momma'll kill him if he gets in any more trouble. I felt like killing him myself." Rita froze as Mitch's voice went silent. "Yeah. Yeah. I'll send you the money to take care of him. I need to handle something else here first, but you'll have it by tomorrow."

He paused again, rubbing a hand through his hair. "Yeah, well, maybe it'll eliminate a problem for everyone. I gotta warn you, he's a real amateur thief with a tough guy attitude. You may not thank me so much when he shows up. See if you can get him to talk about who was behind it. He didn't feel much like talking when I slammed him against the wall." He laughed, and then paused to listen to the person on the other end.

"Yeah, he was scared to death. Probably thought I was gonna kill him right there. Kind of a scrawny punk, but something about his eyes got to me. A smart mouth, but if he's still worried about what his momma thinks, who knows? Be tough, okay? I think he needs it." He paused to listen before adding, "I don't envy him. What a choice, huh? Me, you, or the cops."

Rita started inching back down the stairs before he could turn around. She wanted to hear more, but didn't want to be caught eavesdropping, especially not on this particular conversation.

"Yeah, I hope he makes the right choice, too. And if he doesn't show, call me. The cops'll get him tomorrow. Thanks, Father. I owe you. I'll send you the money to cover the job and the costs...Uh, huh...Bye."

Father? His own father? A priest? Or a godfather like in the movies? What was he going to do to that kid? She turned to leave quietly and was almost out of the garage when Mitch's voice boomed from above. "Hey, Rita, wait a minute!"

"Oh, Mitch." Rita could feel her face turning red and she searched for words. "I saw you were on the phone. I'm in a rush to get to the shop so I thought I'd call you when I got there."

"For what?"

"Oh, to stop by later for Aunt Liz's birthday. I'm arranging a simple barbeque with ice cream and a birthday cake. You know, blow out candles, make a wish, and all..."

"Sure. What time?"

"About five, I guess."

"I'll be there. Who else is invited? I don't want to be surprised like last night."

"Serena and a few of Aunt Liz's friends from the garden club, the down-to-earth characters, not the snooty ones."

"Not Tony I hope."

Rita made a face. "No, I doubt if he'd want to

come, anyway. Unless Aunt Liz bumps into him and works on him. But if he shows up, could you act a little less hostile?"

"Me, hostile?" Mitch raised his eyebrows in mock surprise. "You saw how charming I was last night."

"Well, you didn't slam Tony into a fence like you did that thief last night, or me into a door the first night we met. But admit it, you love taunting the guy."

Mitch descended the stairs two at a time. "Hey, I am a sweetheart except when it comes to protecting something or someone I care about. I don't like Tony. He's a snake. Like one of those cobras that sway to the music and all of a sudden strikes. Hell, I like that punk kid better than Tony."

Rita bit her lip before asking, "And what's going to happen to that punk kid?"

Mitch looked at her blankly. Suddenly his jaw tightened. "Eavesdropping, huh?"

"Mitch, I'm sorry. I didn't mean to. I came up to ask you to a barbeque tonight. I heard you talking and was going to wait until you got off the phone. You weren't exactly whispering and it sounded like you were out to get somebody. I admit it. I kind of froze and listened. And I was getting worried. You said, 'Father' at the end. Your dad? A priest? Or..." Rita's lower lip trembled and her voice got shaky.

Mitch studied her, stone silent. She refused to cry and cleared her throat to continue. "Listen, I'm sorry I accused you of overcharging on renovations. For eavesdropping, too. But I have to know what's going on around here. Something's wrong with Aunt Liz and I can't put my finger on it. A lot of little things are getting to me, the vandalism, having my purse ripped off. Last night I worried about you chasing after the kid, and now it sounds like you're trying to get rid of him."

"What? You've got to be kidding!" Mitch's face

softened and he chuckled. "You thought I was going to hurt a juvenile delinquent like something out of a Mafia movie? Listen, Rita, I'm sorry I snapped at you. I overreacted, but I like my privacy. I wouldn't be living here if I didn't."

"So who were you talking to? It wasn't your dad, was it?"

"No, it was Father Mark at St. Mary's Church in Atlantic City. I kept the kid's license and told him to show up at his mom's parish and ask for help. Get a job. Get off drugs. Whatever, but go straight. I called the priest there to ask him to help the kid out. I'll send a few bucks to pay for the trouble."

"Why?"

"Why not? Maybe there'll be one less dirtbag in the world if he straightens out."

"Mitch, that's so sweet. And you weren't going to tell anybody what a nice thing you did."

He rolled his eyes upward and shook his head. "I am not sweet. I have a soft spot for an underdog, but that's it. End of story. Don't make more out of this than there is. Now get to work before Serena gives you hell. And don't tell the world about this, okay? I don't need a lot of bleeding hearts coming around asking for donations. Then my privacy will be shot to hell."

Rita smiled. "Right, tough guy. See you at five, okay?"

****

When Rita arrived at the store, she was still smiling. Serena looked up from the gift she was wrapping, deftly curled a few strands of long red ribbon, and handed the package to the customer. "I'm sure your friend will love the earrings."

Serena waited until the woman left. "Well, Rita, I'd say from the look on your face, it must have been a good night, huh? So where did you go on your girls' night out?"

"Atlantic City in a limo."

"Get out. No really, where did you go?"

"Well, we had front row seats and Tony Bennett sang to Aunt Liz. Then a dozen roses, dinner for four that cost a fortune, a walk on the beach in the moonlight, my purse got snatched, and I won fifty dollars at blackjack."

"Now I know you're making it up. You don't gamble. You *hate* gambling, and it's impossible to get front row seats at the last minute."

"Not impossible for Tony Jennings."

"Get out of here! You went on a date with Tony Jennings?"

"No, it wasn't a date. He arranged it for Aunt Liz's birthday. His parents go way back with Aunt Liz and Uncle Carlton. I didn't know they were so close, but last night was amazing. Tony thought of everything. Not that he's actually a personal friend, but he somehow arranged with the hotel to have Tony Bennett dedicate a song to her."

"Are you serious?" When Rita nodded, Serena probed, "You said dinner for four. So you were kind of on a double date with Liz and Tony and who?"

"Aunt Liz invited Mitch to come along."

"Mitch? And what did he wear, cutoffs? Dress jeans? T-shirt with the logo of some electrical company or what?"

"No, he was in a tuxedo. In fact, I think Tony was a little annoyed it was exactly like his. Not even rented and it fit perfectly."

"Jealous. Tony's jealous of Mitch. That's a very good sign. I told you he was interested in you."

"Hate to sound like a broken record, but I'm not getting involved..."

"Yeah, yeah," Serena broke in. "I've heard that several times, but this is *the* Tony Jennings. What a catch! Charming, good-looking, and plenty of money for both of you. You wouldn't even have to work at all if you married him."

"Serena, no matchmaking, okay? And if you don't need my help today, I'm going to leave to do a few more errands for the birthday get-together tonight. You'll be there, right?"

"Wouldn't miss it. I'll bring some wine. The new girl hasn't shown up yet so tell me details about last night before you rush off—the purse-snatching and Tony Bennett and the roses. Ooh, and the moonlit walk. And you gambling? I still don't believe that one."

"Well, I didn't tell Aunt Liz about my purse so don't ever mention it to her. Mitch ran after the kid and got it back, so I didn't see any reason to upset her. You know how she worries about me."

"Mitch the hero. What did Tony say?"

"We didn't say anything about it to him either. They were in the restaurant when we left for the boardwalk, and when we came back, they were installed at a blackjack table Tony got the casino to open up for him."

"So tell me more about you and Mitch on a moonlit walk."

The bell on the door rang as a couple wandered in from the heat. "I'll tell you some other time. I gotta run." Rita smiled sweetly and jingled her keys. "Oh, and bring your Tarot cards along tonight. Her friends might get a kick out of your gypsy act."

Serena followed Rita out to the porch. "I'm going to read yours again, too. You say you're not interested in a man, but you have two guys seriously checking you out. You need some cosmic advice."

Rita waved without turning around, but Serena called out after her, "And remember what I said about your astrology chart, too. Your Moon is in Scorpio. Tough position! Terrible karma with men. Always picking the wrong ones if you're not careful. Oooh, find out their birthdays and I'll do their charts. Tell you which one to keep and which one to throw back!" Serena flashed a peace sign and turned back into the shop to help her customers. "Moon in Scorpio, girl. You'd better watch out!" she muttered ominously to herself.

Chapter Fifteen

Rita was thankful to escape from Serena's questions as well as for the Jeep's air-conditioning. The stop-and-go traffic of tourists heading for a day at the beach was brutal but gave her plenty of time to think.

She didn't need tarot cards or an astrology reading to know she'd had bad luck with men. Not that she'd had very many to compare. Her few boyfriends before Kevin had been losers, controllers, or liars. He'd seemed different. Or maybe she'd just ignored the warning signals. She'd been so eager to please, to imagine everything was all right when it wasn't. After the divorce, she'd dated a few guys, but never went out with anyone enough times to call it a relationship. Too busy, she told herself. Or too afraid of getting hurt again.

The bridge was up at Point Pleasant. Another delay. After several errands, Rita pulled into the parking lot of the bakery that made Aunt Liz's favorite carrot cake. One more stop at the deli and she'd have everything for the small party. Touching the extra fifty dollars from the casino in her purse, Rita grinned. Maybe her luck was changing.

****

Back home, Rita unloaded the Jeep quickly and decorated the house without seeing either Mitch or Liz. She'd kept it simple, exactly the way Aunt Liz would like it. Hamburgers, hotdogs, potato and macaroni salads. The watermelon was chilled and there was beer, soda, iced tea, and wine. After chopping some vegetables, she had some free time before the first guests would appear. With four older women, Serena, Mitch, and herself, it would be a quiet evening, an early one, with no talk of financial problems.

Aunt Liz had provided her with a home all those years, and Rita was not going to let her down. She'd take on more clients, work more hours, and visit homes with her portable massage table. She hated going back to that, but it paid extra. If financially pressed, maybe she'd even agree to work for Tony.

But today was for relaxing and celebrating. She'd enjoy one last afternoon by the pool, be up for the dinner party, and sit Aunt Liz down for some straight talk tomorrow.

After a few laps in the pool, she set the alarm on her watch for an hour and stretched out on the chaise lounge stomach down. No one was around, so she unhooked the clasp and untied the straps of her bikini top.

The next thing she knew, someone touched her back. "Hey!" she yelled. She started to get up but remembered her top.

A large hand pressed her down. "Hold it before you give me a big thrill," Mitch's voice ordered from above. "Not that I wouldn't enjoy it, but I don't want you mad at me again. We've got work to do."

"What time is it? What work?"

"Close to four. I brought some stuff for Liz's dinner. Thought you might give me a hand."

"I have everything. It's all under control," Rita mumbled, trying to reach around and tie the top of her suit back together.

"Want some help with that?" he offered.

"No. Well...okay." Mitch hooked it and tied the straps together. "Thanks."

"No, thank you," Mitch grinned.

"For what?"

"Trusting me. For not insisting you do

everything yourself."

"It's a habit. When I do things myself, I know they'll get done, and done right. Someday I'll join a twelve-step program for perfectionists, but right now, I guess I'd better get up and make sure everything's ready for Aunt Liz's birthday dinner." She sat up and slipped on a huge shirt.

"Fine, I'm here to help. Where do you want the food?"

"What food?"

"Lobsters and steamers. Liz loves 'em. And I made my secret family recipe for stuffed clams. The white corn's ready for the grill, but I need another big pot for the lobsters."

Rita scowled. "I told you all you had to do was come. Did you think I wouldn't have enough food? There's only going to be seven of us."

"Better too much than not enough my mom always said. Then you don't have to cook the next day."

"True, and I really shouldn't look a gift lobster in the mouth. I do love them, and I haven't had any in a long time."

Mitch grinned. "Wait till you taste lobsters the way I make them. Sweet, tender, juicy. Not rubbery. You don't even need butter or lemon."

Rita groaned when she looked at her watch. "Good thing you woke me. I must have slept through the alarm."

Mitch showed her how to de-vein shrimp and how much water and spices to put in the various pots. He took charge of the coolers, the barbeque, cooking the seafood, and grilling vegetables. Together they shelled the shrimp and Rita made seafood sauce. Mitch brought out the citronella candles and the lanterns for the deck. "Okay, Rita. Why don't you go change? I've got everything under control."

Rita nodded and smiled. "Yes, I guess you do. Thanks."

Mitch saluted and went back to checking the grill. "Go ahead. Half hour to spare."

Upstairs, she took a quick shower and slipped into a long gauzy aquamarine sundress. She added the silver and turquoise dream catcher earrings she'd picked up years ago on a trip to Arizona. She left her long dark hair wild and loose and hurried downstairs.

Serena arrived in a bikini top and a flowery Hawaiian sarong as red as her hair. She plopped a large box of chilled Zinfandel on the kitchen counter and poured herself a glassful from the built-in spout. "Sorry. I know you folks are used to sniffing expensive corks and comparing years, but this stuff is good enough for me."

"Hey, it's good enough for all of us, but you'll have to watch Rita. She's on a one-drink maximum after last night," Mitch laughed.

"You're in a good mood, Cowboy. I hear you look pretty good in a tuxedo."

Rita blushed. Mitch glanced over at her. "Oh, really? And what else did you hear?"

"Well, I haven't gotten the full story yet, but it has something to do with dancing, a moonlit walk, and winning some money. And quitting while you're ahead. How unmanly of you!"

"Hey, I must be one of those guys women drool over on Oprah."

"Well, it looks like you've got no competition tonight. Except for you, I bet this will be a ladies-only crowd. You know, some of Liz's gray-haired buddies from the Garden Club or church. Where is Liz, by the way?"

Rita sat down near Serena and put her feet up on the ottoman. "She'll be here in a few minutes. She and her friends went to an art show at the Red Bank

Gallery and then to a charity auction at St. Theresa's Church."

Serena said, "Oh, Rita. I forgot to tell you. Liz stopped by asking for donations for that fundraiser the other day while you were out. I gave her a gift certificate for a free massage from your business. Hope you don't mind. I donated a gift certificate for a complete tarot reading, too. Should be interesting to see if we get some new business from it."

"Do you think that's a good idea?" Mitch asked.

"New business? Yeah, I think it's a great idea, especially if they buy something. Why?"

"Well, maybe your stuff, but what if some seedy character wins the massage, somebody Rita wouldn't want to touch?"

"Mitch, get real! Seedy characters at a church auction? I think you ought to get out more. Too much fishing and not enough people."

Mitch passed a platter of shrimp and cocktail sauce to Serena. "Well, fish may stink, but at least you can smell them if they're rotten. Some of the worst people smell the best."

"Can't argue with you there." Serena paused to sample the seafood. "Perfect!" She closed her eyes. "And just in time. I think I hear the guest of honor arriving." Serena looked out the window at Aunt Liz's Crown Vic followed by an old silver Buick. "Places please, for yelling 'Surprise!' But not too loud. Don't want to scare the AARP cardholders. Their hearts, you know!"

"Serena! Don't talk like that!" Rita scolded.

"Sorry, but I don't want any coronaries on my conscience. Now shush yourself!"

Rita opened the door wide, and Mitch and Serena called out, "Surprise!"

Liz smiled and hugged everyone. "More birthday? I don't think I've ever had such a wonderful time. You all are being much too generous."

Rita led Dorothy, Alice, and Helen out to the deck for drinks and brought back an iced tea for Aunt Liz.

Another sound of tires crunching on gravel. Serena pulled back the curtain and turned to the others. "Hey, Mitch! Check out the surprise in the driveway. One of your favorite people!"

Tony got out of his Lexus wearing a white suit with a Hawaiian shirt. "Well, I'll be..." Mitch's eyes squinted as he watched Tony bound up the steps. "Talk about a bad penny. What the hell is he doing here again? Don't tell me he forgot something yesterday."

"Mitch, be nice, okay? Remember Liz's birthday?" Rita whispered and poked him with her elbow.

"Right," he muttered. He walked over to the door and waited until Tony stood in front of it, then yanked it open. "Tony, long time no see. Hey, love the suit, man. Fantasy Island collection? Does it come with a matching little manservant and palm fronds?"

Tony gave Mitch an icy stare and strode past him without a word. He headed for the living room and handed a large envelope with a big ribbon on it to Liz. "Congratulations, you lucky birthday lady! You won the cruise! They drew your name for one of the grand prizes right after you left the auction. Now you and Rita can take a well-deserved break. Three nights, all expenses paid."

Liz sat down and started fanning herself with her straw hat. "How wonderful! I've never won anything bigger than a sewing basket before."

"Hey, Liz, if Rita won't go, maybe you could adopt me," Serena crooned. "When does the ship sail?"

"Next weekend," Tony answered. "I didn't mean

to barge in on you, but I figured you and Rita would want to start preparing for your getaway."

Rita stammered, "I'd love to go, but there's no way I can leave in the middle of the summer season."

Serena urged, "Go ahead, Rita. So you'd cancel a few massages. Isn't that the beauty of being your own boss? I can manage with Kelly's help in the shop now. You deserve some time off."

Aunt Liz looked disappointed. "Serena's right. It would give us a nice chance to have some fun."

What a tempting offer. Two months ago, Rita would have jumped at it, but not now. "I'm sorry, but I'm starting to build my client base. I already have quite a few massages booked. I don't want to cancel and have customers go elsewhere."

She didn't say it might be easier for her to investigate Liz's financial situation if she had the house to herself. And if Liz had money troubles, even if the trip was paid for, Rita didn't want to lose income either.

"What about you, Mitch?" Tony interrupted. "Perhaps you'd like to accompany Liz on the cruise. Ever been on one? You have the required tuxedo."

Liz laughed. "Can you imagine the talk on the ship, Mitch? An old lady like me with a younger man like you?"

Mitch grinned. "I'm sure they'd think I was the lucky one, but I can't go either, even if you're serious. I'll be away Friday, maybe the whole weekend. Why don't you invite one of your friends out on the deck? You'd have a great time."

Liz nodded. "That's a wonderful idea, Mitch. Helen likes to travel but hasn't gone anywhere since her husband died. I'm sure she'd love to go. But how can I leave Rita alone in this house if you're not going to be around, Mitch?"

Mitch glanced at Rita with a twinkle in his eyes.

"If Rita wants me, I could arrange to go away the following weekend instead."

Rita shook her head. "Listen, I survived living alone for the last two years in a crummy neighborhood in Atlantic City. I don't need a babysitter or a caretaker, so don't stick around on my account, Mitch. I'll be fine."

Liz looked uncertain. "I don't know. Can I postpone the cruise until a later date, Tony?"

"I wish I could say yes, but they're booked well in advance," Tony apologized.

Serena refilled her wine glass and interrupted. "Liz, if Rita gets lonely, I'll bunk over here with her, you know, like one of our old slumber parties, right Rita? I'll bring my jammies and my Ouija board."

Rita smiled. "Okay, Serena will be on call. That might be fun! I don't need protection or supervision, but hanging out here with her would be like old times. Are you going to give us the lecture about no parties or boys over, Aunt Liz?"

"I think I can skip that. Now how about supper? It smells delicious, Mitch," Liz raved. "You'll stay, too, won't you, Tony?"

He glanced down at his Rolex. "I'd love to, but I've got to leave. I have other commitments." He bent to kiss Liz's cheek. "Happy birthday, Liz, and have a wonderful time on the cruise if I don't see you before you sail. Give me a call if you need help with the arrangements. Oh, and here's your birthday card." He pressed a gold envelope into her hand and whispered in her ear, "Open this gift later, when you're by yourself."

Liz started to protest, but he simply said, "It's for you. Carlton would want you to have it." Liz quietly slid the sealed envelope into the pocket of her denim shorts.

Waving to the others, he placed his wraparound sunglasses back on his face and smiled. "Rita, may I have a word with you on my way out? It's about the trip."

Rita followed Tony outside and closed the door behind her. "Tony, I don't want to talk about a job, and I can't go on the cruise. Liz will have a great time with one of her old friends."

Tony clasped her hands in his. "I'm not offering you another job. I know you and Liz can manage by yourselves, and I respect the way you're dedicating yourself to building your business. This is purely personal."

Rita glanced down at her hands, wondering when he was going to release them. "You mean about the cruise?"

"Well, no. I think the cruise will be good for her, but it's more than that. She's always been such a strong woman, but she is getting older. Sometimes it's hard to see that even a strong woman needs a little help in accepting reality, in adjusting to changing situations."

"Tony, would you stop beating around the bush?"

"All right. There are two things on my mind. One is that I'd like you to look at Liz not as your aunt, but as a declining older woman. Be objective. Do you think staying in this big house is really the best thing for her, for her health? I'm not sure what her financial situation is, but the taxes on this place must be enormous. I don't know how Carlton managed to take care of his responsibility to Liz, but I want you to check out whatever she's worried about. I'm in real estate. I can help you if you need it."

"And what's the second thing?"

"I'll be direct. I had a wonderful time last night, and I find you very attractive. I'd like you to join me for dinner and dancing some night this week. I think we would be very good together." Rita's mouth dropped open. Tony continued, "We both enjoy fitness, music, and the finer things in life. And you deserve to have more fun. A break from work. You name the place. Anytime. How about it?"

Rita hesitated and chose her words carefully. "Tony, I like you. I think you're very charming and handsome. But from pictures I've seen in the local papers, you date younger women, blonder and richer than I am. Models, even celebrities. We're from two different worlds."

"We don't have to be," Tony whispered as he massaged her hand. "And most of those were photo ops, promoting my businesses. Yes, I've played the field, but turning forty has made me reexamine my life. I want to settle down with a woman of substance. I don't care what your age or your bank account is. And you don't even know how beautiful you are, inside and out."

Rita stammered, "Tony, I don't know what to say. That's so sweet but I'm not dating anyone right now. I'm focusing on building my business. At times, I don't even have the energy to care that I don't have much of a social life anymore. And you know something surprising? Right now, I don't even miss it. I'm relieved when I don't have to dress up. So thank you so much. I'm flattered, but I'm not ready to date. Understand?"

Tony sighed. "Well, if you change your mind, about the job or the dinner, please call," Tony said softly. "And I'll be thinking about you. I can't stop thinking about you. Your ex was an idiot to let you get away." He leaned down quickly and kissed her lightly on the lips before hurrying off toward the waiting car. "Let me know if you ever need anything. Promise?"

Rita stood there a moment and nodded slightly. What a shock. Tony wanted to date her, maybe even settle down. Tony was equally charming to everyone.

Is that why his invitation surprised her so?

His wealthy lifestyle seemed so foreign to her. She wasn't used to having someone else pay for everything when she went out. She laughed to herself. Going to shows, dining out, cruising around in the best cars, giving expensive presents on impulse...were these things so unusual to her because she'd spent too many years doing without and paying off debts?

She wasn't fantasizing about living happily ever after with Tony, but why not change her dating habits? Give someone a chance to develop into a close friend, enjoy some of the nicer things of life, and let a relationship grow. No more rushing in based on an initial physical attraction. Her previous romances had started out on an equal basis, but somehow ended with her paying most of the bills and wondering how a man would allow her to support him. Maybe she should have asked herself, "Why did I allow it?"

"Penny for your thoughts," Mitch said behind her. Rita jumped. She hadn't heard him come outside. "Or would that be too little to offer again?" he added somewhat sarcastically. "What is the going rate for thoughts nowadays?"

"I have no idea. I don't think confusion is worth much at all. Have any spare clarity for sale? I'll buy."

"Confused about what? Ol' Tony holding your hands, looking deep into your eyes, and zooming in for a quick kiss? Of course, I'm assuming this wasn't exactly mutual. At least I hope it wasn't."

"Who's snooping now?"

"Not me. Just curious about why Tony wanted to see you privately. Plus you're missing Liz's party, so I came to get you. Did he tell you what he gave Liz?"

"What do you mean? You know about last night's show."

"No, what he slipped into her hand and she put into her pocket. He said something about looking at it later."

"I don't know what you're talking about. I didn't see anything."

"He's up to something. I can feel it. Find out what's in that envelope. Do some serious detective work for your aunt's sake, if not for your own."

"I'm sure she'll tell me what it is later. Unless it's personal."

"Please, Rita. Find out what he's up to. And I don't like him kissing you. He's after something. I'm warning you." Mitch stuck his hands in his pockets and headed for the house.

Rita stopped short. "Thanks a lot. Is it such a stretch for you to imagine someone like Tony might actually be attracted to me? Is that what you're saying?"

"Of course I'm not saying that, Rita. Any man would be crazy not to be attracted to you," Mitch said quietly. "You're beautiful. You're caring and kind and hard-working. Your eyes light up like a kid at Christmas when you find a ladybug on a rose bush or a piece of sea glass on the beach. So what if you're stubborn as hell? Some people like a challenge."

"Mitch, how about quitting while you're ahead, okay? I don't like being analyzed and I hate being told what to do."

"Sorry, but I'm saying it's Tony who's not good enough for you. Not sincere. He reminds me of a real smooth talker one of my sisters dated. Believe me, I have my own hang-ups about money and snobs, but it's more than that. I can't believe I'm telling you all this, but do you understand what I'm saying?"

Rita sighed. "Yeah, but I'm tired of taking care of other people, you know?" She hurried to catch up with him. "I'll check out the card or present in my own way. I'm sure it's no big deal. And I told Tony no dinner date. God, I hate the whole idea of dating. Now let's go in before they start talking about us."

Mitch let her pass and followed her up the steps. He didn't want to confuse Rita any more by kissing her himself, but he was sure her response to him would be more passionate than the brief touch of Tony that had been on her lips.

"There you two are," Serena announced as they came around the house to the deck. "Master Chef Mitch promised to wow us with his amazing culinary abilities, and when it's time to eat, he disappears with my beautiful friend. You're the only guy left. You can't play favorites, right, Liz?"

Liz nodded. "Right, Serena! But let Rita and Mitch finish setting the food on the table. How about doing a reading with your cards while we wait? Dorothy and Helen want you to tell their fortunes."

"Well, at last you're a believer, Liz. It's about time! Remember I told you there was travel in your cards? And water? And good fortune! And now you've won a cruise!"

"Serena. I always travel and I live by the water. I'm blessed with good friends and a wonderful home. So how could you miss with that one? Can't you be a little more specific?"

"She gotcha on that one," Mitch said, returning with a tray of stuffed clamshells. "Enough talk. Here, try my specialty. After you taste these, you probably won't even want to leave home."

Liz sampled one and closed her eyes. "Hmmmm. The best I've ever had."

"I bet you hear that all the time, right Mitch?" Serena purred. "Here, let me try." She sampled one, then two, and reached for another.

Mitch tapped her hand. "Hey, save some for the rest of us."

Serena zapped him with her towel. "You rat. I

merely wanted to see if they pass the taste test," Serena said. "And Liz is right, Mitch. These are the best. You can cook for me anytime."

"Not only a good chef, but he was so well-behaved around Tony," Rita said.

"Well, the guy didn't stay long enough to get on my nerves," Mitch grumbled and lifted the lid on the barbeque to baste the hamburgers.

"By the way, Mitch, where are you going this weekend?" Serena asked innocently.

"What?"

"You know, you told Tony you couldn't go on the cruise. I thought maybe you didn't want to leave someone unattended, but you said you were going out of town. Where?"

"To North Jersey for a day or so. Maybe I should make it another weekend since Liz will be away."

"Mitch, I'll be fine." Rita interrupted. "Serena will keep me company and I'll keep her out of trouble. So please drop the big brother routine and let's serve the rest of the food. Serena, you predict the future. Mitch and I will work on the present moment."

"Deal!" Serena said and spread her tarot cards on the glass table. She started explaining Native American mythology and interpreting the cards Dorothy and Helen drew. "Helen, I see water and a boat and a good time coming your way!" she said and laughed.

"How did you ever get that from a drawing of a naked lady sitting in a tepee surrounded by wolves?" Helen said.

"Psychic intuition. What do you say, Liz?" Serena looked over at her and winked.

"I say you're a good guesser. Or a good listener. Helen, you've been itching to go somewhere new. I won a short cruise to nowhere. Want to come with me next weekend?" Liz asked.

"Are you sure? What about Dorothy and Alice? Won't they feel left out?"

"Of course not," Dorothy said. "My knees are bad, I get seasick, and Alice wouldn't leave Ned behind. That leaves you. The two of you can dance up a storm. Helen, you know you'll have everybody doing the limbo or some foolishness, looking for a shipboard romance. Plus you've got money to lose gambling. Not me. So live it up."

"Now that that's settled, young lady, what do these cards mean?"

The next few hours flew by as they ate by the pool. When the mosquitoes started to bite, Mitch lit the citronella candles and Rita brought out the cake decorated with a blue dolphin. "Happy 75th Liz!" the frosting announced, but the two fat candles said, "57."

"And thank you to whoever turned around that number. And for not poking seventy-five holes into this cake! You know I used to swim my age in laps every morning until I was about fifty," she laughed. "Now I usually don't count anything except my blessings!"

After they sang the traditional birthday tune, Liz blew out the candles. "What'd you wish for?" Dorothy asked.

"I'm not telling, but it's a big one." They polished off pieces of carrot cake with a final cup of decaffeinated coffee.

"Time for presents!" Serena announced and brought out a tray full of gifts. A rosebush from Dorothy, a new-fangled contraption for cutting quilting squares from Helen, a journal from Alice, some essential oils from Serena. "What else did you get for your birthday, Liz?" Serena asked.

"A box of cheese and sausage from my mom in Florida," Rita said.

"How personal," Dorothy mumbled. "She's

191

probably trying to clog your arteries."

"Now, Dorothy." Liz said. "My sister entertains a lot so cheese is a sensible present to her. And you know she's not in my will. Anyway, I got a wonderful photo album from Rita and a beautiful carved jewelry box Mitch made for me. It's on the piano inside. It even has a tiny music box in it that plays one of my favorite songs."

"Is that everything, Liz?" Serena asked. "Didn't Tony give you something?"

"Tony? I wouldn't expect anything else from him after my wonderful trip last night to hear Tony Bennett. The limo, the dinner. Why would he give me anything else besides a card?"

"He was very generous, wasn't he, Mitch?" Serena asked wide-eyed.

Mitch nodded. "Absolutely," he said in his best Sylvester Stallone imitation. He shot a quick look at Rita before addressing the older guests. "It's dark out now. Would you ladies like me to drive you home?"

Dorothy cast a stern look at Mitch. "Young man, are you implying I'm too old to drive at night?"

"No, but you've had a little wine and I think Liz would feel better if I drove you home safely. If Serena will follow me and give me a ride back, I'll drive your car so you'll have it tomorrow."

Serena rose to get her keys and her bag. "Sure thing. I'll help Rita and Liz clean up the kitchen first."

"No, we'll manage," said Liz. "And I want to thank you all for a wonderful birthday. It will be such a nice memory when..." She got up quickly and dabbed her eyes with a napkin.

"Look at me. Seventy-five, sentimental and foolish." She sighed. "Of course, I've always been sentimental, but I never wanted to be foolish." She got up and shared a round of hugs. "I'll walk you out."

Mitch came over to Rita before he left and whispered, "Here's your chance to talk to her privately. Find out what Tony's up to."

"I'm not giving her the third degree on her birthday!" Rita muttered as she tossed paper plates into a garbage bag and piled the trays full of silverware and coffee mugs.

"Be your charming self," Mitch said and hurried after the women. "Gotta go before Dorothy drives off without me!"

After they'd left, Liz came in and sat down. "Thanks Rita. You and Mitch did a wonderful job. It means so much to me. You'll never know." She stuck her hands in her pockets and closed her eyes. "And now I'm a bit tired. You're almost done here. Will you say good night to Mitch and thank him for me? I'm ready for bed. Take care, dear."

When Mitch came home, Rita was lying on the diving board looking up at the stars. He dragged a deck chair closer and placed his feet next to hers. "Did you find out what he gave her?" he asked.

"Not yet," Rita said, "She told me to thank you and say good night. She was so exhausted; I couldn't bring myself to ask her anything."

"Is something else bothering you, Rita?"

"Well, for the first time I looked at her face and instead of seeing Aunt Liz with her laughing eyes, I saw the wrinkles lining those fine cheekbones, her eyes sunk in a bit. Sad. An old woman who seemed way beyond cheering up with her usual cup of tea." Rita sat up. "That's what I want. A cup of tea with honey. Would you like one, too?"

"It doesn't matter," he mumbled.

"Mitch. What does that mean? Either you'd like a cup of tea or not. What do you want?"

"I don't want you waiting on me. My mom was like that. Always serving everybody else and never sitting still."

"Mitch, I'm not your mom, and if I wasn't willing to get you something, I wouldn't ask. Just say 'Yes' if you want one, or 'No' if you don't. I'm coming back with one for myself either way. So..."

"Yes."

"Yes what?"

"Yes, please get me a cup of tea. I'll even be brave and try whatever kind you're having instead of Lipton. Well, almost anything. No flowers, okay?"

"Okay."

"And Rita? Don't worry too much about Liz. She's had a very busy day. We won't let anything happen to her."

"That's kind of hard to do when we don't know what's going on," Rita said as she got up and headed for the kitchen. "I'm going to have to get to the bottom of this tomorrow, and I'm dreading it."

Chapter Sixteen

When Rita walked into the shop the next morning, Serena sat at her fortune-telling table and held up a copy of the local newspaper. "Guess who's on the front page of the Lifestyle section of *Shore Area Happenings*?" She pointed to the photo and article and grinned. "The headline reads, 'Heavenly Temptations for the Body and Soul.' Then it goes on to say, and I quote, 'Local area gift shop and massage therapy business destined for success…And the brownies are out of this world.' Is this great publicity or what?" Serena folded the newspaper in half and handed it to Rita.

"We're the lead article this week?"

"None other! Of course, you were out that day so they only got a picture of the 'tall, red-headed fortune teller' reading palms and interpreting tarot cards, but I plugged your business as well. Will you look at the size of this photo? This free advertising is a gift from heaven!"

"Great," Rita mumbled and sank down on one of the chairs.

"Earth to Rita." Serena snapped her fingers twice. "Aren't you excited?" She stabbed the picture with her index finger. "I've already had phone orders for five sets of these decks, plus I decided to give a tarot workshop some evening. Okay if I use your sitting room? We can charge a fee for ten ladies, or individuals…don't want to be sexist, at a pop. They're sure to buy incense and CDs and other trinkets before they go. And maybe make massage appointments, too. We've got to get on this right away!"

Rita nodded and drummed her fingers on the Plexiglas. "Uh huh. Right away. That's great."

"Hey, what's the matter? You don't want me to use your room?"

"Oh, no, it's not that. It's Aunt Liz. I'm not sure what the problem is, but something's disturbing her."

"Maybe she's tired from too much birthday. She is getting up in years, you know, though nowadays, seventy-five is nothing."

"I think it's money challenges. Has she said anything to you?"

Serena put down the paper and shook her head. "No, but then I wouldn't expect her to. She's always looking for the silver lining, and so far, so good. What makes you think she's in trouble?"

"Oh, odd remarks here and there. About feeling foolish and making mistakes. There were some past-due bills on the desk I think she was trying to hide, but she claims her accountant took care of them."

"Why don't you offer to help straighten out her finances?"

"I have, but she says it's no big deal. I feel kind of funny. She's always been like a mother to me, especially when she let me stay and finish school here instead of having to move to Florida when Mom remarried. She says she's leaving everything to me someday, and I don't want to seem like some kind of vulture waiting for her to die. Or not trusting her judgment."

Serena reached over and patted Rita's hand. "Calm down, honey. You've done a great job helping me get organized. If anything happened to me now, my kids wouldn't have to go crazy trying to find all my important stuff. You owe it to Liz to do the same for her. Insist on it! What if she had an emergency? Would you be able to write checks for her? Or even know where everything is? You're not being selfish when you do what you can to protect your family. If Liz needs help with her finances, then you have to do it."

Rita sighed. "You're right, but I hate feeling nosy. I wish the problem would go away by itself. But it won't, so if you don't need me right now, I'm going home to go through her desk again while she's at her garden club. She and I will talk about it over lunch and get to the bottom of this mess. I'll be back for my afternoon massages."

"Go," Serena said firmly. "Do what you have to do. I'm fine. Kelly's coming in soon to be trained and help. Good luck sleuthing and give my best to Liz. Me? I'm going to laminate this beauty." Serena picked up her scissors and started trimming the article for display. "See you later."

****

At home, the coast was clear. Mitch had left a note for Liz that he'd be at a construction site a few miles north doing some fancy spiral staircase and wouldn't be back until supper. No interruptions this time. Rita settled down at the old oak roll top desk for a more thorough examination and took a deep breath. *I'm not snooping, just helping.*

She went through each drawer methodically. Old photos, seed catalogs, quilting articles and letters. She flipped through all the pages and between papers to see if Aunt Liz had tucked something inside. Nothing enlightening.

She found a checkbook, but it wasn't much help; the last entry was for a couple of months earlier and the notations in the registry were sparse. No new checks anywhere. How did she pay bills? Were they at a bookkeeping service? Rita started making a "To-Do" list of items to take care of and questions to ask.

She opened the last drawer crammed full of greeting cards and stacks of correspondence that

Aunt Liz had secured with rubber bands. Didn't look like financial things. She was about to shut the drawer when she noticed a gold foil Macy's envelope on top of a bundle of birthday cards. Bold block print lettering announced "Happy Birthday Liz! Have a wonderful trip! Love, Tony." Rita carefully lifted the flap and pulled out a gift certificate for $250 and $500 in crisp one-hundred dollar bills clasped with a gold money clip. "Have fun at the blackjack tables and go in style! And no giving this back! Carlton and my parents would have wanted you to splurge on your special day!"

Rita eased the money back in the envelope and placed everything back in their original positions. She leaned back in the swivel chair and bounced up and down. Why did Tony give Aunt Liz such a big gift? And why didn't Aunt Liz mention it? Where were all the bills that had been crammed in the desk? Damn!

Time for a heart-to-heart chat to find out some answers. Rita grabbed the checkbook and the gold envelope and stuffed them into her purse. "A picnic on the beach clears your head every time," Aunt Liz used to tell her when Rita was a teenager. Rita quickly made some turkey sandwiches, wrapped up some homemade chocolate chip cookies, and packed some bottled water and peaches into a small basket. Seemed like old times, except now she was the one packing the lunch. And dreading a confrontation.

****

When Rita pulled up at the Bayview Park near the Garden Club, it was easy to spot Liz's wide straw hat among the roses. The sun was hot, and the rest of the ladies were fanning themselves and sipping iced tea under the gazebo. "Hey, lady. How about a picnic?" Rita called out as she got out of her Jeep and grabbed the wicker basket.

Liz looked up quickly and smiled. "That sounds

wonderful. A few more weeds here and I'm done. The heat is getting to me."

"You used to tell me to stay out of the sun during the hottest part of the day, remember? And here you are down and dirty in the noonday sun while your buddies are cooling off in the shade. Don't you practice what you preach?"

"Well, plants can't weed themselves, and some folks are more talk than action, as you can see. Anyway, I like getting my hands in the soil and knowing these blooms are here because I helped them along." Liz rose quickly, and lunged forward for an instant. Rita reached out a hand to steady her. "I'm a bit dizzy. The heat, you know." After a couple moments, Liz bent down to dust the dirt off her knees. "Good thing you packed a lunch, because I'm starving. And the way I look now, we couldn't get into any restaurants in this fancy neighborhood."

Rita patted the basket. "This is better than a restaurant. Like you used to pack, complete with chocolate chip cookies."

Liz put her garden tools and gloves into a plastic bucket and stood up straight. "Oh, comfort food. What's up, Rita? Is something bothering you?"

"Let's sit down somewhere in the shade and have lunch."

Liz looked at her with a serious face. "Okay, dear. There's a nice bench under that tree right across the street. And look. No kids on the swings so we can talk in peace." She waved to her friends in the gazebo and called out, "See you next week, all! I'll ride home with my niece." She smiled and whispered to Rita, "You saved me from an hour of conversation about how hot it is, who's in the hospital, and what aches and pains they all have."

They sat on opposite ends of the bench with the picnic basket between them. Rita placed a bottle of water and a sandwich next to Liz. "No mayo or onions. Turkey and tomato the way you like it, right?"

Liz nodded and took a long drink of water. She reached into her huge bag for a moist towelette and wiped the dirt off her hands with a lemon-scented square. She turned and looked directly at her niece. "Okay, Rita, before we eat, what's on your mind?"

Rita knitted her brows. "What do you mean? Can't we just have a picnic like old times?"

"Dear, we can have a picnic, but we can't have old times. They're gone. We deal with the now. So what are you trying to say but not saying? Spit it out. You can tell me anything. You're the daughter I never had, the niece I'll always love. And don't chew your fingernails. I thought you stopped that."

Rita quickly lowered her hand and studied her short, uneven nails. "I never could fool you, could I?" Rita murmured.

"No, so stop trying. What are you worried about?"

"You. I'm afraid if I say what I have to say I'll hurt your feelings. I never want to do that. You and Uncle Carlton were so good to me, letting me finish school here when Mom moved to Florida with her new husband."

"Rita. I will always love you, no matter what, so get to the point."

"I didn't come home to take over, and I don't want you to think I'm some kind of vulture after your house or your money, but I saw some unpaid bills and shut-off notices on your desk and you seem upset. I want to help. If there's one thing I've learned since my divorce, it's how to get out of a financial jam. Are you in trouble? Is there anything I can do for you?"

Liz took a deep breath. "I'm not sure. I never thought much about money. There was always enough when Carlton handled everything. After he passed on, I tried to write the checks for a while, but it was too much. Not that I'm too stupid to do it, but having to pay the bills myself was another reminder he was gone.

"When I got behind, I took all the bills over to the accounting firm for them to pay. Since then, they figure out my taxes and tell me what to sign, same as when Carlton was alive. He trusted them and we did all right, so I've done the same thing. I was upset, too, about the shut-off notices, but the office says maybe I misplaced a bill or something. They'll take care of the problem. I signed some paper that brings in extra money to replace Carlton's pension. So I go out to lunch more, donate more to good causes, and I give more presents. Even had the house fixed up, but I know Mitch didn't charge me enough for all that work."

"What kind of paper did you sign? An investment? Life insurance?"

"I don't remember. It was about six months after Carlton died. I wasn't listening to the details. We've been going to that office for over fifty years so I trust them."

"Maybe they charge too much. What's your yearly income, if you don't mind me asking?"

Liz shrugged her shoulders. "I have no idea. But it covers everything."

"Who handles your affairs if something happened to you, you know, like an emergency?"

"Well, I guess you'd take over, right? You're better at paying bills than your mother or me. Her husband has plenty of money but they're so far away. They never leave Florida to visit New Jersey anymore. You'd take over for me, wouldn't you, Rita?"

Rita nodded and patted her aunt's hand. "Of course. I could kick myself for not insisting you let me help you sooner. But I don't have the power to sign any of your checks or handle anything legal. Who has your power of attorney?"

"Well, Carlton did, but I don't know now. My attorney is one of the most powerful ones in the area. A lot of important people go to him, people with money. Maybe he's in charge."

"Aunt Liz, someone in your family or a trusted friend should have your power of attorney. That means they can make decisions for you and sign legal documents if you ever become unable to take of yourself. You need someone who cares for your best interests. We better visit your lawyer and your accountant and get things clear in your mind and legally straight. If anything happened to you or if you ever need help, I want to be able to take care of you until you're better. And if you want me as your executrix, power of attorney, health care surrogate, or whatever else, I'll do it, but it has to be an official document."

Liz removed the tin foil wrapping from her sandwich. "Dear, I'd love for you to do that, but I don't want you to neglect your own life and business to fix up my mess. I feel like a foolish old woman not knowing these things. Carlton spoiled me and took care of all the money matters so I never learned, and when he passed on, I was too grief-stricken to take over..."

"Aunt Liz, we all need time to heal and we all make mistakes. Stop saying you feel foolish. You're the wisest person I know. I've always wanted to be like you...a gutsy lady who not only pursues her own interests but also takes very special care of the people she loves. So what if you don't balance your checkbook?"

The older woman's chin trembled a bit, but she smiled. "Enough sentimental talk or I won't be able to eat. Let's simply be grateful for what we have - enjoy today, the sun, the sandwiches, and the company."

"Aunt Liz, you can't keep sticking your head in the sand and hope for the best. You don't want to lose your home, do you?"

Liz's eyes followed a sailboat gliding by before she responded. "No, I don't. I guess we'll visit those stuffy old offices and get everything squared away with the three-piece suits there. Between the two of us, we'll take care of it all. 'Save the ranch' as they say. I'm not too old to get a job if I need to, you know. Can you picture me flipping burgers at McDonald's?"

Rita laughed. "Actually, yes, but it's not something I want to see. And the teenagers probably couldn't keep up with you."

"Well, I can do other things. I can quilt. I could work in a florist shop or maybe the library. Or a beach badge checker? Now, young lady, anything else you want to ask?"

"Well, I hate to admit this, but I was worried about you when I saw those shut-off notices and I searched your desk for your current checkbook. It's not there, but this was." Rita pulled a gold gift certificate out of her purse and held it up. "I know he's rich, but isn't it odd Tony gave you such a big gift?"

Aunt Liz twirled her wedding band. "Oh, that. I wasn't sure what to do with the money. I know Tony's wealthy, so it's not a big deal to him. I called him this morning and told him I couldn't accept it, but he sounded hurt, almost insulted. He misses his parents, and has kind of latched on to me. After Tony's mom passed on last year, his dad moved to one of their high-rise condos in Myrtle Beach. Tony's all alone here as far as family.

"So I've decided to keep his gift. If I blow it all on the blackjack table on the cruise this weekend, Tony will get it back anyway, right? It's his cruise business. And who knows? Maybe I'll double the money. I can give it back and still have half left! Any more questions?"

Rita hesitated. "Just one. About Mitch. I know you like him and he's done incredible work in your house. But how well do you really know him? Where's he from? Did you ever check him out? He seems so nice, almost too nice at times, but should you trust him? He comes and goes as if your house is his own, at least before I arrived. Could he have misplaced some of your bills? And are you having financial problems because of all the work he did on the house?"

"Whew! Which question do you want me to answer first?"

"Well, only a year ago, he was a total stranger. Now you treat him like part of your family and you're having problems you never had before. Is there a connection?"

Aunt Liz leaned toward Rita and looked directly into her eyes. "Listen, young lady. There are some things in this life you just know in your heart, in your gut, without question. Like God *is*. He's here, everywhere. The sun comes up in the morning whether or not you spent the night crying your eyes out or sleeping straight through. It may be rainy or cloudy, but the sun is still out there.

"Now, I may not know my bank balance, and I've been accused of being too trusting, but I do know Mitch is a good man, a simple, giving man. As for the remodeling, he charged me so little it's ridiculous. A couple thousand dollars, if that. Some friends helped him out and I fed them dinner. He says he got those beautiful cabinets from some rich North Jersey CEO whose wife didn't like them once they were in.

"And another thing. He's finally coming out of his shell, so please don't ask him about this. Why did he do all this work for free? Probably his way to say thanks for living here and being part of a family. I don't know why, and you don't need to either. Enjoy the sun coming up. Just say thanks to someone who helps you without questioning their motives. Rita, honey, live your life each moment and trust things will work out. Now, enough talk for now. Smile and eat your sandwich! That's an order. Understand?"

Rita felt like an eight-year-old reprimanded by her favorite teacher for daring to ask questions. She wanted to believe Mitch was a good man. But simple? She doubted that very much. Secretive was more like it. What was he hiding?

Aunt Liz leaned over and put an arm around Rita's shoulder, pulled her closer and kissed her hair.

"Okay, Aunt Liz. I guess that's enough for now. But we'll take care of your finances tomorrow so we both feel better."

When they returned home, Liz called and made back-to-back appointments for the next morning with her attorney and CPA. Rita hurried back to work, relieved that tomorrow she'd have some answers. She hoped it wouldn't be too bad or too late to make a difference. Now she had four massage appointments in a row, hour-long ones. At least during a massage, she could shut off her thinking and let her hands take over. She couldn't do anything to change the past, and there was no sense worrying about what she'd discover tomorrow.

Of course, that was simpler said than done.

Chapter Seventeen

The next morning, Liz shoved her financial papers and recent bills into a straw tote bag. Dressed in a sky blue pantsuit with creamy pearls, she looked like a slim senior model from the ad of an AARP magazine. "Ready to go, Rita?" she called out.

"I thought I was until I saw you. You look like the mother of the bride, Aunt Liz. What do you think of my court outfit?" Rita asked.

Liz turned to study her niece coming down the stairs in a gray linen suit with a soft red blouse and three-inch heels. "You could be one of those high-powered female lawyers on TV. At least we look successful. Maybe we'll fool them."

"Aunt Liz. We don't need to fool anyone. We can take care of whatever the problem is." Rita paused to pick up a yellow legal pad. "Do you have everything you need?"

"I hope so. My checkbook, some papers, and more bills. I don't like keeping that stuff around, so I let the attorney and the accountant hold on to whatever they'll take off my hands. They laughingly refer to me as one of their 'paper bag' clients."

"We'll change that," Rita said and held open the door for her aunt. "After dealing with lawyers, accountants, courts, credit card companies, and an ex-husband who seems to have disappeared, I've learned you have to be your own best friend. Don't assume someone else is as nice as you are or is looking out for your interests. Chances are they'll charge you a lot of money to mismanage or steal what you have. And if you don't ask the right questions, you get screwed. I can't believe you trust other people to..."

"Calm down, young lady!" Liz interrupted. "I'm glad you're going to help me, but promise you'll be polite. You know the old saying you can get more flies with honey than..."

"Yeah, well, that's not all flies tend to swarm around!"

"Rita!"

"Okay, I'll start off with Sunday school behavior, but we're going to get to the bottom of this no matter what it takes. The whole truth and nothing but!"

When they arrived at the law firm of Hanifin, Rollins, Santangelo, Stefano, and Co., Esquires, Rita only recognized the location. The old clapboard building had been torn down. In its place stood an imposing brick office complex with three-story white columns. All the prime parking spots were filled or reserved, so Rita pulled into a parking garage and reached for a ticket from a buzzing post. "Wow, a gate, just like in the big city. How long has this been here?"

"A year or so. Maybe more. I never use this garage. Can't stand feeling closed in. I usually call the accountant to say I'm coming and I park in the fire zone, run in, and drop off my papers at the front desk. Anyway, it's not the same anymore since Joe Rollins died. And his secretary Brenda? She retired and moved to Florida after he passed. She always made the best coffee and cookies. These slick young folks always try to serve me some fancy espresso or murky stuff with a funny name. No one drinks plain coffee or tea with milk and sugar anymore."

"You mean you never go in and discuss your finances?"

"Not if I can help it. I lead a simple life. I figure I have plenty of money, more than enough for expenses, my charities, and a few extras, so why talk about it? They're the experts, not me."

They entered the garage's elevator and Rita examined the list of clients posted on an elegant plaque. She pushed the ground floor button for the law offices. "Looks like one-stop shopping. Isn't that your accountant, too?" Rita asked as she pointed to a CPA firm.

Liz nodded but looked preoccupied. "I hate elevators. Too confining, like that dreadful steam room. Next time, we walk around the building."

At last, the doors opened and a quiet bell tastefully announced their arrival. The huge lobby had marble floors and an impressive fountain flanked by large potted ficus trees. They walked over to an antique desk where a young blonde woman in a classic black suit was jotting down notes on a steno pad. A thin headset crowned her golden head of hair neatly tucked into a French twist. Her desk was Spartan except for a Waterford pen set and a leather appointment book. "May I help you?" she asked as Rita stopped in front of her.

"Yes. We have an appointment with one of your lawyers. Whoever took over the Chandler account from Mr. Rollins."

"Let's see. Chandler and Madison. Ten o'clock. That would be Mr. Santangelo. He'll be with you shortly. Please have a seat. May I get you some cappuccino or espresso?"

Rita smiled before glancing at Liz. "How about café latte with extra cream and sugar?" she asked innocently.

"Of course," she rose and turned to Liz. "And you, ma'am?"

"No thanks, dear," Liz answered, "Nothing for me." She headed for a leather sofa and when the blonde was out of sight, touched the potted flowers on the table. "These are real orchids," she whispered. "Things have really changed around here since Joe

Rollins was in charge!"

Rita only had to wait a few minutes until the receptionist returned with a steaming cup and saucer. Royal Dalton china. Rita had paid a couple thousand dollars for a divorce to a newly-graduated attorney with paper cups and second-hand office furniture. How much had Liz contributed to this extravagant decor? Was the latté extra? If the billing clock was ticking, they'd better talk fast and keep it simple.

"Mr. Santangelo will see you now," the receptionist announced and waited for them to follow her down the hallway to his office. She ushered them toward two wingback chairs.

Carmine Santangelo's office was an impressive mix of leather, mahogany, and symbols of success: awards, plaques, and pictures of yachts and golf tournaments, of politicians and celebrities. A large happy family smiled, graduated, and danced in brass frames on the large uncluttered desk. In Rita's experience, it seemed the emptier the desk, the higher the bills. And the more little people slaving away at cubicles out of sight, doing research online or in leather-bound legal volumes, billing their time in quarter hours and photocopies, and always rounding up, not down.

"Mrs. Chandler, Ms. Madison. How nice to finally meet you," said a middle-aged man in a gray pinstripe suit. He strode quickly across the room with his arm extended to shake hands. "I'm Carmine Santangelo, senior partner here after Mr. Rollins passed on. I believe I was away on business when your late husband's will was read, but I've looked it over briefly this morning. What can I do for you?"

When Liz failed to respond, Rita said, "I'm Rita Madison, her niece, and I've recently moved back here. I want to help Aunt Liz get her legal and financial affairs in order. Uncle Carlton used to take care of it all, and we'd like to review her will and whatever arrangements she has in case she needs me to take care of her. You know, power of attorney, ability to pay the bills, health wishes, and so on."

"Of course. It's important to go over these things periodically. Mrs. Chandler, you look wonderful, but you need to be prepared in case of emergencies."

"Yes," Liz agreed. "I'm afraid my niece is worried about a few unpaid bills of mine. And I can't seem to find copies of my will, my current checkbook, and so forth. My accountant has been paying my bills for me, but I'd rather have family doing it, so I want you to put Rita in charge of things in case anything happens to me."

Rita tried to hide her chipped nails as she watched the attorney's long fingers flip through the papers in the Chandler file. A simple gold band on his left hand contrasted with the Rolex watch and an enormous platinum and diamond ring on his right. "Well, the bulk of your estate goes to Rita. There's a ten thousand dollar donation each to the Garden Club and St. Theresa's Church. Here's your handwritten note dated a few months ago stating another ten thousand dollars and the right to live over the garage be granted to Mitch Grant, good friend. That's very unusual, and it wasn't made legal. Our records show we tried to call you regarding this, but no one could reach you. No response to our certified letters, either. No answering machine?"

"No," Liz replied. "I don't like those gadgets. And I just pack up bills and official things and take them to the accountant."

Rita felt her foot start jiggling like it used to when she had to take a test as a kid. "Aunt Liz, let me get this straight. When you die, you want Mitch to go with the property? If I inherit the house someday, you expect me to put up with Mitch for the rest of my life? I don't think you can do that. And why would you want to?"

"Well, I don't want him to lose his home. And he is very handy, you know."

Rita turned to face the lawyer. "Mr. Santangelo, what do you think? Mitch is a boarder...not even a relative. He seems very nice, but he was a stranger until last summer. Would you want your aunt doing something like this?"

The attorney tilted back in his chair slightly, his fingers precisely touching each other in a triangular position as he studied the faces of the two women. "Never. I wouldn't recommend it even for relatives. Impossible to sell the property and hard to evict. If you want to leave him something, there are wiser ways to do it. But we're getting ahead of ourselves here." He tapped his fingers together lightly.

"First, I need to know your net worth and how your assets are allocated to protect them as much as possible: stocks, bonds, real estate, trust fund, whatever. Do you have enough cash to leave anyone money without Rita selling the house? Great location and nice size lot, by the way, but one of the older, smaller homes if I recall. Unless Rita's income is high, she might have trouble paying your property taxes. Estate taxes, too. Let's start with the basics. What assets do you own?"

Liz hesitated. "Well, besides the house, I don't know exactly. Money gets deposited every month into my checking account. I thought maybe you could tell me what I have and what I need to do."

Mr. Santangelo leaned forward and planted his elbows on the desk. "It sounds like a visit to your accountant is in order first. And you should rethink the idea of bequeathing exact amounts. You don't want your niece to have to sell your home to give money to these other people and causes, do you?"

Liz shook her head and he continued. "I'll start

drawing up a new will, a power of attorney, a living trust, a health care surrogate designation, and have you come in to sign them after you check with your accountant and get back to me. Or have him call me and we'll work it out between us. Any other living relatives you'd like to name to take charge? It's good to have a back-up for Rita should anything happen to her."

"I have a sister in Florida, but she married a rich man. They don't need any more money and rarely visit. We talk on the phone, but don't live close enough for her to manage things. Maybe Mitch would help. I trust Mitch. He has a good heart."

"Aunt Liz! Mitch in control of your estate? What does he know about managing money? And what do you really know about him anyway?"

The lawyer shut the file folder and stood up. "It seems you two have a few personal issues to clear up, too. Think it over carefully. Get back to me when you've looked over the sample documents. I'll start my paralegals on the power of attorney and maybe we can get together next week to-"

"Could you make it tomorrow?" Liz broke in. "I'm going on a short cruise this Friday and I'd feel better if everything is in place."

"I can have the power of attorney and the health designation forms ready, but the other documents will take a little more time. Stop in first thing Thursday morning to review those and sign them. After you look over the papers and meet with your accountant, let me know the details of your holdings so we can draw up an appropriate will. I'll explain trusts, too." He walked around his desk and shook their hands again. "It's a pleasure to meet you at last."

"How much will all this cost, Mr. Santangelo?" said Rita, remaining in her chair.

"Normally, all these documents would probably

run a client about five to ten thousand dollars or more, but since your family has been with the firm so long, we'll make it four thousand."

"Can't you make an addendum to my aunt's current will? Substitute my name for Uncle Carlton's?" Rita asked. "The will is pretty simple, isn't it? My aunt has a house, a checking account, a passbook account, a few CDs, and some personal possessions."

"Well, if that's the case, it may be very simple. We don't know yet. And Rita, it's so commendable to see a young person looking out for family. Joe Rollins always spoke very highly of your uncle and aunt. In honor of his memory and being a long-time client, I'm only going to charge you twenty-five hundred dollars. Much less than half our usual rate. We won't make a dime on you."

"That's very sweet of you, Mr. Santangelo, but I'm not a charity case," Liz said as they walked down the hall.

"But you're not rich, either, Aunt Liz, so thank you, Mr. Santangelo, for helping to save her assets." Rita smiled and took Aunt Liz's arm and guided her into the elevator. "Have a nice day," she added as the doors closed.

"Young lady, I've never taken charity, and I don't intend to start now!"

"It's not charity, Aunt Liz. Think of it like clipping a very big coupon at the ShopRite. You get groceries cheaper, and they get your business. I'm sure over the years, you and Uncle Carlton paid for a few of those chairs or marble tiles. Now, let's go to your CPA and find out where you have everything. And no more talk about Mitch for now!"

The CPA office was not quite as large but was equally lavish. Instead of florals or the more typical Jersey Shore décor of sailboats, lighthouses, shells, and seagulls, this one was full of duck decoys, woodsy scenes, and hunter green leather.

Rita and Liz declined coffee from another blonde receptionist before being led to a corner office. An elegantly dressed man looked up from a fat yellowed file and motioned to the two plaid chairs in front of his desk.

"Mrs. Chandler, Ms. Madison, please sit down. I've been reviewing your records. Quite a history here. Not many clients have been with the firm for over fifty years. I'm John Martino. I took over all of the senior partner's clients after he passed on. How may I help you?"

Aunt Liz took a deep breath. "I'm afraid I never was good at managing money. My late husband, Carlton did all that. Since he died, I left all the details to your firm. I don't remember which accountant I dealt with first. A tall young man with glasses. Very polite. He said I had some problems with taxes and such and I signed some sort of investment or thing that took care of it all. I don't remember what he called the account. An annuity? A reversed something. Anyway, my niece Rita is very good at taking care of money and I want her in charge of all my financial affairs. She'll help me put them in order, too. She's going to be my power of attorney, heir, and take care of all the details for me from now on."

Mr. Martino stopped bobbing his swivel chair and folded his hands together. "As your accountant, I must warn you sometimes that is not a wise thing to do, Mrs. Chandler. No offense, Rita. You are probably the wonderful person your aunt thinks you are, but I could tell you horror stories about senior citizens who put their trust in a 'loyal' relative only to find out their beloved child or grandchild left town in a new Corvette with all their money. Then a pile of bills shows up in next month's mail. And every month after that."

Liz's face turned pink. "Mr. Martino, Rita is like the daughter I never had. I trust her honesty as well as her competence. Why, she could have declared bankruptcy and avoided paying all her ex-husband's credit card debts but she didn't. She felt obligated to do the right thing and paid them all herself."

"Well, that's very admirable, and unusual, though perhaps not wise. It's my job to inform and caution you. It's your decision to choose to accept or reject my advice.

"Now about that paper you signed. The young man you mentioned no longer works for us and I see a potential problem. Basically, Mrs. Chandler, you own a home in a very expensive area. You have a few thousand dollars in CDs, a few thousand in a money market account, and a very small pension from Social Security. Never worked long outside the house?" When Liz shook her head, he continued, "Three hundred dollars and change a month doesn't cover much. Are you aware your property tax alone costs you thousands a month?" He wrote down a number and slid it toward her. "This much per month."

"Are you sure? I thought that was the yearly amount." Liz's voice cracked.

"I'm sorry to say I'm positive. Your Social Security isn't even close to covering a fraction of that."

"I don't understand. Carlton earned a good salary as a chemist and a professor, and he said his pension was good. He always paid our bills on time."

"Well," the CPA went on slowly, "it appears that what you called an annuity was actually a reverse-mortgage. You essentially 'sold' your interest in your own home in order to pay off your husband's debts, which were considerable, and to increase your monthly income. In effect, hundreds of thousands were borrowed against the value of your house, which should have been paid off long before your husband retired. You've been receiving a check each month from that loan and paying for your expenses, including those enormous taxes for someone in your income bracket. And your more than generous donations. I hate to tell you this, but within three months, a balloon note will require you to pay back the loan in full." He wrote down the amount and circled it.

"That much? In full?" Liz grabbed a handkerchief from her pocket and dabbed at her eyes. She groaned and took a deep breath before looking directly at Mr. Martino. "How in the world am I going to come up with that kind of money?"

"Frankly, I don't know right now, Mrs. Chandler," he said gently. "You have options, though. I don't know if you can renegotiate the loan and pull out more of the equity for a short time. With the market the way it is who knows? Selling can be hard nowadays and time-consuming, but it may be your best option. You could get enough money for your home to settle your debts and move into one of those nice assisted-living facilities…"

"You mean a nursing home. I may be seventy-five, but I'm too young for that. I want my own home."

"Actually, they're more like hotels than nursing homes. My mom and dad are in one. They love it! Plenty of things to do and all kinds of sports and recreational activities."

"No! That's not for me! I swim in my pool, I walk on the beach, and I help at the garden club and the church, sometimes at the library. This is my home, not just a piece of real estate. There must be another way." Liz pounded her fist on his desk, and her chin quivered.

"Mrs. Chandler, I empathize. My parents felt the same way until they had trouble getting around their two-story home. Looking ahead, it's better for them and better for the family if everyone knows you're taken care of properly. Now they wouldn't want to live anywhere else but the assisted living condo. And they have more time to do the things they enjoy. Think of it. You'd have some money to spare...for travel, your charity work, and helping out your family."

"I don't want to leave my home, and that's that!"

Rita reached out to put her hand on Liz's arm. "Mr. Martino, I imagine my aunt didn't understand what she was signing at the time. Not that she's incompetent. She's not, but she's always hated doing paperwork and left it to my uncle. Who suggested she do this? I would have tried to talk her out of it if I'd known. Isn't there another alternative?"

"For some people, reverse mortgages are perfect. I don't know the details about your particular case right now. I promise you I'll look over everything and get back to the two of you. On your end, contact the financial institutions and have Rita's name added as joint owner of all accounts with assets. Here is a complete list of the accounts you'll need to add your signature on. But as you can see, the totals don't even come close to what the balloon payment is."

Liz blew her nose quietly and shook her head. "What a fool I've been," she said quietly. "Even if I could get a job, I'd never be able to come up with that kind of money."

"Now don't you worry, Mrs. Chandler. You don't have to start working at this stage of the game. You won't lose your home or be thrown out on the streets. Assisted living isn't your only option. You could get a smaller home in a nearby town. Maybe in one of those senior communities. With your real estate, you'll still be better off than most women your age, even after you pay off your debts. And don't beat yourself up for not being prepared to handle the financial details after your husband's passing. It's hard for widows to deal with loss and grief, but you'll be fine. We'll decide what's best for you, do you understand?" The man reached across his desk and patted her hand.

Liz stared at his hand until he removed it. "I'm still capable of deciding for myself." She nodded uncertainly and forced a thin smile as she rose. "Well, no use crying over spilled milk, as they say, right? We'd better get going. I won a cruise to nowhere so maybe my luck is changing. I leave Friday."

"Excellent. Enjoy yourself! Take your mind off these matters. Your niece seems very competent, and we'll get you back on track. Maybe even in a better situation. I'll examine your records and documents thoroughly. Make a few phone calls. May I have your permission to consult your attorney directly?"

"Yes, Mr. Santangelo's on the first floor."

"Good man. We've done business many times. Oh, that reminds me. You'll have to pay for a real estate appraisal, too."

Liz thought for a moment. "I have a friend in real estate that might do it for free. Tony Jennings. His parents and I go way back."

"Great. It's good to have friends in high places and he's very big in this area. Shall I contact him directly about the appraisal?"

Liz nodded but Rita broke in. "Actually, Mr. Martino, I'd like you to touch base with us before you talk with Mr. Santangelo or Tony Jennings. And I'd also like to see a statement of my aunt's account with you and the fees you bill for bookkeeping, tax preparation, and so on. I couldn't find it in this batch, but I thought I saw a bookkeeping bill for one hundred dollars along with the shut-off notices. If that's a monthly fee, it's outrageous, especially if my aunt is getting notices from collection agencies. If I can save my aunt money by assuming the bill-paying and other duties, I will. I'm sure you agree."

"Of course. Once we have your aunt's balloon-note problem resolved and whatever other debts her husband might have incurred as well, it could save her several hundred dollars a year for you to take over as many of the financial details as possible. Remember most of our clients are corporations or have extensive holdings that require considerable financial planning. And Mrs. Chandler could have lost some bills; she often drops them off in a paper bag. Before your aunt leaves Friday, sit down together and make a list of all monthly expenses. My secretary will give you our fee schedule and a printout of bills paid for the past year the next time you come in. We'll know exactly how much income you require and how to solve your current challenge, Mrs. Chandler."

He rose and shook their hands. "Have a wonderful cruise, Mrs. Chandler! We'll get this all straightened out when you return." He ushered them down the hallway to the lobby.

After they had their parking stub validated and picked up some preliminary information at the receptionist's desk, Liz crammed the papers into her empty tote bag and headed for the stairs. "Aunt Liz, the elevator for the garage is the other way."

"I know, but I hate being cooped up in elevators and parking garages if I can help it. When it's only a few flights down, I take the stairs. Gravity helps and it's usually quicker. Can you keep up with me?"

"Aunt Liz, don't you ever get tired of showing off?"

"No," she smiled.

"Stubborn, that's what you are," Rita teased.

"Well, you should know, Ms. I-don't-need-any-help."

Rita sighed. *Not again*, she thought as they walked out into the morning sun and headed for the parking garage. *Another frigging hole to dig out of! A huge one!* It had taken her years of working three jobs and scrimping to pay off a fraction of that amount. How could she possibly get her aunt out of this mess? If the taxes truly were that high, how could they continue to pay them and keep the house?

"Well, Aunt Liz," Rita said aloud. "We've got our work cut out for us, but we'll manage. Right now, you've got to pack for your trip, and I have to get to work soon. Knotted backs await my return."

"After lunch and ice cream," said Liz. "My treat. I'm not broke yet. And who knows? Maybe I'll win big at the blackjack tables on the ship. May I drive?"

"Aunt Liz, you're too much!" Rita smiled and tossed her the keys. "Okay, as long as you promise not to speed! I want to arrive alive."

Liz winked and slid into the driver's seat of Rita's Jeep.

As Rita climbed into the passenger side, Liz started the engine with a roar and adjusted the mirrors. Rita thought she heard a car door slam, and glanced around to warn her aunt of possible traffic, but no one was in sight, no vehicles moving. "Let's get out of here," she said with a silent prayer. "I'm ready for that ice cream."

Chapter Eighteen

Rita skipped the sandwich menu at Jackson's Ice Cream and ordered a deluxe hot fudge sundae, her favorite comfort food guaranteed to hit the spot in times of celebration or sorrow, even if only temporarily. When Aunt Liz started to protest, she said, "I've only got time for a meal or a dessert. I choose dessert."

Their food arrived within minutes, and Rita dug in, savoring the creamy fudge while it was still warm. As soon as their waiter was out of earshot, Aunt Liz leaned over her chef's salad and whispered, "Thank you so much for helping me straighten out this money thing, Rita. You always had a head for numbers like my Carlton. I know there's no blood relation between you two, but you do take after him like that."

Rita nodded and wondered if her uncle had only seemed good at managing money. Yes, she was good at numbers. But a magician? No. She'd been mentally calculating how many massages she'd have to give simply to cover the taxes, and the answer was staggering. She'd raise her prices today, extend her hours, and start booking those "at-home" visits. If these people could afford to pay such astronomical taxes on their second homes, they would certainly not balk at paying double for a house call. Still, even without a calculator, the idea of earning enough money to pay off Aunt Liz's debts felt like trying to bail out a sinking charter boat with a kid's sand bucket.

"Well, look who's here," Liz said, pointing

toward the kitchen. Tony stood by the swinging doors, talking to the manager and making some notes in a small leather planner. "You know, I thought Tony liked ice cream a lot when I kept bumping into him here, but Dorothy told me he owns this place. Oversaw all the renovations and redecorating. I swear whatever he touches turns to gold."

Rita muttered, "Yeah, of course it's a lot easier to have the Midas touch when you've got a pot of gold to start with, isn't it?" She shoveled another spoonful of whipped cream into her mouth and glanced toward the back of the restaurant.

At that moment, Tony looked directly at Rita. He snapped his small notebook shut, said a few words to the other man, and approached their table smiling. "What a nice surprise! My favorite ladies in Mantoloking Sands. All ready to sail, Liz?"

"Almost. A little more packing to do, but what about you?" Without waiting for an answer, she pointed her finger at him and scolded, "I understand you've been keeping secrets from me, young man."

Tony's smile vanished and his eyebrows went up. He glanced at Rita and back at Liz. "Secrets? What kind of secrets?"

"You know. Your latest investment. Better than real estate, the health spa, the Galleria, the French restaurant..."

He shook his head in confusion. "I don't know what you're getting at, Liz," Tony said.

"This ice cream parlor! I know you loved it when you were a little boy, but you never mentioned you were the new owner. I thought you came here for the forty fabulous flavors like the rest of us, not to check on your business."

"Oh, that!" Tony sighed. "I downplay my role here, but it's not a secret. We kept the Jackson family recipes as well as the name. Jennings Ice

Cream wouldn't have had the local history and loyal customer base Jackson's does. And now that the cat's out of the bag, the owner insists on taking care of this." Tony scooped up the check and tore it in half. "Is there anything else I can do for you today?"

Rita glanced at her watch nervously. "Actually, Tony, would you be able to take Aunt Liz home when she's done with lunch? I'm finished and I hate to run, but if I don't leave now, with this traffic, I'll be late for my first afternoon appointment."

Tony pulled out a chair. "My pleasure. In fact, I think I'll have a little something to eat and keep Liz company." He looked around and gave a slight wave to a waiter who hurried over. "Feel free to go, Rita. Sorry you have to run off, but I'm sure you'll bring a smile to some lucky man's face as you always do to mine."

Rita slipped a generous tip under the sugar dispenser and got up. "It's a she, but thanks. For the dessert, too. Bye, Aunt Liz. Call me if you need anything from the store on my way home."

Rita rushed off, annoyed at Tony's attentiveness and compliments...and her own reaction. Why couldn't she just say, "Thank you," instead of wondering if he had a hidden agenda? How crazy! He was charming, handsome, and eligible. Not only that, but he adored Aunt Liz and he was rich. If Tony wasn't her type, who was? And what did that say about her?

Rita gripped the wheel and shook her head as an "Ah-hah!" moment struck. That was it! She was doing exactly what she'd accused Mitch of...judging people like Tony on personal bias. All rich people weren't spoiled and materialistic simply because they had money! Dr. Phil or Oprah would have a field day with that realization! It sounded so dumb. Would they send her to a twelve-step program for people with a phobia about wealthy people?

She exhaled with relief! She didn't need to act like a martyr or repeat her sad story playing a whining victim of a limited ex-husband. *I am an intelligent, attractive, capable woman.* Why be suspicious of a man who was attracted to her, especially one who obviously didn't need what little money she had left?

Besides, her aunt's best interests came first. As much as she hated asking for help, Rita realized she might have to. If Tony had the resources to float a temporary loan so Aunt Liz wouldn't have to sell her house in the near future, why not let him? *I'd never get involved with someone because of his money, but how stupid is it to reject someone simply because he's successful?*

The next time he asked her out, could she let go of her fear of being used and manipulated and say, "Yes?" If Tony lost interest and stopped pursuing her, fine. Or maybe, just maybe, it could be the beginning of something special. Aunt Liz might be right, even Mitch for that matter, about her being too hard on men. How would she ever get to know a man as a person if she kept an angry wall around herself?

She needed to stop the war between her head and her heart, to trust her judgment enough to distinguish between fear and intuition. Sometimes they both felt like giant fists tightening in her stomach. By the time Rita parked her Jeep behind the gift shop, she was tired of thinking. She closed her eyes and took a few deep breaths. *Focus on work.* That would be her mantra today. Maybe for years!

She passed through the kitchen and grabbed a brownie. Some lunch! Two desserts. "Your twelve o'clock is waiting for you," Serena called out as Rita hurried in. "How'd it go with the lawyer and accountant?"

Rita looked around before answering in a low

voice. "Let's say I need to be *very* successful. No vacations or long afternoons off. Book as many massages as you can, and I'm raising my prices. Tonight."

"That bad, huh?"

"We'll find out next week for sure, but I am *not* letting Aunt Liz sell her house. It would break her heart."

"Sell the house? She's been there forever. Anything I can do to help?"

"Well, unless you've won the Pick-6 Lotto Jackpot, I think this problem might be too big for you to solve, but thanks for offering. And don't mention it to anyone, especially Aunt Liz. I've got to find a way out of this."

The afternoon flew by with satisfied customers, and by five, Rita was feeling better. Funny how giving massages could be as therapeutic as getting them. She designed new flyers, brochures, and price lists with significant increases. She'd also devised a "Summer Special" promotion to raise cash quickly and increase volume and clientele.

"You're working late, girl," Serena said as she breezed in a few hours later and plopped on the sofa with her feet up. "I am so ready to lock up and go. But what's this about Liz's house? I can't imagine her living anywhere else. Kind of like my grandfather and this place when it was a little general store. He loved it. It was part of him. When he had to go into the rehab center after the accident, it was the end of him. I promised I'd try to keep it in the family, but it's tempting to sell. I'm property rich but cash poor."

"Well, that's Aunt Liz's situation. She owes a ton of money in a balloon payment on a reverse mortgage and some other notes - more than I earned working three jobs since my divorce."

Serena stood up and jangled her keys. "Well,

keep thinking positive thoughts. I didn't see anything too bad in her cards, and I'm sure you guys will work it out. I gotta go. A possible date. You okay here by yourself?"

"Sure," Rita said without looking up. "I want to finish printing these before I leave. Tomorrow, if you book someone over the phone, use the new price schedule. And I'm offering evening appointments, too. I'll visit clients' homes some nights for double the price, but only for established customers or someone you can vouch for. If they question the price, tell them I have to allow for travel time, gas, and the extra hassle."

"Well, block out the times you're available. But remember what they say about all work and no play!" Serena said, pointing her finger at Rita.

"It's only temporary. I'll work on my social life after I figure out better ways to make money fast."

"I'll lock the front and flip over the 'Open' sign so customers don't bother you. Good night and don't stay too late. And remember to turn on the alarm system!"

By the time Rita finished some leftover pizza along with her new brochures and flyers, it was dark. The phone rang as she was ready to leave. Should she answer it? It probably wasn't Aunt Liz; she'd called earlier to say she'd have dinner at a friend's house. Mitch? She hadn't seen him all day. Could be a potential client. She picked up the receiver. "Shore Therapeutic Massage. How may I help you?"

"What a good question," a husky voice answered. "I'm sure I can think of several ways. Working kind of late, aren't you?"

Rita's heart skipped, her brain raced as she tried to think of a quick response. "Uh, sir, this is only the answering service. May I take a message? Shore Massage will get it tomorrow morning at ten."

"Oh, right. We'll pretend you're the answering service. But we both know better, Ms. Madison. Tomorrow's not good enough. I need a masseuse now. How about I come right over?"

"The office is closed, sir. If you'll leave your name and number, I'll relay your message. Otherwise, I'll have to disconnect. I have incoming calls. Please hold…"

"No need for the charade. I think you already got my message. I'll be in touch, Rita. And don't forget to turn the lights off when you leave. Set the alarm system, too. Better replace that burned-out bulb. Wouldn't want any more vandalism, now would we? We'll get together another night." An abrupt click ended the conversation.

A prank. Her first prank call. Maybe she should have expected it with all the publicity lately, but fear gripped her throat. She thought of calling the police, but they'd probably laugh it off. Still, she double-checked all the windows and doors. Locked. She parted the kitchen curtains and peered out to check her vehicle. Damn, the spot light was out. Was that guy waiting for her in the dark? Why didn't she think to move her Jeep around front?

She was being ridiculous. Rita got her keys, her cell phone, and a huge flashlight out of her briefcase to slug someone if necessary. There was plenty of traffic going up and down Route 35 at this time of night as she exited the front door, wiggled the doorknob, and locked the deadbolt. Alarm on. Everything secure. She heard the phone start ringing again, four rings and silence. Then again, over and over. Could it be the same man? Should she go back in and pretend to be the answering service? If she didn't, the caller would know she had an answering machine, not a service. He'd know she'd lied to him.

She took a deep breath and hurried around the

building, willing herself to stay calm and shining her flashlight across the entire lot. No one hiding, nothing unusual. She pressed the remote key button once, yanked open the door, and slid in smoothly, punching the door lock button instantly. The satisfying "click" locked out all intruders, real ones or phantoms. No problem.

She had to get a grip. It must have been a prank call. No one was lying in wait for her, but she felt like a character in a B movie being watched, stalked. Her hands trembled as she started the ignition and pulled out of the driveway.

She had to get her mind off financial problems and weird people. On impulse, she stopped at the video store a few blocks away and searched the aisles for something funny, something heartwarming. That's what she needed to calm her shaky nerves. She finally narrowed it down to *You've Got Mail*, *Hope Floats*, and *Sleepless in Seattle*. *Big*, too. Three out of four Tom Hanks. Why couldn't she have married someone sensitive and dependable like Tom Hanks? Or the other guy who was loyal and good with his hands? Steady. Handsome. Someone to build a life with.

Which movie would help her forget the fear that had been creeping up her spine when the anonymous caller promised to keep in touch and used her name? Something with a happy ending that wouldn't make her too wistful for the relationship she'd never had.

A low voice behind her said, "Planning on staying up all night?"

Startled, Rita dropped all four videos and whirled around to see Mitch looming over her. "Jeesh, you scared me. What are you doing here?" They both bent to pick up the plastic cases and bumped heads.

"Well, I could lie and tell you I came in for a video, but I didn't. I was looking for you. When Liz came home to a dark house, she wondered where you were. There was no answer when she called you at the office and only voice mail on your cell phone. I spotted your Jeep on the way over. Is something wrong? You seem pretty jumpy. And overloaded with chick flicks."

"Chick flicks? Oh, let me guess," Rita closed her eyes and pretended to concentrate. "You mean a movie not set in a jungle, a prison, a police department, or the Wild West? And for your information, I'm not jumpy. You just startled me."

"Did anyone ever tell you you're a lousy liar, Rita? Your voice kind of goes up and your eyes look down. Look into my eyes and tell me you're not upset about something." Mitch handed her the videos and tilted her chin upwards.

Rita stared into Mitch's eyes and growled, "I can't. I'd be lying if I said that now because I am upset - at you, for popping up and scaring me, and trying to rescue me when I don't need rescuing. Back off! I don't need John Wayne, Rocky, or Rambo tonight!"

Mitch held up his hands in mock surrender. "Well, sorry, Little Missy. Here I am being sensitive and concerned about your safety, and you accuse me of being a macho bully." He paused in the middle of his John Wayne impression and continued when a slight smile appeared at the corner of Rita's mouth. "Seems to me you're jumping to conclusions, darlin'. I said 'chick flick' and you think I only like violent action movies. I bet I could pick out a Western that would have you bawling your eyes out, feeling all warm and fuzzy, and begging to watch it again."

Rita shook her head and grinned. "Nice try, JW, but I sincerely doubt it. And I bet you couldn't sit through one of my favorite movies without complaining and leaving early."

Mitch's eyes gleamed. "I smell victory. You're on.

We each pick one movie and watch them together. If you enjoy my movie, you owe me dinner."

"And if you aren't the least bit touched by the movie I pick out, you pay. But wait. This isn't fair. How will I know if you're being honest? I don't know when you're lying."

Mitch raised his hand to his forehead in a scout salute. "Former Eagle scout, darlin'. Cross my heart and hope to die." He finished with the familiar motions across his chest.

"Please, spare me. I can't take a lightning bolt right now. Hard day. Anyway, I'll get these and buy the popcorn. You get your movie, but I warn you. Nothing scary or you'll definitely lose!"

"And one more condition. When I win, Rita, you have to tell me the real reason why you're so jumpy."

"Mitch! Get your movie, and I'll meet you back at the ranch for dueling movies. I know my way home. I'm a big girl."

"Yeah, I noticed." He winked and headed for the Westerns. Rita rolled her eyes and hoped she wouldn't regret the challenge.

Rita paid for her rentals and left. She quickly unlocked the Jeep and slid in. As she was starting the engine, she noticed a coupon stuck under her windshield wiper. One of her pet peeves, but it looked familiar. "Serena's Body & Soul Gift Shop, 10% off a $50 order." Drawn on the back was a tiny smiley face like the ones she and Serena ended their notes with. "We'll talk again...sooner...or later," it read. It hadn't been there before. She would have noticed it. She looked at the other vehicles parked along the street. Hers was the only one with a paper stuck under the windshield wiper.

Was this Serena's idea of a joke? If so, Rita would have to have a long talk with her. She'd have to remember to ask Mitch about it, too. He'd come in after her. But if he'd seen anyone around her truck, wouldn't he have told her, done something? But who? Could it have been the prank caller referring to their brief conversation? Rita looked around and pushed the lock button on the door. No one in sight. She checked the rear-view mirror as she pulled out and drove away, but no one seemed to be following her.

Rita was glad Aunt Liz was home when she arrived. She'd been thinking that maybe the dueling movies hadn't been such a good idea. She hated to admit Mitch was right. She was nervous. She'd jumped at the chance of being with someone familiar instead of sitting alone in the dark with the remote. Mitch might take it the wrong way, unless Aunt Liz was around to chaperone. "Want to watch a couple movies tonight, Aunt Liz? I've got some good ones."

"No, thanks, dear. I want to get to bed early. I finished most of my packing except for a couple gowns I don't want to wrinkle. We have a busy day tomorrow. Mr. Santangelo expects us at nine to sign the power of attorney and that health paper, and go over a few points. Mr. Martino will go over the checkbook with you. Then we'll go to the banks and add your name to my accounts. He said the complicated things can wait until I get back next week."

"Good. It sounds like you've been busy. How was your talk with Tony after I left Jackson's?"

"Fine. He's offered to give me a good deal on a permanent place in his spa complex. Of course, the spa has more alive people than those assisted living places where you've got one foot on a shuffleboard court and the other one in a nursing home...or a grave. I told him thank you, but I want to keep my home."

"You told Tony about all this? Aunt Liz, I can't believe it! Why?"

"Well, not all the details. But he is in real estate

and knows a lot of things. Like taxes. He wasn't shocked at all at the cost of taxes nowadays. He said to ask him for help if I needed it when I find out exactly where everything stands next week."

"Aunt Liz. I wish you wouldn't tell him your business."

Mitch rapped on the screen door. "Okay if I come in?" Mitch called out.

"Of course, Mitch," Liz said. "I'm going to bed, but Rita wants some company for a movie, if you're interested."

"I know. That's why I'm here. I brought one of the world's best Westerns and a prison movie."

Rita groaned. "We have a little bet about movies, Aunt Liz. You could stay up and be the referee. We both trust you."

"Sorry, I'm too tired. You two have fun." And with that Liz smiled and took her hot tea toward her bedroom.

"What's the matter?" Mitch asked and wiggled his eyebrows. "Don't trust yourself alone with me watching a movie in the dark?"

"Oh, please. Give me a break. I thought she might want to spend time with us."

"So who don't you trust?"

"What do you mean?"

"Well, when I was at the door I heard you say to Liz she shouldn't tell someone her business. Do you mean me?"

"No. Not that I want her telling the whole world what we're up against. She mentioned something to Tony I wished she hadn't."

"What was that, if you don't mind me asking?"

"If I told you, then I'd be blabbing, too, wouldn't I? It's nothing we can't handle."

"Rita, I have nothing to gain from Liz having financial problems. It's the taxes isn't it?" Rita looked down and stuck out her bottom lip slightly.

"You're doing the eye thing again. Play poker with me someday. I'll clean up. Hmmm. How about strip poker?"

"Mitch, I don't want to discuss money now."

"Well, I do. Don't you think if Liz can't afford to stay in this house and pay the taxes I'd want to help? I sure don't want to look for another place to live, and I don't want her to give up this house. She loves it. She's lived here more than half her life. And I'd insist on paying rent, too."

"Really?" Rita looked wistful.

"Of course. I'll take on more jobs and charge some of those overpaid CEOs the going rate. That's all."

"That's sweet, Mitch, but I don't think she can charge you enough rent to do any good, even if you were able to pay it and you could force her to take it."

"I'll take care of Liz and the rent. She's proud, but she's sensible. I agree with you, though. She shouldn't tell Tony anything more about it."

"Well, he offered to help her, too. Kind of surprised me, but then Tony seems to be full of them."

"Yeah, and full of a lot more than surprises. So are snakes. You don't see the fangs when the cobra's dancing, but the venom's still there. Please, promise you'll come to me for help first, okay? You can trust me to take care of Liz's best interests. You must know that by now."

"Well, I'm hoping she and I can handle it ourselves, but I'll let you know if there's anything you can do. I'm compiling a list of her accounts as well as information about the balloon payment due this year and the reverse mortgage." Rita gestured toward the stack of folders on the roll top desk.

"Is that what she got herself into?"

"Darn. I'm so tired. I didn't mean to say that."

"Who am I going to tell? But I can help, and I won't tell Liz you slipped. Now pop the popcorn. My movie first."

"Mitch, it's getting kind of late, don't you think?"

"Six a.m. does come early, but let's make a deal. A half hour of each movie, and then we decide who's the winner, okay?" Rita nodded and headed for the kitchen.

As the bullet-like sounds of exploding popcorn started coming from the microwave, Rita came back out to the family room. "What do you want to..." she started to say, but stopped. She stared at Mitch standing by the desk flipping through the folders there. "What are you doing?"

Mitch shut the file he'd been studying. "Just looking. I've had some experience with balloon payments before. I can probably help if I know what the terms are, the exact language."

"Yeah, well, I came out here to ask you what you wanted to drink and I find you looking at Aunt Liz's personal stuff. It seems kind of...I don't know...nosy...inappropriate."

"Rita. I'm sorry if it looks like I'm snooping. If I wanted to be sneaky, you know I have free access here. I could have done this later or any time you're not around."

Rita stood silent, trying to decide what to say.

"Trust me, Rita. I have nothing to gain financially by Liz selling the house and everything I value to lose. Now let's take a break and watch the movies. Tomorrow's another day."

"Now you sound like Aunt Liz," Rita said and turned. "I'll get the popcorn. With tons of butter."

They sat on the couch with separate popcorn bowls. Rita didn't want to like Mitch's movie, but the scenery was breathtaking and she lost track of time. The story was about a loyal band of ex-Texas Rangers leading a cattle drive. When one of the men rescued the blonde prostitute from being raped by drunken outlaws, Rita tried to subtly wipe a tear from her eyes and sniffled. "Got you!" said Mitch. "Admit it. You're hooked."

"Well, it's better than I thought. I don't suppose you'd believe me if I told you I had something in my eye?"

"Besides tears? No. But if you don't really like it, tell me. You don't have to watch any more," he said as he hit the pause button.

"All right. You win. I need a tissue and I want to see what happens. But not tonight. You didn't warn me it was two videos. And remember, you have to watch the first part of mine or the deal's off. If you like mine, we're even and I don't owe you a thing."

"Or else we go to dinner twice. Now let's get the rules straight. I can't smirk, complain, or roll my eyes or you win."

"Right, and no sighing or bored yawning. And if you get even a little bit choked up, I win, you lose. Agreed?" She held out her hand for a shake. "It's with Tom Hanks and Meg Ryan."

"This should be a piece of cake. I actually like Tom Hanks. He's funny. And she's hot."

"This movie is partly based on one of my all-time favorites, *An Affair to Remember*, starring Cary Grant and Deborah Kerr."

"Never saw it."

"Well, I don't think anyone with a heart could resist *Sleepless in Seattle*. In fact, I should have known Kevin was a creep because he wouldn't even watch five minutes of it."

"Enough talk, especially about your ex. Roll it."

He watched Rita curl up on the sofa, cross her legs yoga-style, and clutch her pillow. "You're going to love this if you let yourself," she whispered as she patted his arm. "Want a pillow to hold?"

"Oh, yes please," Mitch said in a mock falsetto

voice. "Or maybe a teddy bear. Can we do each other's hair, too, or maybe our nails?"

Rita whacked him with the pillow and said, "You're going to lose if you keep up that condescending attitude! Now shut up and watch."

Mitch relaxed and admired Meg Ryan. The boyfriend was a real wuss. What did she see in him? Why would she even consider marrying such a wimp? A traditional Christmas reunion plot with dysfunctional family members. Everybody has some. Yeah, he could endure this movie and win.

He relaxed until Tom Hanks started talking about missing his wife who died. This was getting a bit too close to home. "The magic." When the character said it simultaneously with Meg Ryan, Mitch bit his lip and swallowed. His eyes started filling up with tears; his stomach was tense.

Mitch closed his eyes and remembered how he and Ginger had looked like the perfect couple, hosting elegant parties in their huge house decorated by slick strangers and filled with powerful executives and influential society members. People with perfect hair and designer clothes had networked with others and chatted about corporate deals, golf scores, and where to buy the best cigars. They sipped Louis IV cognac that cost more per bottle than his parents paid for their mortgage each month. He could picture Ginger smiling, looking like a model, adorned in jewelry from Tiffany's.

And suddenly Mitch felt cheated. He'd never had that magic, and never would. Yes, he was angry and sad about Ginger's drowning. His in-laws had blamed him because he'd been out of town, as if he could have stopped Ginger from drinking too much or swimming that night in a friend's pool and never coming home. He swallowed hard and a tear started to slip down his cheek.

"Are you all right, Mitch?" Rita asked as she

clicked the TV off with the remote.

"Yeah, yeah, I'm fine. I must be more tired than I thought." He shook his head. "I'm sorry. I can't watch any more right now. You win. Supper's on me." He started to get up, but Rita pulled him back down on the couch.

"Mitch, you're crying. What is it?"

"Oh, hell. I could tell you I got something in my eye, but you wouldn't buy that, would you?" He paused, clenching his fists and taking a deep breath. "And since I know your curiosity will be in overdrive until I explain, here goes." He swiped at the runaway tear.

"I was married and my wife died a couple years ago. Drowned, actually. No one's fault but hers. She could swim, but she'd had more to drink than she should have. I was away that weekend and didn't have a chance to save her, to even say good-bye. And that's that. End of story."

"Mitch, I'm so sorry." Rita moved closer on the couch and put her arm around his shoulder. "I feel so awful picking a movie with a widower dealing with his grief. I had no idea. I assumed either you never were married, or maybe got divorced. But a widower? You must have loved her very much."

Mitch clutched his hands together. "You know, that's the saddest part. I thought we loved each other at first. Got married against her family's wishes. But over the years I became more of what I thought she wanted me to be, and we grew apart. Too busy doing things, going places, meeting people. She was twelve years younger and insisted on putting off having kids. Whatever magic we had vanished. We'd both been too busy to notice how far we'd drifted apart. After she died, the void seemed bigger, full of unspoken words. She'd slipped away years before and I hadn't noticed. Maybe we didn't even know each other at all."

Mitch leaned forward and propped his head on his hands. "God, I don't know why I told you all that. I never talk about this to anyone. Not even to Liz. My guess is Liz thinks I arrived here brooding with a broken heart, but I think it was more of an empty heart, wondering where the magic had gone. I needed to be alone to try to figure out what went wrong, to start living my life differently."

Mitch looked at Rita. Her eyes were shimmering with tears that overflowed down her cheeks. "You know your chin quivers when you cry? And you get this pathetic but cute scrunched-up expression on your face. Kind of like my little sister's."

"I can't help it. What you just said was so sad, so touching." Rita sniffed and swallowed loudly.

Mitch wiped under his eyes with his knuckles and shook his head. "Now see what these chick movies do? There should be some kind of warning label on them from the Surgeon General or something. You know, like, 'Watching this movie can be hazardous to your mental health. May cause true confessions and uncontrolled weeping. Follow by a comedy or a James Bond movie and call me in the morning.' What do you think?"

He patted her leg and got up. "Well, enough catharsis. Big word for a carpenter, huh? I've got a lot to do tomorrow. And so do you. No time for being mushy, right?"

Rita nodded her head. "Agreed. No mushiness. I'm going to focus on making more money, and I'm going to help Aunt Liz get out of the hole she's gotten herself into. She deserves the best, including some fun on the cruise." Rita got up and followed Mitch toward the door.

"Thank you, Mitch."

"For what?"

"Sharing. And if you ever need to talk, I'm here to listen." She gave him a big hug and stepped back quickly.

Mitch took both of her hands in his and managed a small smile. "Hey, maybe we should watch chick movies all the time."

"Go home, Mitch, before I hit you with another pillow."

"Good night, Rita, and please don't worry. About anything. Not me, not Liz. Nothing. I have some things to take care of out of town for a day or two. I'll say goodbye to Liz tomorrow. You okay seeing her off the next day?"

"Sure." Rita nodded, feeling suddenly awkward as she stood by the door. "Good night."

"Yeah, sweet dreams. Lock the door. And go to bed. No more sentimental movies and tears, okay?"

"You either, big guy."

"And promise me, no mention of my alleged tears to anyone, especially Serena."

Rita paused. "Your secret's safe with me. She wouldn't believe me anyway." She grinned and waved before closing the door.

As she climbed the stairs, Rita remembered Mitch hadn't asked her about what had made her jumpy. And she'd forgotten to ask him about the note on the windshield. Should she phone him and tell him about the creepy call? Maybe she'd tell him before he left in the morning.

Chapter Nineteen

In the morning, Mitch's truck was gone before Rita came down for breakfast. She read the impersonal Post-it note he'd stuck on the refrigerator. "R—Business out of town till Friday night. Please take movies back. Finish another time. M" It sounded like a telegram. After he'd opened up last night about his past, couldn't he have waited to talk to her face-to-face before he drove off? Or at least written his whole name?

A big sign next to the tiny yellow note announced in his neat block printing, "Bye Liz! Get lucky!" next to a rough sketch of a ship, and an ace with a jack of hearts. Aunt Liz grinned and shook her head. "That boy! I thought he might see us off at the dock when we sail, but I forgot to ask. Could you take us to the ship tomorrow morning, dear?"

"Of course." Rita didn't mention the appointments she'd have to reschedule. She grabbed her cell phone and slid it into her tote bag. "I have to get you one of these, Aunt Liz. You might need one in an emergency, especially walking on the beach by yourself."

"Don't waste your money, Rita. I don't need another gadget to figure out. Something that rings in the middle of the supermarket or church service? No thank you! I'd rather use a pay phone if I'm not home."

"But Aunt Liz. Think of how much safer you'd feel..."

"I know you mean well, dear, but please. No more lectures about cell phones. They're annoying."

Liz cleared the table and loaded the dishwasher. "Besides, we have more important things to do. First stop, the lawyer's office to sign papers, then the accountant. I'll do my shopping with Helen later so I don't take up your whole day. Call me when you're ready." She breezed out of the kitchen before Rita could continue.

****

A few hours later, Rita eased her aunt's sedan into a parking space right in front of the lawyer's office. "Careful opening your door," Aunt Liz joked. "Don't want that new Jaguar paint on my classic Crown Vic."

Inside, they refused gourmet coffee and signed the power of attorney and health care surrogate documents spread out on a huge conference table under the watchful eyes of Mr. Santangelo and two paralegals he'd summoned as witnesses. "Mrs. Chandler, you can rest easy now, knowing Rita can act on your behalf and according to your wishes in case you're ever incapacitated." He paused as his employees whisked the paperwork away to copy. "And let me reassure you we'll do our best to avoid having you move unless you want to."

Liz sighed and relaxed her shoulders. Rita remained unconvinced, especially when he added, "There seems to be a minor problem with the bank that financed one of your loans, and the wording on the note could have been more advantageous to your interests, but don't worry. We'll complete and review the rest of the documents next week." He shook her hand and ushered them to the door. "Have a great trip!" he added.

Next stop the accountant. His receptionist set up an appointment for them to go over the records and recommendations the following week, and Rita and Liz were back home in less than an hour. Liz showed Rita where her important papers were stashed in a metal box in the closet and slipped the new documents inside before driving off to meet her friend.

Rita wished she felt as optimistic as Liz was acting. It was early, but maybe Mitch had some answers by now. She checked her cell phone for messages but there were none. Should she call him? What would she say? "Missed seeing you this morning?" It was true, but she wouldn't tell him. And he probably didn't want to hear it, anyway.

She remembered her new mantra, "Focus on work," as she drove to her office. Once she got there, she checked her messages and rescheduled Friday's appointments so she could drive Liz and Helen to the port in Bayonne before lunch and get back in time to avoid losing any income. Much to her relief, there was nothing on her answering machine from that prank caller.

But Mitch still hadn't contacted her. Was he too busy to touch base, or had he decided to reestablish some distance after last night? Rita was still amazed he was a widower. That he'd actually had tears in his eyes when he'd told her. Maybe he was embarrassed about it now.

Rita shook her head and returned to her paperwork. No sense wasting time or energy trying to figure out answers to impossible questions when she had a full schedule. "Focus on work!" she mumbled. To do that, she'd have to forget how good Mitch's hug had felt as well as her urge to erase the pain in his eyes and kiss away his tears.

That evening when she went home for dinner, Aunt Liz said he'd called and said, "Hello." *Only hello*? Rita sat alone on the deck, her cell phone in her hand, and watched the fireflies for a while before heading upstairs. She finally went to sleep, wanting more.

****

The next morning, northbound traffic on the Parkway and Turnpike was light for a Friday, and everything went smoothly at the dock. Only ticketed passengers were allowed to board the cruise ship, so after exchanging hugs with her aunt and Helen, Rita waved and headed back home.

"You're booked solid from noon on, honey," Serena called out as Rita arrived at the shop. "Help yourself to a pita with tuna if you think you have time to wolf it down."

Rita returned from the kitchen and sat down with her sandwich. "Thanks, Serena. I know I should be happy to be so busy and making more money, but right now I feel like a worn-out hamster running nowhere on a little wheel."

Serena laughed. "Yeah, especially when you planned to take the summer off. But no use crying over spilled vacations, right? And speaking of vacations, how did the 'bon voyage' go with Liz and her friend?"

"Wonderful. She gave me a quick hug and told me to be careful before Helen whisked her away. They'll have a great time. She deserves to get away from this money problem for a while."

"Well, you should take a break from worrying, too. You and I are a great team. Business is up for both of us. In fact, our next two clients are double-deckers."

"What?"

"They're friends. Each one is getting a massage from you and a tarot reading from me. Good thing Kelly's here to help out with customers now that you're booked and I'm doing readings." Serena nodded her head toward the storeroom and lowered her voice. "She's a little flaky but..."

Rita laughed. "Sorry, Serena, but that's a scary statement coming from a self-proclaimed Goddess like you who sees the future in everything from feathers on the beach to the stars in the sky. And we're not counting your assorted bags of runes and decks of tarot cards."

"I am offended," Serena said, pretending to look hurt. "You insult my character."

"Serena, I love you dearly, but you know you're a bit left of what the world considers normal."

"Thanks for the compliment, Rita. Now stop interrupting! As I was saying, Kelly may seem to be a bit of an 'airhead' as Mitch would say, but she caught on real quick with the cash register."

"That's hardly higher level math, Serena. The machine tells you in neon green numbers how much change to give."

"All right, but she's eager to learn. And she pops up instantly from the kitchen or back room to help out with customers when I ring this handy bell. Watch."

Serena paused to pound a silver hotel desk bell. Kelly appeared through the beads and smiled at both of them. "What's up?"

"Can you take over out here, Kelly?" Serena said to the thin blond teenager. "It's almost time for my reading."

"Sure thing. Back in a sec," Kelly added and vanished.

Serena whispered to Rita, "Power. Don't you just love it? All for minimum wage and a free room near a beach."

Rita was about to make a smart comment under her breath when the front door opened. Two women in batik print sundresses floated in. One headed for Serena and hugged her. "I felt so incredible after last week's reading and massage I insisted my friend Miranda here simply had to come. She's going through a difficult time...aren't we all, and she's dying to have her cards read."

The woman released Serena and headed for

Rita, arms open for another bear hug. "And you are a miracle worker, Rita! My back hasn't felt this good in years. I may have to move you up to North Jersey after Labor Day or drive down weekends for appointments during the fall."

Kelly took over the gift shop and Rita proceeded with massages, conversations, and referring clients to Serena to buy certain products. At last it was five o'clock, and Rita scanned the appointment book she kept near the gift shop telephone. A half hour to eat and then three house call entries. She wouldn't be done until ten if traffic were bad.

"I wish I could go home right now, but at double my usual rate per session, I can't refuse these house calls," she said to Serena who was busy emptying the cash register and counting money aloud. "Serena, do you know these people personally? I'm not setting foot in someone's house unless I know they're normal."

Serena paused to slip a money wrapper around a bundle of fives. "Well, I don't know how normal any of us is, but I think they're fine. The first one is that old lady who won the gift certificate from the Chinese Auction. She doesn't go anywhere except church and the doctor's office, so she's all excited you're coming. The next one is a referral from Mrs. Curtis, you know, one of those blue-hairs in the garden club? It's a present for one of her relatives who's never had a massage in his life.

"Damn! I messed up." Serena paused to recount the singles. "Oh, the last appointment is for Winslow. Never met him, but he's a big shot builder who's always getting community awards. On the hospital board and donating money to Boy Scouts and the homeless. It's some kind of surprise gift. I forget what the occasion is." She slid the bundles of paper money and rolled coins into a cash box, and left the cash register drawer empty and open.

"Hey, Rita, do you want me to come over later and spend the night? You know how Liz worries about you."

"Thanks, 'Mom,' but I might be too tired to be good company. I promise I'll be alert enough to lock the doors and windows, but I'll be fine alone. Probably get more sleep. Mitch is supposed to be back tonight anyway, so if I need help, he's only a scream away."

Serena closed her eyes and put her free hand on her forehead. "Mmmm. I'm sensing a vision. You alone with Mitch. 'A scream away.' Could we be talking screams of passion with a good-looking, available man? How's that for a fantasy?" Serena teased. "Could that be in your future?"

Rita felt her face turning red. "Will you stop? I admit he's attractive, but I'm focusing on the reality of solving Aunt Liz's house problem, not fantasies. And speaking of reality, I'd better get going. I'm making a copy of these addresses and phone numbers to take with me. I'll leave my appointment book here in case you get any calls for me or need to reach me."

"Suit yourself. See you tomorrow. And be careful!" Serena grinned. "I had to say it. Liz made me promise to take over her mother hen routine while she was gone. Call me if you change your mind about tonight. Or don't, if you're lucky enough to be living a fantasy."

****

A few hours later, Rita slid her massage table back into the Jeep after the second appointment. She remembered why she'd given up home visits. Double the money, but double the work and lifting. And it was harder to set the right mood, too.

Still it was already worth the effort. Rita had acquired two new regular clients. The second one had been embarrassed at disrobing down to his boxers, but he, too, had ended up giving her an extra tip after thanking his wife for the surprise birthday gift.

Almost eight-thirty. Two down, one to go. Her stomach was rumbling, but she'd be late if she took the time to get some fast food. She'd have to wait. Her final appointment was only a few blocks away in Winslow Walk, a new development of Victorian and modern homes crammed together on the last stretch of private beachfront lots in Point Pleasant Beach. Expensive and sold out. Most of the houses were empty with construction debris waiting to be cleaned up or landscaping being finished. A few had curtains and lights in the windows. It wouldn't be long before the entire block would be filled with neighbors. Potential clients if tonight went well.

A couple of SUVs and a Cadillac were parked at the end of the cul-de-sac. Number Seventy-two, lights on, landscaping done. This must be the place. "Winslow" was etched and painted in gold leaf on a small plaque near a fountain in a Japanese garden. So this was the new home of Garrett Winslow, the wealthy developer often featured on the society page donating money to worthy causes. From the looks of this house, he could afford her at-home visit rates.

She parked in the driveway and unloaded again. Massage table, boom box with meditation music, and her bag of goodies—sheets, oils, candles, timer. She knew she should start making two trips instead of one, or she'd be the one who needed a back rub. She could get home at close to ten if she hurried.

Rita leaned her things against the massive urns filled with geraniums at the entrance and pressed the doorbell. Subtle chimes toned from inside along with the pounding beat of rock music. Strange choice of music for an older man. Did he still have teenagers at home?

She pressed the button again. Maybe no one

could hear the doorbell above the music. Though she hated to lose a potential client, especially an important one, she was tempted to leave. She tried the number on her cell phone but there was no answer, only a generic recording asking the caller to leave a message after the beep.

Rita disconnected and rehearsed what she would say before dialing again. "Shore Therapeutic Massage calling. I am at Seventy-two Albert Street at 8:40 p.m. Friday evening, but no one is answering the door. If you had cancelled before my trip out here, your money would have been automatically refunded or your appointment rescheduled. Please contact my office to discuss this matter and reschedule. Thank you."

Rita snapped her cell phone shut and was halfway back to the Jeep when a male voice behind her called out, "Hey, wait. Are you the massage girl?"

Rita stopped and turned to stare at the young man rushing toward her. "If you mean, am I the massage *therapist* from Shore Therapeutic Massage, the answer's yes. I *never* call myself a massage girl."

"Oh, sorry. I guess you wouldn't, not in your line of work." He stuck out his hand to shake hers. "I'm Jim. I'll help you with the table," he added. He grabbed it from her and headed toward the house. "Come on, the party's getting started. You're first."

"Hold it. I'm not here for a party. Isn't this the Winslow booking? An hour massage present for Garrett Winslow?" She studied him a moment. Well-groomed, even preppy-looking in Dockers and a shirt with a buttoned-down collar.

"This is the place. And you're right. It's not really a party. Kind of a house-warming gift for a friend who's getting married. Some of his business associates and friends decided to surprise him with something different. The party's later at Atlantic

City. Oh, the person who recommended you said to tell you Serena said you're the best in the area."

"Serena said that? You know her?"

"Well, not personally, but she books your appointments, doesn't she?"

"Well, yes, but I've had a long day and frankly, I'm not in the mood for surprises. It's late. Have Mr. Winslow stop by or call to book another full hour appointment, okay? Right now, he'll only get forty-five minutes if he's lucky, and the clock is ticking." Rita reached for the carrying handle of her massage table when Jim put it down near the door against an urn of geraniums.

"No, wait. Don't go. I'm sorry about the delay. The music's a little loud and we didn't hear you ring the bell right away. Just give him a shorter massage? If you don't come in, it'll spoil our surprise." He reached into his wallet and pulled out a fifty. "Here's a bonus to make up for the annoyance. How about it?"

Rita sighed. "Well, all right. I don't want to disappoint Mr. Winslow. Do you have a private room where I can set up my table and things? I don't do massages in a roomful of people, you know. And it's more soothing if it's quiet and dark, so could you turn down the rock music?"

"Sure thing." Jim held the door open for Rita. "Go into the family room on the left. I'll bring your table." He clicked the deadbolt and followed her in with her table. "The air-conditioning's on, but we started one of those logs in the fireplace. Mood, you know. Nothing's too good for our boy. Need help setting up?"

"No, it's easy. I'll be ready in a few minutes so you can go get him."

"Be right back," Jim said, and disappeared.

Rita quickly set up the table, plugged in the boom box, and popped in a CD. Ocean waves and flute music. Perfect for the shore. She remembered to put her cell phone on vibrate, then placed and lit a few candles on the mantel. With some finishing touches, the room looked as if it could be featured on one of those decorating shows on cable TV about lives of the rich and famous. Expensive leather couches, mahogany bar, a couple of Llardo sculptures, but no art work on the walls yet. The entertainment center had a space for a wide-screen TV.

"Hey, soft music, candlelight, a beautiful woman," a low voice spoke from the hallway. "I think I died and went to heaven!" Rita turned to see a man dressed in a burgundy bathrobe leaning against the double doors. He was tanned with thinning dark hair; he looked younger than she'd expected from the newspaper photo Serena had pointed to. He smiled and moved closer.

"Surprise!" three baritone voices shouted behind him. The one named Jim patted him on the back. "She's all yours. We figured you needed a little stress relief before the wedding, a last fling."

"Can we watch?" one of the guys yelled. The others laughed.

"Can I be second?"

"How about a fivesome? She's small but she looks like she could handle us."

Rita hesitated and scanned the room for her bag and cell phone. They were on the couch behind her. "Listen, guys, if you're not joking, you have the wrong idea about massage therapy. And definitely the wrong person. Let me clear up any misunderstanding right now."

"Easy, now," the man said in a soothing voice. "They're only kidding, but I understand completely. Massage is very therapeutic. It's good for both of us, right? You give massages and you get money. You give a little more for a house call and we both get a lot more."

Rita backed up and started casually packing her bag. "Listen, Mr. Winslow. I am a licensed massage therapist, not a sex therapist or a hooker, or whatever else you had in mind. I'm sorry if someone gave you the wrong impression, but I only give *massages*, and not on private parts. The house call costs more for the client's convenience and my extra time and effort, not for anything else your buddies thought they were hiring me for."

"Hold, it honey. Lighten up." He put up a hand in mock surrender, almost spilling his glass of wine in the other. "I get the message. No harm done. But seeing as how you're here and looking for extra cash, maybe you'd like to reconsider. How about a little harmless dancing instead? You dance, don't you? Nice slow dance? Maybe get a little more comfortable yourself?"

"Sorry, no dance, no massage. It's late." Rita pressed the "Stop" button on her player, ripped the sheets off the table, and shoved them in her bag. She reached inside and grabbed her cell phone and keys. She slid them into her skirt pocket.

"I know," he continued and held out his glass of wine. "How about some vino? You look like you need a little stress relief yourself." He motioned to his friends. "Go get a glass for the lady, guys. We'll have a little drink." He put his glass on a table and turned his attention back to Rita. "We'll toast to my upcoming wedding and then you give me that massage you were talking about. Strictly a massage, okay? Hey, fellas," he said as he turned to the others, "How about a little privacy for the lady therapist and me, okay? You can see you've upset her."

Rita saw the man wink in the mirror across the room as he strode over to his friends. He grabbed a bottle of champagne and a glass from one of them, shoved them out into the hallway, and shut the double doors.

"Oh, sure, Phil. Have a nice massage. We'll be in the other room."

"Phil?" Rita asked. "Aren't you Garrett Winslow?"

"Who me? No, he's the guy who owns this place. Moving in next week. One of my friends here kind of borrowed the key, and his name."

Rita quickly punched in Mitch's number on her cell phone. Thank God, she'd programmed it. But how could he help her if he didn't know where she was? He might still be out of town. She pressed the button to end the call and selected Serena's number. Pick up, pick up. Fourth ring and the message beep prompt came on. Rita lifted the phone to her mouth and blurted out, "Serena, I'm at the last place, Winslow's, and I need help..." Phil crossed the room in seconds, ripped the phone out of her hand, and tossed it to the ground.

"Come on, honey, just a little dance," Phil took her hand and kissed it. Chills crept up Rita's spine and she yanked her hand away. "The guys don't have to know we only danced. Stay a half hour with me. You might enjoy yourself." With that, he opened his bathrobe with both hands and smiled. He had nothing on underneath.

Chapter Twenty

Rita froze. This could not be happening to her. When the man moved closer, she sprung into action.

"No way, Buddy. I'm out of here!" Rita swung her bag and whacked him in the head. He fell onto the sofa and she bolted to the doors. Before she could open one, he lunged and pinned her against it.

"Not so fast, honey." He held her arms as he pressed his body close against her, rotating his hips and whispering into her ear, his breath heavy with wine and garlic. "I would never force myself on a woman—I don't have to. How about getting out those massage oils again? I guarantee I can make you very happy. I'll do you whatever way you like."

"Never!" Rita yelled. "Help!" she screamed and fought to break free.

Phil grinned. "Scream all you want. There's no one in the neighborhood to hear. Just my buddies and me and the ocean. Your boss told my pals you like it rough. Like to act all prim and proper like you don't want it, but you do. He said you'd play along. Saying no is part of the fun, right?"

Rita forced herself to relax and endure him nuzzling her neck. His hands slid down her arms and took her hands. "That's better, honey. Let's move over to your table and try out a more comfortable position." He started to lead her away.

She smiled and said coyly, "Oh, I've got a special position for you." She yanked him toward her, kneed him in the groin, and pushed him to the floor. He doubled over in pain, and she pulled the door open.

"You'll pay for that!" he groaned.

Suddenly there was pounding on the front door. "Rita? Is that you?" It was Mitch's voice.

"Yes, help me!" she yelled.

The man grabbed Rita from behind and flung her back into the room, smashing her into the sofa. "Is that your pimp?"

"I'm not a hooker!" Rita cried.

Two of his friends rushed in and scooped up the champagne bottle and plastic glasses. "Hey! Let's get out the back before that guy crashes down the door or someone calls the cops. We've got your clothes. Get dressed in the truck. Come on!" Rita heard the thudding of their footsteps grow fainter.

"Hey, Jim! Come on down!" one yelled. "Hurry up! Out the back. We got all our stuff. Meet you at the casino." A door slammed.

The pounding on the front door stopped. Rita heard the sound of glass shattering and got to the hallway in time to see an arm reach through the broken sidelight and unlock the deadbolt.

Mitch embraced her in a hug. "Are you hurt?" Truck engines revved outside and tires squealed. "I'm gonna get those bastards." Mitch pulled away.

Rita hugged him tighter and fought back sobs. "Don't leave me. One of them is still in the house. There were four altogether. They thought I was a hooker. They said they knew Serena. And something about my boss. I should have known better. I should have listened to my instincts. Why do I keep trusting the wrong people?"

Suddenly at the end of the hallway toward the kitchen, a new noise began, the hum of some kind of machinery.

"Stay here, Rita." Mitch whispered. "It's an elevator. I'll see who steps off." He walked toward the back of the house and waited for the door to open. A bell rang, the doors opened, and he disappeared inside.

A great thundering of footsteps filled the foyer as Jim ran down the curving staircase and headed out the front door. Mitch swore and took off in pursuit, returning in a few minutes pushing a slightly bruised Jim with his arm bent behind his back.

"I swear, man, I didn't lay a hand on her. I didn't arrange this."

"Yeah, then who did?" Mitch growled.

"Phil's buddy Nick works construction. He knew where the key to this place was hidden outside and offered to let us use it for a little bachelor party before we headed to Atlantic City. We thought she was a hooker. You know how some of them call themselves massage therapists to look legit?" He glanced at Rita with frightened eyes. "Tell him I didn't hurt you, lady."

"You lied to me," Rita said in a shaky voice. "You said you knew Serena."

"I said Serena said you were the best. That's what our contact told us to say."

Mitch leaned closer and tightened his arm a little. "And who was your contact to get a 'hooker?' "

"I don't know," Jim blurted out. "Nick took care of it. Someone overheard him talking in a local club about wanting to get a little action for a friend before his wedding. He got a call later at the bar from a guy who ran a massage business offering extras on the side for a few hundred bucks. Nick made out a check to Serena Starr for a one-hour 'massage' and left it with the bartender. We got the time and place and said we'd pay the rest when she did her thing. I don't know anything else."

"You gave money to a guy you've never seen before?"

"*I* didn't. I wasn't there, but Nick's check was dated for next Tuesday. If we didn't get satisfaction, we'd stop payment."

"What's the name of the bar?" Mitch clenched his jaw and tightened his grip on Jim's arm.

"I don't know. Some joint in Seaside on the boardwalk."

Mitch turned to Rita. "Call the cops. Maybe it would improve this boy's memory."

Jim's face was ashen. "Listen, I've never been in trouble with the law, not even a parking ticket. Nobody and nothing was supposed to get hurt. It was only a little fun before the wedding, you know? Listen, can we make a deal? Don't call the cops and I'll pay for the broken window. You two take care of it, but don't give anybody my name. My wife would kill me. I'd lose my job. I don't even know this Garrett Winslow, but I'm sure some rich guy like that would press charges. Trespassing. Arranging a hooker. I can't believe I'm the one who got caught and it wasn't even my idea." Sweat was pouring down his face and his chin was quivering. He looked like he was going to cry.

Mitch eased his grip slightly and paused. "Winslow's a big developer, a contractor himself. He only buys the best. Replacing that fancy window will cost almost three grand." Mitch paused. "I know. I'm in construction myself. I could call Winslow and fix it, but why should I? And how would you pay for it? Pocket change?"

"I'll give it to you right now. I have the cash we were gonna blow in Atlantic City later tonight. Please, give me a break," Jim pleaded. "Let me go. I've had it with those guys."

Mitch glanced at Rita. "Well, Rita? Want to call the cops and press charges, or give this guy a break? Your call."

Rita sighed. "Mitch, I hate to see him to get away with it, but I really want to go home. I don't need any rotten publicity, either. Can you fix it so we won't get in trouble with the police ourselves? Or with the owner?"

"I can call Winslow from here. He knows me from a custom staircase I did on one of his construction jobs. If I've already got enough cash in my hand to fix it, he might prefer not involving the police and his insurance company, too. Any other objections to giving this slime bucket a second chance?"

"What's to stop him from doing this to someone else?" She turned to Jim, tears rolling down her face. "You seemed like such a nice young man. How could you do this?"

"I swear, lady, I'll never go along with something like this again. Please don't call the cops." His voice cracked as if he were a junior high kid facing suspension from school.

Rita nodded to Mitch and flopped down on the sofa.

"Okay, Jim," Mitch said. "You got a reprieve. Hand over your wallet nice and easy." Mitch took out a wad of bills and counted out three thousand dollars in hundreds.

"This should cover the temporary repair and replacing the custom sidelight. Smarten up and spend time with your family, not boozing with your so-called buddies. Those dirt bags left you behind to face the music by yourself."

Mitch flipped open his cell phone. "Pray Winslow answers and agrees to let you slide, too." He selected a number from his contact list and hit the send button. "Mr. Winslow? Mitch here...Yeah, from that Bayhead job...Thanks, sir. Sorry to bother you at this time, but it's important." Mitch explained the situation briefly and nodded after a few minutes. "That's fine, sir. I'll take care of it."

Mitch snapped the phone shut. "Well, Jim. You're in luck. He agreed. Said to have you sign a statement saying you and your friends are responsible for the accident and the repair costs. Got a piece of paper, Rita?" She ripped a sheet from her planner and handed it to him. Mitch scribbled a few sentences. "It mentions the three grand already received. Here, sign and date it, Jim."

The young man grabbed the pen, scanned the paragraph, and reluctantly signed.

Mitch handed the wallet back but kept Jim's license. "I'm keeping this for future reference, so drive slow. Believe me, if I get into trouble over this, you'll deal with me, Winslow, and the cops. If everything's okay, I'll mail this to you. Now get going. And don't ever show your face around here again." Before Jim drove away, Mitch took a cell phone picture of him by his truck and jotted down the license plate number.

Rita murmured. "I want to go home, Mitch. Will you drive?"

"Sure, but I'm calling Serena first and I promised Winslow I'd board up the place. Can't leave the house open like this, and I don't want to get arrested if the cops happen to drop in. He'll stop by soon with a locksmith."

After a few minutes, Mitch returned from the garage with a piece of plywood and covered the opening where the stained glass panel had been. "Perfect fit! Winslow's meeting me tomorrow to take care of the details of ordering and replacing the custom sidelight. He called the cops and told them he's aware of the broken window and my truck parked here overnight. Now let's get you home. You look faint."

Mitch loaded Rita's things into the back of her Jeep. "I'll get my truck tomorrow." Rita climbed into the passenger seat. Mitch slid into the driver's seat and turned to her. "Please say something. You're too quiet. Are you all right?"

"Yes, I'm okay, Mitch, thanks to you. I hate to

think of what would have happened if you hadn't come. How did you know where I was? And how did you get here so fast?"

"Well, I got back earlier than I expected and something felt wrong. The house was dark and I thought you'd be home by at least eight or you'd call me. So I phoned Serena and asked her to tell me where I might find you. You know I don't like the idea of you going to private homes, so I made her open the shop and read off the addresses and phone numbers. When she got to the last one, I knew Garrett Winslow hadn't gotten a certificate of occupancy to move into his new home yet, and his wife wouldn't let anyone in her house when she wasn't around. Besides, Serena said she hadn't booked that one. Maybe Kelly had. When you didn't answer your cell, I headed right over. I was almost here when my phone rang twice and stopped. I saw your number on the display and, let's just say, I'm lucky I didn't get a speeding ticket."

"But why would anyone send me to strangers wanting a hooker? That's really sick!"

"A real scumbug. Who hates you this much? Any enemies? Rivals?" Mitch asked.

"Well, the only one who hurt me that much was my ex-husband. But I don't even know where he is anymore. Last I heard he was hitting the tables at Vegas with a rich older woman. But what would he have to gain? I already paid off all his debts. No alimony to get rid of. No kids, no custody battle. I don't know. I changed my will immediately. I don't think I have any life insurance. When I was married, I was always overinsured. One of the downsides of having a husband who's an insurance broker. But I canceled all the policies. At least the ones I knew about."

"Whoever did this is someone who knows you and set you up. If Kelly wrote the appointment down, either she was in on it or she screwed up. She strikes me as kind of flighty, almost like she's been inhaling something stronger than incense. Didn't she know your 'no stranger' rules for home visits?"

"I thought so, but maybe I didn't explain it well enough. She's easily distracted, but too sweet to set me up for anything this rotten. Of course, I'm not exactly an expert on trusting the right people. I thought Jim was a nice guy."

Rita drummed her fingers on the door handle as Mitch neared the final traffic light near home. "You know, Mitch, I'm tired of thinking about the whole thing. I'm so grateful you showed up when you did."

"So am I. After my phone rang twice, then cut off, Serena called me. She said you'd sounded terrified and begged for help on your message before you got disconnected."

"Mitch, I tried to act cool and collected, but I was so scared." She held out her hand. "Look, I'm shaking. I shouldn't have let my guard down. This never would have happened to me when I worked in AC. I knew better than to trust anyone there. But here?"

Mitch reached over and clasped Rita's trembling hand, gave it a small squeeze, and rested it on the seat. "Forget about extra money for now, Rita. It's not worth it. You and Liz will be fine." He released her fingers and turned into their driveway. He shut off the engine and rolled up the windows. "We'll get your things out of the Jeep in the morning."

Mitch came around to the passenger side and helped her out. He rubbed her shoulders and guided her inside. "You're home, safe and sound, kid. And I'm making you a cup of tea."

"Mitch, you don't have to. I'm okay."

"Then why are you still shaking?"

"Well, I didn't eat dinner. Rushing around didn't help. And the whole thing with that horrid man…"

Mitch scooped her up and carried her outside to the back deck. "No arguments. Lie down. Listen to the ocean. I'll be right back with tea and something to eat. I reached Serena before we left Winslow's house and told her you're okay. She wants you to call back. Do you want to talk to her or should I tell her you're tired and need some food and sleep?"

"Mitch, would you call her and tell her I don't want to go over it again right now? We'll figure out what caused the mix-up tomorrow." Rita slumped into the lounge and took some deep breaths of sea air. She wished she could really relax. She kept seeing the man advancing in his bathrobe, leering. The laughter of the others.

She needed a drink. That's what Aunt Liz would give her if she were here. A shot of brandy. She went to the cabinet in the living room and took out Uncle Carlton's dusty decanter of Remy and filled a snifter. She held the base in her palm and swirled it the way she'd remembered her uncle had done every Sunday after a big dinner. Even Liz had given her a brandy the night she'd come home when Kevin had left for good. She gulped it down and winced at the fire trail. After the initial shock and shaking her head at the strength of it, she felt the warmth spreading through her. She exhaled slowly and took the decanter with her outside. Yes, that's what she needed. A little help relaxing.

She poured herself another as Mitch came out. "Hey, what's this? Since when do you drink brandy? Do you know how strong that stuff is?"

"Yes, Aunt Liz and I have one once in a while. You know, it's great for special occasions, like toasting birthdays, getting dumped by your husband, getting mistaken for a hooker. And you know, it's working. I feel better already. Look, my hand stopped shaking." Rita held her arm out, steady for the first time since the incident.

"Well, eat this and drink the tea. It's not good to drink hard liquor on an empty stomach." He gave her a plate with a grilled cheese sandwich and set a bowl of tomato soup on the table near the chaise lounge. He lit a citronella candle.

"Oh, Mitch. Nobody's made me a grilled cheese sandwich in years. And you cut it into four tiny triangles like my mom did when I was little." Her eyes started to water and she gulped the rest of her second brandy, shaking her head. "Wow, this stuff really has a kick, but once you get past the fire trail of the swallowing part, you feel all smooth and cozy inside."

"Hey, no more booze for you, kid," Mitch said and grabbed the decanter. "Getting all weepy over a sandwich? You're over your limit already. Now eat up while I get my plate or you'll end up with a big hangover. Don't wait for me. Nothing worse than a blob of cold, congealed American cheese." Rita pouted but complied, though she did down another quick gulp from the bottle. When he returned, they ate in silence, listening to the waves break on the beach, just being together in the dark.

"This is nice," Rita said when she finished eating and savored her tea. "Thank you, Mitch."

"You can stop thanking me. You know I'm glad to help. Wait till I find out who set you up with those no-good scumbags."

"Hey, we weren't going to talk about it anymore, remember?" Rita put her plate and cup on the end table with some difficulty. She started to get up, but lost her balance. Mitch lunged to steady her, but she fell forward into his arms and pushed him back on his lounge chair.

"Are you all right?"

"Sorry. I guess I got up too fast," Rita stammered as she squirmed on top of Mitch, trying in vain to push herself off a cushion or an arm rest.

"I'd say it was too much brandy, not too fast," Mitch muttered. "And stop poking me. Hold still before you hurt me."

Rita melted into his body. She wriggled up a little, inhaling his scent, soap and man, his T-shirt soft against her face. "You know, Mitch, you smell really good. Did anyone ever tell you that?" She raised her head to see his face in the moonlight.

"Not lately. And you're not staying very still. You've had too much to drink and you don't know what you're doing to me." He rotated his hips against hers, easing the sudden pressure in his jeans. "You'd better stop moving around on top of me. I'm only human, you know, and you need to get to bed. I mean, to sleep. You've had a really bad experience and too much brandy and..."

Rita giggled as she clasped her hands behind his neck and started inching her way up toward his voice. "Oh, I think I had just enough brandy. I am feeling so much better and I didn't mean to fall on you, but as long as I'm here, I want to tell you how much I appreciate you. All the stuff you do for Aunt Liz, yes. But I never had someone, a man, who really looked out for me. I just want to say thank you." And with that, Rita lowered her lips onto his, pressing them gently, then with more urgency, nibbling his lower lip, hearing him moan softly.

She lifted her head and smiled before lowering her face and planting small kisses down his cheek and all over his neck, teasing his earlobe with the tip of her tongue and murmuring his name. He nuzzled his face in her wild curls and massaged her back up and down with his other hand, breathing in the warm scent of sandalwood on her skin, rocking against her as she rhythmically pulsed against the bulge in his jeans.

Her lips were on his once again. Their mouths opened together as they explored each other. He could taste the hint of brandy as her tongue met his, full of wanting.

He broke away. "No," she whispered. "Don't stop. I don't want you to stop. I want some more," she pleaded as she kissed him again.

"Not here," Mitch said hoarsely. "Inside."

Somehow Rita managed to slip off Mitch and sat on the deck, holding her arms up. He pulled her up and lifted her onto her feet in one motion. She smiled and pulled his head down to hers, "I like your kisses. You have great lips. Do you know how great they feel?" And she started kissing him again. His arms wrapped around her back as she melted into his embrace, her hands massaging the back of his head, roving over his neck as she reached up on tiptoes.

Mitch groaned and pulled away, setting her down on her feet. "Yeah, I know how great they feel. Maybe too great. Come on, let's go." He opened the door and ushered her inside, locking the wooden door behind them.

Rita turned and stroked his arms, under his shirt and massaged his shoulders. "You have such nice skin, too. You have one of the nicest bodies I've ever worked on, hard, muscular, but so soft when you relax. I didn't want to tell you that before. You, with your big ego and all, you would have teased me forever. Know what? You are the first client I ever felt like kissing. That's unprofessional so I didn't. I never ever get involved with a client. But I never dreamed your lips would feel so..." and she lifted her head to touch them with hers again. "Come on down. I can't reach them."

He leaned forward as she reached up again. He pulled the drawstring of her wrap-around gauzy skirt and it fell to the floor. He bent to slip his hands under her buttocks and lifted her up until her legs wrapped around his waist and they could see eye to eye. She smiled and lightly kissed his forehead, massaging his temples and feathering kisses over his cheek until she opened his mouth with hers. "Stay with me tonight, Mitch. Please? It's been so long since I felt this good. I don't know if I ever felt this good. Please stay," she whispered in his ear and nibbled on his earlobe.

"Rita. I don't think…"

"Don't think, Mitch. You always tell me I think too much. Take me upstairs. Now."

Mitch turned off the light and carried Rita upstairs, placing her gently on the moonlight-covered quilt. He stood looking down at her in her tight knit top and black bikini bottoms. She stretched slowly like a cat, peeling the shirt off in one fluid motion and flinging it across the room. She patted the bed beside her as he gazed down at her.

"You are so beautiful. I can't believe I'm here looking at a wild sexy woman wearing a skimpy black lace bra in her little girl room."

"Mitch! I'm not a little girl. I want you. Please?" Rita grabbed his T-shirt and yanked it out of his jeans. "Come on, Mitch," she taunted. "I bet you can play real nice." She suddenly grabbed his arms and pulled him toward her. "Here. Let me give you a nice massage. Take off this shirt. It's in the way."

Mitch pulled off his shirt slowly and looked at Rita's eyes shining in the moonlight. She looked so small and vulnerable. He cupped her face in his callused hands and smiled. "I want you, too, honey. But I don't know if this is a good idea. What about tomorrow? You've had too much to drink after a rough experience. I don't want you to look at me in the morning and think I took advantage of you."

"Don't you want me?" Rita's voice wavered and her eyes glistened.

"Oh God, Rita. I want you so bad you'll never know. But not like this. Not after too many drinks and feeling scared. I want you to make love to me, to Mitch, not because you're lonely or scared or feeling a buzz from some brandy. I know you. If we make love now, you'll never forgive me, or yourself. I can't let you do that. You're too important."

A couple tears slid down her cheek. Rita flung herself down on the pillow and sniffed. "If I'm so important, why don't you want to be close to me?"

"Rita, I do. But not like this. You know you're driving me crazy. I never thought I'd feel like this about anyone again. If I didn't care, I wouldn't stop to think about the consequences, but I don't want to mess up this time. Now, move over and get under the covers. And put on a T-shirt shirt or an ugly nightgown or something. I'm going to get you two aspirin and a glass of water or your head's going to feel like exploding tomorrow."

Rita groaned and started to crawl under the sheet. She grabbed her favorite faded New Jersey Devils shirt from under a pillow and pulled it on after struggling to get her bra unhooked and flinging it across the room. She rested her head on the pillow and closed her eyes. She felt worn out and light-headed. The darkness seemed to spin so she sat up and opened her eyes. "I don't feel too good, Mitch. The room is moving a little like a merry-go-round, and when I shut my eyes, I see swirling colors."

"What do you expect after gulping down two or three shots of brandy on an empty stomach? Here. Take these aspirin and drink the water. Preventive." He waited until she swallowed. "Now move over," he ordered. "I'm not leaving you alone in this shape. I hope you're not a bed hog."

Rita moved over. "Moving around is the last thing on my mind now. If I don't move my head, I don't feel woozy. Can you give me a spoon hug?" she turned her back to him as he removed his jeans and slid under the covers in his boxers.

"Okay, but no funny business. No taking advantage of me while you're under the influence, lady."

"Right," Rita murmured as she snuggled her backside into his pelvic area. She giggled a little, and mumbled, "Well it's nice to know you're still interested. Are you sure you don't want to give in to temptation, huh? I could try not to move my head."

Mitch growled and eased back a little from her as his arm enclosed her waist. "I don't know if I'll be able to sleep like this, but I'll give it a shot. I'm trying to be noble, but it's hard."

Rita giggled. "Yeah, I noticed. I wish I didn't feel so dizzy. Can I have one last kiss?" she asked as she started to turn around and couldn't.

Mitch kissed her on the neck. "That's it for kisses for you tonight. I'll give you a rain check till tomorrow."

"I get the feeling you don't trust me, Mitch."

"Or myself. Not half-naked. Now shut up and relax. Deep breaths. Good night, Rita."

"Good night, Mitch. I don't think I can sleep like this either, but please stay here a few minutes, okay? And thank you." She sighed, grabbing a pillow in one hand and enjoying the warmth of his arm over hers.

"For the last time, you're welcome. Now go to sleep." Mitch whispered near her ear. His breath tickled and sent tiny shivers down her spine.

"Sure you don't want to play, Mitch? Because if you don't stop breathing like that on my neck, I'm going to turn around and..."

Mitch backed his head away from hers and squeezed her hand. "Not tonight. When you make love to me, I want it to be a conscious choice, not the aftermath of too much brandy. Now be still. You're safe and you need to sleep."

Rita drifted off.

Mitch lay in the dark a bit longer, listening to the ocean.

Doing the right thing had never been so damn hard.

Chapter Twenty-One

The note on the pillow was brief. "I'm downstairs. You owe me. Wake me. Mitch." Not "Love, Mitch" but he'd drawn a little heart by his name with two eyes and a smile. And there was a tiny little carved angel with a ponytail holding the note down. Rita smiled. It was like getting a valentine back in second grade from the fair-haired boy nobody knew you had a crush on.

Rita brushed her teeth and slipped into a silk robe before heading downstairs. Mitch was sprawled on the sofa with only his boxers on, one leg tangled in a sheet. She eased onto the couch next to him and snuggled her back into his chest. His arm slipped around her and he pulled her close. "What took you so long?" he murmured into her hair. "I missed you."

"I guess I was more tired than I thought."

"I like this robe. Sexier than that old T-shirt you wear. Silky," he whispered as he pulled the slippery tie and slid his hand over her breasts. Rita shivered as his rough hands played with the tips, now small and hard.

Rita tried to twist around, but Mitch held her tight. "Not yet. I'm not done exploring this side." His fingers slid down her belly and skimmed lightly over her thighs, gradually working closer and closer to the dampness between her legs. When he finally touched her there, she thought she would explode. "You are so ready." He started softly, gently, rhythmically pressing harder, pulsing his fingers further down inside her like an external heartbeat, all the while caressing her hair, nibbling her earlobe.

Rita could feel his erection against her backside. "Mitch, I want you."

"I want you, too, but we may not be ready for this."

"Mitch, I've never been more ready in my life."

"I don't mean that way. I don't have any protection. Do you?"

Rita groaned. "Damn! I don't believe it! You get me all hot and bothered after years of doing without and I *still* have to do without?"

Mitch nuzzled her neck while his hand teased and stroked below. "Well, sorry, Babe. I guess we're going to have to wait. Do you remember how good getting to first base was?" In one quick move, he flipped her over and pulled her on top of him. He kissed her hard as his hands traveled slowly down her back. "And second base? And third? Where exactly where they?" he teased as he massaged her buttocks. His erection nudged at the moistness between her legs and she gasped. He pulled back. "We know where home is, but for the first inning, maybe we'll explore the general area with our hands or..."

Rita eased her hand between them and traced the tip of him. "You're talking to an expert when it comes to massage," Rita whispered. "Perhaps you'd like a little demonstration," she added and started to exert rhythmic pressure on him. He moaned.

Tires crunched outside on the gravel driveway. Rita froze. "Oh, my God! Who could that be on a Saturday morning? I bet it's Serena checking up on me." Rita jumped up and ran to the door. "Oh, no! Worse. It's Tony."

"What the hell is he doing here?" grumbled Mitch.

"I don't know. Get up! Quick! Put on your pants. A shirt. Look like you're cooking breakfast. No, slip out the back door. I don't know. Do something. I've got to get real clothes on." Rita tore off her robe and ran to the laundry room.

"What the hell do you care if he knows we're together, Rita?" Mitch yelled after her. "Are you stringing him along? Tell him to stop sending flowers and candy. No more lunches. No more job offers. You want me to tell him?"

Rita returned, struggling into a fuzzy blue sweatshirt, dressing and moving at the same time. "No, Mitch. I don't need you to do my talking for me. And no, I'm not stringing him along."

"Then why don't you want him to know we're together?"

Rita tugged up her sweatpants and planted a light kiss on Mitch's chest. "Mitch, you're the one I want, the one I trust. But I don't like other people knowing my private business. Neither do you. So *please* get up!"

Rita glanced out the window again. "What if he's here to tell me something happened to Aunt Liz on the cruise, something he doesn't want me to find out over the phone? Oh, God!"

"Calm down!" Mitch pulled on his shorts, slipped his head through a navy polo shirt, and padded barefoot into the kitchen. "Look, sheet hidden under the cushion, man dressed, and innocently making a pot of coffee. Don't look so flustered and he'll never guess what he interrupted." The doorbell rang. "Want me to answer it?"

"No, I'll get it," Rita breezed by. "How do I look?"

Mitch gave a wolf whistle. "Real seductive in those baggy sweats. He'll know for sure what we were up to."

The bell rang again as Rita opened the door. "Tony. What brings you here this early? Is it Aunt Liz? Is something wrong?"

"No, she's fine. I apologize for not calling first, but I stopped by Serena's shop and heard you had a bad experience last night. Want to join me for breakfast or a drive to take your mind off things?"

Rita bit her lip before answering. "Well, I, uh, don't know what to say."

"How about 'no?' " Mitch boomed from the kitchen.

Tony jumped at the sound of the male voice and his mouth dropped open. "Oh, I apologize for intruding. I had no idea. I should have known a beautiful woman like you might not be alone."

Rita opened the door wider. "Tony, it's only Mitch. He's here for breakfast, watching over me while Aunt Liz is away." She paused to smooth her uncombed curls. "So you've heard from her?"

"Yes, she's a bit tired, but at her age, that's to be expected. You know I've been looking out for her, but I'm here to talk about you, not Liz. When that young cashier told me about your unfortunate encounter last night, I wanted to make sure you were all right. A woman alone has to be careful."

Mitch nodded as he appeared behind Rita. "Damn right. Never know who's out to get you, right, Tony?"

"How true." Tony studied Mitch without another word and looked back at Rita. "Well, Rita, your watchdog's here, so I'll be on my way. Remember, if you're ever in trouble and Tarzan here is busy, I'm only a phone call away." He pulled a business card out of his pocket and put it in her hand, enfolding hers in both of his. "My private line and cell are listed, too."

"You didn't tell Aunt Liz about my, uh, close call, did you, Tony?"

"No, but she knows something happened. Liz called to leave a message for Serena while I was there and Kelly started gossiping about your unpleasant incident. I knew you wouldn't want Liz to worry while she's away, so I took the phone and reassured her you were fine. I promised I'd stop by to check on you." He kissed her hand and released it. "A promise is a promise."

Rita stuffed his card in her pocket and shrugged her shoulders. "Thanks, Tony, but you can see I'm fine now. And I already have plans for today. We were about to eat breakfast and then Mitch needs to run to the drugstore, right, Mitch? Do you need a list, or will you remember?"

"Oh, I'll remember." Mitch smiled and turned quickly. "And speaking of breakfast, I gotta get back to the frying pan. So long, Tony," he added and headed for the kitchen.

Rita stepped outside and glanced at the vintage caramel-colored Porsche 911S in the driveway. "Nice wheels, Tony. How many cars do you own? I don't remember seeing this one."

"Three, plus a motorcycle. Want to take a quick ride around the block?"

Rita hesitated. "I'm tempted, but starving and my pancakes are getting cold."

"Well, anytime you want to take a spin, or go out, call me. You have my card. Please use it. For business or pleasure. And take care of yourself."

She watched as he zoomed away. Part of her had wanted to hop in that impractical car just for five minutes, but not with Mitch waiting inside, waiting for more than someone to share a stack of pancakes.

Which little inner voice should she listen to? One warned her not to risk losing her heart again. The other urged her to trust her gut that everything could turn out fine.

Rita turned and cautiously walked on the stones in her bare feet. Pulling the screen door open, she heard Mitch talking loudly to someone on his cell phone. "Can't I come up later? I appreciate you making the time to go over this stuff with me, but I didn't want to leave till lunchtime." He paused and listened. "Okay, I know you're swamped. I remember what it was like. Yeah, I'll get everything together and leave town in an hour or so. Somebody's picking me up and driving me to my truck. A small repair job... Yeah. Thanks. See you soon." He punched the "Off" button and muttered. "Damn! Why does everybody have lousy timing?"

"What's wrong?" Rita asked from the kitchen doorway.

Mitch dropped the spatula. "Damn, you startled me! The world's greatest banana pancakes are almost ready! Sit down and tell me what ol' blue eyes wanted."

"You heard him. He stopped in to tell me Aunt Liz was upset when Kelly blabbed something about my scary home massage experience. Fortunately, Tony smoothed things over so she wouldn't worry about me."

"Yeah, I'm sure. 'Smooth' is his middle name."

"What's bugging you?"

"I'm frustrated, okay? I thought we'd have the rest of the morning together but I have to go now. Winslow's picking me up here in a few minutes and driving me to his house. I'll give him the cash and finish the temporary window repair from last night. Then I have to drive up the Parkway to meet some of my contacts. They're willing to give us some free advice for Liz, and believe me, their suggestions are worth their weight in gold. I hate to rush off, but I have to get up there ASAP."

"I'll come with you. I want to know what they're saying, too. And I may have background information they need."

"Sorry, sweetheart. I think it's better if I go alone. No pressure to make it a social visit, no curiosity about getting to know you. They trust me completely. They don't know you well enough to speak freely or to ask the tough questions."

"Mitch, that's not fair. Can't I go along for the ride and stay in the truck?" Rita reached across the table and massaged his hand. "Who knows? Maybe we'll get a chance to finish what we started."

He smiled. "Everything good is worth waiting for, isn't that what they say?"

"No, they say, 'He who hesitates is lost!' "

"Rita, you know I'd rather stay here and make love to you, but I want our first time to be special. And we need to take care of Liz first, okay?"

Rita withdrew her hand and drowned the pancakes on her plate with maple syrup. "Of course. You're right. I know we have to do that. But you owe me big time for being patient, assuming I don't have second thoughts while you're gone."

Mitch leaned over to kiss the back of her neck on his way to the range to flip the last three hotcakes. "Honey, I can't wait till this mess is all cleared up, believe me. And I'm calling Serena to get her to stay with you."

Rita stopped cutting her pancakes with her fork and narrowed her eyes. "I don't need a baby sitter."

"I know, but you could use a good friend to keep you company. She's one tough broad, and I want somebody here that cares about your safety. Whoever set you up used her name and business. Who knows? Maybe she's the one who needs a baby sitter."

Rita pushed her plate away and sighed. "You know, I never thought of that angle. By hurting me, someone hurts my best friend, my business partner. She did mention feeling some kind of pressure to sell the property. She's hurting for money, too. You think she might be the target, not me?"

"Could be. I don't know." Mitch looked at the clock and gulped down his orange juice. "Be observant, be careful, but no heroics, okay? Promise me you'll call the cops right away if you even think you might be in danger."

He grabbed the phone and kissed the top of her head. "I gotta run, but I'm not leaving till I reach Serena and know you won't be alone. Would you get me those copies of Liz's papers to take along? My friends need to see the exact language of the documents she signed and what her assets and liabilities are."

"All right, we'll do it your way." Rita sighed and took her plate to the dishwasher. "Serena's number's programmed. Tell her I'll meet her at the shop in about an hour."

Rita went to the desk to retrieve Aunt Liz's paperwork. She wondered if the reality of making love to Mitch could match her growing fantasy of what almost had taken place. If only Tony hadn't interrupted. If only Mitch didn't have to leave. If only Aunt Liz weren't in such a financial mess, maybe she would be in Mitch's arms right now instead of getting things together for him to take on a trip.

Suddenly an image of the Tower card flashed in her mind, dark and ominous. This house was no fortress and she didn't like admitting she felt safer with Mitch around. She wanted him close enough to reach out and talk to, to joke with, to touch. She didn't want him to leave, but she reminded herself he'd be back soon, and things would be wonderful. *I've been hanging around Serena too long. They're only cards.* Still, the thought of having Serena stay over was comforting. She didn't want to be alone.

Mitch was looking out the window by the door when she returned and handed him an envelope of Aunt Liz's papers. He smiled and stuffed it into an open briefcase on the foyer table. "Wow, Mitch. I'm impressed. Real leather, isn't it?" Rita asked.

"Yeah. An old present." He grabbed her and crushed her lips with his, warm and wanting. A horn honked twice. Mitch pulled away and framed her face between his strong hands. "I gotta go now. Winslow's here to take me to my truck and work on fixing that sidelight. I'll call tonight. Be careful and lock the windows when you go out. That's an order!" The hug they shared was too quick. He left with his briefcase and a duffel bag and hopped into the waiting Land Rover. He waved as they drove away. She managed a smile and a wave, glad he hadn't seen the tears she'd wiped from her eyes.

Back on the deck, she curled up on the chaise lounge and looked around. Even in the warm sunlight, she shuddered. Could someone be watching her? Remembering her yoga practice, she closed her eyes and let the heat and stillness soak into her skin. *Let go past experiences and future expectations. Inhale peace, exhale tension,* she thought. To the east, seagulls cried and a distant radio pounded an angry beat over the gentle splash of waves rolling onto the sand. After ten minutes of trying to relax, Rita gave up and got moving. With all the tourists in town, Serena was bound to need an extra pair of hands in the store. If she were busy waiting on customers, maybe she wouldn't be missing a certain muscular carpenter right now.

She smiled. Six weeks ago, she would have been happy to see Mitch disappear and never come back. Now she couldn't wait for him to return. She carefully closed and locked all the windows and put on the air-conditioning. Fresh air fanatic Aunt Liz would have a fit if she were here. Rita exhaled and felt better knowing the house was secure as she headed for Serena's Body & Soul Gift Shop.

****

By the time Rita arrived home after dinner with Serena, she was more than anxious to talk to Mitch. The light on the new answering machine flashed, but his message was short and impersonal. "Got here okay. Reviewed the papers with friends, but I'll have to be away a day or two more. Be back as soon as I can. I owe you, remember?" Rita replayed his message a couple times to hear his voice.

"What does he owe you?" Serena snorted from the doorway. "And how many times are you going to listen to that tape? Did something happen between you two?" She paused before continuing, "I doubt if he's doing all this just to protect Liz!"

"Serena, stop badgering me or you're gonna need protection from me! Now would you make some popcorn while I get the DVD ready?" Rita went to the windows and yanked on the cords. The blinds slapped into their resting place on the sill, shutting out the darkness and the downpour outside, but not the feeling something wasn't quite right. She wished she knew where Mitch was. Even more, she wished he were with her right now, not miles away.

Serena dozed off during the film and grumbled when Rita flicked off the TV and woke her. Rita managed to steer her into the guest bedroom next to Liz's and tucked her lanky friend in for the night with a comforter and a smile. Without makeup and flashy jewelry, Serena looked more like the gangly, freckled adolescent who'd always been there for her.

After crawling into her own bed, Rita sighed and grabbed the phone. It was almost midnight. Should she call Mitch or not? When the phone suddenly rang, Rita almost dropped the receiver in shock. Smiling, she pressed the "Talk" button. "You're a bit late, but you must be psychic. I was lying here thinking about you."

Silence.

"Mitch, are you there?"

Rita clutched the phone and waited for him to say something. One last try. "Hello? Anybody there?"

"I'm close by," a raspy voice whispered, "And I'll be thinking about you, too, saying your little girl prayers during the storm. 'Now I lay me down to sleep, I pray…' How does that go? Oh yes. Something about keeping your soul if you should die before you wake…Sweet dreams, if you dare. Pray the lights don't go out…again." An abrupt click.

Rita's hand trembled as she dialed Mitch's number.

Please answer.

"Hello?" he mumbled.

"Mitch? Is that you?"

"Rita?"

"Yes. I hate to wake you but I had a weird phone call just now and I…"

"Are you all right? Is Serena there?"

"Yes, she's in the guest room. But I got this horrible call." Rita fought for a deep breath. "I thought it was you, but the guy on the other end scared me to death."

"What'd he say?"

Rita repeated the ominous words and could hear the concern in Mitch's assurances. "Probably a wrong number or maybe a random teenage prank. He didn't use your name did he? Did he say anything personal?"

"No, not like the call I got at the shop awhile back. That guy knew my name but he never called back."

"You never told me about that. Was it the same voice?"

"I don't think so. But that thing about if I should die before I wake. That was so scary! I hated that prayer when I was little. My mom made me say it every night, and I tried to stay awake for fear of dying before morning. It's on a sampler my mom made for me. I put it in the attic. How could he know I hate that creepy prayer?"

"Rita, honey. Calm down. It's a coincidence. Do you know how many kids probably hate that prayer?

But just to be safe, walk downstairs with the phone. Wake up Serena and check all the windows and doors again. If anything doesn't look right or if you hear anything strange, call 9-1-1. Lock yourselves in the guest room, call me, and wait for the cops. Otherwise, just stay together and get some sleep. If that scumbag calls you back, say nothing. Hang up and call for help." He paused. "Rita?"

She cleared her throat. "I'm okay, I'm heading downstairs."

"Honey, do you want me to drive back right now? I've arranged some important meetings about Liz first thing tomorrow, but if you need me, I'll make it back and forth with a few hours' sleep."

"You'd be worn out. I wish you were here right now, Mitch, but I can't let you do that."

"Well, I'll stay on the line with you while you and Serena check out the house. I'm not saying goodnight till both of you feel secure."

Rita felt foolish waking up her friend, but it calmed her to talk to someone in person. As soon as they examined the doors and windows together, Serena made some peppermint tea, a sleep aid she called it, while Rita told Mitch everything was fine.

"I'll be back as soon as I can," he said, "And remember, you and I have some unfinished business to take care of."

Rita smiled and whispered, "Maybe we do, if I haven't changed my mind by then." When he didn't respond, she added, "You know I'm kidding, right?"

"Yes, honey, we both know what you really want."

"Men! You're all alike."

"Rita, if that were true, you'd already know what we'd be like under the sheets, on the sheets, in the shower, and on the dining room table. Just because I haven't acted on my urges doesn't mean I don't plan to."

"This hard-to-get act for a guy is intriguing, you know?"

"Getting someone isn't hard. Keeping them is. Now good night, Lady. I'll be thinking of you."

"Good night, Mitch. And thanks for holding my hand long distance."

Chapter Twenty-Two

Rita woke to bright sunlight flooding the guest room. Had she overslept? She glanced at the digital display flashing 12:00 a.m. and groaned. The power must have gone off during the thunderstorm. Her brain shook off remnants of dark dreams like cobwebs, images of twisting ivy choking the life out of a crumbling castle and coming after her. What day was it? Sunday. No massage appointments until the afternoon, but Serena had to be at work earlier. Was she still here?

Rita hurried to the kitchen and found a scrap of paper stuck on the refrigerator. "Didn't have the heart to wake you. *Some* of us have to work this morning. Later...S"

The phone rang. Rita hesitated, hoping it wasn't her late night caller. After the fourth ring, she picked up the receiver.

"Rita? Are you there?" Serena yelled in her ear.

"Yes. Thank God it's you and not that creep. What's up?"

"Never mind the creep. I need you at the store right away before I kill a different one!"

"Serena, what's wrong?"

"You name it. The power was out. Spoiled food and the health inspector drops in without warning. Since when do they work on a Sunday? Kelly didn't show and a tourist bus is due in soon. Can you come in now?"

"Yeah, I'll leave right away."

"Thanks, girlfriend. Wish me luck. Bye." Serena disconnected before Rita could respond.

Rita pulled her curly hair into a quick ponytail and took a one-minute body shower. She threw her make-up bag into her drawstring purse and slipped into a sundress and sandals. A morning without coffee and no time to stop. Less than five minutes after Serena's call, Rita pulled onto Highway 35. "Wonder Woman would be proud," she muttered as she applied some eye shadow and mascara at a stoplight. Now if only traffic would cooperate.

By the time she reached the shop, a tour bus was pulling away. Strange, the "Closed" sign was on the door. What was going on?

Rita parked on the side of the building and went in through her own entrance. She heard angry voices coming from the kitchen and pulled out her cell phone. She unlocked the door between their businesses and grabbed an umbrella from the stand. It wasn't much of a weapon, but it was something.

Serena's voice boomed, "Listen, Buddy. I don't know where you found that roach, but it wasn't in my kitchen! And the refrigerator's not the right temperature because the power went off last night during the thunderstorm. I don't know why the door was open, and I know I have to throw all the milk and butter and mayonnaise away. Do you think I want to poison myself *and* ruin my business? There are easier and less painful ways to commit suicide you know."

"Miss, no need to overreact," said a short balding man in a white coat, busy making notations on a checklist. "So you failed one health inspection. It's not the end of the world, now, is it? Clean up your act and I'll be back in a week or so, but for now, you're out of the food business. You've got your witchcraft stuff to fall back on, right?" He signed his name with a flourish, tore off a copy, and handed it to Serena.

"Overreact? This is how I make my living, you

283

pompous little weasel. What kind of health inspector waits for a power outage to drop in and inspect the refrigerator anyway? And on Sunday? Any fool knows things happen and you have to throw out food. Although right now, I feel like serving you a fungus sandwich slathered with spoiled mayo."

The man pulled a day planner out of his jacket pocket and sighed. "And any fool should know not to insult the only inspector in town. My calendar's booked. I'm so busy I may not be able to squeeze you into my schedule until...let's say, Labor Day Weekend?"

He paused and smiled before continuing. "Some of the locals think this town would be better off without your tawdry little shop and massage parlor anyway. We don't need your kind of women around here. Men can go down to Atlantic City if they want to pick up some hussy or a kook."

"Oh, yeah? Well I guess you'd probably know since any woman in her right mind would expect you to fork over some money to let you touch..."

Before Serena could dig her hole any deeper, Rita parted the hanging beads and stepped into the kitchen. "Serena, maybe you'd like to ask the gentleman here to come back another day to re-inspect? I bet he wouldn't want a witness repeating what I just heard to his supervisor, right, Mr.-" Rita paused to scan the inspection report. "Benson? You know how people frown on affirmative action violations nowadays."

The man gritted his teeth and studied his small calendar. "Well, I, uh, suppose I could come back this week. Considering the power outage, the refrigerator is a minor matter. If it's functioning. But the cockroach. Now that's another story."

Rita nodded. "A story. My thoughts exactly. Maybe you'd like to talk to the exterminator. He was here yesterday and everything was fine. He goes by strict EPA regulations. We haven't seen a pest around here the whole summer until you showed up. So how about erasing the bug thing, too? It might be hard to explain where you actually found your specimen. Then maybe we won't file an affirmative action suit against you and your office."

The man turned red and grabbed the paper from Rita. He recopied part of it on another form on his clipboard before ripping the first one neatly in halves. "The information on temperature violations and spoiled food stands. No serving food for three days or until I return. And everything must be absolutely perfect or I'll close your operation down permanently. I didn't address the issue of the anonymous call about a tourist getting sick from one of your brownies. Rest assured, I'll have my own witness with me. Maybe my friend the fire inspector. Everything strictly by the book. Good day." He removed the "Satisfactory" health inspection certificate from the wall and replaced it with a glaring "Unsatisfactory" sign.

Glassware rattled as Serena slammed the door after him. "Pompous little bastard! Insinuating my cooking made someone sick? Planting a roach behind the refrigerator? And slinging around accusations that I'm some sort of witch or slut! What a morning! Whenever I don't take the time to check my cards or meditate the whole day gets screwed up."

"Serena. Get real. If you'd read your horoscope or said your morning mantra, are you telling me you would have calmly resisted the urge to cut him down to size?"

"Possibly."

"And did you have to call him short? You're six feet tall and he's a runt. Probably had sand kicked in his face his whole life, and you have to rub it in?"

Serena grinned. "Okay. I admit I got carried away. Thank God you stopped me before I got started questioning the size of his manhood and how much he'd have to pay to use it! It's so much easier to have peace of mind when you don't feel like giving some fool a piece of it. I was so pissed.

"The weird thing is that when Inspector Clean arrived, I was already tossing out all the spoiled food. The power went off. I was being responsible. It was like he was determined to close me down before he even stepped in. I left up the "Closed" sign because I wasn't ready for the tourists and I didn't want them hearing that jerk accuse me of keeping a dirty kitchen. Damn. You know that group is good for buying a ton of coffee, brownies, and good luck charms for their weekly trek to AC. And to top it off, Kelly left a message *thanking* me for the day off."

"You didn't give her the day off?"

"No, why would I do that?"

"Well, if you didn't, who did? Could someone be trying to ruin your business? Think about it. The power outage happened to everybody, but you'd never leave the refrigerator and freezer doors wide open. What about Kelly?"

"She's spacey, but both doors open? I don't think so."

Rita walked over and examined the back door. "Serena, it doesn't look like a forced entry. Nothing scratched or broken. Who else has a key besides you, me, and Mitch?"

"Only Kelly." Serena slammed her fist on the counter. "Damn! I just remembered. Kelly told me she lost her key on the beach last week. She swore she didn't have a name or address attached to it, so I let it slide. Maybe she lost it in the parking lot. If I have to change all the locks and get new keys again there goes another week's profit!"

Rita shook her head. "This stinks! Benson said someone made an anonymous phone call to his office. But why? And who? Could Kelly be in on some scheme? Maybe she's not as scattered and sweet as she seems."

Serena shrugged. "I don't know. It's more likely she's too much of an airhead to handle responsibility. I'll deal with her when she shows up tomorrow." Serena slammed the sponge into the sink from across the room.

"But first things first. I need an expert on health and fire regulations. I don't intend to be shut down for good, not when we're starting to do so well! And I better not need a new friggin' refrigerator. I don't have that kind of money."

"Don't panic. I'll call Mitch. He'll help get you ready for the white glove inspection. If he ever gets back here."

Serena rinsed out the sponge and started wiping melted ice cream out of the freezer. "Well, our cover story for the next three days is that the kitchen is closed due to appliance and electrical problems. Plus, we'll redecorate the dining corner. I'll jazz up the menus, up the prices a bit, and paint. How about a rainforest mural? Or Native American? Maybe give catchy names to the food: Brazilian brownies, Sedona Special-tea, and Peace of Mind Punch.

"And speaking of peace of mind, that self-righteous little health inspector better keep his big mouth shut about the roach he brought along or I'll have his job. If I hear one lousy rumor about sick tourists, I swear I'll put his name on one of those funny voodoo doll kits I don't believe in and stick pins in it anyway. Nobody is going to put us out of business, right?"

"Right you are, partner. Now how can I help? I've got a couple hours before my first client."

"Call Mitch and see when he'll be back. Like you said, he'll know how to get ready for that jerk's next visit. I'll call the exterminator. I need a letter confirming no evidence of creepy crawlies on

Saturday. I could use a hand with this mess, too. We had better make a 'To-Do' list for this project. We'll show 'em!"

Rita gave Serena a quick hug. "Yes, we will!"

Back at her office, she dialed Mitch's cell phone number. Damn. Voice mail again. She left a message without saying what she really felt—she missed him, and more than just his voice. Was she asking for too much? He was already on a mission to solve Aunt Liz's financial problems and now Rita wanted him to help Serena, too. Compared to the tough decisions Aunt Liz would have to make when she returned, Serena's health inspection troubles were minor... unless they were somehow connected.

Rita took a deep breath and looked out the window. She whispered to herself, "Who's the real target? And why?"

Chapter Twenty-Three

Monday morning and still no Mitch. As she drove up the Garden State Parkway to pick up Aunt Liz and her friend Helen at the cruise ship, Rita replayed her brief conversation with him the night before.

He'd said he was close to resolving Liz's "cash flow problem" as he called it. He wouldn't tell her details over the phone, but he promised to be back after lunch. He'd even gotten on the line with Serena and reassured her he'd help her pass inspection with flying colors. Rita had finally slept through the night. No strange calls, no crises.

Aunt Liz and Helen both looked tired but happy. As usual, Aunt Liz had befriended someone who needed help in the form of a ride to her riverfront home near Red Bank. "I hope you don't mind, dear, but Irene's husband died recently and I volunteered your services to drop her off on the way. She's asked us to stay for lunch."

"Well, Aunt Liz, Red Bank's south of here, but it'll take another hour to get off the Parkway and make an extra stop. Can't she call a cab or a limo?"

"Rita, are you assuming all widows who live on the water are rich?"

Rita thought about her own aunt's situation. "No, of course not. And if she's a friend of yours, we'll manage." She lifted Irene's suitcases to the top of the Jeep and strapped them on with a length of rope she carried in the back. "But I'll pass on lunch. I'll give you forty-five minutes to bond and eat while I browse in some of those trendy little shops on Broad

Street."

After carrying Irene's bags inside a stately brick home with a long porch, Rita smiled and declined lunch again. "I'll be back in forty-five minutes, Aunt Liz."

Rita turned down Broad Street and tried to find a parking space close enough to the shops she wanted to explore and maybe grab a quick sandwich at the Broadway Grill. No such luck. She vowed if she ever owned a Mercedes, a Jaguar, or a huge luxury SUV like many of the patrons, she'd learn how to park the blasted thing. The way they hung their expensive bumpers right to the edge of the line, it was as if they were begging some poor sucker to risk denting their chrome or scratching their paint.

She gave up and made a u-turn around the block to try the other side of the street. It was then she spotted a familiar red truck with surf fishing pole holders parked in front of the post office. It had to be Mitch's. There couldn't be two rusted trucks like that in the world. What was he doing here? Wasn't he in North Jersey, maybe New York? Or at least on his way back to Mantoloking Sands?

Torn between eating quickly and satisfying her curiosity, Rita turned the corner and parked a block away on a side street. She jogged back to Broad Street and ducked into a funky clothing store. She grabbed a free local advertising newspaper and stood by the window pretending to be checking out the ads. The truck was still there, but where was he? What if she had to leave and get Aunt Liz before she found out what Mitch was doing here?

She didn't have to wait long. Moments later, Mitch came out of the post office going through a stack of mail. Mitch in a three-piece gray suit with a crisp white shirt and a solid red tie. A red handkerchief peeked out of his coat pocket in a perfect satin triangle. And his hair was cut. Not

short, but definitely professionally cut, his wavy
black and silver hair full and flowing to the top of his
collar. No more ponytail. What was he up to?

How could she follow him? He dumped some
papers into a nearby trashcan before throwing the
rest of the mail into the cab and locking the door. He
paused a moment to check himself in the mirror,
shook his head and frowned. Raking one hand
through his hair, he strode off down the street and
hustled up the steps to the First National Bank of
Red Bank, taking two at a time. What was he doing
here?

"May I help you?" a young sales clerk with
multiple piercings asked from behind her. Rita
jumped and mumbled something about having to go.
She quickly crossed the street and headed toward
the post office, keeping an eye on the bank in case
Mitch should appear. At the trashcan, she tossed her
flyer in, and then looked around. No one was
watching. She leaned over and picked it back up
along with a few other pieces of paper. Two were
addressed to "Resident," one from Home Depot, the
other from a local memorial park for a plot or a
crypt. The third was an invitation to GM Ventures
Inc. to apply for a pre-approved, zero-percent
Platinum business credit card. "GM? Grant Mitch?
Ginger Mitch? Why does he get his mail here?"

Hoping to find out, she ducked inside the post
office and approached the older woman behind the
counter. Rita placed the credit card mailing Mitch
had discarded on the counter. "Excuse me, ma'am.
Do you know the man in a suit who left here a
moment ago? He dropped this mail outside, but he
was walking too fast for me to catch up with him."

The clerk took the envelope and felt its
thickness. "No real credit card in here, but nowadays
with identity theft, most people shred these offers
instead of tossing 'em in the garbage. Mailboxes are

full of these. No wonder so many people are in debt up to their eyeballs. But thanks, anyway. I'll put it back in Mr. Mitchell's box, in case he wants it."

Rita looked puzzled. "Mr. Mitchell? You know, I thought he might be someone I used to go to school with, but my friend's last name was Grant."

"Yeah, well it's probably him, but you've got it backwards, hon. It's Grant Mitchell, not Mitchell Grant."

Rita's mouth dropped open. "Are you sure?"

"Positive. He's been here quite a few years. Don't remember exactly how long, but why don't you ask him yourself when he comes back? That's his truck out there." She pointed outside.

Rita hesitated. "I don't have time to wait. Maybe I'll drop him a line now I know his box number."

"Well, he only stops by once a week, so if it's urgent, leave a note on his windshield."

"You remember his truck? Is he a friend of yours?"

"Oh, no. He's pleasant enough and very polite, but kind of shy. I remember the truck because his wife always drove some fancy car, one of them expensive Italian ones you can't spell. Not him. Unless he was with her, he'd pull up in that old truck, even in a suit like today. She died, you know. Drowned I think. Too bad. Not that she was ever that friendly. Always treated me like hired help, she did. Never a 'good morning' or a 'how are you?' from that one. She always looked perfect, though, like one of them models on magazine covers in the beauty parlor. You know what I mean? Skinny girls with fake boobs in overpriced clothes slit down to there?"

The woman shook her head. "Oh, my lord. Where's my manners? Here I am gossiping about the dead with a stranger. Can I get anything for you, hon?"

"A sheet of stamps, thanks."

As the woman was making change, Rita tried to think of what to do. Should she stand by the truck and confront Mitch? Wait in a nearby store and see what he did next? Follow him from the bank? Hide and say nothing until later? Maybe they could have lunch and he'd tell her a perfectly good reason for his masquerade. But what about his name? Why did he go by Mitch Grant if his name was really Grant Mitchell? Was he hiding something?

She had almost decided to wait by his truck when she noticed it pulling away from the curb. Damn! Now what? Run after it waving her hands wildly? She watched him disappear down Broad Street. He turned left. Toward the Parkway and home?

She couldn't follow him anyway. Not with twenty minutes left to kill before she could go pick up Aunt Liz. She popped into the health food store and grabbed a veggie pita and some tea that promised eternal energy and renewal. She sat down on a bench and wolfed down her natural food as she inhaled carbon monoxide from idling cars looking for the perfect parking spot. Still ten minutes left. She crossed the street to the Angel Shop and splurged. Thirty-five dollars for a white resin garden angel peering into a gazing ball.

"Is this your first time?" the cashier asked as Rita slid her last fifty on the counter, remembering the days when she used to have credit cards. *Thank you Kevin, wherever you are!*

"My what?"

"First purchase in our shop?"

"Oh, yeah. First time."

"Well, dear, fill out this card and you get ten percent off your next visit and a free guardian angel pin right now." *Good gimmick. Serena'd like that. What the hell! A guardian angel couldn't hurt.* Rita scribbled her name on the card and reminded herself to calm down. *Go with the flow. All that shit that was so easy to say and so hard to do.*

A vision of Aunt Liz's disapproving face popped into her mind. "Rita," she'd say as if she were talking to a naughty child. "Not that word, please." Well, what would Aunt Liz think when she found out Mitch had even lied about his name? Why was he leading a double life? "Trust me," he'd said. "Have I ever lied to you?"

At last, it was time to get Aunt Liz, and then drop off Helen on their way home. Rita prayed Mitch would be there. She'd mention her side trip to Red Bank and that she'd seen his truck. Would he squirm? Make up a story? Or would there be a logical reason for what he was doing there looking like a banker or a hotshot attorney? She wanted to believe him. Her heart told her to trust, but her head was already nagging at her for being so stupid again. *Why lie about your name, for God's sake?*

On the ride back, Rita nodded occasionally as Helen chattered on about the food, the activities, and the wonderful music on the cruise ship. "And the doctor was so nice to Liz when she had her dizzy spell and heart palpitations."

"Your what?" Rita snapped.

Liz patted Rita's arm. "It was nothing, dear. And Helen, you promised you wouldn't mention it!"

"I'm sorry, Liz. I forgot. But what difference does it make? You're fine now. Hasn't happened since February, right? And it should make her feel better to know how nice everybody was in case we want to do this again next year."

"So, tell me about the dizziness," Rita prodded.

"Well, it was the night we ate at the captain's table. I felt fine during dinner. Even got to dance with a handsome young man who looked like one of those Italian counts on the cover of a romance novel. Someone proposed a couple of toasts after a spin on the dance floor. Maybe it was the champagne or a touch of seasickness. The doctor gave me some pills to take."

Rita shook her head. "I swear you two need a chaperone if you go again! Maybe someone tried to slip something into your drink."

Liz chuckled. "Rita, no one tries to take advantage of a woman my age. Still, I steered clear of alcohol the rest of the trip. And I didn't take the rest of the pills and felt fine."

Rita pulled into Helen's yard and deposited the elderly woman and her bags into the house.

"How did you ever put up with her incessant talking without throwing her overboard?" Rita asked as she backed the car out of the driveway.

"She has a good heart, Rita. She's very lonely since her husband passed on. This trip was good for her."

"Yeah, well, you think everybody has a good heart. Sometimes I think you're only seeing what you want to see, whether it's there or not."

"Young lady, what's bothering you?"

"Let's wait until we get home."

"After one more stop. Ice cream up ahead. You need a hot fudge sundae."

"Aunt Liz. I need to fix my life. And yours. I don't need a hot fudge sundae!"

"Well, you may not need a hot fudge sundae but I do. After I get home and weigh myself, I won't be having desserts for a long time. Humor an old woman. Then we'll get serious."

Rita sighed and pulled into Jackson's Ice Cream, relieved not to see any of Tony's vehicles. "Make it two," she'd said as the waiter took Aunt Liz's order. "With extra whipped cream."

They savored their ice cream in silence until the waiter brought the check and slipped away. "So what's troubling you?" Aunt Liz asked. "Is it just money?"

Rita didn't know where to begin. As she reached into her purse for her wallet, she pulled out one of the crumpled flyers she'd fished out of the trashcan by Mitch's truck in Red Bank. "Well, this for one thing."

"You're upset about getting a coupon offer from a Memorial Park? I may be old but I'm not planning to die anytime soon. Are you?"

"No. It's not addressed to me. It's Mitch's."

"You think Mitch is going to die? Dear, that's only an ad. Everyone gets those in the mail."

"I'm not worried about him dying. It's his mail I'm worried about."

"You're confusing me. What are you saying?"

"While you were visiting in Red Bank, I saw Mitch in a fancy suit. He came out of the post office and tossed some mail into the trash. This mail."

"And you picked through the trash to get some flyers? I think I'm more worried about you than Mitch, dear."

"Aunt Liz! Listen. It turns out his name is Grant Mitchell, not Mitch Grant. This is addressed to GM Ventures in Red Bank. Initials G-M-V. Grant Mitchell or Ginger Mitch? Get it? His dead wife's first name? I don't know. The postal clerk has known him for years."

"Well, what did Mitch say about it?"

"I didn't get a chance to ask him before he drove off. And I've been dying to find out what's going on ever since. Last night he told me he thinks he's found a way for you to keep the house, everything's fine, and hinted he may love me. And today I discover he's not who he said he was."

"He loves you? Oh, Rita. I'm so happy for you! He's such a good man."

"A good man? Do good men lie about their names? Pretend to be someone they're not?"

Liz paused. She smoothed and folded the brochure neatly and passed it back to Rita. "Well, I'm sure there's a perfectly good explanation. Maybe GMV is some kind of construction company."

"GMV? What do you know about them? Have they contacted you about the property?" The tense male voice got their immediate attention. Tony stood by their table ripping up the check their waiter had left. He gave a slight bow before continuing. "My treat. And excuse me for eavesdropping, but I couldn't help overhearing you say something about 'GMV' as I walked up. Have they made you an offer?"

"An offer?" Rita said tentatively.

"You know, for your property." He looked around the restaurant and pulled another chair up to the table. "By the way, Liz, welcome home. You look wonderful considering your little episode on the ship. The captain was very concerned. Are you sure you're okay?"

"Yes, and thank you so much for everything. I had a lovely time."

"You're more than welcome."

Rita sat a little straighter and looked at her watch. "Tony, I want to get Aunt Liz home for a nap, but what were you saying about GMV?"

"Well, ladies. I'm going to be blunt. Whatever offer GMV has made on your property, I'll beat by $100,000. And if you sell it through me, you can buy a luxury suite in my assisted living/spa at construction cost." He lowered his voice and leaned forward. "I know you're in some financial trouble, Liz, and I think you're making a wise decision to sell. As wonderful as it is to own a house, you'd both have more peace of mind without major problems, responsibilities, and taxes. In the spa, you'll have access to the beach, the pool, and the health facilities but no headaches."

Rita's eyes narrowed. "Tony, you don't even know what the offer is. And why shouldn't we sell to GMV?"

"Rita, my family has been in the real estate business in this area for fifty years. We're reliable."

Rita felt the hair on the back of her neck stand up. "And GMV isn't, is that what you're saying?"

"Who are they? Some shadowy holding company that owns a single piece of property next door to you. They don't even respond to requests for information. The partners are impossible to reach. Once that old Victorian burned down, you'd think someone would be eager to sell or build. There's not much beachfront property left, but who's going to buy a small lot like that where you can only build on the tiny existing foundation? Sell your house to them and I guarantee they'll knock it down to put up some massive modern atrocity. But if you've decided to sell, I know some interested buyers who like your house as is."

Liz sighed. "Tony, I appreciate your concern, but I'm not selling my home to anybody. And I'm too tired to discuss it now anyway."

Tony reached over and patted her hand. "I understand it's a tough decision, Liz, but think of the advantages. Your life would be easier and Rita would be free to live hers, without worrying about your health or struggling to support you and pay your taxes, even if she could." He glanced at Rita and smiled. "I confess one selfish motive. I'd like to be closer to Rita, too, but either way, I'm here to help you both." He cleared his throat and rose from the chair. "Please be careful. I don't trust out-of-town corporations like this GMV that I don't know, and I'd hate to see either one of you get hurt."

Liz watched Tony leave. "Maybe I am being selfish trying to hold on to the property."

"Then I'm being selfish, too," Rita murmured. "I

love your house, and I don't want you to let it go, either. But what about Mitch?" she whispered. "If he's the head of GMV, why didn't he tell you about owning the property next door?"

Liz shook her head, "I have no idea, but I'm sure he must have good reasons. I may be old, Rita, but I'm not blind. You love him, don't you?"

Rita twisted a long curl and whispered, "Yes, but..."

"Then no 'buts.' You be straight with him. Ask all the tough questions you need to and follow your heart. I don't know who to believe anymore, except you and me. So let's get home and figure out what we're going to do next."

****

There was no sign of Mitch or his truck when they arrived home. Liz relented and stretched out to rest her eyes. Rita stirred restlessly, flipping through a magazine without seeing it. She felt so powerless, anxious to see Mitch yet dreading a confrontation. Dreading what else she might find out. What other secrets was he hiding? And where?

His computer. His closets.

Rita grabbed Aunt Liz's household keys and headed for the garage. She hurried up the steps and let herself in, feeling like a criminal. Justified, but a criminal. She turned on the computer first, only to be stumped by a password request. She tried all combinations of his name and initials, even "Ginger" and his license plate number. Birthday? Dog's name? Mother's maiden name? She shook her head. She couldn't answer any of those questions about Mitch Grant, let alone Grant Mitchell. How could she love a man she hardly knew?

She shut down the computer and checked to make sure the mouse was exactly where it had been on the mouse pad. She quickly looked through the drawers, stopping now and then to look out the window and listen for any sounds of a vehicle on the gravel.

Closets? In the back hung his expensive tuxedo. A couple of Armani suits protected in expensive carry-on luggage. Shoeboxes. Two held pairs of Italian designer shoes practically unworn. And then, one filled with photographs.

Rita dropped to the floor and carefully examined a few pictures. Mitch as a youngster surrounded by four teen-aged girls. A smiling blonde with perfect legs. A wedding photo in a silver frame engraved with "Ginger and Mitch" and tiny hearts, the groom with long salt-and-pepper hair beaming at the beautiful blonde with perfect features, gently feeding her a piece of cake. So young. Pain stabbed her heart.

"Looking for something?" Rita jumped at the sound of Mitch's voice from the doorway.

"Oh my God, you scared me. I, uh, didn't expect to see you," she stammered. "I mean, I thought I'd hear you coming down the driveway…"

"I guess you were too absorbed. Funny, I expected you to be happy to see me. Not snooping through my stuff."

"Yeah, well you know what else is funny? This morning I would never have dreamed I'd be here searching through your things. All I thought about was throwing my arms around you as soon as I saw you. But you look a lot different since the last time I saw you."

"What do you mean, different? You mean the haircut?"

"Nice cut, but I saw that earlier today. No, I mean your clothes. You look like Mitch the carpenter again. Quite a switch from the three-piece suit, Mitch. Or should I call you Grant?"

Mitch pounded his fist on the doorframe. "Shit! I was going to tell you about that as soon as I thought it wouldn't matter to you. 'Grant' was a sissy name in a working class neighborhood so I went by 'Mitch' all through school and it stuck."

"Right, and what else haven't you mentioned? What about GMV Inc.? Does that name ring a bell? It sure meant something to Tony this afternoon. He offered Liz enough money for a lifetime residence in his health spa to sell the house to him instead of GMV." She took a deep breath. "So Grant, do you own the property next door or not?"

Mitch let out a long sigh. "Yes, but it was never about real estate. I've never been after Liz's property."

"So if it wasn't about real estate, then what made you worm your way into her life...not to mention my heart? 'Trust me,' you said. Which you? The guy with the tool belt or the one in the business suit?"

"Honey, I can see why you're upset. I'd be doubting me, too. But know one thing, Rita. I'd never do anything to hurt either you or Liz. Someone else is trying to do just that, and I think I know who and why. Where's Liz? Is she okay?"

"She had a little health challenge, as she calls it, on the cruise ship, but seems to be all right. She's lying down."

"We have to go talk to her. Someone wants the two of you out of this house by any means, and it's not me. Did anyone give her pills?"

"The doctor on the ship did, but you know how Aunt Liz avoids medicine. She probably threw them overboard."

"Well if she has any left, we're going to have them tested. Remember the incident in the health spa's sauna? Let's say there've been a few untimely deaths of older people the past few years in this area. And Tony seems to be involved."

"Mitch, you've got to be kidding. You suspect

Tony of bumping off old ladies? And if you're accusing Tony of drugging Aunt Liz on the ship, aren't you forgetting he was in town the whole time?"

"No. Think about it. We know he has a financial connection to the cruise line, and Liz conveniently happens to 'win' a free cruise. What if her name was 'pre-selected' to get her out of town and to get you alone?"

Rita paused. "Mitch, you wanted the same thing. Why should I believe a man of mystery I only met this summer...who's kept some major secrets? I've known Tony since high school."

"Rita, you don't know him at all. I don't have time to explain in detail now, but he's at the fringe of a lot of investigations...real estate swindles, shady deals, 'accidental' fires and insurance fraud, and gambling debts, to name a few. Maybe even involved in some sudden deaths of husbands of elderly women who ended up selling their properties to Tony."

Rita put the box of photographs back in the closet. "And what about you? Do you have more secrets I should know about?"

Mitch leaned over. He took both of her hands in his and pulled her off the floor. "It's no secret I love you, Rita. The question is do you love me?"

Rita lowered her gaze. "If you'd asked me this morning I would have said 'Yes' without hesitation."

"And now?" Mitch put his hand under her chin and gently lifted her face.

"I don't want to love you."

"That's not what I asked."

"I don't know what to think."

"Hell, I'm not asking you to think. I'm asking what you *feel*."

"Mitch, considering my track record and everything I've just found out about you, how do you think I feel? Confused. Angry. Betrayed again. I feel like a fool who always picks the wrong guy to love. Codependent ever after or something like that."

"Stop your damn analyzing. Do you love me?"

"Yes...but I feel like such a sucker because more than anything, I want you to be Mitch again, just simple Mitch. I want you to hug me, to love me. I want to believe you love me, too, and everything will be okay."

"Come here," Mitch whispered as he pulled her close and surrounded her in his arms. "I want that, too. You have to believe me."

"I want to. But how? Tell me how I can trust you when I didn't even know your real name until a few hours ago? Maybe you're all bad guys. Why should I believe you and not Tony?"

"You'll have no doubts when you see him in action tonight. Come on." Mitch brushed her lips softly with his. "First we have to let Liz and Serena know what's going on. My friend Don works for the feds and he's setting up the house to tape a conversation between you and Tony. I didn't like the idea of you confronting Tony, but with protection from the feds, you'll be safe. The local authorities aren't involved. One of them may be on Tony's payroll. So far only minor stuff, but when the stakes are higher, who knows?"

"Mitch, this seems pretty far-fetched. Can't we wait?"

"No more waiting, no more secrets. You've all been targets, and when the feds say it's time to close in, we can't wait. Right now, we have to talk to Liz and get you ready for Tony's little visit."

"Why in the world would Tony come over?"

"Because you're going to call him."

Chapter Twenty-Four

"What? Are you crazy? If Tony's the monster you claim he is, can't they arrest him and leave me out of it?" Rita hurried to keep up with Mitch as they headed toward the main house.

He opened the door and ushered her inside. "Best way to flush him out is for you to invite him here. He's overextended and getting desperate, but the feds need evidence, not suspicions. You're going to offer him the way out of his predicament and then change your mind. If Tony threatens you, the feds will swoop in and arrest him to play 'Let's Make a Deal.' They're interested in catching the big fish, his silent partners and connections. Now calm down before we wake up Liz. I don't want her upset."

"Don't want me upset?" Liz stood in the foyer, her arms folded over her chest. "Too late for that. Now start explaining, young man. Is it Mitch or Grant?" she said. "And why are two gentlemen with FBI badges in my kitchen? Scared the hell out of me. They wouldn't let me call anyone or leave until you arrived."

Two men in dark suits appeared behind her. "Sorry, Mitch. We thought you said it was clear to set up the equipment."

Mitch closed the door behind him and turned to the older woman. "Liz, I'm sorry you're upset. You have a right to be, but I can explain everything. This is Don, an old friend from high school who's now a big shot in the FBI. And this is his partner. They're here to help you out of this jam—and catch a criminal."

"Since when do I need help from the FBI? And who are you? Do you really own the property next door?"

Mitch sighed. "Legally, I'm Grant Mitchell, but everybody calls me 'Mitch.' And yes, I own the eyesore garage next door and the foundation of the old burned-down Victorian. That's why I was walking the property when I first met you. You thought I was a poor, homeless person camping out. I was amazed it didn't matter to you...and that you were so trusting and generous to give a stranger a place to stay."

Liz leaned against the wall. "You always said I was too trusting. I guess you were right."

"I know you're hurt, but I'll prove you were right to trust me."

"Lying's a funny way of proving you're honest, isn't it?"

"Liz, I lied by omission. I didn't correct you when you assumed I was homeless. But I don't want your property. I don't need it. I just want to be close to you...and to Rita. I want to protect you from people like Tony who prey on kind souls like you. You're not the only ones he's hurt. Don't you want to stop him?"

Don's cell phone beeped. "Stanton here. Yeah, we're almost ready. Everything functioning?" He listened. "Your end, too? Okay. How about surveillance on the Amazon redhead?" He laughed. "Yeah, I heard she's a piece of work! Tell Johnson to save some brownies for me, but I'll skip the rolling pin intro and the ice pack..." He winked at Mitch. "Right. The niece is going to make the call soon...Yeah. That'll be the signal to move in."

Rita nudged Mitch and motioned to the man shoving the cell phone back in his pocket. "What's with the secret agent man act? And what was that about a redhead and a rolling pin? Is Serena okay? I want to talk to her."

Don nodded to Rita. "Go ahead, but call your friend's cell phone. She's in her apartment. No bugs there. Somebody tapped your business lines, but we didn't want to remove them and tip our hand. Ms. Starr embarrassed Agent Johnson by whacking him on the head with her rolling pin before he got a chance to explain he was there to protect her. She appears to be trying to make it up to him with chocolate."

Mitch handed Rita his cell phone. "Reassure her but make it short, okay?"

Rita sat down on the couch in the living room and punched in the number. "Hi, Serena? Are you all right?" She paused and chuckled. "Yeah, I heard about the rolling pin. Good reflexes. Did they tell you about Tony?" She nodded at Mitch gesturing her to hurry up. "Yeah. I'll be careful. I've got guardian agents watching over me. Plus Mitch. Listen, I can't talk long...Love you, too." She passed the phone to Mitch's outstretched hand. "She wants to speak to you."

He listened for a moment. "You know I won't let anything bad happen to her, Serena. Sit tight and try to play nice, okay? And don't attack any more of my friends."

Mitch's grin faded as he turned to Rita. "Serena's fine. And you will be too, but Don needs to go over what you're going to say to Tony when you call him to come over."

Liz sat on a nearby rocker. "Mitch, why do you want Rita to meet Tony if he's a criminal? These FBI men say they're going to escort me someplace safe, but I'm not leaving Rita behind without some answers."

"Let me explain, ma'am," Don interrupted. "When Mitch asked me for my opinion about your situation, I recognized the name as part of an investigation the Bureau's been conducting on some of his associates for years. They're involved in scams and deals that go beyond state lines. Gambling, fraud, real estate swindles, money-laundering, and embezzlement for starters. Maybe even murder. When Ms. Starr's grandfather refused to sell his property to Tony, the next week his bike was run off the road. We don't think the death was an accident. Or that it's a coincidence Tony gets friendly with recent widows or heirs of terminally ill patients."

Liz shook her head. "But he seems like such a nice young man. So helpful and successful. His mother would roll over in her grave if she knew her son was mixed up in anything shady. And his dad in Myrtle Beach? He's going to be shocked."

"Could be broke, too. Tony's a big spender, and he's overextended on all those businesses, restaurants, and spas he's acquired since his father retired. If Tony doesn't come up with the quick cash to cover his gambling and business debts, he's headed for a hole with six feet of sand over his head."

"You mean, someone will kill him?" Liz gasped.

Don nodded. "Tony's painted himself into a corner with Alphonso DeLaurio. Tony brokered DeLaurio's purchase of the house next door to you with the promise you would sell, too, and they'd add to their family compound. No one reneges on a promise with Alphonso and lives to tell about it. Tony's a dead man if he doesn't clinch this deal and deliver your property to Alphonso."

Liz drummed her fingers on the arm of the rocker. "So Tony's facing possible bankruptcy, prison, or death. Can't you arrest him now and persuade him to testify without Rita getting stuck in the middle?"

"No, we need her. Tony's coming over soon. Rita's going to agree to sell him your property, and then change her mind at the last minute. It should push him over the edge. As soon as we have enough lies and evidence on tape, we'll move in from another room and arrest him. Then we can pressure him into ratting on his cohorts to save his own skin."

Liz shook her head. "I don't like it. Won't Rita be in danger?"

"Tony isn't armed. We are. Heavily. He has a couple guns registered to him, but to our knowledge, he never carries them. No history of violence. It's not Tony's style. Besides he's not expecting trouble from Rita - just an easy way out if she's willing to sell. Believe me. We're poised to move in right away. We won't let her get hurt."

Liz looked over at Rita. "Are you sure you want to do this, dear?"

Rita shrugged. "I don't want to but I'm sure I have to. If he's behind all our troubles and has done this to other people, he has to be stopped."

"So are you ready, Rita?" Don asked.

She nodded. "Nervous, yes, but ready to get it over with."

Mitch put his hand on her knee. "You're strong, Boss Lady. You can do this!"

Rita sighed and turned to Don. "So what do I say when I call? Won't he expect Mitch here?"

"Tell Tony Mitch isn't back yet and you've been thinking over his real estate offer. You can't sleep and you'll feel better if he comes over and talks to you about making a deal."

Mitch interrupted. "Tell him you realize you're being selfish when you see how old and frail Liz is getting."

Liz snorted and threw a pillow at Mitch.

Don glared at Mitch. "It's just a story, Mrs. Chandler," he resumed. "Anyway, Rita, tell Tony you've decided there's no other way to bail your aunt out of her troubles. Be brief."

Rita bit her lip. "But what happens when he

sees Mitch's truck in the driveway? He'll know I lied."

"Mitch parked blocks away. Rita, remember to let Tony do most of the talking. We'll be listening and recording. Cameras are hidden in here so stay in the living room." He pointed to a flower arrangement on the mantel.

"You mean I'll be on video?"

"Yeah. Here, look over these questions," Don said and handed her a piece of paper.

Rita skimmed over the list. "Oh, God! I can't remember all this! I want to go into hiding myself."

"You don't have to memorize it," Don said. "Reread them a few times before he gets here. Work a few into the conversation. Let Tony do the talking and he'll dig his own grave. Act confused and tired, you know, do the weak female routine."

Rita gritted her teeth. "I don't do that role. Ask Mitch. If I pull that off, I'll deserve an Oscar."

Mitch grinned. "Well, Meryl, go for it. Just don't say too much or you'll get upset. I know you."

"Gee, thanks for the vote of confidence!"

Mitch put his arm around her shoulders. "Rita, I didn't mean it that way. You'll do fine. You know how Tony loves to hear himself talk. Remember, you're doing it for Liz."

Another agent appeared from the hallway. "It's time to move Mrs. Chandler and Mitch. Tony's at home." He held out his hand to Liz. "Ma'am, if you'll come with me, the car's waiting. You, too, Mitch."

Liz gave Rita a quick hug and kiss. She turned to the agent. "You gentlemen better take good care of my Rita or you'll have to deal with me."

Mitch gave Rita a forceful kiss and whispered, "I don't want to go, Jersey Girl. You stay tough."

She hugged him tightly. "Right. And remember, Cowboy, you owe me something."

Don cleared his throat. "Hate to interrupt, but

Mitch and Mrs. Chandler have to get out of here."
He waited until they left. "Rita, we're ready
whenever you are. Showtime starts when you make
the call."

She reluctantly took Tony's card out of her purse
and picked up the receiver. She punched in the
numbers and frowned when he answered on the
third ring. "Hi, Tony. It's Rita." She paused and
clasped her hand to her heart. "Yes, I know you're
surprised to hear from me. I, uh, don't know where
to begin. I've been thinking about your offer to buy
this house. Maybe you're right. It's time we faced
facts. Aunt Liz might be better off if she sold the
property. I'm ready to meet you at the spa tomorrow
and talk about it."

Don shook his head vehemently and mouthed,
"Not tomorrow. Now!" Rita waved him off as she
listened.

"Tonight?" she said. "I don't know. I hate to
bother you after hours and I'm exhausted. Aunt Liz
is staying at a friend's house, Mitch is still out of
town, and I was going to have tea and go to bed
soon." She paused and twisted the phone cord. "Well,
I suppose if you get here in fifteen minutes, we could
talk about it over tea." She listened and nodded.
"Thank you so much. Bye."

Rita's hand shook as she passed the phone back
to the agent. "Oh, my God! I wish Tony hadn't
answered. I am so nervous. What if he senses
something's wrong?"

"He won't. He expects you to be shaky and
vulnerable about signing away your family home.
Bravo on your acting reluctant to see him tonight.
Great touch! Thanks to his good lawyer friend
Santangelo, he also knows you have your aunt's
power of attorney. I'll bet he comes with a contract
offer in his briefcase. Pretend to go along until the
last minute. Then throw in a couple zingers. Sound

wavering, unsure. Rattle his cage. Visualize those drunken creeps he set you up with to save his sorry ass, excuse my language. Remember, he thinks you're nothing but money in his wallet."

"Tony was behind that, too?" Rita clenched her fists and shuddered. "What do I do when he gets here?"

"Sit him down on the couch. Breathe. Try to relax. Say whatever you feel will get the bastard talking. He'll try his best to convince you to sell, but if anything goes wrong, we're here to protect you. We'll monitor you the whole time, only ten feet away in the guest room. If you feel like you're in danger, holler and we'll come to the rescue. Otherwise, we'll arrest him outside when he gets in his car. Understand?"

Rita nodded.

Don fell silent and adjusted his headset. "He's on his way. ETA seven minutes. You mentioned tea. Fix it and bring it out here. Sit where you are now and stay put for the cameras. We have to get into position." He ushered her toward the kitchen. "It's showtime!"

"Please don't say 'Break a leg,' okay?"

Don gave a thumbs-up sign and grabbed the list of questions from her hand. "You don't need these. On with the show."

Chapter Twenty-Five

Rita watched the clock on the mantel and massaged the pressure points of her hand. One more minute. It seemed like a lifetime before she heard the roar of Tony's car approaching. She waited for the doorbell to chime, took a deep breath, and headed to the door. It felt like walking the plank in a pirate movie except the shark at the end was real.

When she opened the door, Tony stood there smiling, briefcase in hand. "Rita, I got here as fast as I could. Are you all right?"

"I'm fine, Tony, but tired of facing reality." She stepped aside and motioned to the living room. "Please, sit down. Let's get this over with. Aunt Liz finally agreed she needs to sell, but she's too emotional and worn out to talk about it now. She left to stay at a friend's place. I'm having tea. Would you like some?"

"Yes, thank you." The carafe trembled as she filled two china cups. He waved off the cream. "I take it like you, with honey and lemon, right? But you look like you should add a bit of brandy to yours. You're shaking."

"No, I don't need brandy. Money? Peace of mind? That's what I really need, not brandy. I've been giving your offer a lot of thought. It's selfish of me to want to hold on to this house when Aunt Liz would be better off in your complex. The trip was a bit much for her. She can't come up with the money to pay the taxes or the balloon note, and she's ready to sell. She's given me the authority to act for her, but it's so hard...so final."

Tony set his briefcase next to the tea tray and unlocked it. "I understand how painful it feels now, but you'll both be so much better off without all this stress. And what a gift it is for you to take care of the transaction on her behalf so she doesn't have to deal with more than she can handle."

Rita sipped her tea as Tony withdrew some papers. "Tony, before I sign anything, is there any other alternative to selling? You have a lot of connections, don't you? Could you arrange a loan or something for her?"

"Well, yes, my family's been in business here a long time, but I can't arrange something that's doomed to fail. You simply don't have the income to support further loans. You'd keep getting behind and eat up the equity in the house. Your aunt could live twenty happy years in a more practical place. She can't afford to stay here. What does your accountant say?"

"Do you know Mr. Martino?"

"I've heard of him. What did he advise?"

Rita sighed. "To sell. Said it's the smart thing to do, especially if she's going to live a long life, which she's not going to do if she's worried about money."

Tony reached over and took her hand in his. "Rita, I know it's difficult to give up your family home, but what else can you do?"

Rita's chin quivered and her eyes filled with tears. "Nothing, I guess. If you draw up the papers tomorrow, I'll have our attorney, Mr. Santangelo, look them over. I only met him once, but he took over Aunt Liz's account and she seems to think he's okay. Pretty plush office, though. Are you familiar with him?"

"Santangelo, you say?" Tony paused shuffling the documents in his briefcase as if trying to picture the man. "I've heard he's quite competent. Of course, I believe you get what you pay for. My own lawyer is out of town, but it's good we have different counsel. Sharing a lawyer would be a conflict of interest. If you want to get the process started, contracts of sale are fairly standard. I have one with me you could sign tonight. I ran a quick market analysis, too. I think you'll find the proposal more than fair." He placed a contract in her lap and reached for his tea. "Take a look."

Rita scanned the first page of the papers and gasped. "More than a million dollars!"

"Oceanfront property. Rita, can't you see selling is only difficult for sentimental reasons? After paying off her sizable debts, Liz will still have money in the bank. She won't be cash poor or worried about bills. She can even buy a smaller house near the bay if she insists on a water view. One that's close to the church or the garden club so she wouldn't be driving as much. A whole new beginning for her. And for you."

"Well, I knew the property was worth a lot, but seeing all those digits! I'm feeling a bit out of my league. Are you sure this is right? I mean, is this the going rate for a four-bedroom house on a single oceanfront lot?"

Tony sighed. "Actually, it's about $100,000 more than what it should be for a single lot, but I have a buyer in mind for this property; he is unusually anxious to get his hands on a piece of property like this. And to sweeten the deal on my end, Liz can lease a unit at the health spa and assisted living complex at a reduced cost. Or buy in at construction cost. You couldn't ask for a better solution, except maybe winning the lottery." He laughed and passed a pen over. "Sign by the Xs and help her out. Help yourself."

Rita bit her lip and looked at the pen. "I don't know. What's the rush? Maybe I should do more research before I sign anything. How do I know it's not worth more or less? Not that I'm questioning your honesty or competence, but I have to look out for Aunt Liz." She fell silent as she read. "This language is pretty complicated. Can you explain this section to me? The part about the buyer and the terms?" Rita pointed to one of the pages and handed it back to Tony to read.

She poured some tea and watched him study the page quietly. "Tony, I've never owned real estate and I'm not sure what questions I should ask before I sign. And I'm not clear about who you're working for."

Tony hesitated. "The buyer wishes to remain anonymous at this time."

"Isn't that odd?"

Tony shrugged. "You meet all kinds of people in this business. As long as they have the money, who they are doesn't matter at this stage."

Rita looked puzzled. "Actually, what I meant was who are you working for, Aunt Liz or the buyer? That always confuses me."

"Well, as a dual agent, I'm serving you both. As the agent for the seller, my primary interest is Liz. The fact that I'm closer to you than some stranger from out of town should make you feel safe. And you know what? I can't afford to drop the commission entirely, but since we're talking about a substantial amount of money, well, for an old friend, I'll only take two percent instead of the customary five or six." He made some changes with his pen and initialed the papers before passing them back.

Rita stared at the papers in her hand. "That's very generous, Tony, but there's one more thing, I know it sounds silly, but Aunt Liz wants to meet the buyer and his family before she sells. I mean, can you guarantee they won't level this place? That would kill Aunt Liz, no matter how much money she gets."

315

Tony sighed. "There are no guarantees, but they swore they wanted to maintain the charm of the place. They want a retreat, not something that looks like a glass and concrete hotel on Miami Beach."

Rita flipped through the contract again. "I still don't get it. If you're the real estate agent, why is your name on this contract as the buyer?"

"I told you this businessman requires anonymity. He intends to buy the land from me for the same price after I acquire it. He's willing to pay top dollar for his privacy."

He studied Rita's face gravely. "You know, this isn't going to work if Liz can't let go of the house. Yes, it's full of memories, but selling a house isn't like giving away a child or a pet for adoption. Believe me I know how old ladies can be sentimental about their possessions, but Alphonso wants this house."

"Alphonso who? Is that the prospective buyer?"

"I, uh, well...Yes, but I can't divulge his last name. I shouldn't have mentioned his first name either." Tony clenched his teeth and exhaled slowly. He placed the contracts back in the briefcase and snapped it shut. "I'm sorry, Rita. I don't mean to sound harsh, but you seem to be wavering now. It's been a bad day for me, too. You should understand bad days. You've had your share of those lately."

Rita nodded. "Tell me about it. God, I am so tired of dealing with everything going wrong."

Tony turned and took her hands in his. "Rita, bottom line: Liz can't afford to keep this house and neither can you. And frankly, with everything you've been through, I don't understand why you want to keep trying. Why slave away trying to help her keep it when you can see you'd both be better off selling?"

"But..."

"No more 'buts.' Face it, Rita. Liz needs an assisted-living facility. She's an older widow who's too stubborn to be sensible. What if she has a dizzy spell swimming alone here? Or falls during a power outage and breaks a leg or hip? You can't be here around the clock to watch over her."

"I guess..."

"And what if something happens to you? Who's going to take care of her? How much longer can you go on trying to make a living and bailing her out? Aren't you worn out dealing with lawyers, accountants, vandalism, health inspectors, unreliable employees, crank calls? My God, being mistaken for a hooker!"

Rita stared at Tony. "What health inspector?"

"You know, the health inspector who gave you a hard time."

"I didn't tell you about that."

"Of course you did. You mentioned it earlier. How else would I know about it?"

"Good question, Tony. Serena and I swore each other to secrecy. Didn't tell a soul except Mitch. We don't need that getting around. So how'd you find out?"

"I don't recall. I must have heard it from someone else, then. You know how people gossip."

"Right. And do you chat with Mr. Benson regularly?"

"Who's Mr. Benson?"

"The little weasel with the white coat, the clipboard, and the traveling roach. Was he checking in at your ice cream parlor today?"

Tony knitted his brow. "You know, I think there was a surprise inspection today. I guess he mentioned something about a refrigerator going bad or a power outage. Someone ill? I don't remember the details." Tony drummed his fingers on his briefcase. "Rita, I think you need some time to think. Get some sleep. You're not making much sense. I'll drop by in the morning to see Liz and you can both sign these documents then or at Carmine's office.

This is your best offer. Take it or leave it. If I were you, I'd take it."

"No, wait. You said, 'Carmine's office.' So you know our lawyer's first name after all. And what else did you say? What did you mean about dealing with unreliable employees?"

"Everyone has them. You had that talkative blonde teenager who worked in Serena's shop. She was causing problems, am I right?"

"You said 'worked' as in past tense."

"Works, worked. What's your point? That type comes and goes, doesn't show up on a good beach day, loses the keys, doesn't even phone in. You don't have to be psychic like your friend to know what minimum wage people are like."

"Well, Tony, she *used* to work for us before she left a message on the answering machine and disappeared. Did she drop in at your ice cream parlor to chat, too? Serena and I were the only ones who knew about her missing keys. Maybe she's been working for someone like you who wanted our business to fail. She was the one who booked that hooker job."

"Rita, what are you insinuating? Did you ever consider maybe it was your buddy Mitch who set up that little bachelor party scam so he could play hero and rescue you?"

"Oh, my God, it's been you all along, hasn't it? How could you do that to me? I didn't tell Kelly everything about the bachelor party. And Mitch would never tell you. Kelly was working for you all along, wasn't she?" She covered her mouth with her fingertips. "The crank calls...you?"

Tony's face relaxed in a crooked grin. "I don't know what you're talking about, Rita. Maybe with some rest you'll feel better. Think more clearly. But I'm not a man to be crossed. If you don't sign these tonight, Liz will sign them in the morning."

Rita stared at him. "Why, Tony? What makes you think we'll ever sign those papers now?"

"What a clever woman you think you are! And a lot more trouble than I figured. Too bad Mitch didn't slam you harder into the door the first night you came here. It would have taken care of everything."

"What? How could you know about that?"

Tony snickered and leaned over to play with the curls of her ponytail. "I was there watching. You two ruined everything that night. The perfect plan. Every detail figured out. A power outage. Liz safely away at the spa. The handyman out of town with his truck conveniently disabled. I'd even insisted she leave a message on his cell phone so he knew she was safe at the spa with a friend. He had no business showing up. And then you arrived on the doorstep early, too. You weren't expected for days! Both of you wrecked my plan."

"What plan?"

"If I'd arrived a half hour earlier, or if you'd waited until the following week to appear like Liz expected, everything would have been fine. But no, you showed up before I could arrange an unfortunate electrical fire to start when the power came back on. The old homestead would have burned to the ground, leaving only memories and land. No one hurt and better for everyone. She would have moved into my spa and sold me the lot in a heartbeat. She couldn't afford to rebuild and I would have bought the unimproved land for less. Now I'm in a bind. And it's your fault, yours and Mitch."

"Hold it. You've set fires to collect insurance or force people to sell their homes?" *When were the FBI agents coming to get this madman?*

Tony chatted on, evidently ignoring her growing nervousness. "On occasion. Helps cash flow. Sometimes inspires unwilling clients to sell. You have to be careful to change your pattern, though. I used the careless teenager scam with the old Victorian next door, so I couldn't use it here, too. And you know what's funny? The place burned to the ground and the owners never tried to collect the insurance. I couldn't even find out who the principals were. No answers to my inquiries or my offers. That was a dead end. But I can't give up this deal. I owe too much money to very serious people."

"Tony. This is all wrong! If you owe a lot of money, I'm sure you can sell some of your cars, your restaurants, your properties. Your interest in the cruise line."

He stood and shoved his hands into the pockets of his tailored khakis. He looked down at Rita. "Sorry to say everything's leveraged. I'm afraid it comes down to you or me. If I don't buy and deliver this house as promised, I'm either dead, and I mean that literally, or broke. Since that idea upsets me more than removing you from the picture, you lose."

"You're going to kill me?" *Okay, Don, when are you going to swoop in?*

"It'll be painless, I promise."

"Tony, no. I won't tell anyone what you've said. I'll sign the papers. I understand you've been under a lot of pressure. We both know Liz can't afford to keep this place going, and I'm sure your offer is the best we can do. Give it to me. Where do I sign? We can be partners."

"I thought so at one point in time. Even considered marrying you. You're quite beautiful, you know. But you have too much substance and integrity. You never would have fit in. I might get you to look the part, but as my father used to say, 'Some people can't rise above their waitress mentality. Or operate below their scruples.' You don't know how to keep your full lips shut, or who to kiss with them."

"You won't get away with this."

"Of course I will. You didn't notice me dumping the contents of a capsule into your tea as you were shuffling papers back and forth and reading that contract. Try standing up. You'll be dizzy."

Rita rose to her feet, swayed and sat down again. "I don't feel so good."

"Yes, I know. Unfortunate, but necessary. Don't fight it, Rita. This is the best thing for everyone. You'll trip and fall in the pool and drown. Or miss one of those steep steps leading up to your lover's garage apartment and break your pretty neck. Mitch will be devastated when he discovers you. Or how's this for a nice twist: *he* gets blamed for your death. I'll generously give Liz enough money to cover your funeral expenses, and I'll get this property for a song. I'm sure a grieving old widow won't want to live every day where her favorite niece died. Game's over."

"What did you put in my tea? The room's kind of spinning."

"A strong sedative. Same kind Liz got on the cruise. If you'd signed right away like a good girl, you could have gone to bed and lived. Now it will look like you were upset and helped yourself to a couple of her sleeping pills before your unfortunate accident. Unless you'd rather cooperate. How about one last chance?" He clicked the briefcase open and handed her the contract and his Waterford pen. "Sign where indicated, Rita. Keep your mouth shut and you'll wake up tomorrow."

Rita took the pen and scribbled, struggling to stop her hand from shaking. Tony grabbed the papers and examined them, turning red at what she'd scrawled. "Go to Hell, Tony! RM"

Rita lunged for the carafe and threw hot tea in Tony's face, followed by the carafe itself. She scrambled for the front door, screaming for help as loudly as she could.

"It's too late to escape now." Tony tackled her from behind, forcing Rita to the floor with such force the breath was knocked from her. Rage and desperation drove Tony as his hands wrapped around Rita's neck. Already short of breath from impacting the floor, Rita fought to pry his hands from her neck as her vision dimmed.

Where were the agents? What were they waiting for? Murder on tape?

"Want to say your favorite prayer first? You know how it goes. If I should die..." Tony laughed. "Rita, Rita. When will you learn to stop ruining everything? You're not supposed to struggle. Just drift off to sleep before you die."

Before he could pull her back to her feet to drag her outside, footsteps thundered behind them. "Freeze, Jennings! Let go of her arms. Slowly. Now!"

"Or I'll kill you myself," boomed Mitch's voice.

"Ah, the hero handyman," sneered Tony.

Rita lay face down on the floor, waiting, frozen in fear.

The metallic click of a gun's safety release near the base of Tony's skull inspired him to ease his hands off Rita. He rolled off and got up slowly, his hands in surrender.

Rita scrambled to her feet and ran to Mitch. Tony took a step back and flashed a sinister smile, chilling and silent. His burning eyes stared at Mitch. Then at Rita. One of the agents read Tony his rights as another one cuffed his hands behind his back and guided him outside.

Rita's body was still shaking with shock. "What took so long? I thought you guys would never swoop in!" she cried. Mitch wrapped her in his arms and hugged her to his chest.

"You sound like Mitch," Don said. "Good thing I put him in the van across the street before Tony arrived or he would have charged in before we got all we needed. By the way, you were great! Now relax. An ambulance is on the way. We didn't see him slip anything into your cup. Bad camera angle."

"I didn't drink it."

"We saw you drink it."

"No, I switched the cups. If he had drunk his tea, he would have been doped up."

"Hey, Mitch. Smart lady here. Better watch yourself around her! Won't be able to fool this one."

"Fooling her isn't in my plans."

"By the way, your aunt is fine. We tried to convince her she'd had enough excitement for one day, but she insists she wants to come home. We'll bring her back as soon as we take Pretty Boy away."

Rita pulled out of Mitch's embrace, but kept hold of his hand. "What'll happen to him? Somehow I can't picture him in jail. Bad cuisine, common criminals. Of course with his good looks, he could be very popular."

Don shook his head. "Or end up very dead, is more likely. The people he's been running with won't go down alone. Thanks to Rita getting Tony to implicate himself, I think he'll be willing to testify against his pals. He's definitely going to be out of this area for good."

"You mean the witness protection program?" asked Rita. "I don't ever want to see his face or hear his voice again. But what about plastic surgery? Do they actually do that? What if he changes his face and comes back for revenge and I don't recognize him? He's a sick man."

"Rita, Tony prefers life in the shadows to no life at all. We're happy to use him to convict some bad guys, to clean up some government corruption. We'll never let him loose. The man has no morals. I'd bet his only regret is that you weren't killed to keep his house of cards from tumbling down.

"We're almost done here. The equipment will be

out in a few minutes." Don shook Rita's hand. "Pleasure doing business with you, Rita. If you ever need a job, come see us. You're a natural!" He winked at her and shook Mitch's hand. "And you, Mitch, don't be a stranger any more. Keep in touch. I'll keep you both posted. But I promise you this. You'll never have to worry about facing Tony again."

Chapter Twenty-Six

Mitch grabbed Rita's hand. "Come on, let's get some fresh air. We need to talk. There's something else you'll never have to worry about. I've got to explain before Liz returns." He paused to pat the cushion of the chaise lounge by the pool. "Sit."

She reached to pull him down with her and took a deep breath. "Mitch. I love you. I'm not going to let you pull away or hide any more. Not tonight. Not ever. I realized when Tony intended to kill me I wanted to live. Not just stay alive, but I want to live and be with you. I'd rather be with you anywhere than to struggle to keep this house for Aunt Liz without you. I know she feels the same way. People are more important than things. We can make new memories in a different house. Tony was right about one thing. Letting go of this place could be a new beginning. This is my childhood dream home, but as long as you're with me, we can make our own dream home anywhere...and make our individual dreams come true, too."

Mitch leaned over and kissed her gently. "I love you, too. And you have nothing to worry about. Here." He pulled a piece of paper from his wallet. "It's the balloon note. Paid in full."

"I don't get it. Who paid it?"

"I did. That's the other secret. I have more money than I'll ever use. I live simply and made some good investments. After Ginger died, I collected on a million dollar life insurance policy I never wanted in the first place. Sold our empty houses full of expensive furniture and bad memories before I came down here. I'm also what's left of GMV. Its last holding is the property next door."

"I don't understand. Why did you lie to Aunt Liz about being poor? Why not just tell her the truth?"

"I was going to, but it was easier to let her believe the conclusions she'd jumped to. I met her when I was walking the property after the fire. I was still blaming myself for leaving Ginger the weekend she died. Ginger's dad had given us the Victorian next door on our tenth anniversary. She'd seen it on a Sunday drive on the shore, and her daddy loved to indulge her. He was proud of me, too, and of all the money I'd made after I left construction. I had a knack for knowing when to buy and sell, seeking out small businesses to invest in. For a few years, it was fun. After a while, I got tired of spending all my time making money, playing golf with people I didn't like, and going to parties with people my own folks considered snobs." Mitch shifted on the chaise and pulled Rita closer.

"I'd been trying to decide what to do with the property even before someone burned it down."

"I don't understand. Tony said he did it to force a sale but it didn't work out. It was such a lovely house. Were you going to move here?"

"I didn't know what I wanted then. I only knew what I didn't want. Reminders, hurt, pain, phony people. People after my money. Pressure and 'told you so' comments from my family. Divorced women trying to comfort a rich man and fill a gap in their social lives. I'd intended to stay down here and sort things out. Then the fire. You know, Tony did a great job of arson. Police were sure it was an accident caused by careless teenagers having some fun at a vacant house."

Rita massaged Mitch's hand with her fingertips as he went on. "In a way, I really was homeless when Liz offered me a place to stay and something to do. She was so kind I just wanted to be around her. At first, it was a place to hide from my family and my wife's family. They never got along. Former business associates, too. I felt good working with my hands again, doing honest work. Didn't have to socialize with phonies, just work on their houses once in a while."

"Is that why you disliked Tony?"

"Yeah. Reminded me of the crowd my wife ran with. She spent her time drinking and shopping. Or playing tennis and golf. I blamed myself for not being at that party to rescue her. Maybe I worked too many hours, didn't spend enough time with her. Even wondered if I could've stopped her from drinking so much if I'd moved her down here away from them. But you know what? I bet she would have taken up with Tony's crowd and kept on drinking, checking her pictures on the society page every Sunday with two aspirin, black coffee, and a bad hangover."

"Are you going to tell Aunt Liz about all this?" asked Rita.

"I don't know. She hates being on the receiving end of a favor or gift! I could let her believe the lawyer found some assets Carlton left her. That happens sometimes. Or should I tell her the truth? That I paid off the loans and will set up a trust fund to pay her taxes every year, plus clear up the other debts. She might hate that. You know what a stubborn broad she can be. What do you think?"

"I say, 'How about giving a stubborn old broad a hug and a chance to say thank you?' ", a familiar voice said. Rita and Mitch turned to see Liz standing by the sliding glass door.

Mitch walked over and scooped up the small woman. "Glad to. You mad at me? How much did you hear?"

"More than enough to know I'm lucky you

wandered into my life. And Rita's. How can I stay mad at you, you big tease? If I didn't love you like the son I always wanted, do you think I'd ever let you get away with calling me a stubborn old broad?"

Mitch laughed. "I didn't say 'old.' You did!"

"So what do I do next?" Liz asked.

"We'll get you a new lawyer and a new accountant. Yours happen to be unethical friends and business associates of Tony's. They could have told you that you own a double lot. You'd never have to sell your home if you subdivided and sold the lot where the pool is. And that balloon note? They should have explained what you were signing after your husband's passing. I imagine they'll end up spilling some secrets to the feds, too, if they want to avoid a scandal and criminal charges."

"I guess I forgot to practice what I preach: you can't judge a book by its cover. Tony seemed like such a caring person, maybe put on a few airs, but we all have our faults...like being stubborn."

Mitch interrupted. "Growing up with four older sisters, I got used to being outnumbered by stubborn broads. Feels like being home. So if you'll both have me, I'd like to create a family compound of our own here."

Rita whacked Mitch's arm playfully. "What is this, a group proposal? Aren't you supposed to see if I'm interested first? Or is this another real estate deal? Aunt Liz, what if he only wants us around to make three lots in a row like a kid playing Monopoly?"

Mitch laughed. "No, I don't want a business merger and I'm not playing games. I want us to be a family. What do you say, Liz?"

"Mitch, I'm delighted, but right now, my only plan is to go to bed. Stubborn old broads hate to admit when they've had enough excitement, but smart ones do. 'My momma didn't raise no fool,' as they say. Good night, you two. And no fighting!" She gave Rita a quick hug and left. "Be happy!"

Mitch sat down beside Rita again. "Well, kid, what's it going to be? Do you think you can love a rich handyman as much as you wanted to hop in bed with a poor one?"

Rita nodded. "As long as the man in bed with me is you. I have to admit I've acted like such an underdog for so many years, it's going to take a little time to get used to giving up all that struggle. A shift to really feeling good, not overburdened by responsibility. And having an equal partner, one who cares. Right now, as long as you're beside me, that's all that matters."

He kissed her hard on the lips, then softened and pulled away. "There's a lot more I want to give you, but I'm tired."

"Are you going to bed, too? I don't believe this!"

"Why not? Aren't you coming along? I'm not going to bed to sleep, woman. I'm tired of waiting to get there...or maybe a private spot on the beach, with you."

Mitch pulled her into his arms. "How about a blanket and some wine and a nice picnic on the beach? Just the two of us...as soon as the crowd leaves."

"That depends. Did you ever get to the drugstore to make that purchase?"

Mitch smiled and kissed her neck. "You bet I did. Someday I can see us welcoming a fourth member, a little one, into the family, but for now, we could do some serious practice for that project...if you're interested. How about it, Massage Lady?"

Rita laughed and kissed him on the lips. "You're on, Handyman. I'll get the wine and glasses, you get the blanket!"

A word about the author...

Born in Buffalo, New York, Karen Bostrom moved to South Florida at an early age and was raised to love learning, storytelling, and being open to new experiences. Always an avid reader and writer, she is thrilled to be achieving her dream of being a published romantic suspense novelist.

Now living in New Jersey, she is a member of Liberty State Fiction Writers, Sisters in Crime-Central Jersey, RWA, and NJ Romance Writers. With the special man in her life, she enjoys many Jersey Shore attractions such as beaches, boardwalks, wineries, and ballroom dancing!